Pra

FIONA LOWE

"With the perfect mixture of romance, sadness and Australian/American wisecracking, *Boomerang Bride* is one of the best romance novels this reviewer has read in a long time."
—Maria Planansky, *RT Book Reviews*, 4.5 stars

"*Boomerang Bride* is a lovely romance with fantastic characters and a very happily ever after…. This story is fantastically written and I loved the witty dialog between Matilda and Marc. My favorite part is the ending—the epilogue is beyond fantastic and made me smile for the rest of the day after I finished."
—*www.thebookgirl.net*, 5/5

"*Boomerang Bride* was just sheer magic to lose myself in…. charming, beautiful and heartwarming, *Boomerang Bride* is a romance for everyone!"
—*www.maldivianbookreviewer.com*,
5/5, Caliber Seal: *OUTSTANDING READ!*

Boomerang Bride

FIONA LOWE

CARINA PRESS™

Recycling programs
for this product may
not exist in your area.

**CARINA
PRESS**™

ISBN-13: 978-0-373-00205-4

BOOMERANG BRIDE

This is the revised text of the work, which was first published by Carina Press
in 2011.

Copyright © 2011 by Fiona Lowe

Revised text Copyright © 2013 by Fiona Lowe

This edition published by arrangement with Harlequin Books S.A.

® and TM are trademarks of the publisher. Trademarks indicated with ®
are registered in the United States Patent and Trademark Office, the Canadian
Trade Marks Office and in other countries.

www.CarinaPress.com

Printed in U.S.A.

Dear Reader,

I'm so excited to introduce you to *Boomerang Bride!* This story grew out of a collision of ideas sparked by moments in time starting with me riding a ski lift on my own. As I gazed out at the Australian snow gums and the pristine snow, an image of a bride holding a wedding cake and staring into a shop window pinged into my mind. I had no clue why, and the image wouldn't budge.

Two days later I heard a TV snippet about a con man scamming a European heiress and I got an email from a man in Nigeria telling me I had won the lottery.

Three weeks after that I heard the song "Bridal Train" by The Waifs—the story of their grandmother who married a U.S. sailor during WWII. At the end of the war, the U.S. Navy commissioned a train to collect all the Australian war brides from around the country and gathered them all in Sydney before they set sail for the U.S. It got me thinking...what if you'd grown up hearing the great romantic adventure-cum-love story of your grandmother, and your mother had her own, as well. Stories like that become family folklore and set up an expectation.

Suddenly I had a reason for my heroine, Matilda, to be standing in an ancient wedding dress, holding a cake and staring into an empty shop window ready for her great adventure. Of course, absolutely nothing goes to plan!

I've lived in Wisconsin, and every cross-cultural confusion that happens to Matilda happened to me! Although Australians and Americans speak English, it often feels as if we're speaking a different language, which leads to some very funny misunderstandings.

I hope you enjoy *Boomerang Bride.* If you'd like to hear the song "Bridal Train" and see photos of the real towns that inspired Hobin, then head over to my website at www.fionalowe.com. I love hearing from my readers. You can contact me at fiona@fionalowe.com or hang out with me on Facebook (fionaloweromanceauthor) and Twitter.

Happy reading!

Love,

Fiona *x*

For Norm, Sandon and Barton for their suggestion that I
"write a big book," and for their support while I did it. I love you guys!

To Jude, Doris, Libbey, Cindy, Elizabeth and Maureen
for making an Aussie so welcome in Wisconsin.
And with thanks to Norma, who patiently answered my questions,
to Charlotte, who loved the story and translated "Aussie" to
"American-speak," and to Rachelle, who explained how small-town
Wisconsin policing works. I couldn't have done it without you all!

Boomerang Bride

Books have always been a big part of Fiona's life—her first teenage rebellion was refusing to go on a hike with her parents because she was halfway through *Gone with the Wind*. As an adult, Fiona read her way around the world, always trying to read a book that related to where she was at the time...the Brontës in Yorkshire, Jane Austen in Bath, *The Godfather* in Italy, Michener in Hawaii...you get the picture. It was when she was living in Madison, Wisconsin, and at home with a baby, that she started writing romance fiction. Now multipublished with Harlequin, Mills & Boon and Carina Press, she's won a RITA® Award and a R*BY award, as well as being an *RT Book Reviews* Reviewer's Choice finalist.

She loves creating characters you could meet on the street and enjoys putting them in unique situations where they eventually fall in love. Fiona currently lives in Australia, which is a lot warmer than Wisconsin, and she attempts to juggle her writing career with her own real-life hero, a rambling garden with eighty rosebushes and two heroes in the making.

Fiona loves to hear from her readers. You can contact her at fiona@fionalowe.com.

She also hangs out at www.fionalowe.com, www.facebook.com/ FionaLoweRomanceAuthor and twitter.com/FionaLowe.

CHAPTER ONE

The petite bride stood stock-still, her chapel-length beaded train sagging in the damp gutter while her white fingers clutched a two-tiered wedding cake. She stared long and hard into a vacant store window.

It wasn't a usual fall sight in Hobin, Wisconsin. Brides tended to marry in spring. Even then, Hobin was hardly the bride capital of the state or the United States. Hawaii took that prize with its tropical sandy beaches and swaying palm trees, surprisingly acing Hobin's snowbound winters and late-spring flowerings.

Still, in the last one hundred and fifty years, many a local bride had stood in the old log church but none that Marc Olsen could remember had stood alone on an almost deserted Main Street, late on a Sunday afternoon. But then again apart from his annual Thanksgiving visit, he'd been gone from Hobin a long time and things might have changed.

He glanced up and down the familiar wide empty road with the same shop fronts that he'd known as a kid. Nope, nothing had changed. The realization both annoyed and soothed him. He took a second look, this time casting his gaze around trying to locate the groom. A stray bridesmaid or ring bearer. Anyone?

No one.

He was used to oddities—he'd shed his small-town boyhood years ago, moving to New York City where a bride alone on a street wouldn't even make a ripple in the bustling Broadway crowd. But in Hobin it was more than odd. The bride wasn't moving. Perhaps it was performance art. In Hobin? Nah.

Completely intrigued, he gave his curiosity free rein. It was all about curiosity and had absolutely nothing to do with the fact that investigating the lone bride would further delay his cross-six-state journey and postpone his arrival at his sister's house. He knew that once he stepped over Lori's front stoop, the snare of family would clamp on to him like the grip of a Denver boot, which was why for the last twelve years he'd always arrived with a set departure date.

He crossed the street in a few brisk strides, with the chill of the air easily penetrating his light cotton shirt. He regretted not grabbing his cashmere sweater from his Porsche.

The bride had her back to him and as he got closer he realized the wedding dress hadn't come off the rack, but nor was it a Vera Wang creation. The faint sepia color hinted that many years had passed since it had first elegantly draped itself over a bride. Now the dress hung from sharp and narrow shoulders which seemed undecided about their posture, hovering between rigid and rolled back, and decidedly slumped.

On hearing his footsteps, she swung around, the unusual cake with its delicate lace icing wobbling precariously on its sugar pillars.

He grinned, deciding she was a cross between the bride in *The Rocky Horror Picture Show* and Miss Havisham. The round neckline of the dress sat flat and puckered as if seeking breasts to give it the form it deserved and a strand of uneven-sized pearls graced a slender neck which moved into a pointed chin. Stray wisps of wayward auburn hair stuck to hollow cheeks, and a smattering of freckles trailed across a snub nose that some might at a pinch call cute. Black smudges hovered at the top of her cheeks but it was hard to tell if they were caused by fatigue or the remnants of day-old mascara.

He'd never seen a more homely bride in need of a makeover. This was definitely performance art. It seemed a shame that she'd gone to all this trouble on the one day of the week country people spent at home with their families.

"You seem to have lost the chapel." He extended his arm indicating the direction. "It's another mile down the road."

Marc was used to a wide-eyed reaction from women, often followed by a come-hither smile. He knew this was nothing to do with him per se, and everything to do with the random collision of DNA combined with his Nordic heritage. He often wished he wasn't the walking cliché of blond hair and blue eyes but he wouldn't trade his height for anything. But this woman's vivid turquoise gaze hit him with a clear and uncompromising stare which combined irony with hovering hints of bewilderment.

"Yeah, thanks for the tip." Flat, elongated vowels clanged against the crisp fall air, falling from a mouth that on second glance was surprisingly plump given all the other sharp angles on the rest of her body. "I didn't think men did directions."

The truism made him laugh. "We happily give them. We

just don't ask for them." Her accent intrigued him. "You're not from around here?"

"I guess that depends on your definition. If ten thousand kilometers is outside the county limits then no, I'm not from around here." She held the hexagonal iced cake out toward him. "Hold the cake for me."

As an award-winning architect, Marc was more used to giving orders to his staff and contractors rather than taking them. But this situation was completely bizarre and he found himself receiving the cake without a murmur, his fingers gripping the gold-embossed foil board.

"Don't drop it."

The comment reminded him of growing up in a houseful of organizing women. "Are the English always this bossy?"

Surprisingly well-shaped eyebrows shot skyward. "The English are far too polite for their own good. Australians, on the other hand, call a spade a spade." She fisted a large amount of material into both hands and lifted the skirt free of the sidewalk, the action exposing slender ankles as she marched up to the shop window.

Surprise jolted him. Given the state of her hair and makeup and the whole "disarray bride" look she had going, he'd expected to see heavy work boots on her feet. Instead, a tiny strap of golden leather sparkling with rhinestones daintily caressed her slender foot and coiled up past a shapely ankle before disappearing tauntingly underneath the satin dress. He idly wondered what the rest of her legs looked like. "So you're a Down-Under bride?"

"I'm definitely down." The muttered words seemed more for herself than him as she pressed her face to the window and peered into the empty store. She spun back toward him, confusion bright in her eyes. "This *is* 110 West Main Street?"

He tilted his head to the faded numbers above the door. "That's what I'm reading."

White teeth tugged on her plump bottom lip as she firmly shook the door handle with her ringless left hand.

"Are you lost?"

"I didn't think I was. This is Hobin, Wisconsin, isn't it?"

"Since 1856."

"I expected it to be bigger."

He gave a wry grin. "Most people do but not a lot has changed in over one hundred and fifty years."

She took another look through the window. "And I expected this building to be a house not an empty shop."

The cake surprisingly weighed as much as two house bricks and he readjusted his grip. "This building has always been a shop, but it's been empty since old Mr. Erickson passed away more than a year ago."

"So where's Barry?" She visibly sagged, and the material of her dress rose up, as if trying to envelop her. "I can't believe I've been up thirty hours, flown halfway around the world safeguarding Nana's cake, and driven hours only to arrive and have the wrong address. This didn't happen to Nana." The words poured out on a rising inflection, ending on the hint of a wail.

Her general dishevelment suddenly made a bizarre sort of sense. He had three sisters and knew intimately that their brains, although equally intelligent, ran along a completely different track from men—a track that never ran straight. Australian women were obviously no different. "Don't tell me you've flown all the way from Australia in a wedding dress?"

She rolled her sea-green eyes and shot him a look that severely questioned his intelligence. "No, Blondie, I haven't. I put it on at the service station in the last town to surprise Barry."

Blondie? No one had given him a nickname since high school. He matched her eye roll with one raised brow. "Surprise him or scare him?"

"Hah hah, and I'd been told the Yanks didn't have a sense of humor." She crossed her arms against the cold and tossed her head. "I was going to bring my personal hairstylist and makeup artist with me but I thought Posh and Paris needed them more."

He laughed. It had been worth crossing the street just for the entertainment but he could see that she was barely keeping her teeth from chattering and was obviously lost. "Who is it you're looking for?"

"Barry Severson, importer and exporter, and my fiancé."

Marc had never been engaged and had no intentions of ever getting that closely entangled with any woman but some things were well-known facts—a groom met his overseas bride. "Why didn't he meet your plane?"

Her moment of spunk faded and an aura of fragility hovered around her making her seem smaller than her five feet four inches. "Because, like I said, I'm a surprise." She plucked at the folds of satin. "You know, the girl jumping out of the cake, only I'm the bride jumping in holding the cake."

He tried to keep his disbelief out of his voice just in case he'd missed a vital piece of information. "You're arriving unannounced to get married?"

She shrugged. "It seemed like a good idea last week when I was at home in Narranbool."

It sounded completely crazy and he'd always thought Australians had common sense. But this woman—who right now looked more like a child playing dress-up—obviously lacked that gene. Her vulnerability tried to tug at him but he immediately shrugged it away. He'd given up looking after needy women years ago. Still, the good manners drilled into him as a boy won out. "You can use my cell to call him."

A spark of hope lit up her almond-shaped eyes making the blue-green color shimmer like phosphorescence. Her smudged makeup combined with her thick, dark lashes gave her a sultry "bedroom eyes" look that was unexpected.

"Thanks, but this town isn't very big so you'd know where Barry lives, right? I'd still love to surprise him and you've already proved yourself to be good at directions." A cajoling smile danced along her face hinting at what she might look like when she wasn't totally jet-lagged.

"I'm sorry but I haven't lived here for years so I don't know your Barry."

She abruptly straightened up and hooked the train over her arm, the action all purpose and intent. "But you know someone who would know, right?"

He sighed, wishing he'd stayed in the car, wishing he'd ignored the whim to investigate. Wishing he'd stayed focused on the task at hand like he always did because although Lori and his sisters would spend the entire holiday grilling him on his life, unlike this woman, none of them was a nutcase. He *really* didn't want to get involved. But her expression was so full of expectation, so certain he could solve her problem that it took him straight back to when he was seventeen and pretty much raising his sisters. They'd specialized in similar looks.

When his friends had all been heading off to college he'd

been up to his neck bussing tables and working every odd job that came his way, trying to be the head of the family when the man who'd so loved the job had died. Died way too young when his tractor had rolled, crushing him underneath its bright green metal, stealing a husband, a father and the essence of the woman who'd loved him.

Over the next five years Marc had cut out and stapled Halloween costumes together, negotiated the bewildering aisle of feminine hygiene products in the supermarket—who knew a basic product with *one* job came with so many different names and capabilities—and mediated over everything from clothing disputes to boys. They borrowed his dress shirts, used his razor and lost his favorite sweatshirt. He'd marched pimply pubescent boys out of bedrooms and enforced every dating curfew even though it had meant enduring slamming doors and screams of "It's so not fair." Many times he'd yelled the same back.

At twenty-two he'd finally got away. Now he had an easy and dependent-free city life where not even a goldfish required his help. A place where no one else's toothbrush ever sat beside his, no one borrowed his clothes and the only person he shopped for was himself. He never got involved and that wasn't about to change.

Take the bride to Norsk's. The idea immediately relaxed him. If he took her to the diner he could leave her with Astrid who'd sort things out and he'd still make it to Lori's in time for supper. "I know exactly the person to ask, but can I put this cake down first?"

Contrition creased her forehead. "Oh, sorry. It's deceptively heavy, isn't it? But that's what you get when you combine over three kilograms of the best Australian sun-dried fruit with rum, whiskey and brandy." She reached forward to lift the second tier off its pillars and the ill-fitting dress fell forward.

He caught the hint of creamy lace and hoped Barry was going to appreciate all the effort she'd put into this insane escapade. "That's a lot of liquor."

A rich, full-bodied laugh carried back toward him as she walked toward a silver hatchback with a distinctive black-and-yellow rental company sticker. "Nana's cakes were legendary and always full of booze. It acts as a preservative and that's why they can travel so well. There's a special box for it in the boot."

"Excuse me?" His ears were adjusting to her accent but he thought she'd just said *boot*.

She popped the trunk open and lowered the top tier into a box.

"That would be the trunk," Marc corrected.

"Really? I guess that's because it would have originally carried trunks." She relieved him of the cake and carefully placed it into the second box. "Nana had a real trunk with a curved top and I used to love playing in it when I was a little girl." A dreamy look crossed her face and she seemed to lose herself in memories.

He leaned against the car. "So why is it called a boot in Australia?"

The dreamy expression faded, overtaken by something far more prosaic. "Probably because of the convicts with their stolen booty." She straightened up and extended her hand, her freckles more pronounced with the cold. "Matilda Geoffrey, direct descendent of convicts."

He smiled and gripped her hand. "Marc Olsen, direct descendent of Viking marauders. Let's go and ask the town oracle about this fiancé of yours."

★ ★ ★

Norsk's had been a Hobin institution for as long as the oldest resident in town could remember, and then some. With its high pressed metal ceilings and deep wooden booths, plus extended hours from six in the morning until ten at night, it was the unofficial town hall where the most important deals—both financial and social—took place. Plus it sold the best food in town and was famous across the state for its potato lefse.

Marc opened the door and ushered Matilda inside, checking that the door didn't jam the dress before she'd moved through. She'd come this far with her madcap scheme, the least she deserved was to have a clean dress. The aroma of hot, strong coffee combined with the deep-fried scent of fat and brown sugar washed over him, immediately making him smile. As a kid he'd saved his pennies and bought the mouth-watering Norwegian rosette pastries by the bagful.

A cry of surprise greeted him, followed by the bang of a swing door and brisk firm footsteps. A big-boned woman, her buxom frame covered by a huge old-fashioned white apron, rushed toward him, her arms outstretched. Astrid was the current owner of Norsk's and a good friend to his mother. She was also the woman who knew everything there was to know about everyone in Hobin and the tri-county area.

She wrapped her arms around him. "Marc, you're home. Your mama said you were coming and here you are." She pinched his cheeks as if he was seven and her scent of soap and spices enveloped him, taking him back in time when he'd been small and the most complicated thing in life was to make the difficult choice between gingerbread and chocolate-chip cookies.

Astrid admonished him, "It's been too long. You really should come more often. Your mother worries."

He gave an understanding shrug, having had the same conversation every November for years. "She'd worry about me if I lived here."

"True, but she'd worry different." Astrid's pale blue eyes studied him closely, as if he might disappear again before she'd had her fill. Slowly, her gaze drew away from him and she caught sight of Matilda. Her hand immediately shot to her throat. "Oh, as I live and breathe, I never thought I'd see the day." She spun around so fast that her bun of carefully wound gray hair wobbled. "Listen up, everyone," she shouted in her "order-up" voice. "Marc Olsen's home and he's brought a bride."

Heads turned, legs of chairs scraped against the floorboards and the jukebox fell silent. People rose to their feet, surprise shining on their faces and comments tumbling from their mouths.

"How wonderful."

"No way."

"Who's going to tell Sue-Ellen?"

"She gave up on him years ago and married Brent Larsen. You went to the wedding, remember?"

Hobin loved a bride and loved a wedding, and that enthusiasm seemed to blind them all to the fact he was in casual wear and his so-called bride was wearing a gown clearly from five decades earlier. Not to mention the combination of her pale face with run mascara that made her look like a Goth. Nonetheless, Marc's back was slapped, and hands pumped his own as he raised his voice, trying to speak above the noise before the story went from "just married" to "they're expecting a baby and moving back to Hobin."

"I'm not marrying *him*."

The hands dropped away and the chatter stopped instantly as Matilda's Australian accent silenced everyone.

He'd noticed she often ended her sentences on a high note and in this case it made her sound like marrying him was the worst possible thing in the world. But ego aside he shot her a grateful look as he caught sight of the clock. It was time to sort this out so the bride and groom could be reunited and he could get to Lori's.

"Everyone, this is Matilda Geoffrey and she's just arrived from Australia today to surprise her fiancé, Barry Severson. But there's some confusion over his address so can someone give Matilda directions?"

"Barry Severson." A murmur went around the diner while blank faces stared back, oscillating between the Australian bride and himself.

Ray Peterson, a local farmer, chipped in. "There's Barry Everett just out of town on the highway. He runs the agricultural equipment co-op and he's single. Perhaps he's your man."

"Barry Hillestad just opened that Sparkle Clean carpet business." John Wolf tugged thoughtfully at his beard. "And he's been advertising for staff. Mind you, he could do with a wife," he added helpfully.

Marc swallowed a groan and glanced at his watch. At this rate they were going to be subjected to the occupation and marital status of every Barry in Hobin.

Matilda agitatedly tucked some hair behind her ear with one hand while she straightened her dress with the other. "Barry's got a business in town importing giftware."

"Peggy Hendrix has the only gift shop in town, dear." Astrid's brows pulled down into a V of concern and she shot Marc a questioning look.

Matilda's expressive hands fluttered out in front of her. "It's more than a shop and I think that's the confusion. He's had the shop for a while but now he's leased a large warehouse in the business park so I think he must have moved everything there and is concentrating on expanding his business."

Business park? A sinking feeling settled in Marc's stomach. He might only visit once a year but his sisters' emails would have mentioned something as huge as a business park starting up in town. An empty shop had just been joined by a fictitious business park.

The mutters amongst the customers started to sound concerned.

Marc drummed his fingers against the diner's counter as he tried to marshal his thoughts. "Matilda, when did you last speak to Barry?"

"Two days ago. I rang him on his mobile just before I got on the plane…" She must have caught his confused expression and immediately corrected herself. "I called him on his cell phone but he couldn't talk because he was entertaining clients at the microbrewery."

The closest Hobin got to a microbrewery was Ray's homebrew. Not that it wasn't a legendary drink, it was. Every year for the last decade Ray had taken home the State Fair blue ribbon for the best-tasting milk and his not-so-secret ingredient was giving his Holsteins a sip of his beer while they were being milked.

Astrid shoved her hands deep into her apron pocket, gazing at her feet for a moment before looking up and opening her mouth, only to close it again. The usually plain-speaking woman inclined her head toward Marc as if to say, "You have to tell her."

Fantastic. Just great. He swore under his breath, his plans of leaving Matilda with Astrid unraveling faster than rope being pulled by an anchor. He should have just stayed in the car. Now he had to tell a woman of doubtful emotional status, who'd traveled halfway around the world to get married, that her fiancé's story about his business and life in Hobin was a pack of lies, and that no one in town had heard of him. Oh yeah, he really wanted to put his hand up for that.

He remembered the tears of his sisters when they'd been dumped by boyfriends. Boyfriends not fiancés. The chances that anyone would take this news well were slim. Especially a woman who'd got on a plane with an ancient dress and a cake that wouldn't pass a breathalyzer test. *Crazy* didn't seem strong enough a word.

The urge to turn and walk out the door made his feet tingle. He could still do that. He could walk away. After all, she'd find out soon enough on her own without him telling her. If she had any sense at all—which he sincerely doubted—she'd have started to put the pieces together and work it out all by herself. Besides, he was now seriously late for supper at Lori's.

Oh yeah, like that's ever worried you before.

"Marc." Astrid's tone said it all.

He had no choice but to break this woman's heart.

CHAPTER TWO

Fifteen pairs of unknown eyes bored into Matilda plus one pair of eyes the exact same vivid blue as the outback sky that had always shone above her right up until thirty-odd hours ago. But despite the familiar and reassuring color, those eyes were a heartbeat away from belonging to a total stranger. A stranger with a very critical gaze, and for the first time since she'd left Narranbool, she felt totally alone and misunderstood.

Okay, so she looked a bit untidy, but it wasn't like today was the wedding. She'd just wanted Barry's first image of her in three months to be as a bride. Just like Nana and Grandpa Hank all those years ago. Barry would get the symbolism because they had wedding plans—heaps of wedding plans. For the last month most of their emails had focused on that topic and she had eighty-five of them filed in a "wedding" folder with subject headers ranging from dates and places right down to the menu options. So when her immigration papers had come through unexpectedly early thanks to Grandpa Hank's ancestry, it had made all the sense in the world to hop on a plane. She'd dropped a few pointed hints in an email the day before she left and Barry, who was utterly simpatico, would have picked up on them.

My love expands across the oceans until you're here with me. Barry had the soul of a true romantic unlike the Viking in front of her who clearly thought she was stark, raving bonkers. Well, his opinion didn't matter. No one's opinion mattered except Barry's and he'd totally understand why she'd come *and* he'd be thrilled.

He would be. He had to be. She squared her shoulders against the tiny shivers of apprehension that had started shooting through her on and off from the moment she'd driven into town. In the last hour, each shiver had increased in frequency and intensity, dragging at her, and making her doubt everything. But she refused to allow demon doubts to plague her. It was just tiredness and jet lag playing tricks and everything was going to work out just fine.

Her stomach churned acid against nothing and she swallowed hard. This was body-over-mind stuff and she rejected her body's lack of belief in her plan. Of course she'd done the right thing. This was the dream and right now she only had the dream to hold on to and, damn it, she was clinging to it like a life preserver. After all, the dream had worked like a charm for Nana and for her mother so there was no reason to expect anything different for herself. The Geoffrey women had always lived the dream—it was their destiny to travel for love. This current situation was merely a hiccup in her predestined journey and just a bit of confusion over addresses. Within the hour she'd be having a hot cup of tea with Barry and laughing at how she'd let a few niggling doubts shake her up.

The tall and indecently good-looking Viking had said

someone here would know where Barry lived, but no one was saying anything and all this staring was starting to freak her out. The time had come to step back into the game and take control. Smoothing down the front of Nana's wedding dress, she stared back at them all with a smile and broke the strained silence. "I know my passport says I'm a 'non-resident alien' but I didn't think I really looked like one."

She'd expected a chuckle or even a laugh but all she got was the shuffling of feet. She tried again. "After all, the dress isn't green."

The Viking's generous mouth twitched but his smile stalled as seriousness took over. "Ah, Matilda."

"Yes?" She'd never considered herself short but she had to tilt her head to look up into his face which was disconcertingly flawless and in perfect symmetry. She'd never trusted handsome men whose "godlike" beauty overshadowed everyone around them. No, it was far better to trust in mere mortal men like Barry. Handsome in the Hollywood style he wasn't and he could even be called short and dumpy but his emails were virtual poetry.

The Viking shoved his large hands into the tops of his jeans pockets. "There's no business park in Hobin."

No shop, no business park. Every cell in her body shot out a surge of adrenaline, and a prickle of anxiety swept her from head to toe. *Stop it.* She must have heard wrong. She breathed in deeply and started again. She'd only been in the States a few short hours but already she was used to people not understanding her accent. "Maybe you call it something else over here. I'm talking about factories and warehouses, and they tend to be built on the edge of towns."

His gaze bored into her both frank and direct. "That's right.

We're on the same page, but the only things on the edge of Hobin are cornfields and cows."

She rubbed the throbbing sensation in her temple as she searched her memory for snatches of conversation with Barry and snippets of emails. *"Baby you won't believe how fast the business is growing. With your injection of capital I'm moving the stock into a bigger place. It won't be long now and we'll get married."*

Her brain fought to think clearly. "Perhaps he's made it sound a bit grander than it really is. Maybe it's more like he's rented one of the self-storage garages I passed on the way in?"

"I don't think that's the case."

His deep voice, the straightforward gaze full of judgment and superiority really started to grate. Not to mention the effect it had on her stomach which had gone from churning to full-on pulverizing-blender mode. Her red-hair temper flared. "How would you know? You said you don't even live here." She swung around in desperation, seeking help from the others. "Someone in this room has to know Barry? He's coached the junior soccer."

Fifteen gray-haired heads shook from side to side and fifteen faces continued to stare at her with a mixed expression of extreme interest and traces of pity.

"This is stupid." Her frustration peaked and all her plans of surprising Barry turned to dust. She threw up her hands. "I give up on the surprise. I'll just ring him and tell him I'm here." She tossed her head back in an almost defiant action which she knew was silly but she hated having to ask for help, especially from the Viking who obviously thought she had a kangaroo loose in the top paddock. "Can I borrow your phone, please?"

"Sure." He fished the neat, black smartphone out of his

pocket and pressed a button before passing it to her. "Just touch in his number and you're good to go."

"Thanks." She could feel everyone's gaze fixed on her and her heart pounded hard against her ribs. Being the center of attention had never been her thing so she took a few steps and slid into an empty booth, welcoming the protection of the high wooden walls.

She closed her eyes for a moment and thought of Nana. As she heard her grandmother's voice in her mind and relived the story she'd grown up hearing over and over again, she started to relax. *And Tildy, darling, when your Grandpa saw me walk down the gangplank off the ship that had sailed all the way from Australia, he waved so hard and stood so tall that I knew right then everything was going to be just fine.*

Everything would be fine for her too. She was a Geoffrey. This was her future and her long-time-coming chance at happiness. She quickly punched in Barry's mobile phone number and pressed the phone against her ear.

A woman's recorded voice vibrated in her ear. *The number you have dialed has been disconnected and is no longer in service. If you think you have dialed this number in error, please check the number and try again.*

She dragged in a deep breath. She'd let tiredness and frustration get to her, making her inaccurate. This time she carefully pressed the numbers slowly, checking each one on the liquid display before she continued. Again she pressed the phone to her ear, willing the connection time lag to speed up.

The number you have dialed has been disconnected...

She punched the off button. For the third time she let her fingers automatically trail across numbers as familiar to her as her own name. The same American accent told her the same story. *No longer in service.*

The pounding in her head sounded as loud as a jackhammer and she had to pull on every reserve to concentrate. Something must have happened. Perhaps Barry's phone had been stolen and he'd emailed her to tell her he'd had to cancel the account. With shaking fingers she scrolled back to the main screen, and brought up a browser. Seconds ticked by like hours as she watched the little blue circle turn around and around but finally the familiar icon appeared and she located her email account. She clicked on the Inbox and three bold and black messages came up.

Mail System Delivery failed: returning message to sender. A message that you sent could not be delivered to one or more of its recipients.

All three emails had been sent to Barry just before she got on the plane. Sent to the same email account she'd used for months.

This is a permanent error.

Her hand gripped the small multimedia device so hard it should have cut into her hand but she was oblivious to that pain as she tried to force air into a rigidly tight chest. No phone, no email, no shop, no warehouse. No Barry in Hobin. *No Barry.*

A scream sounded in her head. This wasn't possible. He couldn't have just vanished. Barry existed. He had an address. He had a business. He had such plans for their future and she'd invested in them and...

She gulped in a breath as silver spots danced in front of her eyes. Somehow against a head pounding with half-completed thoughts, she managed to enter her ID number into the login page of her new U.S. bank. It was like being plunged into a slow-motion film sequence as the page painstakingly loaded, and the lines of figures formed across the tiny screen. She only had eyes for one line—the balance of their recently opened joint account.

Zero.

A permanent error.

Oh God, what had she done?

She closed the internet browser, removing the uncompromising zero from view, and laid down the phone. Her stomach tried to eject its contents and every breath hurt. She desperately wanted to sink under the table, huddle into a ball and hide. Hide out and pretend this was just a bad dream and she'd wake up really soon, standing behind the counter at the Narranbool post-office-*cum*-general-store, dressed in her signature work outfit of black pants and a short-sleeved blouse, having swapped her nursing uniform to run the business for Nana two years ago.

Only it had stopped being Nana's business the moment she'd died not quite nine months ago, and last week Matilda had handed over operations to the new owners. Handed it over so she could come and live the dream, and start her new life in Hobin.

We'll build a life here and work together. She pressed the heel of her palm hard against her forehead to try and stop the violent and excruciating pounding as realization changed from a trickle to a full roar. A new life in Hobin wasn't going to happen. Barry was a fake.

Anger flooded her, knocking over every other emotion. Fury burned at Barry and raged at herself. How had she let this happen? The last few months of her life lay in dust at her feet, now the remnants of a huge con. She'd opened her heart, shared her hopes and dreams and that bottom-dwelling scum had fed on them. Now Barry-the-Bastard had vanished, stealing her money and her dreams.

Her brain creaked between disbelief and reality. Everything she'd believed in had been a sham. She'd been well and truly played by a con artist in the very same way as so many women before her. Women she'd been so derisive of when she'd read about similar situations in the newspaper.

Oh, Nana. It wasn't supposed to be like this. Tears prickled at the back of her eyes and it took every ounce of energy that she had not to openly weep. Crying would have to wait. Right now she had to walk out of this café with her dignity intact. She refused to be a victim in a café full of strangers. Especially not in front of the Viking who had pegged her as a crazy fool from the start. No way would she give him the satisfaction of knowing that he'd been right. And she'd been oh-so very wrong.

No one needed to know the truth. She could do this. She could get out of the café and into her car without anyone thinking anything more than she'd been a diversion in their normally quiet Sunday evening. She was wearing Nana's glorious dress from a time when true love really did exist and she'd exit in style. Forcing every muscle in her body to work just a little bit longer, she stood up on rubbery legs, picked up her train and then the phone.

Drawing on every school drama lesson, she swept out of the booth and glided down the center of the café with her head held high, ignoring all the well-intentioned stares. Her heart hammered so hard she thought it would bound right out of her chest and roll down the aisle before her, and her head spun dizzily making walking on high heels an occupational health hazard.

You can do this. "Hey, Blondie, thanks for the use of your phone. I'm all sorted now." She slapped the sleek black device into his palm and shot him her best quelling look. "Just as *I* predicted it was a misunderstanding and I've confused Hobin Road with the town." She gave silent thanks to the GPS which had announced every hamlet and town she'd driven through on her way from Chicago, providing the chance for her to sound far more knowledgeable about Wisconsin geography than was accurate. "So I better hit the road if I'm going to get to Wausau. Barry sends his thanks for helping me out and so do I." The bell above her head rang as she wrenched the door open, and the tinkling noise was the only sound breaking the stunned silence behind her.

Digging deep, she turned because everything came down to the exit. "It was lovely meeting you all. Thanks so much for your help. Goodbye."

She lifted her skirt, stepped over the threshold and out into the unknown, welcoming the icy air as it bit painfully into her exposed skin. She'd done it. Everything was a complete mess, her dreams lay in tatters and she was stone broke, but she'd exited with her pride intact. Hollywood would have been proud of her.

The door of the diner shut and silence prevailed for about five seconds before people drifted back to their seats and resumed their meals. Everyone quickly slipped back into the previous discussion of milk prices, the scandal of the proposed middle-school band uniform change, and what size Thanksgiving turkey was big enough without the leftovers dominating the menu for the following week.

"Well, thank goodness for that," Astrid exclaimed. "I was so worried for that girl and I'd convinced myself that Barry didn't exist, so it's good to be wrong for once." She winked at Marc before heading back behind the counter, busying herself with making fresh coffee. "Those Australians are adventurous though. Fancy coming all this way to get married. But then again I remember my mother talking about an Australian woman she knew who married one of our marines in the war and then came to live in Green Bay. Can you imagine that?"

Marc ignored the rhetorical question knowing his answer wouldn't be welcome. But please, who in their right mind would trade the sunshine of Australia for the frigid winters of Green Bay? Women lost every iota of common sense when they fell in love, leaving them wide open for disaster. It had happened to his sisters time and time again and to his mother in a different sense, losing a part of herself when his dad died. At least today's disaster had been averted and there were no hysterical tears to mop up.

Relief trickled through him at the lucky save. Hobin had reverted to its slow and predictable self and he had five days in town which was more than enough time with his family before he headed back east. All was right with the world.

"I better get moving." He pocketed his phone which had been surprisingly silent given how late he was running. He'd thought Lori would have called at least twice by now asking him if he'd come via Canada.

Astrid handed off two plates of burgers to waiting customers. "Give Lori my love and make sure you come in for breakfast tomorrow and tell me all your news."

He knew better than to argue. "Will do." He flicked the collar of his shirt up in an attempt to keep the keen and biting wind at bay and moved down Main Street at a brisk jog. As he opened his car door he noticed the silver rental car had gone. An image of flyaway auburn curls and flashing turquoise eyes, filled with ironic humor, flashed in his head.

Hey, Blondie. He couldn't help but smile—she'd been an entertaining diversion and Barry had no idea what he was letting himself in for with that one. The woman was both crazy and foolhardy, but she'd provided more entertainment in one hour than he usually got in Hobin in five days. He'd get plenty of mileage out of the story over dinner and a glass of Australian Merlot when he got home to New York.

He pulled his sweater off the passenger seat and caught sight of the large box of Legos he'd bought for his nephew. The toy was as much for himself as it was for Kyle and it would be a good distraction over the next few days. He and Kyle could retreat to the basement when the house filled with women trying to feed and organize him.

Flicking on the heater, he rubbed his cold jeans-clad thighs, these days more used to the feel of the fine black wool of a tailored suit than the work-ready denim of his childhood. These days his casual wear was more urban chic but when he'd been packing he'd found these jeans buried at the back of his wardrobe, discarded a year ago after the weekend build for Habitat for Humanity. Wearing them had been a whim, pretty much like checking out this whole bride thing.

He moved the gear shift into Neutral, started the car and checked over his shoulder before pulling out and heading down the county road. The sun sat low in the sky, and he pulled on his designer sunglasses, hoping a deer didn't decide to stray from the woods and cross the road. He knew from experience that a hit deer was an uncompromising beast, able to inflict irreparable damage on a vehicle. The streets of New York were a lot safer than Northern Wisconsin.

The road curved, the Porsche purred and he lost himself in the smoothness of European engineering, racing through the gears and enjoying the drive. Normally he flew in to Madison and rented a car, not prepared to risk his own vehicle on salt-drenched roads should the snow fall early. But this year the urge to drive had seemed the answer to a wave of restlessness that had been with him since the end of the summer, and no amount of work or exercise seemed to be able to shift it. So after checking the weather stats and noting snow hadn't fallen before Christmas for three years, he'd decided traveling by car was a pretty safe bet.

Driving on the back roads, through groves of aspens and paper birch trees losing their final golden leaves, he'd taken in the ubiquitous red barns that dotted the brown fall landscape, and watched the farmers bringing in their crops and bedding down their fields for winter. He'd originally thought he'd stick to the interstate, avoiding the farms, avoiding memories, but surprisingly the bucolic scenes had been an unexpected highlight of the trip.

Now his journey was at an end. As he glimpsed the welcome flag fluttering from under Lori's mailbox, he slowed and pulled into her long gravel driveway. Surrounded by maples and oaks and a scattering of walnut trees, the low-slung ranch house nestled into the curve of the block, using the fall of the land to accommodate a large basement which doubled the size of the small home. Large picture windows caught all the precious winter light and in full summer the foliage of the garden acted as natural blinds, shielding the house from the sun. A chimney built from local quartzite sandstone interrupted the long lengths of beige clapboard, providing a change of texture and a rich variation of earthy color. Neat but dormant flowerbeds bordered the path to the front door, having already been put to bed for winter. Flower season was seriously short this far north.

Except for the stone work, a nod to the memory of Wisconsin's famous architect son and Marc's hero, Frank Lloyd Wright, it wasn't his style of house. But Lori had worked hard to make it hers after her louse of a husband left her with a king's ransom of a mortgage. Marc had offered to buy the house outright and free Lori from the financial burden but she'd insisted on paying him back and he'd had to settle on giving her an interest-free loan. On the first of every month the repayments appeared on his bank statement. Unbeknown to Lori, he'd invested the money and now it was working hard generating Kyle's college fund.

The gravel driveway acted as a doorbell and usually the moment his car wheels touched the crushed rock, Kyle raced out the white front door to greet him, quickly followed by Lori. He parked in front of the garage, killed the engine and lifted his travel bag off the backseat. Still the door remained closed. He checked his watch. It was well past six and he'd expected to be met with a hug and a "what-time-do-you-call-this" look. Then again, he'd expected at least two "hurry up" phone calls, as well. Although none of his sisters had lived on the farm in years, like many Wisconsinites they kept to the routine of an early supper time. He, on the other hand, was always late.

He opened the front door—locks in Hobin rusted from under use—and stepped inside. A small black suitcase sat by the coat closet, a jacket resting on the extended handle. He put his bag down next to it and called out in his best attempt at a New York twang, "Hey, sis, did you cancel the band?"

Running feet thudded down the hall. "Hey, big brother!" Lori flung her arms around his neck. "I'm sorry. I didn't hear you arrive. I was just—" She hugged him hard and then stepped back, gazing at him with familiar blue eyes but with unfamiliar black shadows underneath them. "It's good to see you. Did you have a good trip?"

His usually bubbly younger sister seemed distracted and subdued. "I did. Sorry I'm late but you'll get a kick out of this story. I stopped in Hobin because—"

Lori crossed the hall as if she hadn't even heard him and called down the basement stairs. "Kyle, come say hi. Your uncle's arrived."

As she turned back, he caught strained lines around her mouth and her hand gripped the banister overly hard. A forced smile touched her lips. "He's grown so much since last year that you'll hardly recognize him."

A lanky teen, half boy, half man, shuffled up the stairs, shoulders slumped forward, hands pushed hard into the pockets of a red hoodie and his dark head tilted down, staring at his large feet. His olive skin, courtesy of his father's genes, gave the illusion of a permanent tan, the envy of many a female in Wisconsin who had to pay and pay often for the same look. As he reached the top step, he slowly raised his head and wide, brown eyes filled with boredom peered out at Marc through a veil of hair before dropping back to his feet.

"Hey, kiddo." Marc stepped forward ready to hug him but suddenly stopped when he hit the aura of teenage antipathy.

He immediately regretted using the word *kiddo*. He quickly regrouped and extended his hand for a man-to-man shake.

Kyle's hands stayed in the hoodie pockets, his eyes glued to the ground. "Hey."

In the space of twelve months, the enthusiastic kid who used to beg Marc to shoot baskets before he'd even got out of the car had vanished, leaving behind a stranger in his place. Feeling ridiculous with his hand stuck out in midair, Marc raised it and gave the boy's shoulder a quick squeeze. "Good to see you."

Kyle's shoulder shrugged his hand away. "Yeah."

Marc expected Lori, the usual manners police, to reprimand her son but instead she marched toward the kitchen calling over her shoulder, "You must be starving. Come wash up, and then tell me about the trip."

He glanced back to speak with Kyle but he'd already turned and was walking down the stairs leaving Marc alone in the entrance feeling like he'd walked into the wrong household. He followed his sister into the kitchen and did a double take.

Lori was the most house-proud woman he knew and despite working and raising her son on her own, her home was always immaculate. But today dirty dishes sat in the sink and the central counter was covered with a mix of half-unpacked groceries, opened jam jars and peanut-butter-stained knives. The tabletop was littered with newspapers dating back three days and evidence of a previous meal that must have involved peas lay squished and scattered on the floor underneath the table.

"There's liquid soap by the sink and a hand towel on the cupboard rail." Pushing the papers up one end of the table, Lori then grabbed some glasses and plonked the gallon milk container into the center of the table. She crossed the kitchen, opened her oven and, using mitts, pulled out two TV dinners, which she slid onto plates and set them down on placemats. The meal looked completely out of place on a table that normally groaned with dishes of steaming vegetables, creamy mashed potatoes; fine, roasted beef and a boat of fragrant gravy.

Every one of her actions vibrated with unusual agitation and was completely out of character. Marc frowned as he dried his hands.

"Come sit." Lori poured him some milk. "You must be hungry."

He pulled out the chair and sat down opposite his sister. "What about Kyle? Isn't he eating with us?"

She shook her head and pushed a pale green bean around the plate. "He ate already."

His increasing sense of dislocation heightened. Lori always made a fuss of meals and sitting down together, especially the night he arrived. The chaotic kitchen, the once-frozen meal in front of him, Lori's complete distraction—none of this added up.

He left his silverware sitting crookedly by the placemat. "What's going on?"

Lori gave him a wry smile. "You know November's always crazy for me. The run-up to the fall play was, as usual, a nightmare and I've been living in the Drama department. But it came together as it always does and the kids did a fantastic job." She trailed her fork through the white blob that hinted at potato origins.

Lori had directed the fall play for the last six years but she'd never looked this tired. "No, what's really going on?" He extended his arm to encompass the kitchen. "I've never seen the house like this, not even when Carl left."

She dropped her fork, the metal clattering against the stoneware. "I've got some news."

Her quiet tone sent a chill along his spine. "Are you going to tell me?"

Hesitation swirled around her as she took in a long breath. When she spoke, she did so very quickly. "I've got breast cancer and I'm going into the hospital tomorrow for surgery."

Her words drilled into him hard, sharp and unrelenting as his brain bounced between disbelief and total realism. Cancer. *No.* Words seemed deeply inadequate. "Hell, Lori...the hospital tomorrow? But that means..." He did a quick calculation in his head. "How long have you known?"

She didn't shy away from his gaze. "I had the scan and biopsy ten days ago and the results came back the next day."

"Ten days!" He couldn't believe it. "But we've spoken on the phone since then. Why didn't you tell me when I called you to say I was driving and arriving today?"

Her chest rose and fell and she spun a ring on her finger. "Because you wouldn't have come."

"That's ridiculous." The words flew out on bluster, loudly defensive. "Of course I would have come."

She raised a brow, giving him the exact sardonic look he knew he was capable of. "No. You would have stayed in New York, thrown money at the problem and sent a nurse."

The words of denial rose to his lips only to stall. He wanted to yell, "I would not!" but she knew him too well. He came home once a year on a flying visit, caught up with his mother and sisters over three days and then left, barely staying long enough for any Wisconsin marsh mud to stick to his Italian leather shoes. "Well, I'm here now. Do you need a nurse?"

She shook her head, a sad smile clinging to her mouth. "No, I don't need a nurse."

"Are you sure?" Paying for a nurse to care for Lori after her surgery was the least he could do.

"I'm sure." She took a sip of milk.

He ran through the family logistics and realized a nurse wasn't necessary. "I guess even with Sheryl taking that job out on the West Coast it still leaves Mom and Jennifer fighting each other to help out."

"I haven't told them." Lori's fingers fiddled with the cotton edges of the placemat.

"Why not?"

She sighed. "You know how Ty took that job in Chicago and has been doing the weekly commute? Well, his company is sending him to a tiny country I've never heard of called—" she hesitated and wrinkled her nose in concentration "—Brunei. Apparently they've got oil. Anyway, it's a two-year contract so Jen and the kids are going too. They leave on Thanksgiving and I don't want to tell Jen because she has enough to deal with right now."

Astonishment socked him. Apart from going to college, his sisters had always chosen to live in Hobin and suddenly in the space of three months two of them had moved away. "But I emailed her earlier in the month and she never said a word."

Lori shrugged apologetically. "She wanted to tell you in person so act surprised."

He smiled at the first sign of the bossy sister he knew. His siblings had always been hopeless at keeping secrets and growing up he'd been custodian of so many stories it got hard to keep track. "So no Sheryl or Jennifer? It probably suits Mom better to be able to care for you on her own and not be bossed about by those two."

"Actually, Mom hasn't been well herself. She's having dizzy spells to do with her blood pressure so she's not driving right now."

This information layered in on top of the other unanticipated news, causing a slippery slope of bewilderment to build inside him. "She always says she's fine when I ask."

Lori shot him a pitying look as if he was completely clueless. "Of course she tells you she's fine. You're far away and she doesn't want you to worry. I don't want her to worry either so I'm not telling her until after the surgery." She laced her fingers together, knuckles gleaming white. "After I know the full extent of…what I'm dealing with."

Cancer. She was dealing with cancer. A traitorous condition that had the modus operandi of a stealth bomber—unseen and deadly. He hated not knowing how bad it was, if it had spread widely or what Lori faced fighting it.

His brain was so caught up with processing the impact of the illness that it took a while for Lori's words to really sink in. "So you're not telling Mom or our sisters, yet you're telling me you don't need a nurse to help you after surgery and perhaps through chemotherapy?"

Her mouth took on a mulish line. "I don't need a nurse."

He ran his hand through his hair. "What about Gracie, then? You've been friends since kindergarten."

"I'm not telling anyone in town until I know more."

"That's not practical. Without Mom, Sheryl or Jennifer, you're going to need someone here to help."

"That's right." Blue eyes filled with fear and uncertainty,

but backed with determination, stared him down. "I need you, Marc. Kyle and I need you to stay for a while past Thanksgiving."

The ties that bind pulled in taut with a jerk across his chest, lashing him tightly and holding him firmly in the chair. Family ties. The years rolled back in an instant. *You'll help, won't you, Marc?* Teenage memories roared through him, pressing down with their obligations and responsibilities. "Are you sure it wouldn't be better to tell Mom?"

She shook her head, the action vehement and decisive. "No, not yet."

He loved his sister dearly but every part of him railed at what she was asking. He hated being the custodian of secrets. He didn't know anything about caring for a woman post-surgery and the thought that Lori was so sick scared him rigid.

And Kyle? Hell, he didn't even know the sullen boy who was downstairs. Every part of him screamed "no." Every part of him said, "go." This wasn't what he'd come home for, this wasn't part of the annual plan. For years he'd used short, sharp visits to keep him free of family stuff having done his time from seventeen to twenty-two.

Lori leaned forward, her eyes pleading and her fear palpable. "Marc, you *will* help, won't you?"

Cancer. Given any other choice he would have run. Hell, he wanted to run right now, but once again he had no choice so he swallowed hard and said, "Sure, sis, I can stay for a bit."

Family. He felt the responsibilities sucking him down into a black hole. His years of "time off for good behavior" had just come to an abrupt end.

CHAPTER THREE

Weak rays of early-morning light permeated the thick coating of ice on the windshield, waking Matilda from a fitful sleep. She stretched and immediately hit her funny bone on the cup holder. The pain shot up her arm, joining all the other aches and pains that throbbed in her limbs which were not used to being curled up so tightly trying to keep warm. Her head banged, her skin screamed for the heat of a shower, for the cleansing touch of soap, and her stomach growled in hungry protest.

Last night had been the longest and coldest of her life. After leaving the diner she'd gotten into the car and driven until tears blurred her vision, forcing her to stop. She'd pulled into a rest area and had stayed put, sleeping in the car because she had no money to waste on a motel room.

Her freezing fingers numbed by cold, shock and fatigue, hadn't been able to reach around to her middle back and undo all the tiny buttons on Nana's dress. As she hadn't been prepared to rip the precious gown, she'd left it on and pulled her hand-knitted, wool sweater over her head followed by her polar fleece jacket. Underneath she'd shoved her legs into a pair of bright, striped long johns and her feet into two pairs of fleecy socks. By midnight, with teeth chattering, she'd covered herself with her oil-skin coat and all the clothes from her suitcase but none of them had protected her from the insidious cold that had seeped into her and was now bone-deep.

The night had passed excruciatingly slowly and across the hours she'd experienced almost every emotion possible. The anger and despair about Barry came in suffocating waves. At other times, complete terror struck her as loud and totally unfamiliar sounds came out of the inky darkness. At home she was used to sleeping out in her swag under the outback southern stars, and she enjoyed listening to the nocturnal scratching of bilbies, the electrical static sound of the sugar glider and the barking of koalas. But she hadn't recognized any of the sounds she'd heard last night. Something had squealed and squeaked in the dark and even worse than that, something big like a bear had bumped the car and she'd been a pathetic excuse of a girl and screamed.

In between moments of darkness-induced fear and creating vivid and detailed plans about how to emasculate Barry-the-Bastard if she ever found him, she had long tracks of time to think about what she was going to do. She had less than forty-five dollars to her name, no return ticket to Australia and a car that was due to be handed back to the rental company today. Ironically, the insistence of the U.S. immigration department that she prove financial security and independence so she wouldn't be a burden on the American taxpayer had been her total undoing. She'd transferred all her money and then on Barry's advice, had put it into a joint business account.

He'd sagely told her this was the best way to gain higher interest as well as protecting her future by becoming part of a business. A business she was now certain was fake.

That left her with the clothes she stood up in and nothing to sit down in. All of Nana's inheritance had vanished along with Barry-the-Bastard. Her parents, who'd never placed any value on money and material possessions, were busy working in a remote village in the highlands of Papua New Guinea and impossible to contact. Even if she could have phoned them, they didn't have the funds to help get her home and would have been stunned she'd even asked. They'd raised her to be independent from an early age so they wouldn't think they needed to bail her out at thirty. *This is your life, Tildy. Chase your dreams.*

Chasing ridiculous dreams had got her into this mess. She glanced down at Nana's dress that was wrapped tightly around her legs, the off-white evidence of her greatest folly.

No one wants me, Nana. I'm never going to marry.

Yes you are, darling. Forget Jason. The man of your dreams is out there waiting for you. Keep the faith and follow the dream.

Then Nana had died, leaving behind a hole in her heart the size of the Great Sandy Desert and a lovingly decorated wedding cake. A cake that had bored into her grief day after day, an unrelenting reminder that she was the *only* Geoffrey woman without a life-altering great love. She was the failure.

Men left her. She'd spent two years of her life creating a home with her live-in boyfriend, only to have him up and leave her for a hospital job a thousand miles away with no invitation to follow. *Don't come with me, Matilda. It's best to end it now.* People she loved left her. It was as simple as that and it had happened yet again.

Anger at herself almost choked her. Bloody hell, for all her post-Jason determination to leave the dream alone and live a sensible and independent life, she couldn't even spot a blatant con. Barry had taken her for one hell of a ride. With great skill he'd zeroed in on her emotional weak spot and she'd been oblivious to it all. Too busy missing her grandmother, desperately needing to believe in the dream and with Nana's words ringing in her ears, she'd let him make decisions for her that had now cost her everything. Love. *Hah!*

Love for her was the greatest hoax and so was the dream. She would never put any faith in either again. She sure as eggs was never again putting any money on love. Love worked for other women but not for her. From today, she, Matilda Geoffrey, would only ever depend on herself, because that was the only safe way.

Her tummy burned from a combination of hunger and acid stripping off the lining, while the thoughts in her head went around and around on a continuous loop, getting her nowhere. Like most of her life she was once again on her own. Now she needed a plan. So far the plan consisted more of what she was *not* going to do rather than what she was going to do. No way was she going back to Hobin. If she was virtually destitute she could be that in a town where absolutely no one had met her or knew what had led her to this point. She had enough on her plate without facing Hobin and having to explain over and over what a fool she'd been.

First she had to get out of the dress and into real clothes. Then she'd drive to the next town and buy the cheapest breakfast on the menu. With food in her stomach she would test her new green card and get a job.

She pulled off her sweater and jacket, and bit her lip against the sting of cold on her skin. Struggling with the buttons on the dress, she managed to undo a few more but the confines of the car made it too hard to get out of the dress. She needed more room so she pulled on her sturdy elastic-sided boots and opened the car door.

Pulling the dress up to her knees in case there was mud, she stuck her feet out of the car and heard a snap. The same thing happened when her other foot touched the ground and she stood up. Glancing down, she saw that she'd just broken a sheet of ice that had crusted over a puddle. She'd never seen this before. In Narranbool the temperature hovered in the high nineties for a large part of the year, and the only ice to be found there was in the drinks.

It had been dark when she'd arrived the night before but this morning the vista was vastly different. Hers was the only car in the parking area and the sounds of the woods the only noise. Yellow and orange leaves turning a murky brown lay in uneven piles at the base of bare trees for as far as the eye could see. Crisp frost touched everything, leaving a thick white coating. Tall, thin, leafless trees surrounded her, the bare wood stark against the gray sky. A pang of homesickness for the evergreen eucalypts with their colorful gnarly bark washed through her. *Be tough, Matilda.*

She needed food before low blood sugar reduced her to curling up in fetal position and freezing to death. She had to get the dress off. To avoid getting the hem muddy, she bent over and pulled the skirt over her head, hoping to be able to wriggle out of the bodice now she'd freed a couple more buttons. Material cascaded around her, burying her face and she immediately realized why brides had bridesmaids.

She tugged at the neckline trying to ease the dress upward.

Heaven knew her breasts were not going to be an obstacle and slowly the material started to move. Cold air whizzed around her thermal-clad legs, sneaking in at the waistband. With her butt in the air and her head down, she struggled, easing the bodice inch by inch over her head. Satin clogged her mouth and nose and she blew out, trying to shift the material and drag in a breath.

The muscles in her upper arms burned hot as she continued with her task, her head thumping with the rush of blood but at least she was making slow progress. She pressed on, ignoring the fire in her arms. The dress suddenly stalled, fixed tight around her head and her arms, refusing to move in either direction. Through the layers of wedding dress she heard a car engine.

Panic fizzed in her gut like carbonated bubbles. She wanted to dive back into the car but she had no idea where it was having turned around a number of times when she'd been pulling at the dress. She was all alone in the north woods, tied up in a dress and unable to move. An image of the woman from the movie *Fargo* running through the woods with a straitjacket over her head bounced in her brain.

"That's an interesting look. They say you learn something every day and who knew Australian brides wore thermal underwear."

She groaned with a mixture of embarrassment and relief, instantly recognizing the deep and melodic, yet slightly mocking tones of the Viking. Slowly, she straightened up, letting the dress fall back over her legs, desperately trying to hold on to a shred of her dignity. Not that she had much, especially as she was going to need his help getting the stuck dress off her head.

She raised her chin and spoke through the bodice, her voice

muffled. "And it's my role in life to educate. This is a simple physics lesson. The aperture needs to be the same diameter as the object that has to fit through it." She heard his footsteps crunching against the frost.

"And let me guess, if it isn't, the object gets stuck."

"Got it in one." Her arms screamed in protest as the dress held them fast above her head.

"And would the solution lie in widening the aperture?"

She could picture him standing in front of her with a bemused smile on his face. Meanwhile, she could hardly breathe. Her skin burned from cold and humiliation, and her arms were going to explode any minute. Forget dignity, she had none. "Listen up, Blondie, just undo the damn buttons!"

Marc laughed as he walked around Matilda and faced a line of buttons snaking down her very straight back. He had to admire her chutzpah; she must be frozen solid but she was still dishing it out. He'd been on his way into town to collect some last-minute items for Lori from the drugstore when he'd recognized the silver hatchback. The one that should have been in Wausau. The one he should have driven past, but intrigue had made him pull over and investigate.

He'd been greeted by a curvaceous pink-blue-and-green-striped behind and Matilda still wearing that damn dress. Was this guy of hers into some kinky dress-up fantasy so she hadn't taken the dress off? But if Barry had been here she wouldn't be asking him for help with the dress. He stepped in close, questions buzzing on his lips, when the scent of pure soap and sunshine tickled his nostrils, immediately driving out all the questions. He wriggled his nose against the sensation, blaming the cold for playing tricks on him. It couldn't be anything else because Matilda, with her sharp features and bossy manner, was not his type of woman in any way, shape or form.

Blowing on his fingers he concentrated on the job at hand. "Right then, here we go." His large hands carefully eased the tiny buttons through aging button-loops, slowly exposing more and more creamy skin, the color of Wisconsin milk. Unexpected warmth stirred in his groin.

His fingers slid open another button and suddenly the wide expanse of skin gave way to ivory satin covered in tiny silk flowers. A crisscross of satin ribbon laced down her back across smooth and teasing skin stretched across a straight spine. A wave of heat rocked through him, making his fingers itch, eager to explore skin he was certain was soft and supple.

For once he was thankful for Wisconsin's cold. If he had to unbutton a dress past a tantalizingly sexy corset outlining every feminine curve and swell, but at the same time silkily taunting that it protected forbidden fruit, then at least he was outside with the freezing cold keeping his libido in check. A libido that had been absent for quite a few weeks.

His tight pants mocked the thought.

"Take your time. It's not like I'm freezing here." Matilda's muffled voice managed to sound bossy.

"You want me to accidentally rip something?" Irritation at himself threaded through his voice as he tried to speed up his fumbling fingers and at the same time chant multiplication tables to reduce the package in his pants.

"No!" Her teeth chattered. "Sorry, go as slowly as you like."

But taking a long, slow approach to undressing this woman wasn't something he wanted to do. "Try this." The last three buttons yielded more easily than the previous five and the dress tumbled down over her head, exposing her face and a chaotic tumble of auburn hair.

She sucked in a long breath before swinging around to face him. "Thank—"

Her quick movement caused the dress to slide forward off her shoulders, and although she made a quick grab for it and pulled it tight against her chest, he still caught a brief and surprising glimpse of two soft mounds of skin that the wedding dress had not even hinted at.

Clutching the dress to her front she moved sideways toward the car. "I'll just put some other clothes on."

He smiled and crossed his arms. "You do that and I'll wait here." *Not wise. Don't get involved. Lori needs you to drive her to the hospital.* But he had plenty of time to spare before he had to leave for Wausau and after the way Matilda had swept out of the diner last night leaving the impression she was off to start her married life, she now had some explaining to do. She was like a boomerang; she kept coming back.

She stopped dead, dismay darting across her face before morphing into a more social expression. "You've been a great help but I don't want to hold you up any longer. So please, feel free to go. I'll be fine from here on."

This is your chance to leave. He ignored his common sense and stayed put. Last night she'd thanked everyone for their help, said she'd be fine and yet she was still here and it looked like she'd slept in her car in freezing conditions. "Really? This from a woman who spent the night in a car in a wedding dress *without* a groom and in an area infested with bears."

Her eyes widened and fear streaked through their blue-green depths. "So that really would have been a bear that rocked the car last night?"

He'd been joking about the bears. Damn it, but he'd been right about her spending the night here. Heaven knows what or who had rocked her car. The woman was a walking disaster and a menace to herself. "Get dressed and then we'll talk."

Despite the fact she must be freezing she squared her shoulders. "We don't have anything to talk about, except perhaps about why you're here. I thought you didn't live in Hobin."

"I don't. I live in New York City but I'm visiting family. *Helping family.* More to the point, shouldn't we be talking about why *you* are here?"

Something flickered in her eyes but quickly faded as she tilted her chin. "At home we drive on the left-hand side of the road and because I was tired and it was dark, I thought it would be wiser to drive to Wausau this morning. Safety first you know."

The lie was transparent but he decided to see how far she'd go with it. "And it didn't occur to you to call Barry to come get you?"

"I tried to, but my phone doesn't work here."

"You could have driven back to town and called or checked into a motel?"

She tossed her head. "They were all booked out."

She wasn't giving up. "Is that so?" Had it been Wednesday that might have been true but three days out from Thanksgiving, Hobin normally had some rooms available.

"Yes. Look, I'd love to chat for longer but I'm freezing. I need to get dressed and get to Wausau." She shivered and the dress slipped slightly, exposing some lace.

Lace that he knew rode across small but round breasts. Not that he had any interest in them or the rest of Matilda Geoffrey. She was a catastrophe on a stick and he had some serious doubts about her ability to separate fantasy from reality. Who in their right mind would camp overnight at a rest area in November? But she was a foreigner, alone, and she needed protecting from herself.

What was it about him and needy women? It was as if he sent out a navigating signal that led them straight to him. An idea flashed in his mind and he fished his phone out of his pocket, immediately scrolling down to the log. "So you'll drive to Wausau where Barry will have breakfast waiting for you?"

"Got it in one, Blondie." She extended her hand. "Thanks and goodbye."

Instead of taking her proffered hand, he pressed the call button on his phone and put it on speakerphone. The sound of a phone ringing split the air, immediately followed by the standard disconnection message. The disembodied words trailed off and he raised his gaze to stare straight at her. "You have no idea where he is, do you?"

Her pale face blanched but her shoulders stayed rigid. "Not a clue in the world." Then her eyes flashed with unexpected insight. "Is it always this important to you to be right?"

He ignored the comment. She could talk—he wasn't the one who'd crossed the world to get married to a guy who'd vanished. "Get dressed and come back into town with me for a shower and breakfast."

She raised her brows. "That's quite an offer, sir, but I don't even know you."

She'd deliberately misconstrued him and he sighed. "You know that's not what I meant."

"Really? How would I know that? I don't know anything

about you. For all I know you might be plotting to run off with everything I own, including my cake."

He should just leave her to freeze. Matilda was turning into the most infuriating woman he'd ever met. "Oh yeah, the alcoholic cake was top of my list, quickly followed by the fluorescent thermal underwear." This nonsense had to stop. He marched over to her car and pulled the key out of the ignition.

"Hey, what are you doing?" She leaped toward him, dress, skin and corset flashing in a blur.

He tried to ignore the bubble of heat that socked him. "For God's sake, put some clothes on and then we'll drive into town."

She opened her mouth to speak but quickly closed it. Scrambling into the car, she slammed the door hard behind her, the crash of metal against metal loudly declaring, "Do Not Disturb."

As if he'd even be tempted to peek—irritating, bossy, almost flat-chested women did nothing for him. It was purely out of Midwestern politeness that he turned his back.

Matilda couldn't believe how much a hot shower, clean clothes and a huge plate of pancakes, bacon and eggs could improve things—relatively speaking anyway. Astrid had kindly let her use her bathroom and now her body wasn't working one hundred percent on trying to keep her warm, her brain had thawed. True, her plan never to come back to Hobin had been well and truly nuked, what with the Viking, who seemed to be on a grumpy Sir Galahad mission, having found her out. Right now she was totally ticked off at him for taking her car keys and she planned to get them back as soon as possible, but perhaps not until after he'd paid for breakfast. When a girl had nothing, practicalities had to come first.

He'd insisted on driving her to Norsk's in his car as if he didn't trust her not to drive off in her own vehicle in the opposite direction. She supposed he had a point although why he was taking such an interest in her she had no clue, but every part of her was on alert. Barry might have taken everything she had but that was yesterday. Today she was nobody's fool.

She sneaked a peek at the Viking over the thick, ceramic coffee mug. His eyes were cast down, studying the newspaper, and the blond strands of his hair reflected back the winter sunshine in a dazzling light show. The man was extraordinarily handsome and she didn't trust him as far as she could throw him. Who trusted a man with a car worth more than the average Australian's annual salary? It was the flashiest thing she'd ever seen in her life. The only other time she'd sat on leather was on the back of old Betsy, a horse she'd adopted at age ten during her parents' flirtation with commune life. In a mostly itinerant childhood the commune had been the closest place she could call a home, excluding Nana's.

The waitress paused at the table with the coffeepot and Matilda extended her mug for a refill. "This is seriously good coffee."

The young woman smiled shyly at her, before sneaking an eyelash-fluttering peek at Marc. "You're welcome."

The man under scrutiny smiled at the waitress, folded his paper neatly and then leveled his clear, blue gaze directly at Matilda. "Are you done?"

A involuntarily shiver whooshed through her, completely disconcerting her with its effect of half delight and half apprehension. "Done?" She had no idea what he was talking about.

He inclined his head toward her empty plate.

"Oh, have I finished? Sorry, sometimes I swear we don't speak the same language. Yes, I'm done, so if you could return my key and drive me back to my car, I'll be on my way."

He shook his head. "I let you walk out of here last night and you nearly froze so the key stays with me."

Righteous anger flared. "You can't do that."

He shrugged. "Well, I have."

Her forefinger tapped the tabletop. "I'm sure that's theft and if I went to the police station they'd side with me."

He leaned back toward the booth behind him and turned his head. "Hey, Eric, you remember Matilda. She slept in her car last night at Larsen's rest area."

A round-faced man with two chins and a silver badge on his shirt poked his shoulders out of the booth. "Sounds like a clear case of vagrancy to me, Marc."

His brows rose. "That's what I thought." The music of "Waltzing Matilda," the quintessential Australian song about a swagman or in this case, a vagrant, whistled in her head. This town had shades of Narranbool; small and where everyone knew everybody and outsiders were treated with suspicion. John Dunstan, the town's policeman, had always grabbed a coffee from the store each morning and while Matilda had frothed the milk for his cappuccino, he'd often settled small points of law with the other customers. Well, two could play at this game.

She leaned sideways and spoke to the police chief. "Excuse me, but he's confiscated my car keys so I can't leave the car park. I'm sure that's detainment against my will and that can't be legal."

The policeman chewed slowly on a piece of toast before

answering. "If you were making a nuisance of yourself then Marc has the right to make a citizen's arrest."

"A nuisance?" Her voice rose. "All I did was sleep the night in my car. At home I get out my swag and sleep out all the time."

"I don't know what that is, miss, but here in Wisconsin, sleeping in your car in *November* sounds like vagrancy." He aimed a look at her that combined paternal concern with legal correctness—both said she'd chosen the wrong season. "Then again, you could treat this like a good Samaritan act, what with Marc giving you breakfast and all. But whatever you decide it is, you need to come on down to the station today. We just need to know that you're able to support yourself and that you have someplace to stay. I don't want to have a frozen Aussie on my books." He caught the keys that Marc tossed to him and then leaned back inside his booth, ending the conversation.

The Viking stayed unexpectedly silent which was disconcerting. Matilda crossed her arms over her breasts, trying to stop her agitated and bounding heart from leaping out of her chest. Three clicks of the police computer was probably all it would take to find out she was close to destitute. Why hadn't she driven back to Chicago? A big city like that wouldn't even notice another homeless person. But no, she'd stumbled into a small town where anyone new was not only noticed but scrutinized to within an inch of their life.

She squinted and gave him what Nana used to call her killing look. "I didn't expect a kangaroo court in Wisconsin."

He matched her position of leaning back with crossed arms. "All you have to do is show him your passport and financial position, or evidence that you have a job and a place to stay, and then you get your keys back."

"Geez," she grumbled. "Does Hobin always treat its guests like this? No wonder you're not on the tourist trail."

His lips twitched as if they wanted to smile. "Will that be a problem?"

"Getting the town on the tourist trail? Until people like you stop making citizen's arrests over nothing it will be." She took another slug of coffee, wondering how long she could keep up this defensive banter. It was exhausting always having to keep one step ahead of this bloke. Despite taking her keys and giving her a lecture in the car on the perils of Wisconsin weather and north-woods' bogeymen, he surprisingly hadn't actually asked her anything about herself or about Barry. For her part, she hadn't volunteered any information and she planned to keep it that way. The less everyone knew the better because publicly sharing her stupidity wouldn't change a thing.

Marc scrunched his napkin into a tight ball and his knuckles gleamed white as he dropped it into the middle of his empty plate. "I have to go to the drugstore."

She wondered at the tension that suddenly circled him but she was too relieved that he was leaving to think much of it. "No worries. You go and do that and I'll go and buy myself a phone card." Not that she planned to but she needed some space away from those penetrating sky-blue eyes so she could think clearly. She needed to work out how she was going to convince the policeman and the Viking she had means, so she could get her car back.

Marc casually opened a leather billfold and dropped enough money onto the middle of the table to cover the breakfast bill, along with a generous tip.

Relief that her small stash of money could stay intact for a bit longer settled the butterflies in her stomach. "Thanks very much for buying me breakfast. It's just the sort of thing a Good Samaritan would do."

He fiddled with the notes. "Not exactly."

"No?" She tried to remember the story in the Bible but her memories of Sunday school were hazy.

His high cheekbones seemed to sharpen. "Good Samaritans don't have strings attached to their actions but I do. Now you're clean, fed and warm, it's time to tell me about Barry."

The unexpected question smashed into her like an outback road train and all she could hear in her head was the screech of failing brakes and the crack of crumpling metal as her strategy of avoiding the subject of Barry hit the wall.

CHAPTER FOUR

Marc watched the color drain from Matilda's face but her eyes flashed brightly as she rolled her shoulders back and tilted her chin upward—all of them familiar actions he was coming to associate with this crazy woman when she was pressed into a corner. But he ignored the strange tug of feeling that his curiosity had just trampled on her privacy. The woman needed saving from herself and this was just part of the rescue.

She sucked in her bow of a mouth and then cleared her throat as if she'd made a decision. "I met Barry in an online chat room six months ago. I thought he wanted the same things out of life as I did and we talked about our future. I came over to marry him but it seems he's changed his mind so end of story."

His gut had been right. This woman needed rescuing. "You came all this way to marry a man you've never met in person?"

Her eyes sparked indignantly and she shot him a searing look. "As much as it makes you feel superior to paint me as a complete moron, Blondie, I have met him. We spent three days together in Sydney, a couple of months after we'd met online."

"Still. Three days?" He made an effort to try and sound less critical. "Surely that's not enough time to get to know a person let alone commit to a lifetime together."

Pressing the forefinger of her right hand against the thumb of her left hand, she spoke. "No? Explain then Grace Kelly and her prince who fell in love at first sight." She moved her forefinger, numbering off. "Paul Newman and Joanne Woodward whose eyes met across a crowded room, and my grandmother who fell in love with my grandfather in less than a week and was married to him for fifty-five years."

He quickly dismissed her examples. "They might have fallen in love quickly but they would have spent real time together which is totally different from online time."

Her cheekbones sharpened on her elfin face. "Grandpa Hank was an American GI and he proposed to Nana on day seven and married her on day ten, the night before he was shipped out to fight on the final assault on the Pacific in the Second World War. Nana, along with fifteen thousand Australian war brides, came over here to start her married life at twenty-two. She hadn't seen Grandpa for over a year." She leveled a steely look at him. "And it worked."

Things started to fall into place. Yesterday she'd mentioned her nana's trunk and cake. The whirlwind romance between her grandparents had probably become part of her family's folklore. "The dress you were wearing, it was your grandmother's, wasn't it?"

She nodded. "Nana always talked about me wearing her dress and making my cake."

"So why didn't she come with you to see you get married?"

Matilda pushed her hair back behind her ears in an abrupt and jagged movement. "Because she died nine months ago."

Her sadness hit him hard in the chest, combining with his feelings for Lori. "Oh, I'm sorry."

She blinked rapidly. "Yeah, it wasn't nice. She'd been sick for a while and although she was a battler, she couldn't win against the cancer that eventually invaded every part of her body. She died two days after she finished my cake."

His brain churned through the information, sparking questions at every turn. "But you hadn't even met Barry at that point so why did she make you a cake?"

"You weren't supposed to notice that detail." Her cheeks pinked up, and for the first time since he'd met her she looked slightly embarrassed. Sighing, she shook her head. "Look, I know you think I'm bonkers."

She held up her hand as he opened his mouth to politely lie. "On the bare facts it does look completely irrational but my grandmother and my mother both had a great romantic adventure. Nana had complete faith that I would have one too which is why she made the cake. After she died I think I must have resurrected Nana's dreams for me—you know, a way to hold on to her for a bit longer." She shrugged. "Barry seemed perfect. Obviously it was all too perfect, fiction even, seeing as he has never lived where he said he did. I didn't see it coming."

Marc surprised himself with the need to offer her something to ease her self-deprecation. "Grief can screw with your head."

Her mouth flattened. "Yeah, tell me about it. I thought because I'd cared for Nana, nursed her through the last few horrid weeks, that I'd be okay. You know, be relieved that my darling Nana didn't have to suffer anymore, but when she died there was this huge gaping hole and just an endless empty feeling that dragged at me. I mistakenly thought Barry sort of filled that space. He certainly knew the right words to say."

He recognized the feelings of loss but when his father died he'd been kept so busy that he'd hardly had any time to think about that empty space. "This guy's obviously taken you for a ride." An insidious thought struck him. Guys like Barry usually had an agenda. "He hasn't taken anything else from you, has he?"

She tilted her head, humor valiantly trying to shine. "What, something like my virginity?"

"There are some men who prey on women."

"It's kind of you to be concerned about my reputation but no. Daniel Mack had that dubious honor as I did for him at the Bachelor and Spinsters ball. It was the end of my second year at university and neither of us knew what we were doing although I'm sure he's had a lot more practice since then than I have." As she ran her fingers down the ridges of the glass sugar bottle, her bottom lip seem to quiver before she dragged her teeth against it and forced out a brittle smile. "Actually, it was Barry who insisted we wait until our wedding night."

A surge of unanticipated rage jetted through him, directed at the unknown Barry. Matilda didn't deserve to be treated this way and the man was not only a bastard, he was also a fool. Sure Matilda wasn't the tall, willowy and exceptionally well-dressed woman he always dated and she was full of sharp angles, but she was still all woman.

The memory of small, soft, creamy mounds of flesh peeking out of a lacy corset thudded through him making his palms tingle. He cleared his throat. "You should track him down and sort this out."

A wave of tension ripped into her. "No! Why on earth would I want to put myself through that? I mean, he's obviously changed his mind, not to mention his phone number, as well as lying about where he lives. I'm not *that* desperate that I'd make someone marry me who doesn't love me. No way am I putting my hand up to be humiliated again. No, it's time for new plans."

Surprise bounced through him. Most of the women he knew would have demanded—what was the psychobabble term for it? Closure. "So, you're heading back to Australia?"

"Hmm. That's probably the best solution." Her top teeth snagged her bottom lip and then she abruptly slapped her palms against the tabletop, making the silverware jump. "We've both got jobs to do. You have to get to the chemist." She shook her head. "I mean the drugstore and I have to check in with Eric and get my keys back. Thanks for breakfast, Blondie." Pulling her purse on to her shoulder, the action all bristling business, she stood up and extended her hand.

He rose to his feet, and accepted her hand in his, surprised at the firm grip which was out of context with her recent behavior. "It's been interesting."

She winked at him. "You obviously need to get out more."

"Sweetheart, I'm a New Yorker. I get out plenty."

"Of course you do." She turned and with a backward wave walked toward the door.

He laughed, watching her retreating back and enjoying the way her hips swayed and how the soft denim of her jeans molded to a pert backside. Crazy as a loon and always needing to have the last word in that bizarre and clipped accent, she was the most intriguing woman he'd ever met. His phone beeped, immediately grounding him in time and place. Matilda was now Eric's problem and it was time for him to concentrate on Lori. He needed to get her prescription filled, buy her some luxurious toiletries and drive her to the hospital.

Matilda tightened her coat around her as she wandered along the main street of Hobin which was book-ended by two churches, in stark contrast to most Australian country towns which were bordered on all sides by pubs. Always referred to as the top pub and the bottom pub, they tried to outdo each other and their positions at either end of the main street meant they caught passing trade in both directions. She wondered if the churches vied for passersby, as well. Both buildings had seriously tall steeples, although she suspected one was slightly higher than the other.

Unlike Narranbool with its hugely wide verandahs to protect against the fierce glare and heat of the outback sun, Hobin's shops were flat-fronted with very few awnings. There were lots of other differences between the towns. The Aussie town only flew the flag on Australia Day but here, the American flag fluttered from the lampposts as an everyday occurrence. Shop windows were all decorated with pumpkins, gourds and variegated corn, which she assumed must be connected to the harvest and autumn, and again so very different from home. But in Australia the seasons were hardly distinct enough to be celebrated like they were here. Glorious houses with pitched roofs, turrets and wraparound porches nestled between brown brick two-storey shops and Matilda itched to see inside these homes, so architecturally different from what she was used to. But she wasn't a tourist and she had no time to waste.

Show him your financial position or evidence that you have a job.

The Viking's deep voice resonated in every part of her, setting up a rabble of butterflies furiously batting their wings against her gut. Handsome beyond what was legal *and* a control freak, he had a way of looking at her that made her feel both lacking and jittery. But she had no time to think about him. She needed to find herself a job. She started scanning the shop windows for any Help Wanted signs. If she had a job by lunchtime she could go to the police station with her head high and no one need know about her empty bank account. No one need know she'd been conned out of more than a wedding. But most importantly, the Viking would never know.

He didn't need any more fuel to add to his already blazing fire that she was a total and utter nutter. But finding a job this morning meant staying in Hobin and continuing to meet Mr. Marc Olsen, something she really didn't want to have to do. With one flick of his sky-blue eyes he managed to set off the most disparate range of emotions she'd ever experienced and she hated that. Hated that bubbling sense that she was careening out of control. Hell, everything else in her life was out of control and she needed to find some firm ground and regroup. And that meant leaving Hobin.

But she couldn't leave Hobin without a job. The Viking was just visiting town and therefore would be leaving soon so basing a decision around avoiding him was just stupid. Small-town Hobin had all the hallmarks of a safe town, unlike the urban stories that circulated back in Australia about dangerous American cities and guns. Hobin had traces of Narranbool and she was intimate with small towns which could be to her advantage. Besides, working here would be short-term. Very short-term. Just long enough to save some money and work out what she would do next. Perhaps she should see some of the country she'd planned to live in before she flew home. After all, why let a major personal disaster get in the way of world travel? She refused to let a conniving con man steal everything from her.

She passed two antique shops with spotless windows, unsullied by any Position Vacant signs and moved along the street, unconsciously humming the famous Gloria Gaynor tune, "I Will Survive." Half an hour later, having traversed both sides of Main Street, she'd drawn a blank. It seemed no one needed any staff or perhaps they did but they hadn't gotten around to putting a notice in the window. She squared her shoulders. She'd do another round but this time she'd go into each shop and ask if they had vacancies, although the way she was feeling it would probably be more like begging.

She'd start with the grocery store because she had some experience from Nana's shop. She was about to cross the road when she realized there was one other shop on her side of the street. Gold lettering arced across the glass, spelling out Hobin Gifts. The window display was a mixed affair, with two small tables, each dressed quite differently. The first had scattered maple leaves surrounding large silver charger plates which sat against polished oak, and all of it pulled together by a circle of family photographs dating back a hundred years.

The second table held a white linen table runner scattered with pinecones and a wreath of holly decorated with tiny golden baubles, all of which surrounded a golden column candle. The two displays vibrated with warmth and promised wonderful family times around a table. Christmas was coming and people needed gifts. The thought rocked her with its clarity. Retailing and Christmas went together like Vegemite on toast. This would be the place to start in her job quest.

She pushed open the door and walked inside. A woman wearing an apron with a picture of a gourd overflowing with produce and the words Happy Thanksgiving stenciled around it was chatting to a customer. At the sound of the bell the customer drifted into the back of the shop and the assistant turned and greeted Matilda with a smile. "Hello, can I help you?"

Matilda smiled in a way she hoped didn't scream desperation. "I hope so. I'm looking for a job."

The woman blinked. "Pardon?"

Matilda was still surprised at the startled expressions that her accent generated; after all she did speak English. "I'm Matilda—Tildy—and I'm keen to work in your lovely town. With Christmas coming, I reckon you're heading into a busy time."

Recognition flashed in her eyes. "Oh, you must be the bride from Australia Astrid was telling me all about. Welcome to Hobin. I'm Peggy Hendrix." The woman, who looked to be in her forties, extended her hand.

Matilda accepted it, and returned the shake deciding it was best to admit to being the abandoned bride as she doubted there were any other Australian women in town. If she glossed over the broken engagement and followed on with a question about the job, she might just avoid an interrogation on the whole fiasco. She had a sense that Hobinites, unlike Australians, were inherently polite and probably wouldn't say, "So the bastard dumped you?"

She nodded. "Yes, that's me. Seeing as things didn't work out quite as planned and Hobin is such a pretty town, I thought I might stay awhile and work here. Your sensational window display caught my eye."

Peggy glowed with the compliments. "Well, it's a busy time what with Thanksgiving on Thursday."

The word *busy* sounded good, and hope surged, dousing all the anxious tendrils that had tightened inside her. "Brilliant. I can start now."

Peggy's expression looked pained. "But unfortunately Hobin isn't like the towns in Door County where all the folk from Chicago come to vacation and do their Christmas shopping. I'm very sorry but I don't need any extra help."

Hope receded like the dramatic pull of a tsunami just before the wave struck. "Do you know of anyone who's hiring for the Christmas rush?"

"Honey, if this was Chicago or Madison I'm sure the shops would be hiring but this is Hobin." She shrugged as if that explained everything. "Thanksgiving is the biggest holiday weekend of the year and people tend to shut their stores for a couple of days while they visit or entertain their relatives. Heaven knows, as mayor I've pleaded with them to stay open but they're stuck back in the eighties." She threw her hands up in frustration as if this was a long and ongoing issue for her.

Acid surged into the back of Matilda's throat as images of Narranbool shut down tighter than a drum over the Christmas period assailed her. For three days every year a cannon could have been fired down the main street and the only thing that would have been hit was a crow. No wonder there were no Help Wanted signs in any of the windows.

Panic trampled on anxiety. Now she was completely and utterly stuck. Without proof of a job or evidence of money she couldn't get her keys back. She couldn't avoid spending the night in the Hobin jail cell or avoid the entire town knowing her story and no way could she avoid the Viking's grinning "I knew it" expression.

The young woman Peggy had been talking to when Matilda arrived wandered from the back of the shop clutching a bridal magazine in one hand, and a dusty garter in the other. "Peggy, do you have anything for weddings other than this garter?"

"I'm sorry, Vanessa, but I usually don't get any wedding stock in until March." She waved her arm around the small space that groaned with stock. "Right now I'm fully stocked for Thanksgiving and Christmas."

The young woman pouted with disappointment. "But I'd hoped to get most of my wedding organizing done while I was home for Thanksgiving because once I'm back in Philly, work is going to be crazy." She sighed. "And I really wanted that tiara you had last spring."

Peggy shook her head sadly. "I can't even order that one in for you because my supplier can't source it anymore."

The conversation wafted around Matilda and slowly the words penetrated her dread. For the last three months she'd lived and breathed wedding planning and had spent hours on the internet discovering every bridal accessory, every style of table decoration and every type of invitation ranging from the wonderful down to the downright weird. Plus she had a tiara in her suitcase that she no longer needed. A tiara she might possibly be able to sell.

She cleared her throat. "Sorry, but I couldn't help overhearing. Exactly what sort of tiara did you have in mind? Seed pearls, rum pearls, rhinestones, crystals, brushed metal?"

Vanessa walked over to Matilda, enthusiasm for the topic shining on her face. "The one I liked had tiny flowers made of fine silver and each flower was decorated with tiny pearls and crystals."

"I *really* don't think they make that one anymore," Peggy reminded her.

Matilda tried hard not to bite her lip. Selling a tiara that was similar to the one described, but was also a tainted remnant of a cancelled wedding, would take a bit of skill especially if the potential buyer was superstitious. Still, Vanessa sounded bonded to the idea of the tiara and Matilda desperately needed money so it was worth a shot. "Do you have access to the internet here? If you do, I can show you a picture of something very similar to your description."

"Oh, Peggy, can we use your computer?" Vanessa chattered in excitement.

"You bet." Peggy walked to the counter and clicked on a laptop computer, bringing up a browser.

Matilda's fingers flew across the keyboard, typing in the URL and sending up a silent but quick request that as her life was already in the toilet, the least that could happen was that the tiara she'd purchased remained the very last one available. If Vanessa really wanted the tiara then she'd have to buy it from her. "Is this what you're after?"

Vanessa leaned forward, intently studying the picture on the screen. A moment later she let out a squeal of delight. "Yes, that's exactly what I'm looking for, thank you so much. I'll order it now."

Matilda held her breath while Vanessa clicked on the order button.

"Oh, no. It's no longer available." Vanessa sat down hard on the high stool, totally dejected.

Be casual, not needy. "By sheer coincidence, I actually have that tiara in my suitcase and I no longer need it."

Peggy clucked her tongue and gave Matilda's shoulder a kind squeeze.

Matilda pressed on. "It's still in its packaging and perhaps it was destined for you, via me. Fate has a funny way of working out."

"What do you mean you don't need it?" Vanessa studied her hard.

Crunch time. She took a deep breath and let it all spill out in one continuous breath. "I thought I was getting married to an American I met online. Dumb I know, but you learn, right? I bet you've probably known your groom for longer than six months and you've actually spent more than three days with him which is why I think this tiara is a lot more yours than it ever was mine."

"Oh. I'm sorry, how awful for you." Vanessa continued to stare at her. "To plan a wedding and then have it not happen..."

Matilda hated the pity but she held the other woman's gaze, willing her to want the tiara with a pull stronger than superstition. "I made a stupid mistake but this tiara was made to be worn and it deserves to have its day of glory and not be tinged with my foolhardiness."

Vanessa turned slowly back to the computer, clicking around the website, examining other headpieces while Matilda bit her tongue, keeping her desperation in check, knowing that often the sale was more in what you didn't say.

"It *is* the one you have your heart set on," Peggy chimed in unexpectedly.

Vanessa nodded absently as she fixed her full attention on

Matilda. "So you have an entire wedding set and no wedding?"

It wasn't the question Matilda had expected. "Not exactly. I have my dress, the tiara, a cake and a stand-by list that was ready to be set in motion when I arrived here. You know, order the invitations and the bonbonniere."

Vanessa's expression blanked. "Bonbonniere? What is that? It sounds like a terrorist attack."

Matilda laughed. "It's a gift you put on the tables to thank the guests for attending your wedding. I was going for silver yo-yos."

"Oh fun! We call those wedding favors. Did you find all this stuff on the internet?"

"I did."

"Could you help me with all this because I really only have these few days and I don't have any time to waste? I'd pay you."

Yes! A job.

Peggy's sharp intake of breath pierced her joy, instantly grounding her. Vanessa was in town for a few days but Peggy had a business to run all year-round. Matilda desperately needed the money but sometimes short-term gain shot a girl in the foot. She chewed her lip in thought. "I can certainly sell you the tiara for the same price I paid for it. But I'm thinking that as you came to Peggy planning to buy your accessories and favors then what if I help you find what you want but we order it through Peggy?" She turned to the store owner. "That's if it's okay with you?"

Peggy beamed at her. "I think it's a wonderful idea. I'll contract you to do Vanessa's wedding and we can hammer out the details later. Matilda, you just got yourself a job."

The vision of the prison cell receded slightly and inside she was squealing, *I've got a job. I've got a job.* Somehow she managed to sound coherent. "Awesome. Thank you. Let's start now." She brought up another internet browser.

Vanessa clicked down on a pen and started writing on a yellow legal pad she'd picked up off the counter. "I'm thinking you chose that tiara because it matched your dress. Are you interested in selling that too?"

The question came out of left field. "I…um…it was my grandmother's dress."

"Ohh, a vintage wedding dress, how perfect!" Vanessa's smile split her face. "I'm getting married in the old log church which is why I so wanted that tiara. You know, it's Old Worldly and it suits the church perfectly. I don't want to be just another bride in a strapless gown. I want my wedding to be different, to stand out, which is why I'm planning a vintage wedding." Vanessa studied her from top to toe. "We're similar sizes, although I am bigger in the chest. Can I see the dress and try it on? Please."

No! Every cell in her body vibrated in protest. She'd loved Nana's dress from the first moment she'd seen it when she was four years old. For twenty-six years she'd dreamed of the day she would wear it, but today she was far from home with less than fifty dollars to her name and a dress she didn't need. Perhaps the ultimate irony of her life was that for all the years she'd held on to Nana's dress it wasn't because she would wear it as a bride but because it was to save her from destitution.

The dream which yesterday had cracked into a thousand pieces finally shattered and fell far into a deep, black hole. How had she been so blind as to let her life get to this point? The sob she held back filled her chest like a lead weight, but there was no point going back over old news. She sat up a bit straighter and breathed in deeply. Parting with Nana's dress totally sucked but it was absolutely necessary if she was going to survive. Survival had no place for sentiment and no place for a dress she'd never wear.

"Vanessa, honey, Matilda might not want to part with her grandmother's dress." Peggy spoke quietly, her amber eyes filled with feeling.

Mustering every scattered bit of inner strength, Matilda forced her cheek muscles to move into a semblance of a smile. "Unlike me, Nana had breasts, so it'll probably fit Vanessa a lot better than it fit me. Nana only ever wanted her dress to be worn by a happy bride and it comes with a story of a great love and a long and happy marriage."

"I can't believe this. Half an hour ago I was so down and now!" Vanessa clapped her hands like an excited child. "Can we go and try it on right away?"

She thought fast, picturing everything she owned locked in the trunk of the rental car still sitting at the rest area, and the keys with Eric at the police station. She was not going to explain all that so she took control instead. "Seeing as we're at the computer, let's sort out the invitations, favors, toasting flutes, guestbook and the bridesmaids' gifts. After lunch I'll bring the dress and tiara over to your place for you to try on. How does that sound?"

"Peachy."

Oh, yeah, just peachy, but in her case, more like the pits.

CHAPTER FIVE

"You can go."

Marc straightened the pen and notepad on the bedside table in the hospital ward, wanting to take Lori at her word and immediately rush out of the building. Hospitals made his skin prickle and he'd rather be fighting for his own life than watching helplessly while others fought their own battles. "I think I should stay."

Lori fidgeted with the edge of the bedsheet. "No, really, you go. Kyle gets out at one today and I'd like for you to be in the house when he gets home and you need to allow time to visit Mom before she gets suspicious."

"But what about when you get out of the operating room?" Half of him wanted to be here when she came back to the ward and the other half of him didn't.

She sighed. "We've been through this. My doctor will call you when the surgery is over. Tomorrow you come and collect me and take me home. I think it's best that way, don't you?"

He had no clue. The fact that Lori was so sick had totally

rocked him and he was still trying to wrap his head around the word *cancer* and what it meant. He poured a glass of water, uncertain if it was for him or just for something to do with his hands. He passed it to her. "If you're absolutely sure."

"I'm sure. In fact I'm certain." She shot him a familiar smile, one he hadn't seen since his arrival yesterday. "And, hey, they're giving me drugs soon so I'll be fine. Right now Kyle needs you more than I do and don't worry, it's my turn when I get home."

And that terrified him. An image of Lori covered in bandages socked him hard. The nurse had spoken to them both earlier, outlining the care Lori would need in the first two weeks post-surgery. He'd zoned out at "drain tubes," horrified at the pictures. Nursing wasn't his thing and never had been. When any of his sisters had hurt themselves that was the one thing he'd always tried to hand over to someone else. There was something about blood that made his stomach lurch, which was why he'd offered to hire a nurse. But Lori had been insistent that she wanted everything kept very private.

He kissed the top of her head. "Love ya, sis."

"You too, bro. Give Kyle my love. Oh and make sure you show Mom all those photos of your latest project like you always do so she doesn't suspect anything, okay?"

"Can do. I've just finished a heritage conversion."

"Go you." Lori waved as he turned and walked out.

Visiting his mother was the easy bit. She'd make coffee and he'd fire up his laptop showing her the pictures of how a run-down turn-of-the-century building was now the marble façade of multimillion-dollar apartments in downtown Manhattan. But Marc didn't know whether staying with Lori would be easier than being with Kyle. The boy had hardly spoken to him since his arrival and had refused all entrees to conversation. The Lego gift still sat in his car, mocking him with the fact he'd missed his nephew's leap from childhood into antsy adolescence. He glanced at his watch and ran a schedule through his head. He'd start with the filial visit, then buy food supplies from the grocery store and lunch-to-go from Norsk's. He'd grab a bag of rosettes as well because what kid didn't enjoy those?

Throwing his jacket into the back of the car, he lowered himself down, feeling his seat belt tighten firmly against him, just like his family responsibilities. He deliberately shifted his thoughts, centering them on the car which always gave him a great deal of satisfaction. The familiar natural scent of soft leather wrapped around him but this time added in was the crisp fresh scent of a sea breeze. An image of Matilda, all huge green eyes and flyaway hair, rumbled through his thoughts as he pulled out of the parking lot and headed back to Hobin.

He raced through the gears overly fast, surprised that his brain would make that connection. The scent probably belonged to Lori, who was the last passenger in the car. *I don't think so.* But it didn't matter who the scent belonged to, Matilda would have left Hobin by now. Still he'd thought that last night and she'd unexpectedly turned up. Earlier, when he'd finished at the drugstore he'd glanced up and down Main Street but he hadn't seen her, which was a good thing. He had enough on his plate with Lori and Kyle without adding an Australian with attitude into the mix.

Hey, Blondie. And she had attitude. Usually when he spoke, people listened. He'd earned that right with hard work, two prestigious architecture awards and being one of the youngest people ever to be made a partner in Evans, Gaynor and Associates. Yep, he was the one who called the shots. He was the one in control. He had to be because there were no shortcuts in architecture or people got hurt, and it wasn't often that people questioned him.

He unexpectedly found himself smiling at the memory of Matilda standing with her arms in the air and the wedding dress fixed tightly around her head. She'd been behind in the game in every conversation they'd ever had but it hadn't stopped a list of instructions and a litany of sass pouring from that lush mouth; the only soft thing on a body of sharp angles.

You glimpsed soft.

He fought the memory and planted his foot on the accelerator. He was always very careful when it came to dating women. He only ever went out with career-minded women who understood the game. Good times, good fun, great sex and no expectations of a future. He kept his life complication-free. He'd fought too long and hard for his independence and he wasn't sharing it with anyone. Love only opened up opportunities for heartache and stifled life with responsibilities. No matter how curvaceous the butt, or how soft the breasts, pursuing a woman who'd planned a marriage with a guy she'd only ever spent three days with and had just been dumped by, well, that was just asking for trouble.

And for a woman who had just been dumped she seemed remarkably accepting. That he didn't get. Where was the weeping and wailing and gnashing of teeth? Where was the desire for revenge that relentlessly drove so many women when relationships failed? It didn't make sense and it didn't seem normal, but then again, nothing about Matilda was sensible or normal. Nothing at all. With that logic it also followed that it made no sense for him to be even thinking about her.

He glanced left as he passed the rest area where he'd found Matilda this morning. A family, probably on their Thanksgiving pilgrimage, was chasing a dog and getting some exercise before the next leg of their journey. There was no sign of a silver hatchback which meant Eric had checked her out and Matilda had left town and was heading back to Australia via Chicago. Something akin to relief moved through him. He flicked on the radio and the rock of AC/DC thumped through the car as he headed first to his mother's and then the Piggly Wiggly.

Holding three very full shopping bags in each hand, Marc walked back toward the car planning to dump the groceries and Lori's magazines, and then pick up lunch. As he delved the depths of his pockets, searching for his keyless remote, he heard the tinkle of a shop bell and automatically turned around.

Matilda Geoffrey, her torso wrapped in her bulky cream Aran sweater, her hair tumbling around her face in a mass of auburn curls, and with a new swing in her step, strode out of Peggy's gift shop. She stopped right in front of him, a smile dancing on her very kissable lips. He lost the grip on one of the shopping bags.

She bent down and retrieved the bag before it and the contents rolled down the street. "*People, Good Housekeeping* and *O Magazine?* Interesting choice of reading matter, Blondie, and here I had you picked as a sports fan."

He grunted as he loaded the bags into the car, ignoring the rush of blood to his groin. "You proved your nonvagrant status yet?"

This time she grinned and leaned against his car. "Or at the very least with a car like this, I thought you'd be a petrol head. Who knew you were such a sensitive, new-age type of guy? Not many Australian blokes would be seen dead with a stash of magazines like that so perhaps America is the new world after all."

He slammed the trunk closed. "I thought you might enjoy reading them in the Hobin jail cell tonight, that's if Eric doesn't personally escort you out of town for being a general nuisance."

She raised a shapely brow. "Someone's tetchy. Having trouble settling into small-town holiday life after the big smoke?"

He thought of Lori and Kyle and frustration collided with guilt but he wasn't discussing his life with Matilda. "I thought you were going directly to see Eric and then to the airport but here you are again. You're the boomerang bride."

Her eyes crinkled up at the edges as a smile lit up her face. "Very good. Alliteration combined with a national symbol, I'm impressed. I'm also impressed by Hobin. I've been checking it out and all the lovely shops. The one at the very end of the street has an interesting combination of stock."

"You mean Grayson's Farm Equipment and Antiques? The antique part of the business being the old rusted farming equipment that Stefan Grayson hasn't been able to sell." He gave a wry smile. "No one's ever been brave enough to tell him that antique doesn't mean broken, rusted and bent."

She looked thoughtful. "I'm sure there's a market for some of that stuff. The small hand-plow in the window would look fantastic with some paint and a clump of petunias growing around it."

He doubted it. "Maybe, but definitely not in Hobin. Some of that stuff has been gathering dust in the store since I was a kid."

"Well it really is antique then." She pushed off the car with a wink. "I'll let you get on with your job and I'll get on with mine. See you around." She almost skipped down the street.

Job? Nah, she'd used that expression at breakfast and he was certain she meant errand. Still, if he'd learned one thing it was that Matilda was unpredictable. He pressed the lock on his keyless remote and caught up with her. "You're running errands, right?"

She nodded. "As part of my job, yes."

He spoke without thinking. "*You* have a job?"

Her chin tilted up, indignation on the rise. "Don't sound so surprised. I happen to have plenty of skills an employer would find useful."

He riffled through his memory bank trying to make sense of this change in plan and came up blank. "But you said at breakfast you were heading back to Australia."

"Ah, no, actually I didn't. You assumed I was heading back to Australia but I've thought about it and it seems silly for me to dash home just because my plans didn't work out." Her eyes glittered overly bright. "Let's face it, to really experience the American way of life I need to be more than a tourist. Hobin is so quaint that I thought I'd stay awhile."

Unease skittered through him which he promptly squashed. It was nothing to him if she stayed or left but even so he found he was both irked and interested. "So what's the job?"

She pulled her wayward thumb, which had migrated to her mouth, away from her teeth. "I'm subcontracting to Peggy and helping Vanessa Jacobson organize her wedding."

He stopped dead and stared at her. Here was a woman who'd crossed the world to marry a man, had been spectacularly dumped less than twenty-four hours ago, had shown no signs of wanting revenge and was now working to plan someone else's wedding. He had sisters and this was just plain wrong.

"I would have thought organizing a wedding for someone would be the last thing you'd want to do."

She shrugged her narrow shoulders as her forefinger brushed her top lip. "Who doesn't love a wedding and Vanessa needed the help. I learned a lot planning my wedding so it seemed the natural thing to do."

There was nothing natural about it. He'd expected her to collect her keys from Eric straight after breakfast and leave Hobin as fast as she could, keen to avoid a place that would remind her of everything she'd just lost. Yet she was still here and she'd been job hunting. Did she need money? No, that was crazy as she'd already collected her car so Eric had been satisfied with her financial status.

He glanced along the street wondering where she'd parked her rental car. "Where's your car?"

Air shot out of her nostrils in a sharp harrumph. "Exactly where *you* made me leave it."

A flash of concern bit him. "No, I just drove past the rest area and it's not there."

"What!" Her pupils dilated, the inky discs almost obliterating the stunning green. "Everything I own is in that car. Nana's dress, my tiara…money. Everything." Her shoulders sagged and her head fell forward for a moment before rising up and snapping back.

"You!" Her forefinger shot forward like a loaded gun pressing hard against his chest. "You made me leave it and now it's missing, making me homeless and penniless which I wasn't before you interfered." Her voice spiraled upward. "What is it about American men? Are you all hell-bent on making my life a living misery?"

He wrapped his hand around her jabbing finger before she bored a hole into his sternum and gently placed her arm by her side. "Calm down, there'll be a rational explanation for this."

"Calm down?" A blazing bolt of white-hot anger hurled from her eyes. "You commandeer my car, force me back into Hobin on some misguided Sir Galahad trip, grill me on my life and now you lose my car, but I'm the one that has to calm down? Listen, Blondie, this is *your* mess and you have to fix it."

Memories of his sisters' rants assailed him and he smiled; this was familiar territory. He recognized this sort of behavior and could deal with it, unlike her previous stoicism. "There's a logical explanation. Eric expected you to call in straight after breakfast and when you didn't show he probably had the car brought into town. This means all your possessions will be safe, which is lucky for you because leaving money in the car was really unwise."

She stomped her foot. "Give me a break! Who was it who hustled me into town so fast I barely had time to grab any-thing?"

He tilted his hands, palm upward. "Hey, don't shoot the messenger. You were the one who was frozen. Come on, we'll go straight to the station and it will all be sorted out in under ten minutes." He indicated the direction with his arm and she fell into step beside him, a grumbling and seething mass of auburn outrage.

He shot her a sideways glance. "You know, you really should be thanking me."

Her dark brown brows flew skyward, her expression one

of complete skepticism. "And how did you come to that conclusion?"

"All this anger of yours should be directed at Barry but he's vanished so I'm merely helping you out by letting you vent." He flashed her a smile. "It's so much healthier for you than holding it all in."

She folded her fingers against her palm, slowly forming a fist. "Physical release is also healthy so can I assume you're my punching bag?"

"Now, now, Matilda." He stared down at her and gave her a wink. "Violence only creates more problems."

"At this point in my life, Blondie, I'm willing to risk it."

Laughing, he opened the door of the station and ushered her inside before walking straight to the desk. "Hey, Brian, is Eric around?"

The police officer looked up, surprise and interest racing across his face. "Marc, it's good to see you." He extended his hand, his grip firm and friendly. "Back for Thanksgiving and for some of Lori's wonderful cooking?"

Marc nodded with implied agreement. He knew Lori wanted to keep the news of her cancer very quiet and he wasn't going to be the one who broke her confidence. Lori and Brian had been at high school together but never in the same circle of friends and he doubted they were close now. Who Lori told her news to was up to her. "Good to see you too."

He caught Brian's intrigued gaze and warm smile moving past his shoulder, and realized he was scoping out Matilda. On impulse he draped his arm casually around her shoulder. Ignoring her stony look, he drew her closer to the station desk and to him. "Brian, this is Matilda Geoffrey from—"

"Australia," Brian interrupted. "You have to be the bride Eric was talking about. We expected you earlier."

Matilda immediately ducked out from under Marc's arm and moved to stand a foot away from him, sending a beaming smile at Brian. "What can I say? Yes, that's me but my friends all call me Tildy."

The police officer shook her hand. "Welcome to Hobin, Tildy."

"Thank you. I must say *most* of the town has made me feel very welcome." Her sideways glance at Marc packed a punch. "I'm sorry I've been delayed but I got caught up discussing my new employment contract with Peggy Hendrix."

Tildy? Irritation streaked through Marc. She'd just volunteered her nickname to a virtual stranger, and yet he'd shared three conversations with her and she'd never confided that to him.

Brian's attention centered one hundred percent on Matilda. "I guess you've come to collect your keys."

Marc interjected, feeling the need to stake back a claim in the conversation. "Not just the keys but the car as well. It's no longer in the rest area so Eric must have had it brought here."

Brian frowned as he turned back to Marc. "We did expect Ms. Geoffrey—"

"Tildy." The Australian accent sounded friendly yet firm.

"Yes, ma'am, but on official business I have to call you Ms. Geoffrey." He turned back to Marc. "We expected her to call in earlier this morning and as we've both been busy and the morning got away, neither of us have had time to go and get the vehicle."

Marc's complete certainty that the car would be safe and parked at the back of the station tilted underneath him and some New York abrasiveness slipped out. "And you're certain of that?"

Brian looked affronted and his usual easygoing and polite demeanor slipped slightly. "Yes, Marc, I am extremely certain of that."

"Sorry." He ran his hand through his hair. "It's just I drove past the rest area half an hour ago and the car wasn't there, so where is it?"

Matilda threw her hands up in the air, her voice rising. "It's obvious it's been stolen."

"That isn't obvious at all," Marc retorted, needing to believe it.

Matilda peered at Brian's badge. "Lieutenant Rogerson." With her accent, the title came out sounding like *Left-tenant*. "Marc Olsen took my car keys this morning and insisted I leave my rental car at the rest area. Now it's missing along with everything I own, leaving me homeless and penniless. Can you arrest him on that?"

Brian shook his head, his smile slightly conspiratorial. "No, ma'am, but let me call the car-rental company to find out if it's been returned." He picked up the phone and dialed.

Matilda, muttering something about moron Vikings, stalked to the water cooler and flicked on the tap, filling a paper cup.

Marc crossed over to her as much to reassure himself. "There'll be an easy explanation to all of this. Hobin isn't New York. It's northern Wisconsin where good people probably thought the car had been abandoned and contacted the rental company who came and picked it up."

Her eyes rolled. "And *you* think I'm as nutty as my grandmother's fruitcake? No matter how well mannered people are in this part of the world this isn't Fantasyland. You know, I was doing just fine on my own but you had to put your overbearing oar in and interfere. I have to ask you, do you do this to all the strangers you meet or did you just decide to pick on me?"

"You're misconstruing my actions. You have no idea about Wisconsin weather. You slept in your car in freezing conditions and damn it, I was only trying to help."

"Is that what you call it? Remind me never to get on your unhelpful side." She tossed the paper cup into the trash can.

Brian put down the phone. "The car hasn't been returned so at this point I am assuming it's been stolen. I've put out an APB on it and when I hear something I'll let you know. Ms. Geoffrey, I need a contact number for you. Where in Hobin are you staying?"

A strangled sort of a wail sounded from her throat. "I don't know. I hadn't got that far. I was going to find a place when I retrieved the car and my possessions."

Marc immediately opened his wallet to appease his guilt and pulled out two hundred dollars and his business card. "Take this to buy yourself some clothes and toiletries and I'll pay your hotel bill until things are sorted out."

Her eyes widened at the crisp notes in his hand before her fingers closed around the money. "Payola money, eh? Well, most of me wants to throw it back at you but I do have a practical streak so I'll take it."

Brian tapped his pen on the counter and looked directly at Marc. "It's Thanksgiving."

He shoved his wallet back in his pocket. "Yes, Brian, I'm well aware of that. It's the reason for my annual visit."

The sarcasm wasn't lost on the officer but he continued calmly. "It's also the Halverson Family reunion."

"That I didn't know, but thanks for the update on the Hobin

calendar of events." No wonder Lori had never shown any interest in this guy; he was hardly quick.

"There isn't a commercial bed available for sixty miles."

"Sixty miles, that's…" Matilda's brow furrowed in concentration. "That's one hundred kilometers! I have a job in Hobin and no car. How is that supposed to work?"

Marc sighed and pulled out his phone. "I'll rent you a car and arrange a line of credit for you."

Matilda clapped her hands. "Oh this is deliciously ironic isn't it?"

"What is?"

She tilted her head and gave him a knowing look. "That you've made me the vagrant you presumed me to be, and now you're paying to keep me off the streets."

He should have known not to get involved. He should have just driven past the rest area on his way to town. Still, he supposed it could be worse. In the grand scheme of things it was only going to cost him a thousand dollars or so and that he wouldn't miss. But he'd learned his lesson and this was the last time he was ever trying to help anyone again. Especially sarcastic Australians with a mouth designed for sin.

"Ms. Geoffrey has to stay in town, Marc." For the first time Brian's voice had the tone of a person in authority and Marc paused, phone in his hand. "Seeing as your actions have precipitated this situation then the best solution is for Ms. Geoffrey to stay with you."

Indignant words tumbled over each other, each striving to be the loudest and sound the most insistent.

"I can't stay with him."

"That's ridiculous. I'm staying at Lori's place and it's not my house to invite guests."

Brian gave Matilda a kindly look. "Marc might have lived in New York for a long time, Ms. Geoffrey, but he was raised right and I can guarantee your safety."

"But—"

Brian silenced her with an upheld palm and turned his gaze to Marc. "Call it legal responsibility or Hobin Thanksgiving hospitality, but either way, as far as the police department is concerned, Ms. Geoffrey stays with you until her car and possessions are found."

Just great. In less than twenty-four hours he'd gone from carefree architect on a road trip to caregiver to his sick sister, uncle to a surly nephew and now he had to share a house with a crazy and cranky Australian. Marc decided right there and then that the holiday season totally sucked.

CHAPTER SIX

Everything hurt. Voices surrounded Lori, sounding far far away and echoing toward her through a fog of pain that encased every part of her. She tried to think past the pain but everything wobbled and thoughts kept slipping away before she'd managed to find purchase. What had happened? Why couldn't she move? She fought to think but the cloak of agony made it impossible.

Kyle. The image of her son formed in the mist of her mind. Panic immediately followed. Where was he? If she hurt this bad then was he hurt too? She tried to open her mouth but it was so dry that her tongue had glued to her palate. She tried to move, to raise her shoulders from the bed but visceral pain, the color of fire, tore through her.

A cool hand touched her arm. "Just lie still, Lori."

"Kyle." With superhuman effort she managed to force out the word before a wave of nausea came over her, rolling her stomach up into the back of her throat.

"Kyle's at school, Lori. Remember, you're in the hospital

and you're just back from surgery. Everything went well and your surgeon will speak with your brother. He'll tell Kyle, remember? That was the plan and now your job is to sleep."

For the briefest moment the fog cleared and all the trauma of the last ten days sped back, filling every cell with its brutal and terrifying message. Breast cancer.

Why her? She'd done the right thing, religiously doing self breast examinations each month. Well, most months. Hadn't being left alone to raise a child been enough to deal with? And why now? Why did cancer have to strike now? Kyle at fourteen needed his mama more than ever now he'd hit the bewildering years.

Snippets of the conversations she'd had over the last two weeks with doctors pounded her. Tough decisions needing to be made, decisions she had to make on her own, just like she'd been making since Carl walked out the door saying he hadn't loved her for years. But this decision was the toughest she'd ever had to make and she'd made it for Kyle.

Her hands crept from her sides, fingers splayed, and slowly she moved them until she felt the roughness of bandages and the flatness of nothing—the place her breasts had once been.

She cried out, an agonizing high-pitched sound that scraped across her like a blunt knife. Then the fog moved in again, blanketing everything, and the pain receded. She fell thankfully into the oblivion of medicated sleep.

Marc turned hard left, his tires spinning on the gravel at the entrance to Lori's driveway. The distinctive yellow school bus had just passed him, heading in the opposite direction which meant Kyle had been dropped off ten minutes ago. Shit! He'd lost track of time. Kyle should have been front and center in his mind—instead he'd let his mind wander at the first glimpse of a pair of intelligent green eyes that teased and sparkled and made him feel horny, exasperated and restless all at once.

Belatedly he'd remembered Kyle. He'd immediately left the police station and Matilda, throwing her instructions to buy what she needed and wait for his return. He'd hightailed it to Lori's but not quickly enough.

He walked through the front door tossing his keys on the hall stand. "Kyle?" he called through the house but there was no response.

Taking the basement stairs two at a time he opened the door at the bottom. Posters decorated the plasterboard; NBA players mingled with the latest heavy metal musicians, as well as pictures of scantily dressed models ripped from a lingerie catalogue. The corner of a Lego poster peeked out from behind the women in bikinis and was the only reminder of the boy Marc had known. "Kyle?"

There was still no sign of him so he walked around the large air-hockey table, a Christmas gift he'd sent the year before, and finally he saw the teenager sitting on a couch with distinctive white earbuds in his ears. As he got closer he could hear the thub-dub of rap.

He tapped him on the shoulder. "Kyle."

The boy looked up, his eyes shuttered and his face expressionless.

"How are you?"

Kyle shrugged, the first sign of communication he'd shown.

"Can you take those earphones out so we can talk?"

Kyle silently pulled them out, his animosity pounding against Marc like waves against the sand.

"I'm sorry I wasn't here when you got home."

"Whatever."

Marc wasn't certain if his apology had been accepted or not. "So how was school?"

"The usual."

As he wasn't familiar with Kyle's school day that answer didn't tell him anything. "Do you have much homework?"

"Some."

He pushed on, desperate to find a way to make contact. "Do you need any help with it?"

Dark brown eyes rolled. "No."

"What about lunch?" Weren't teenagers supposed to be hungry all the time? Perhaps they could connect over food?

"Had it."

Marc blew out a breath he hadn't known he'd been holding. "As soon as the hospital calls I'll let you know." He reached out and squeezed the boy's shoulder, wanting to reassure him, wanting to reassure himself. "Your mom's going to be okay."

Kyle's only response to this was to push the earbuds back into his ears and flick through a copy of *Sports Illustrated*.

Marc stood for a moment, feeling out of place and out of his depth. Should he keep going with this virtually one-sided conversation? The kid obviously didn't want to talk right now and he still had the problem of Matilda. "I'll let you get on with your homework. I have to go back into town and pick someone up who's going to be staying the night with us." Surely that would get a reaction?

Nothing.

Marc jotted down his cell number onto a yellow sticky note and stuck it to Kyle's MP3 player. "I'll be back in an hour or so but call me if you need me."

Kyle didn't look up.

★ ★ ★

Matilda gnawed on her thumb, already regretting her decision to leave the warmth of Peggy's store and stand on the corner waiting for a very grumpy Viking to collect her. Soon after the pronouncement that she'd be staying with him and his sister, he'd abruptly left her at the police station. He'd marched out the door, his long legs eating up the ground so fast she'd expected flames to blast out of his expensive shoes. The man was a clotheshorse from the fine heritage stripe of his shirt and tailored woolen jacket, down to the soft leather of his loafers. Dress sense wasn't something she'd ever admired in a man before, but she was learning fast the wondrous tingling effect generated by well-cut trousers on a toned body.

A moment before he'd turned into a general issuing orders, she'd seen him glance at his watch, heard the soft under-breath swearing and had instantly recognized the reaction of someone who'd let time get away from them. She assumed he had to be somewhere else and was late. Even so, for someone on vacation he seemed totally strung out but then again, that's how most people started their holidays which is why they needed them so much in the first place.

When the door to the station had slammed shut behind Marc, Brian had smiled at her. "Don't worry. Marc will honor his word, Tildy, and his sister, Lori, is a lovely lady. I'll be in touch the moment I hear anything about your car. Meanwhile, enjoy your shopping."

She'd thanked him and left, wondering why it hadn't even occurred to her that the Viking, a virtual stranger, would leave her stranded. Hell, she should be so lucky! It was his interfering that had got her into this mess.

Matilda Jane, take responsibility. The fact you're penniless and stranded in America lies at your own feet.

She pulled her thumb away from her mouth, jammed both hands into the pockets of her too-thin coat, and jumped up and down trying to keep warm. As much as she hated to admit it, the Viking's interference with the car had worked to her advantage apart from the loss of all her belongings. She now had a place to stay and a bit more money in her pocket than she had this morning so there was some semblance of luck on her side.

Staying with the Viking alone wouldn't have been wise given her inability to read men, but staying with him and his sister made it a safe proposition and a win–win situation. Her sordid secret of losing all her money to a con man was safe. Hobin was on her side as a victim of theft, and Mr. Marc Olsen, having lost her car was now definitely behind in the game. Yes, she held the superior position which was a vast improvement on her previous "crazy Australian bride" status.

Hopefully whoever stole her car wouldn't be interested in the contents of the trunk and when they abandoned it— as Brian had explained was the usual modus operandi of car thieves—all would be safe. She just had to bide her time. Fortunately she'd been able to send Vanessa home with a huge list requiring many decisions, so the bride had plenty to think about and her disappointment caused by the current displacement of the tiara and dress had been tempered.

The sleek lines of the now-familiar black Porsche pulled up next to her and the window soundlessly wound down. Piercing blue eyes swept from the top of her head to the tip of her toes and tiny pops of sensation started exploding inside her, each one sparked by the touch of his gaze. She bit her lip hard against the heady feeling. This wasn't good on so many levels. She'd just been brutally dumped and robbed by Barry so shouldn't her body be shut down, immune, numb? Hadn't she lost yet another part of her heart to a man who'd used and left her?

Barry took your trust, your money, but not your heart.

She didn't want to agree but since yesterday whenever she thought about Barry all she could feel was rabid anger and bitter betrayal. The uncompromising truth was that all he'd ever wanted from her was money, and knowing that hurt most of all. A part of her had shriveled and died when she thought of the night in Sydney when he set her aside from him, quoted poetry and cited the "eroticism of waiting," which had all been complete bullshit and code for she wasn't even attractive enough even for a con man to have sex with her.

But now, even knowing all of this, it wasn't enough to stop her body from betraying her and going completely haywire whenever the Viking looked at her. Which was insane because it was obvious from his expression that her presence infuriated him. He with his designer clothes and glossy magazine good looks was way out of her league, yet another reason to ignore her wanton body. She was done with men and totally done with a crazy, antiquated and out-of-date dream. The best way to deal with the Viking was to keep things light and superficial, give her body time to get back to its sensible self and then she'd be fine. Just fine. Really fine in fact.

She leaned forward toward the open window, trying not to show her admiration of the sleek vehicle. "I hope this excuse of a car of yours has a heater that works."

His eyes narrowed, zeroing in on her bagless arms. "Where's your shopping?"

Her fingers closed around the drugstore bag in her pocket, feeling the outline of a traveler's toiletry kit and two pairs of undies. "I've got the basics in my pocket." Along with the precious change from two hundred dollars. It was never too early to start saving when you had nothing.

A deep crease appeared across the bridge of his noble nose and then the car suddenly went silent. He opened the door, his feet hitting the pavement, and then the rest of his long body unfolded into its full height of six foot plus. He gazed down at her, new lines of strain creasing the corners of his eyes along with a matching expression of exasperation. "You need clothes."

"There's no point buying clothes when my car will probably turn up by tomorrow. Brian said it's likely that whoever took it will dump it when it runs out of petrol. I mean gas." She tilted her head. "At home we have cars that run on gas but that's LPG which is what you call propane, right? Really, with all these different words for the same product, it's amazing we can communicate at all." She laughed, hoping to distract him because the longer she held on to those almost two hundred dollars, the more control she had over her panic about her lack of finances.

He grunted. "And if the car's been stolen to be used in an armed robbery then it will probably be torched and never seen again."

She didn't want to think of that. It was bad enough being far away from home with her life in tatters without adding in the fact she didn't have her clothes, her favorite lipstick or even her jar of Vegemite for breakfast. But most importantly she didn't have the two items that would earn her much-needed money.

He rubbed the back of his neck. "Look, you need clothes, especially with Thanksgiving looming."

Peggy had filled her in on Thanksgiving traditions but she hadn't realized there was a dress code. She swallowed hard at the thought of her one hundred and eighty dollars disappearing on a cocktail dress she'd only wear once. "Do I have to dress for Thanksgiving?"

"Turning up naked would probably cause a fuss from the women, although I'd have no objections."

Twinkling eyes belied his deadpan expression and a traitorous streak of heat whirled through her. "In your dreams, Blondie. What I meant was, do I have to buy a good outfit? Seeing as your sister is hosting me I want to do the right thing."

The twinkling light faded from his eyes, replaced by a serious look that seemed to deepen the strain on his face. "Hobin's clothing choices are limited but my sister likes Gracie's so we're going there." He rested his wide palm against the small of her back with firm and determined pressure, his heat immediately permeating her thin coat and burning through to her skin.

With him gently pushing her forward, she started walking up the street. The weight of his hand, combined with her fatigue, made her light-headed and she fought against the feeling by assuming her protective mode. "Are you always this pushy?"

"Are you always this difficult?"

She tossed her head, her hair swinging around her face. "I'm not difficult. I just know what I want."

"Oh, and that's been real reliable for you recently."

His knowing gaze challenged her to disagree but she had nothing. Damn it, she'd walked straight into that one.

With a grin, he opened the door of the women's clothing store and she had little option but to step inside.

An elegant woman immediately crossed the store, her eyelashes fluttering and gold bangles tinkling on her wrist. Her wolfish gaze arrowed past Matilda, straight to the man behind her. "Marc Olsen, how are you?" Her voice purred out the words, her elongated R's rolling on a slow wave—the quintessential Midwestern accent which Matilda was slowly becoming accustomed to.

"I'm well, Gracie. How's business treating you?"

Matilda noticed he'd neatly skirted asking Gracie how she was, which effectively kept the focus off the personal. Interesting. It wasn't the first time she'd noticed it. This morning when the waitress had smiled at him in a wide-eyed way— all bright smiles and coquettish eye-darts, the younger version of Gracie's more sophisticated flirting—the Viking had smiled politely, replied with some social chitchat, but all of it was packaged up in a wrapping of reserve. Lucky them. In a complete stroke of irony, he had no qualms about grilling her on her lost groom and her life choices, when she would have much preferred to be the recipient of his distance.

Leaving them to chat, she drifted through the shop ignoring a small selection of stylish and expensive fitted winter jackets, soft cashmere sweaters in every color imaginable and the most glorious array of scarves she'd ever seen. But as tempting as they were, she needed sensible, serviceable, warm clothing and fashion didn't come into it. At those prices, fashion couldn't come into it. She found the farther she got into the shop, the more the clothes became practical and everyday, and much more what she needed. Ignoring the internal girly-girl who was currently having a tantrum, complete with a full-blown pout, she reached the discount rack and bins and riffled through the remaindered purple and orange turtlenecks undoubtedly rejected on both color and size.

When Matilda had three garish turtlenecks and a pair of corduroys over her arm, Gracie walked toward her holding a dress with a scoop neck and fine lace sleeves that were almost transparent. "These burnished colors would suit your coloring and with the use of a jacket and a pair of heels it can go from day to night in a moment. It's ideal holiday wear."

"I'm sure it is." She was certain the dress could be all those things that Gracie described and more. She caught sight of the figure on the price tag and out of habit automatically converted it despite the fact she had no Australian dollars left and the exchange rate was now irrelevant. In either currency, the amount would feed a family in Africa for a year.

Stifling a groan she smiled politely, feeling the tension at the edges of her mouth. "It's lovely, but it's not really me. I feel more comfortable in this range." She swung her arm out to encompass the general stock.

Gracie sighed, a well-worn sound, and Matilda had the distinct feeling her comment had just scratched a sore point that never really healed.

"But you're an international jet-setter, not a Hobin farmwife. I have enough trouble convincing them to step out of their frumpy comfort zone and believe me, I've been waiting a long time for a cosmopolitan customer like you." Her expression screamed, "Don't let me down."

Matilda pictured her life in Narranbool and her current destitute state. Somehow she managed not to laugh out loud at how far from a jet-setting life it really was. "I really don't think I've got the need for a dress like this."

Gracie's brows rose in a shrewd spike. "While I was buying coffee at Norsk's I heard that you're staying at Lori's and working with Peggy. Lori bought her dress a few weeks ago and holiday season invitations will soon come your way. You're going to need a dress." She turned, smiling at the Viking. "Won't she, Marc?"

"Try it on." His deep voice rumbled around the shop.

Was he kidding? Or did he just want to appease Gracie? Was that part of his style—superb manners and gracious politeness except when it came to her?

"Yes, do try it on." Gracie pushed the garment into her arms and turned her toward the dressing room.

The door closed behind her. Hobin might be ten thousand kilometers from home but it was channeling Narranbool. Within a couple of hours word had got around about who she was, where she was staying and who she was working for. Obviously Thanksgiving was a huge deal and she'd be treading on toes if she wore her jeans. But even with her one hundred and eighty dollars she couldn't afford the dress but she'd placate them both by trying it on. Then she'd politely refuse.

The dress fell effortlessly over her shoulders, hugging her as if it had been designed with her in mind, and even hinting at a cleavage which in itself was a miracle. Nipping in at the waist, it then flared out like the skirts of the 1950s before falling to her knees.

The girly-girl applauded. Gracie was good. The color made her hair glow russet and her eyes shine large in her face. Even the black rings under her eyes generated by the last two days seemed less defined.

"Do you need a hand with the zip, honey?" Gracie enquired from the other side of the door.

"No, I'm fine." She pulled open the door and walked out with a twirl, perversely leaving her work boots on her feet.

"Hello, New York. Grunge meets haute couture." Marc's rich full-bodied laugh vibrated through her, doing strange things to her gut.

Gracie pursed her lips and immediately reached for a basket of shoes. "Take those horrible boots off and try these heels." The assistant fussed around her.

"There's no point. Since *someone* insisted I leave my car in an unsafe place and now it's been stolen, I don't have the money." She shot an accusatory look at Marc. If this story was going to fly then he had to be her fall guy.

But disappointingly, the Viking didn't react. Instead his attention was fixed firmly on reading a text message on his phone, accompanied by a deep V carved into his normally smooth forehead.

Gracie hustled her into the shoes and then stood up and looped a small necklace of beads around her neck. As she fiddled with the clasp she leaned in close to Matilda's ear. "Honey, Marc Olsen's a big-shot New York architect and the price of this dress is small change for him. He lost your car so the least he can do is buy you a dress."

Matilda had never understood why so many women saw men as cash cows for their exclusive use. She'd always had her own money and paid her share. *Until Barry.* Oh God, until Barry when every tenet she'd ever lived by had gone disastrously pear-shaped. Even Barry had initially insisted they keep their accounts separate and it was only after she'd offered to help with the business expansion that he had, with snakelike guile, accepted. She now realized with the clarity of retrospect that she'd fallen neatly into his well-laid trap of "fleece the gullible Aussie."

Men and money. No, she wasn't going to combine the two again. It gave men too much power over her.

The two hundred dollars Marc had given her at the police station had been like a one-off emergency payment, similar to travel insurance, but a dress was in a totally different league. "But I don't need the dress."

"But I need the sale." The mask of friendly efficiency slipped and Gracie's *sotto voce* held an edge of despair. A second later she turned toward Marc, her saleswoman voice once again bright and breezy. "Now, Marc, don't you agree, this will be the perfect dress for Lori's party?"

The Viking stiffened for the briefest of moments before his slow, lazy smile slotted back into place. "It's perfect party wear."

A party. Matilda's chest tightened. Oh God, if her host was having a party then she really did need this dress. She cursed Barry-the-Bastard for stealing all her money on the eve of a major holiday with social responsibilities. Why couldn't it have been during a slow time of year? She craved her independence but right now poverty didn't provide that luxury. On the one hand she could refuse outright to take the dress and avoid being in debt to the Viking and that was her preferred option. But that left her socially outcast at a Thanksgiving function thrown by the woman who was giving her a room and food, not to mention disappointing Gracie.

Not that she owed the shop owner a thing but there'd been an edge of desperation in her voice which had resonated with Matilda. She recognized it as being very close to mirroring how she felt right now—powerless, out of control and impotent as life swirled around her, dragging her down. Working for the last couple of years in Nana's shop, she knew all about the challenges facing small-town businesses and how tough it was to turn a profit. Was Gracie finding it hard to make her lovely shop pay its way?

The Viking slid his phone into his pocket and leaned against the counter, his previous tension vanishing. In its place was a casual ownership of his surroundings that the rich and successful have in spades, along with a critical gaze. "If your jeans are representative of your other lost clothes, just take the dress."

Her red-haired temper sparked. Not everyone could afford to be as well dressed as him. The spark flared into flame, burning at every good intention of not taking financial advantage of the fact he'd lost her car. Right then she realized the Viking had never actually apologized for its loss. Just like a famous Australian prime minister, the word *sorry* had never crossed his lips.

With vivid clarity she knew exactly what she had to do. *In for a penny, in for a pound.* She was taking a stand not just for herself but for Gracie as well and she'd hit him in the back pocket, right where it was going to hurt most. Sucking in a deep breath she smiled. "Okay, I'll take the dress but I also need pants, blouses and some warm tops and footwear."

Gracie beamed.

Half an hour later with a warm winter coat, a week's worth of new clothes that far exceeded her meager and currently lost selection, Matilda stood surrounded by shopping bags joyfully staring at an obscene total on Gracie's cash register. Now that had to hurt. Surely that would teach Mr. Marc Olsen not to interfere in her life or at least make him show some remorse for losing her car.

"How do you want to pay for that, Marc?" Gracie asked.

Without a murmur, Marc laid down a platinum credit card, the clack of plastic loud against the wooden counter. His expression however was unexpectedly devoid of any discernable emotion—certainly no sign of reluctance or pain at the amount of money he was about to part company from. In fact nothing dented his handsome features.

The dress is just small change. Gracie's words hit her like a ton of bricks. *Fool.* Revenge turned bitter in her mouth, burning the back of her throat. What represented a shirt-load of money to her was just play money to this man. She'd let her temper get the better of her and cloud her judgment. Hadn't she learned a thing in the last twenty-four hours? She'd run with an ill-thought impulse but instead of a sense of victory she rapidly experienced a loss of much-needed control. She'd just put herself in debt to the Viking and it didn't feel good at all.

CHAPTER SEVEN

Marc's feelings of culpability about the loss of Matilda's car had lessened somewhat now she'd spent a big chunk of his money and shopped in a style he was completely familiar with—single-mindedness and vigor. Most of the women he knew used retailing as therapy and it seemed Matilda was the same. With three sisters he understood women better than they understood themselves and, despite his initial reservations, it was both gratifying and relaxing to know this woman was no different. Except for someone who had six bags of beautiful clothes, she didn't look all that happy.

She marched purposefully ahead of him, as if she was in charge of the situation and just automatically assumed everyone else around her would fall into line with her plan. With sheer obstinacy he squashed his adopted New York speed and followed behind at Hobin pace. He planned to do things his way.

When he reached the Porsche, Matilda's hand was gripping the driver's door handle. A surge of protection for his pride and joy moved through him. "Don't even think about it. No one gets to drive this car except me."

She looked over at him, shaking her head with a smile. "You're such a control freak. But you can relax. I've got no interest in driving your car. If it was a Lamborghini, then I might be tempted but it's just a plain old Porsche."

Derision about the car wasn't a common reaction but he'd caught Matilda red-handed wanting to drive, and she wasn't one to back down. He leaned over the top of the car and met her twinkling gaze. "So it would offend you to drive it?"

"I suppose if I *had* to drive it I could force myself."

"So tell me, if it would be such a hardship for you to drive it, why are you trying to open the driver's door?"

Her confused gaze darted from his face to the car window and back again and then her eyes crinkled up, her lips parted against white teeth and she started to laugh.

A huge belly laugh swept around him, pulling at him to join in but he didn't get the joke. "Care to share your amusement?"

She patted the top of the car. "You can relax, Blondie. Your precious car is totally safe. I'm on automatic pilot. In Australia this is the passenger side of the car." Still giggling at herself she walked around the vehicle.

"Oh right, just like in England." He opened the door for her.

She paused on her way into the car, resting her hand on the door, her ringless fingers pale against the dark paintwork. "And Asia and large slabs of Africa. It's so weird sitting on this side of the car as a passenger. My hands want to grip a wheel and my feet automatically press on imaginary pedals. Twice this morning I tried to brake when you took those bends too fast on the way into town."

"I did not. This car corners like a dream."

"Yeah, well the way you take those corners it needs to." She got into the car and fastened her seat belt.

She clearly didn't understand that this particular vehicle was designed for speed and that bends represented the opportunity to fully explore the driving experience. He slid in next to her. "I'll have you know that I have an impeccable driving record."

"Good for you, mate." She patted his arm dismissively as if he was a seven-year-old with a merit award.

For the tenth time today he asked himself why he had stopped at the rest area. Most people would sit back and enjoy the precision engineering in glorious silence. But his passenger was a completely unpredictable Australian so he pushed in a CD. A strident and loud jazz trombone solo filled the car, precluding conversation.

Matilda failed to take the hint. "So to Americans, which is the more important family holiday, Thanksgiving or Christmas?"

"I've never really given it much thought."

"Do you come back here for both?" She pushed off her boots and turned sideways, tucking her feet underneath her.

He shook his head. "Just Thanksgiving. I come back to Hobin for a few days every November, visit my family and give thanks that Hobin hasn't been home for twelve years."

"Oh, now that's heartfelt." Her face danced with interest. "Let me guess, you were so keen to leave town you ran away and joined the circus?"

Her lighthearted teasing hit with uncanny accuracy which he immediately deflected. From now on he'd stick to the basics. "At times college was a circus. I went to college in Madison before heading to graduate school in New York state."

"This leaving home and 'going to college' is a rite of passage for Americans, isn't it?"

"I don't know about that." She was questioning some of the quintessential American ways and he realized he'd never really given them much thought.

She wound strands of hair around her fingers. "I think it must be. Either way it's very different from home. Unless you're a rural kid, the average Aussie goes to university in the city where they live and they stay living at home. Parents try moving them on at twenty-three but the newspapers are full of horror stories of parents leaving home because their adult children won't leave."

He shot her a grin. "So when did your parents leave home?"

She gave a tight laugh. "They packed their bags and left on numerous occasions."

Something in her voice made him frown but he didn't follow up. He'd already broken his own self-imposed rule when he'd taken her car keys and look where that had got him. He had enough on his plate with Lori and Kyle. "Tough houseguest are you?"

"The worst." She tossed her head and her hair swung around her like a veil. "You have no idea what you're letting yourself in for."

"Believe me I know. I have three younger sisters, which is why I live alone." He pulled into Lori's driveway and cut the engine while his head ran through a to-do list that seemed to grow longer by the minute. He got out of the car thinking about the call he'd got in Gracie's and how he needed to tell Kyle his mother was out of surgery and that it had gone well, if *well* was a word you could apply to such a thing. Automatically he walked around the Porsche and opened the passenger door.

Matilda stepped out, her expression questioning. "You're frowning. You have told your sister about me?"

"Lori has always had an open-door policy for waifs and strays so you'll fit right in." He didn't plan to tell her about Lori being in the hospital. He had some time before his sister was discharged and by then, if there was a god, Matilda's car would be found and she'd be gone. He took the path of least resistance and tweaked the truth. "She's away at the moment."

The freckles on Matilda's nose suddenly seemed darker as her face paled. "Hang on a minute, that changes things."

He opened the trunk and pulled out her packages, wanting to get inside out of the chilly late-afternoon air. "It doesn't change a thing."

"Yes, it does. I can't stay here alone with you. I hardly know you."

He slammed the truck closed, his temper flaring. Why did she have to complicate every single damn thing? "You hardly knew Barry but that didn't stop you planning to marry him."

Her chin jutted upward. "Yeah, well I'm a lot wiser now."

Something in her voice jabbed at him. It wasn't grief which would have been expected. Instead it was more like hard-edged disillusionment. "Don't worry, your virtue is safe. My fourteen-year-old nephew, Kyle, is here to act as chaperone."

A flicker of something like relief flooded her face before she faux-wiped her brow with the back of her hand and shot him a look from under arched brows. "Phew, because my chastity belt is in the boot of my car."

An image of a satin-and-lace corset slammed into him, pumping his blood hard and fast through his veins—an unstoppable force of lust that confused the hell out of him. So what if she had the most amazing colored eyes. She was the complete opposite of the women he dated, not that he'd dated that much recently. Perhaps that was the problem and now his body was lusting after anything female. Matilda Geoffrey talked too much, questioned him too often and was completely high maintenance. The type of woman he avoided at all costs.

He pressed the car lock. "Even if your chastity belt wasn't in the car you have nothing to fear as mouthy Australians are not my fetish."

"Really?" Her intelligent eyes sparkled the color of the sea around Hawaii. "And let me guess, long leggy blondes with big breasts would do it for you?"

"Only the quiet ones."

Her laugh rained over him as he marched toward the house wistfully thinking of his female-free apartment in Manhattan.

Lori's house was a home. A very feminine home. Lacy window dressings, throw cushions, knick-knacks and magazines clearly stated this house was the domain of a woman. The Viking looked out of place and extremely tense in the small house as if one poorly judged movement from his large toned frame would bring the bric-a-brac tumbling.

Matilda decided he belonged in a space with cathedral ceilings where natural light spilled in spinning golden rings around him. A god among mortals. But right now he looked like a very stressed god and she took pity on him. "If you show me where my room is, I'll dump my stuff and make up my bed."

He nodded briskly and walked down a short corridor before turning left into a room that had a computer desk in one corner and a sewing machine in the other. Swatches of material were pinned in bunches to a corkboard and outfits that looked like costumes hung from a small rack. Advertising posters of well-known musicals and plays adorned the walls and a two-seater couch was positioned under a window.

Marc put her bags by the door and started pulling cushions off the couch. "I'm sorry, but the pull-away bed is the only spare."

"No worries. It wasn't like I was an expected guest." She didn't want to be extra work for anyone and she put her hand out for the sheet he'd pulled out of a cupboard. "I can make the bed."

He flicked the sheet out toward her and she lined up the folds with the edges of the mattress the way she'd been taught and folded it under with crisp hospital corners. She noticed he did the same. "You know your way around a bed."

"I do." His eyes shimmered a darker blue for a fraction of a second as his gaze seemed to absorb her.

A tremor of sensation streaked along her veins and every warning bell clanged loudly. Not that she needed protection from him but she surely needed protection from herself. She immediately changed the subject to a much safer topic. "Seeing as your sister is out of town how about I cook tea for you and your nephew."

He glanced at his watch, his lips twitching. "Is your definition of cooking boiling water?"

The question came out of left field. "I'm not Jamie Oliver but I can do a bit more than boil water."

"You said you'd cook tea. Isn't that just boiling water and adding a tea bag? Kyle and I are hungrier than that."

She swore she was in a parallel universe. On the surface

things looked familiar, the words sounded similar and yet everything was so very, very different. She put the pillows in position and explained. "I'm talking about tea, the evening meal, not a cup of tea. That's a cuppa."

He threw a quilt onto the bed. "Here it's supper."

That made sense. She often had a cup of tea and a snack before she went to bed. "So a cuppa is supper?"

"No, a cuppa isn't supper."

"You don't have a cuppa at supper?"

He grinned. "Not generally, no."

She plonked down on the now-made bed totally confused. "Then what do you have for tea?"

"Supper."

"But you said you were hungrier than that."

He sat down next to her, his weight causing the bed to tilt her closer to him. She smelled citrus and wood mixing with all male strength and power, an intoxicating combination. Then he smiled. Dimples carved into his cheeks, chasing away the serious expression he'd worn more often than not since she'd met him. He looked and smelled divine and her concentration completely collapsed.

She started to laugh. Half out of confusion and half out of hysteria for the crazy swirling sensations that battered her whenever she was close to him. "Let me try and get this straight. If a cuppa isn't supper and tea isn't a cuppa…" But the giggles took hold and she couldn't think at all. She fell back onto the bed, tears of laughter running down her cheeks. "I have no idea what we're talking about."

"This reminds me of Abbot and Costello's, 'Who's on First?'" His rich laughter joined hers as he lay back next to her, his arm brushing hers.

Delicious tingles raced up her arm but somehow she managed to splutter out, "So what's your evening meal called?"

He raised himself up on his elbow, dancing blue eyes gazing speculatively at her. "Supper is the evening meal."

She met his look, fascinated by the multihued shards of blue. It was like looking into a kaleidoscope. "Which in Australia is a bedtime snack."

His fingers trailed across some stray strands of her hair, before tucking them gently behind her ear. "And tea in America is a drink not a meal."

The soft caress of his fingers ricocheted through her but instead of her alert system going into overdrive, her body completely betrayed her by giving an internal groan of pleasure and turning every limb liquid. His hypnotic eyes held hers, drawing her in and then sucking her into their depths. For the first time since she'd arrived in the United States she felt safe, which was insane because *nothing* about this man was safe, nothing at all, so she kept talking. "I'm dying for a cup of tea. I haven't had one since I left home."

"In this part of Wisconsin coffee is the brew of choice."

His breath tickled warm against her skin and she snagged her bottom lip with her teeth against the surge of heat that fired her skin from her toes to her scalp. Surely it was just a hysterical reaction to the total rejection by Barry. "Coffee is okay for an early morning starter but nothing comes close to the soothing taste of tea in the afternoon when the chaos of the day surrounds you."

His gaze seemed fixed on her mouth and his head tilted closer. "I'm not even sure Lori owns a whistling kettle or tea bags."

"No kettle?" It came out as a squeak as the stubble on his

face grazed her cheek, his lips hovering dangerously and deliciously close to hers. "Doesn't she know that a cup of tea is the panacea for all ills?"

The sparkle in his eyes that held her captive vanished so quickly that Matilda felt bereft for herself and pain for him.

"Uncle Marc?"

He abruptly pushed up and away from her, the action so fast that he was on his feet before her brain had time to decode the disembodied words spoken from the doorway. As she rose up from the bed she caught sight of a teenage boy slouching against the architrave.

Marc's usual composure of a man at ease with himself and the world looked decidedly shaky. His voice sounded rough. "This isn't what it looked like—"

Yeah, right. They'd been ten seconds away from locking lips and she didn't know what upset her more—the fact she'd been rescued in the nick of time from her own stupidity or that the kiss had been interrupted.

Kyle gave his uncle a justifiably disbelieving look that only an adolescent can give to an adult caught red-handed.

For some reason she wanted to rescue the Viking but at the same time gain back the distance of friendly antithesis they'd shared from their first meeting. She knew enough about teenagers to know that her accent would mark her as different and therefore, by default, slightly more interesting than most adults. She played to her strengths and started with a cliché.

"G'day. I'm Tildy. You must be Kyle. Pleased to meet you, mate." She shot her hand out toward the youth and smiled.

Kyle looked momentarily nonplussed before accepting her hand. "Hi. Your accent's awesome."

She caught the Viking's brows shooting skyward but she kept her attention fixed firmly on Kyle.

"Thanks. I've just arrived from Australia and your uncle's had my car stolen and because there's no accommodation in Hobin, the police said I have to stay here. I hope that's okay with you?"

Kyle's gaze flicked between the two of them before resting on Marc, his look half impressed and half incredulous. "You had her car stolen?"

Self-righteous indignation rumbled across Marc's high cheekbones. "No, I left her car at—"

"He stole my keys." Matilda shot Kyle a conspiratorial look as they walked out of the room toward the kitchen. "It seems New York has rubbed off some of your uncle's small-town values and he has no qualms about theft."

Marc's grunt of exasperation sounded loud behind her. "And this coming from someone descended from convicts."

She ignored him and kept talking to Kyle as if they were the only two people present. "On top of losing my car and all of my possessions, he refused to let me drive his car."

Kyle nodded in understanding as they arrived in the kitchen. "Yeah, well don't feel too bad, he won't let *anyone* drive it. I asked once."

"You were twelve!" Marc expostulated before leveling his gaze at her. Steel-gray storm clouds gathered in his eyes. "Shouldn't you be cooking supper and earning your keep?"

Matilda smiled. Gone was the banked heat in his eyes replaced by high-level frustration. Yes, everything between them was back to normal—grudging toleration. This time she planned to keep it that way.

★ ★ ★

Matilda couldn't get over how much satisfaction she'd gotten from preparing a simple meal. She supposed it was the normality of the event compared with the last two days, where not one second had been normal. She had the kitchen to herself after a very tense Viking had taken a reluctant Kyle into another room, mumbling something about helping him with homework. Kyle hadn't looked impressed but when had the average teenager ever been impressed by having to study.

You were. She acknowledged the truth, but she wasn't sure that hadn't been more to do with trying to get her parents to notice her via good grades than the joy of learning. Even her career choice of nursing probably came from the seeds of an idea that it would be a way to be valued by her parents—joining them in third-world countries and working together. But that hadn't happened because just as she'd graduated she'd finally realized her parents were a team of two and they didn't require anyone else in their life, not even a daughter. *This is your life, Tildy. Chase your dream.*

But her long-held dream of a family and a great love had crashed and burned and she was the only Geoffrey woman to fail. And what a spectacular fail it had been, leaping blindly off a cliff, and crash-landing in Hobin, homeless and penniless. Now she needed to accept her destiny wasn't a great love story, but a life alone. Nana had been wrong.

Never again was she begging for love to watch it walk out the door, never again would she allow herself to be seduced by the dream and absolutely never again would she put her happiness in the hands of someone else.

She tried to shrug off the cloak of regret and claim back the semblance of peace she'd gained by pottering around an unknown woman's kitchen. She didn't recognize a single brand name of any food in the pantry but the kitchen set-up had been spookily similar to what she was used to. Rummaging through the freezer and the pantry, and knowing that teenage boys had voracious appetites, she'd gone for the old favorite of Spaghetti Bolognaise and garlic bread.

With no idea where everyone was, she walked into the hall and yelled, "Tea's—" She automatically corrected herself, "Supper's ready."

She expected the thundering feet of hungry men—she'd cooked for shearers, firemen and emergency workers during bushfires—but silence greeted her. She checked the front room and then walked down the hall. With the exception of her bedroom, all the other doors were closed but she could hear a murmuring behind one of them so she knocked.

The Viking opened the door, his height and breadth almost filling the doorway, leaving a small gap where she glimpsed his phone and a laptop computer on the bed, its screen glowing brightly. Deep lines edged his eyes, his well-cut hair had the signs of being plowed through by fingers more times than the style demanded and he looked even more tired than she did, which was saying something as she was jet-lagged and had slept in a car the night before.

The man didn't look like someone enjoying his vacation but she wouldn't ask because if she did she risked being told and that would undermine her safety zone. Instead she smiled breezily. "The meal's almost ready. I just need a bit of a hand from you and Kyle for the last-minute things. Where is he by the way?"

He sighed as he stepped out into the hall, closing the door firmly behind him. "In his lair."

"His bedroom?"

He shook his head. "No, the basement."

Surprise skittered through her as she walked back up the corridor with him. "A real basement, like a room under the house?"

A wry smile hovered on his well-formed lips. "That's generally what a basement is. You don't have those in Australia?"

"No, I've never known a house to have one. The closest we have to people living underground is in the opal mining town of Coober Pedy, but then they're there to escape the heat and they don't have a house on top of them." She watched him knock on the basement door. "I'll have to wangle an invitation from Kyle so I can see it."

His brows drew down and he grunted as he disappeared through the door. "Don't hold your breath."

She continued walking and once back in the kitchen, she set out the garlic bread and parmesan cheese. Kyle walked silently into the kitchen with Marc following closely behind. Both of them looked tense. "Kyle, can you tell me where the cutlery and serviettes are kept?"

Her question yielded a blank look. "Pardon?"

She explained, wondering if it was her accent. "Knives, forks, spoons and paper things you put on your lap."

"Oh." Realization lit up his face. "Silverware and napkins. They're in the drawer over there."

"Excellent. Can you set the table, please, and your uncle can pour us some drinks."

Five minutes later they were all seated around the table, a table thick with silence other than the strained politeness of asking for items of food and drink to be passed. Marc seemed intent on eating rather than engaging her or his nephew in conversation and the boy had his head down more than up. Kyle's behavior she understood. Teenage boys usually grunted in monosyllables but after nursing and working in the store at Narranbool, Tildy had learned that if you treated kids with respect and showed some interest in their lives they eventually warmed up. She had no such insight into the Viking's silence.

Sprinkling parmesan cheese onto her pasta, she smiled at the teenager. "So, Kyle, do you follow football?"

"Some." The word came out softly.

"I have no clue about American football. I'm not even sure why they call it football when it seems to be all hand passes."

He gave a half smile. "There's punting."

She pushed on. "Yeah, but that's just chicken feed. Aussies can kick a football eighty meters." Again she got a blank expression and she realized she had to convert. "That's—"

"Two hundred and sixty feet." Marc supplied the answer as he reached for some garlic bread.

"No way." Kyle sounded skeptical.

"Yes, way." Tildy smiled. "In fact, one of our players, Ben Graham, signed on with the NFL when he retired from Aussie Rules because he could kick a long way. What team do you support?"

"The Packers."

She forked some salad onto her plate. "Are they any good?"

"Yeah!" He nodded almost enthusiastically. "They've won more league championships than any other team."

"Awesome." She wondered if Marc might join in, mentioning who he supported but he didn't. Instead he put his knife and fork together on the plate and scrunched his napkin.

"Thank you for the meal, Matilda, but if you'll excuse me,

I need to make some business calls. Leave the dishes. I'll do them later."

The "excuse me" was perfunctory and, without hesitating, he rose from the table and left the room.

She watched him leave in surprised silence, a zip of irritation shooting through her. For someone who was visiting his family he certainly didn't seem very connected. She turned back to the boy. "Would you like some ice cream, Kyle?"

The boy shook his head, lapsing back into silence.

She tried to draw him out with a few more open questions but clearly he didn't want to talk. He kept glancing at the phone as if he was expecting a call or could it be he wanted to make a call? "Would you like to leave the table?"

He nodded, stood and as he walked past her out of the kitchen, Matilda could almost smell the sadness on him and she resisted the urge to reach out and give him a hug. But hugging wasn't something you did to young boys you didn't know. Plus she no longer trusted her intuition. Hell, her radar was so out of whack she'd allowed her life savings to be stolen and on the coattails of *that* disaster had almost kissed a total stranger.

But tomorrow was another day.

She'd go into Hobin in the morning and—

She suddenly realized how far out of town she was, which meant she was dependent on the Viking for transport. Sitting in the small interior of his car, so close to all that testosterone-laden gorgeousness, was too close for her peace of mind. Perhaps Vanessa could pick her up so they could finalize the wedding order. The sooner she accomplished that, the sooner she would get paid. Money was her only way out of this house and Hobin.

Glancing down at her favorite albeit faded jeans, she was reminded of the clothes she'd bought this afternoon. She wanted to take them all back to the shop, get a refund, repay Marc and get out from under that obligation. But that meant Gracie, who needed the sale, would lose out and she still needed the dress for Lori's party. Thoughts zinged in her head, bouncing around like a kangaroo on speed.

An idea as bright as the neon sign outside the Spotted Cow lit up her mind—*eBay. That* was the solution for the clothes. Gracie kept the sale and she repaid the money without having to dip into the funds she'd make from Vanessa's wedding. Her brain was on a roll and more plans spread out as clear as if they were printed on paper. If she washed her jeans and shirt each night she'd be fine to wear them the next day even if the car took an extra day or so to be found.

She relaxed into her plan. All she needed now was a celebratory drink. Forget champagne, she'd kill for a cup of hot, fragrant tea.

Rising slowly, she gave the pantry one last inspection, picking up every container looking for leaf tea or tea bags but Marc had been right. Every conceivable type of coffee bean and coffee blend graced the shelf but not tea. She'd have to settle for a hot chocolate. She poured the milk and set it inside the microwave before pressing a gazillion buttons until she finally managed to start it. Tiredness clawed at her and she stared at the cup as it rotated on the carousel, mesmerized by the action.

A loud, shrill ring made her jump but it wasn't the microwave. She let the phone ring, figuring as this wasn't her house Marc or Kyle needed to answer it. But it continued to ring. Reaching out she picked up the phone.

As she spoke the words, "Hello, Lori and Kyle's house,"

running footsteps thudded on the stairs and Kyle appeared in the kitchen, his face pinched.

"Is it Mom?"

She shook her head as the words of a male voice on the other end of the line were drowned out by a PA announcement of a "code blue." It sounded very much like a hospital and although she didn't know what blue meant, no code was good news. "I'm sorry, can you repeat that?"

"It's Doctor Wernitzski and I'm trying to contact Marc Olsen."

"Just one moment." She put her hand over the mouthpiece. "It's a doctor wanting to talk to your uncle. Can you get him?"

The boy stood perfectly still, fear stark on his face. "What's wrong with Mom?"

Goose bumps rose and raced down Matilda's arms and she immediately called loudly down the corridor, "Marc, phone."

She's away at the moment. Marc's earlier answer to her question about his sister rang in her ears. She'd assumed the woman was away on a business trip seeing as she was soon to host a Thanksgiving party. But the expression of alarm on the teenager's face was reminiscent of the look that relatives of patients wore, the look she was familiar with from years of working in hospitals. A barrage of images flashed in her mind—the tension at dinner, the strained look the Viking had worn all day. No, that was crazy. If Marc's sister had been in the hospital the whole town would know and she would have been housed somewhere else.

Marc strode into the kitchen and picked up the phone, his face drawn. Kyle never took his eyes off the phone as if willing it to divulge its secrets.

Immediately, all the ducks lined up. Out of instinct, Matilda slung her arm around Kyle's rigid shoulders and spoke quietly. "Is your mother in the hospital?"

His silent nod gave her the answer.

Her shaky lifeline that had five minutes ago seemed so safe and secure collapsed around her. How could she possibly stay here now?

CHAPTER EIGHT

The oven clock glowed green, showing 02:00. Marc sat in the dark kitchen, the only other light coming from the moon which cast long shadows across the small space. He'd tried sleeping but whenever he gave in to it, the sleep had been as restless as the tossing and turning he'd done while he was awake. When he'd closed his eyes, he'd dreamed of Lori covered in bandages but when he'd gone to speak to her she'd morphed into a redheaded woman with chaotic curls and a soft, welcoming mouth. He'd lowered his head toward those tempting lips but the moment he'd got close she'd vanished with a laugh and a sullen Kyle appeared in her place, staring at him with reproachful eyes.

He ran his hand through his hair for the zillionth time and stared out the window into the darkness. Things in his usually ordered world wobbled precariously. He was the adult in the house, yet he'd been the one to act like a teenager when he'd tried to steal a kiss from a woman who drove him crazy. He couldn't believe that Kyle had arrived upstairs at that precise moment. He sighed. Kyle's reaction to the phone call from the hospital bothered him. The kid was obviously upset, yet he refused any overtures from Marc to talk about it. Even if he had, Marc had no idea what he was going to say to him.

Before supper he'd told Kyle that his mother was comfortable and the surgery had gone as expected. His nephew had listened politely and then pushed those damn earbuds back in his ears as if he wasn't concerned at all. So Marc had been pretty shocked when the kid had gone white with fright at the doctor's phone call, but again, once he'd been told his mother was okay, he'd silently disappeared into his room for the night.

Damn it all, Matilda, a total stranger had got more out of Kyle in an hour than he had in twenty-four. That made no sense. She made no sense. She should be bereft and grief-stricken after having her life turned upside down but instead she had an infectious laugh, twinkling eyes and a scandalous mouth that didn't match the rest of her compact body. A mouth that glistened plump and red like a cherry, just demanding to be kissed.

But it could also be set firmly in disapproval which it had been after he'd hung up with the hospital. She hadn't asked any questions, in fact all she'd said was, "Kyle needs to know his mum is okay." But the real statement lay in what she hadn't said, which reflected clearly in her eyes. "The kid needs support." Did she think he didn't know that Kyle needed support? Hell, he knew and he was trying but he had no clue how to help when the boy wouldn't talk to him.

He heard footsteps and expected Kyle to appear but the preceding flash of pink put an end to that thought.

A rumpled Matilda, wearing a pair of Lori's pajamas with the sleeves and pant legs rolled up, and a sleep crease marking her cheek, wandered into the kitchen. She looked about fifteen and vulnerable which for some reason annoyed the hell out of him. He reminded himself she was bossy and opinionated.

A startled look streaked across her face when she spied him sitting in the dark. "Oh, hello."

He leaned back in his chair. "Couldn't sleep?"

She nodded. "My body clock is still in Australia and one minute I was asleep, and then next I was instantly wide awake. It thinks I should be busy doing other things rather than sleeping and my brain is going nonstop." She yawned and slid into the chair opposite him, her elbows on the table and her chin resting on her hands. "Are you up because you're worried about your sister?"

He deflected the question. "You Aussies are direct, aren't you?"

She shrugged. "No point beating about the bush. Why didn't you say she was in the hospital when Brian was instructing that I had to stay here?"

"Because Lori doesn't want anyone to know she's in the hospital. Not yet, anyway." He sighed. "Not until she knows what she's dealing with."

Understanding crept into her eyes, which in the moonlight looked as dark and soft as moss. "So I take it the same went at Gracie's and you really didn't need to buy me that party dress?"

"It was easier to buy the dress than risk a rumor but you're right, Lori won't be hosting a party this year."

She chewed her bottom lip and his blood temperature kicked up a degree or three.

"What she's 'dealing with' is code for cancer, right?"

He flinched at the word, hating his reaction.

Contrition wove between her freckles. "Sorry. Sometimes I forget people aren't as familiar with the big C as I am."

He remembered her conversation at breakfast. "Your nana?"

"Yeah, Nana and others."

She seemed to sink into deep thought and he let the silence wash over him, trying to get a handle on his own feelings. The reason Lori's doctor had called was to set up an appointment for her discharge in the morning. In a few hours she'd be home and he'd promised to take care of her but that was before he'd realized what was involved. The thought of nursing his sister scared him shitless. Added to that he also had an antsy teenager, a homeless Australian and he needed to create time to finish the designs he'd brought with him on vacation.

Vacation. He stifled a derisive laugh. This was no vacation. Hell, it was much harder than work.

The responsibility of Lori and Kyle weighed heavily on him, mostly because he had no clue what he was doing and it dragged him back to when he was seventeen and had felt much the same way. The urge to involve his mother or bring Sheryl over from California tempted him constantly, but for some unknown reason Lori didn't want them caring for her. He loved his sister and her illness scared him rigid, but hard as it was for him not to have other family support, he'd respect her wishes. He wasn't happy about it, but he would do things her way.

Matilda traced the wood grain pattern on the table with her forefinger. "Look, I know I was going to stay here until my car was found but seeing as your sister is in the hospital I think I should find somewhere else to stay. Peggy or Gracie can probably help me out."

No! "No, you can't do that." His words tumbled out brusque and fast, shocking him as much as they did her, going by the stunned look on her face.

Her well-shaped brows shot skyward, disappearing under her curly bangs and he realized that telling Matilda Geoffrey she couldn't do something was like waving a red flag at a bull. He immediately qualified. "I don't know where you come from but this is a small town and if you go asking Peggy or Gracie for help it will put the spotlight on me and Lori. I couldn't care less but my sister lives here and right now I'm trying to respect her privacy."

She still looked uncertain. "I know small towns, but me being here doesn't feel right. This is a family situation and you and Kyle need to be here on your own."

No way did he and Kyle need time alone, that much he knew. So far the only conversations they'd had were one-sided with him doing all the talking. He doubted time alone would change that. As much as he hated to admit it the only time Kyle had looked remotely happy since he'd arrived had been the occasional moments talking to Matilda and when he'd been eating her delicious food.

She twirled some hair around her finger. "Plus I have this job and it would be better for me to be right in Hobin." Her mouth slowly curved into a wide smile and she winked. "I could always say you were impossible to live with. People would understand and Lori's secret would be safe."

A feeling of lightness washed through his doom and he leaned back, resting his hands behind his head. "Nah, that wouldn't work. Even though I no longer live here, Hobin still thinks I'm their most eligible bachelor so no one would believe you."

Her gaze flicked to his chest before promptly returning to

his face. "You're forgetting I have a broken heart and I'm no longer looking for a groom."

But she didn't look broken-hearted. She did however look determined and in the short time he'd known her he knew that she acted on ill-thought-out impulses and if she wanted to leave she would. He also knew he didn't want to be in the house alone with Kyle. If he was brutally honest he didn't want to be alone with Lori either and an idea struck him. "What if I paid you to stay?"

Her plump lips gaped in surprise. "You didn't want me here in the first place so why would you pay me to stay?"

He dragged his gaze away from her mouth, hauling it up to her eyes, and smiled. A smile he knew would carve dimples into his cheeks, giving him an engaging look that had paid dividends for him with women in the past. "Even the simple meal you put together tonight was gourmet compared with what I can cook."

She tilted her head and gave him a long look. "Flattery got you places in the past, has it?"

She'd seen right through him. "A little bit. So what do you say?"

Her clear and steady gaze didn't waver. "I've already committed to Vanessa."

He frowned, suddenly worried that she still might leave. "What do you need to do both jobs? More money, a car, what?"

She stilled. "Money just flows out of you, doesn't it?"

"I've worked hard for it and now it works for me."

Her gaze narrowed slightly, taking on an intense and calculating look. "If this idea's going to work then I need a laptop computer, a cell phone, an internet connection, plus the use of a car."

He immediately relaxed, wanting to whoop with the ease in which he'd got what he wanted. "Deal."

She blinked as if she hadn't expected him to meet her request. "O…kay…deal."

Her small hand slid into his, the grip remarkably firm yet soft and enticing at the same time. But it wasn't her grip that really held him; it was the bead of moisture that trembled on the plump edge of her bottom lip. Wet, tempting and outrageously kissable.

Heat filled him and right then he realized he'd just broken his rule of living alone and had signed on to share a house with the owner of the sexiest mouth he'd ever laid eyes on.

"If you have any questions or concerns, just call my office."

Lori watched her doctor leave the room, her head so foggy and woozy that it wasn't able to form a single question although she knew she must have a million. Her stomach swished back and forth as if she was on a boat. The back of her hand throbbed painfully where the IV had just been removed and two drain tubes protruded from her side. Apparently she was ready to be discharged.

She took a deep breath and forced herself to glance down under her T-shirt at the mastectomy bra that covered her flat chest. She squeezed her eyes tight against tears. Her one extravagance as a single parent had always been pretty lacy bras. Now she had no breasts and the plain utilitarian pressure bandage pressed firmly against her, reminding her of that fact every single moment.

"Ready to go?"

Marc's hand touched her shoulder and she looked up to see him holding her small suitcase. Behind him a nurse was arriving with a wheelchair. She didn't want to leave. She didn't want to have to go through those double doors and face a world that was pretty much the same as it had been yesterday while she had changed so much. "I guess."

He nodded, his expression serious and he bent down, preparing to put his arm under hers.

The nurse yelped, "Not like that, Mr. Olsen. No pulling by the arms."

He dropped his hand as if he'd been scorched and stepped back, his face a blank mask. She caught the muttered oath before the more audible, "Sorry."

The nurse moved in, fussing about, assisting her into the wheelchair, checking her drain tubes and tucking a blanket around her.

She wanted to rip out the tubes and hurl the horrible blanket away. She hated that she needed help. Hated that she had no control and she hated the way Marc was looking at her as if she was a scarred stranger.

Staring straight ahead, she let her mind float on the remains of anesthesia gases—a collage of images some real, some memories, all colliding and morphing without the boundaries of reality. Then the fog suddenly lifted. She heard the nurse's voice firing a litany of instructions and Marc's deep voice rumbling with monosyllabic replies as the rustle of discharge papers changed hands. She realized they were talking about her as if she wasn't in the room with them. As if she was a problem.

Her hand gripped the arm of the wheelchair. "Take me home, Marc. I want to go, now."

But she didn't really. Going home meant taking all this with her and that made it way too real.

Matilda downed a big mug of coffee, trying to kick-start her brain, which wasn't ready to be awake, even though it needed to be. It was almost lunch time but all she wanted to do was crawl under the covers and sleep. Yesterday, survival had defeated jet lag. Today, with temporary housing and two jobs, the adrenaline had subsided some and the jet lag whooshed in.

She'd even failed her first morning as a housekeeper, having got up to find the house empty. Breakfast dishes littered the sink and a note with her name on it was stuck to the fridge, held in place with a magnet advertising Hobin Pizzas. "Back by noon. Lunch for three. Marc."

She'd rolled her eyes at the directive. Of course it would be lunch for three as there were only three of them living here. Written in a clear and decisive script, the note displayed the hallmarks of a man used to directing employees and she guessed that was exactly what she was. Staff. Engaged to cook, clean and tidy up after two blokes while the woman of the house was in the hospital. Still, it came with full board, giving her a bit of breathing space to find her feet, even if it did involve being in a house with a man who could grace the cover of any magazine and sell out the print run. A man who was intimately familiar with women falling at his feet and very used to getting his own way. The fact he'd asked her to stay had everything to do with making his life easier. The fact it made hers slightly less unstable was just dumb luck.

She didn't know the exact procedure Lori had undergone but given the tension in the household last night, she'd worked out it wasn't minor surgery. She figured she probably had five days living here as a housekeeper before Lori would be discharged home. Then she'd have to leave because if the woman hadn't told her family and friends about her illness then she wouldn't want a stranger in her house knowing.

But five days was good. She could handle the Viking for five days. Vanessa's wedding would be sorted out and she'd have her clothes back and money in her wallet. She could get to Madison or Chicago and hopefully find some retail work in the pre-Christmas rush. Nursing would pay better but she hadn't taken the time to sit the examination to allow her to practice here because the plan had been to work with Barry in the business.

She hoped the slimy bastard got an incurable rash all over his weedy body.

Don't think, keep busy. She threw herself into domestic duties, washing sheets, making beds, vacuuming carpets and she spent five minutes lugging a full laundry basket of wet washing around the garden looking for the clotheslines. There wasn't one. The sky hung like a thick, gray curtain against the sun and the faint rays barely penetrated. Cold nipped at her hands, wrists and the back of her neck, the only exposed skin, and she carted the washing back inside realizing the huge machine next to the washing machine must be a clothes dryer. It wasn't something she'd ever needed in Narranbool as the abundant hot sun had always dried the washing.

As she dusted and straightened, she gleaned Lori was a drama teacher, a quilter and a keen photographer. Photos of family, friends and scenery were displayed in an eclectic array of frames scattered along the mantelpiece, including a group photo of six—Lori, Kyle, Marc, two other women of similar ages and a statuesque older woman. With the exception of

Kyle, they all shared the same blue eyes and striking Nordic features. The date recorded the photo being taken this time last year. So there was more family than just Marc. Did they all live elsewhere too?

The crunch of car wheels on the gravel made her turn. Marc was back. A shiver of anticipation shot through her like an arrow heading straight down before spreading into a warm tingle between her legs. *Stop it.* She couldn't wait until the shock of the last few days wore off and she'd beaten the jet lag because right now her body wasn't helping her out at all. Calm and aloof was the key to dealing with the Viking. She kept dusting, expecting to hear the clink of his keys on the hall stand and firm footsteps on the carpet. Instead, the chime of the doorbell sounded.

Smiling at the fact that "Mr. Control-Everything" must be locked out, she hauled open the door saying, "Forget your keys, Blond—oh, hello, Lieutenant." She clapped her hands together in joy. "You've found my car."

"Morning, ma'am. Ah, no, I'm sorry there's no news about the stolen vehicle. That's not why I'm here."

Disappointment slammed into her but was immediately deflected by her realization that the policeman looked extremely uncomfortable. She glanced over his shoulder and was surprised to see Kyle standing a couple of steps behind, his eyes fixed firmly on his feet.

A policeman and a teenager. This couldn't be good.

"Hey, Kyle." She gave the boy a reassuring smile. He didn't respond.

The lieutenant cleared his throat. "Ms. Geoffrey, I need to talk to Mrs. Perez."

She stared blankly at him for a moment.

"Lori."

"Oh, right, Lori." She lightly bounced her fingers off her forehead as if she was forgetful. "Sorry, I couldn't remember her surname."

"Could you get her for me, please?"

She caught a flicker of movement from Kyle, anxiety loud and clear on his face. "She's not here, I'm afraid."

The police officer frowned. "Kyle told me she wasn't at school today so I assumed she'd be home which is why I brought him here." He turned to the boy. "Kyle, do you know where your mother is?"

Matilda's heart went out to the boy whose palpable distress swirled around her. He knew only too well where his mother was. She had no idea why this family was keeping such a huge secret from the world but if that was what they wanted to do then she wasn't in the position to question it. "She's at a conference, isn't she, Kyle?"

Kyle's head shot up, bewilderment in his eyes before gratitude slipped in. He nodded slowly.

She threw Brian a self-deprecating look. "At least I think that's what Marc said, something about a drama teachers' convention but I'm hopeless on details. He's not here either, but can I help?"

A conflicted expression washed over Brian's face before he spoke. "I found Kyle wandering along the road. He claims he missed the bus but he should be at school. Thanksgiving vacation doesn't start until the end of tomorrow."

Kyle didn't utter a word.

The kid wasn't giving her much to work with. "You duffer, Kyle. You're not having a good morning, are you? First the headache at breakfast and now missing the bus." She shook her head slowly as if to say, "teenagers eh?" and then she smiled at Brian. "If you leave him with me I'll make sure his mother and uncle talk to him, plus I'll have him clean up his room and then he'll wish he'd gone to school. How does that sound?"

The lieutenant hesitated, clearly not happy but resigned. "Kyle, you're a good kid but I don't want to find you out of school again, okay? Your mom's going to be disappointed."

"'Kay." Kyle muttered his reply without making eye contact and brushed past Matilda into the house and straight down the stairs.

"I *promise* I'll make sure his mother and uncle both talk with him."

"Thanks." He scratched his head. "It's out of character for Kyle. He's always been a great kid."

She smiled wanly. "I'm sure he still is. It's just puberty can be a confusing time." *So can having a sick mother.* She expected the policeman to turn and go but he stood on the stoop as if he was reluctant to depart.

His expression softened and Matilda caught a glimpse of the man he might be out of uniform. "Lori's done an amazing job raising him on her own and I really admire her for that." He hesitated as if he wanted to say more but then his shoulders rolled back and the professional policeman returned. "The moment I hear anything about your vehicle, I'll be in contact."

"Thanks a lot." She closed the door giving a silent vote of thanks that she'd got away with a lie and went directly to the kitchen to prepare lunch. She'd give Kyle a bit of time alone and then she'd go check that he was okay. She tasted the minestrone soup and added some freshly ground pepper before slicing and dicing the sandwich fixings. All the time her mind whirred and she kept wondering if the reason Brian hadn't reported Kyle to the school had more to do with how he might feel about Lori. Or was it just small-town policing at work?

It was probably community policing. She mused along similar community lines. Did housekeeping extend to getting involved in the dynamics of the household? She wasn't sure about the ethics of that but she was absolutely certain that the current plan of "pretending things were normal" wasn't working out for Kyle. From her nursing experience she knew that shielding teenagers too much always backfired because imaginations usually came up with worse scenarios than reality served up.

No matter what Lori's prognosis, Kyle needed to visit his mother in the hospital this afternoon and the moment Marc arrived home she'd tell him that whether he wanted to hear it or not.

CHAPTER NINE

Marc walked Lori from the car, feeling her weight against him. It had been a fraught drive from Wausau and although he'd tried to avoid every pothole and rough road surfaces, Lori had often flinched.

"Home, thank God." Lori breathed out the words on a whoosh of relief.

Half a dozen times on the journey home, he'd gone to tell her about Matilda but she looked so frail and had kept closing her eyes as if the effort to keep them open was too much, so he'd bailed. Now as he helped her through the connecting doorway from the garage and into the house, the aromatic combination of garlic and marjoram came out to meet them.

Lori gripped his arm. "I asked you not to tell anyone and you promised."

He dropped his keys onto the hall stand and sighed. "I've kept your promise."

She looked skeptical. "Then who's cooking because I know for sure it wouldn't have been you?"

As if on cue, Matilda's voice sounded from the kitchen. "Hey, Blondie, you and I have to talk." She walked around the corner into the entrance hall, wiping her hands on an apron that covered the same jeans and long-sleeved T-shirt she'd worn yesterday.

An arc of disappointment thudded into him and he realized with some surprise that he'd been looking forward to seeing her in the new clothes she'd bought, especially the skirt which would show off her legs and slender ankles. He'd only glimpsed her legs briefly but even covered in striped thermals he'd appreciated the curves.

She stopped abruptly and blinked twice before stepping forward slightly. "Oh, hello. You must be Lori."

"You said you wouldn't hire a nurse." Lori sagged against him, her voice full of the pain of betrayal.

He raked his free hand through his hair, wishing he'd explained it all in the car when Lori had been sitting down. "I didn't hire a nurse. It's a really long story but the short version is that this is Matilda, our temporary housekeeper from Australia."

Matilda wound a stray red curl slowly around her finger, her brow creased in thought and her perfect-pout lips unexpectedly silent.

His nostrils flared, immediately recalling the scent of mangoes he'd inhaled from her hair yesterday and his fingers tingled at the memory of the soft strands caressing his skin.

She quickly dropped her arm by her side. "Actually, I'm also a nurse, which is just as well as your sister looks like she's ready to faint." She moved quickly to Lori's side and issued a list of snappy instructions. The next minute she was gripping his wrists with unexpected strength and their arms had fashioned a chair for Lori.

They carried his sister into her bedroom. Lori's gray color scared him and a combination of helplessness and guilty redundancy rolled through his stomach, quickly giving way to sheer relief when Matilda's hands pulled back the bed linen, plumped pillows and helped bring Lori's legs up onto the bed. When she'd tucked the quilt around their patient, she immediately checked Lori's pulse. Through all this his sister remained silent and the moment her head hit the bank of pillows she closed her eyes.

Matilda touched her hand lightly. "I'll be back in a minute with some water, to check your dressings and to help you get into your nightie so you're more comfortable. Is there anything else you need?"

Lori shook her head, eyes shut tight refusing to look at either of them. "I don't need either of you. Go away."

Marc wrung his hands. "Lori—"

But Matilda caught his arm and pressed her finger to her lips. Pushing him out the door, she shut it quietly behind her.

He followed her into the kitchen and the moment his foot touched the linoleum floor he opened his mouth, not quite believing his luck. "You're a nurse? Who would have thought?"

Green sparks ignited in her eyes. "I'll take that as a compliment."

Quicksand sucked at his ankles. "Sorry, it's just that—"

She crooked a brow. "Women who are so gullible to cross the world to marry a man who vanished can't possibly be intelligent?"

"I didn't say that."

"No, but with you there's always more in what you don't

say." She bent down to pick up some pasta that had fallen on the floor and her jeans pulled tight across her sweet behind. His groin reacted immediately.

She tossed the pasta in the trash. "It's lucky for you that I'm a nurse. What were you thinking bringing a woman home from hospital less than twenty-four hours after a mastectomy? She needs to be in the hospital longer than that!"

"Hey, don't make me the fall guy." He pressed his palms down on the island counter, annoyed she would think him that irresponsible, and frustrated that he even cared what she thought. "You think I wanted to bring her home this early? I expected her to be in the hospital longer but I didn't have a choice. When her doctor rang last night he said she was at a lesser risk of infection here. That and her HMO only covered her for a short stay."

Her brow creased. "HM—what?"

"Health Maintenance Organization."

"Oh, like health insurance? Still, twenty-four hours! That doesn't sound like maintaining health to me." She threw her hands up and paced around the kitchen more agitated than he'd expected, pausing only to stir the soup. She looked up at him, concern etched in her velvet green eyes. "You heard what she said. She's furious with you and she doesn't want me in her house."

He jumped on that statement fast, worried Matilda was going to reconsider working for him. "Yeah, well she's going to have to put up with it because I can't do this on my own." He rubbed his neck, still bewildered by how fast his ordered life had been turned upside down. "They gave me stuff for wound care and I have to call twice a day to tell them how

much goop is in the drain tubes coming from where her..."
He couldn't voice what had been taken from his sister.

He took a deep breath. "I'll pay you double standard nursing rates if you stay."

She set the large cooking spoon down on the ceramic rest, empathy clear in her gaze. "This isn't about money."

Concern sliced into him at her quiet words. "What is it then?"

She lowered the heat under the pan. "I'm not registered to work in the U.S. as a nurse."

He grasped at straws. "But you're qualified as an RN in Australia, right?"

She nodded. "It's been a couple of years since I worked in a hospital, but yes, I'm fully qualified and can handle Lori's care."

Everything steadied again. His gut unclenched and the abject fear that had filled him from the moment he'd laid eyes on Lori in the hospital room—fear that he'd inadvertently hurt her—faded. Matilda was one hell of a surprise package and he sent a vote of thanks up into the ether for her arrival. Lori now had the nurse she needed. Kyle had food, someone to make sure clean clothes were on hand and that he got to school on time. He'd made sure everyone was well looked after and if things continued going well, he might actually be able to find some time to sort out the Matheson account which needed attention yesterday.

He smiled. "That's great. You go help Lori get settled and don't worry about me. I can get myself lunch."

"Really?"

"You bet." He reached into a cupboard for a bowl.

"You can manage to ladle already prepared soup from a

saucepan?" Her hand touched her chest in sarcastic amazement "Wow! Next you'll be telling me you can eat a sandwich that's been made for you."

His hand stilled on the bowl. He was used to her teasing but this was different. It had an edge. "Am I missing something?"

"Someone. You're missing someone." Her voice rose and her accent broadened. "There's a scared little boy downstairs so stressed about his mother that he wagged school today."

He had no idea what *wagged* meant but he could guess. "But I dropped him off at school on my way to Wausau."

She spoke slowly as if he was an imbecile. "You might have done that but he obviously didn't stay *at* school. The lieutenant, the one who's looking for my car, dropped him home half an hour ago."

The bowl clattered onto the bench. "Hell."

"Hell's right and it's what Kyle's going through so here's the plan." Her body language screamed "Nurse-in-Charge." "I'm going to get your sister sorted and you're going to talk to Kyle. Next you're bringing in a lunch tray and the three of you are eating in Lori's room so you can all have the conversation you need to have. The one that involves Kyle so he knows what is going on. Then she'll be exhausted and need a nap while you spend the afternoon here with your nephew."

Her precise instructions rained down on him, not unlike the demands of his sisters over the years, but at the same time he hardly recognized this practical, organized woman compared with the deluded bride he'd picked up half-frozen yesterday. No matter how much it galled him to hear it, he had to concede she was right.

He couldn't believe that Kyle had skipped school.

He sighed, wishing he could just morph himself back to

New York, back to his office where he knew how to be an architect and knew exactly what he was doing instead of the floundering feeling he had right now. But Lori and Kyle needed him and he had to go be the big brother and uncle. He just wished it came with instructions.

"I probably shouldn't have even thought I'd be okay having Marc do this." Lori looked away from her chest, her eyes not able to linger on the place where her breasts had once been.

Matilda paused with gauze in her gloved hand, about to re-dress the drain tube. Seven hours ago her patient had declared she wanted nothing to do with her but after an afternoon sleep and pain medication Lori had accepted her ministrations without a murmur. "It's probably not something you'd want your brother to see."

Lori swallowed. "Or any man."

She immediately clarified. "I wasn't thinking of it like that. I meant that because you're siblings you'd both be embarrassed."

Lori shook her head. "Nothing embarrasses Marc. He grew up fast when Dad died. He delayed college and pretty much kept things together while Mom worked, and with three younger sisters, he's seen and dealt with a lot."

Matilda absorbed this bit of news and tried unsuccessfully to align it with the man who'd told her he couldn't cook and needed a housekeeper. The man who'd looked horrified at the thought of having to deal with drain tubes.

Lori fidgeted with the top sheet. "My husband left me when I had two breasts, so can you honestly tell me there is *one* man out there who'd find me attractive now?"

Taping the gauze in place, she measured her words carefully. "I've never seen you before your surgery but even with post-anesthetic hair, you're a beautiful woman."

"But with no breasts." The strangled sob vibrated around the room.

"So we find you a leg man." She sat down on the bed, welcoming the faint curve to Lori's lips. "There's a lot more to you than boobs. But I understand going from a double D to this is a shock. You have the choice of reconstruction or if you don't want to go that way, you can use prosthetics and be a different breast size every day depending on your mood. Just think, you can be a woman of mystery. Me, I'm just plain flat all the time."

Lori gave a watery smile. "Finding two leg men in Hobin—now that could be a big ask."

She patted her hand. "I'm off the dating scene completely so there's no contest. When we find him, the leg man is all yours."

"Marc told me about the wedding."

"Right." Of course he would have told his sister as a way of explaining why she was in the house but she hated people finding out and judging her as hopeless before they really knew her. She tossed her head against the hurt of her own stupidity. "More of a lack of a wedding, really. See, you just can't trust boob men."

Blue eyes with the same intense look as the Viking's, but with a glimmer of understanding, stared at her. "You're remarkably together."

"No, I'm just bloody angry and grateful I realized what he was before I made the huge mistake of marrying him. Barry Severson, if that's even his real name, is a bastard best forgotten," she said with feeling as she stood up. "Do you need anything?"

Lori shook her head and stifled a yawn. "I think I'll sleep."

"Good for you. I'll go feed the men in your life."

"Tildy?"

She paused with her hand on the doorknob. "Yes?"

"Thanks. I know it sounds wrong and I feel really guilty but it's easier you being here than my mom or sisters. They'd fuss too much."

Matilda thought of her own mother who'd never fussed over her, and how as a child she'd dreamed of having her undivided attention for just one day. "I can fuss."

Lori stilled. "Can you fuss over Kyle for me?"

"Consider it done."

Marc stood frowning at the plans spread all over Lori's dining room table, his concept for the latest development project he was spearheading, and tried to muster up some enthusiasm for it. Not a lot showed itself and he rubbed the back of his neck. He loved his work, in fact he lived and breathed it but just lately it didn't excite him the way it always had. The Matheson account was a pointed reminder.

"Kyle's gone to bed. Lori's asleep and I've made us hot chocolate."

He glanced up as Matilda slid into a chair opposite him, setting down two mugs of steaming drinks. Her hair had slipped out of its utilitarian band and bounced off her shoulders in a riot of untamed curls. A bulky woolen sweater now covered her T-shirt, stripping her of any discernable female shape, but her scent and her mouth screamed one hundred percent, in-your-face, lush femininity. If he'd spent more time thinking about the plans in front of him rather than the way she nibbled her plump lips when she was thinking, he'd be a hell of a lot closer to his deadline.

"Are you cold? I can turn up the heat if you want." He accepted the mug with a nod of thanks.

"No, I'm fine now I've got my jumper, I mean sweater." She laughed. "Kyle's been educating me about words. We worked out that Australians pash. The English snog and Americans mack."

"He's fourteen. What does he know about macking?"

She looked at him over the rim of her mug. "The point is he's fourteen and even if he hasn't pashed, macked or snogged I can guarantee you he's thought about it."

So have I. Watching the way her soft mouth moved over the words and hearing her accent tackle "macked," sent his imagination into overdrive. Would she taste as delicious as she sounded?

He consciously moved his thoughts back to Kyle and macking. He was immediately struck by the irony of the situation— he did actually have something in common with his nephew after all. He sat down, still not able to absorb the rapid change from young boy to teen. "Last year we built Legos together."

She shrugged. "This year you still can."

He did a double take. "You just told me he's thinking about kissing girls so I can't see that he'd possibly be interested in Legos."

"Ah, but that's the beauty of teenage boys. They go from boy-man to boy-child in a heartbeat." She leaned forward, her eyes sparkling. "The rules pretty much go like this. You don't suggest playing board games or Legos in front of his friends, but at home, suggest it and if he says no then start building Legos yourself. I bet he drifts over and joins in."

Marc wasn't convinced. "You seem to think you know a lot about boys. Did you grow up with little brothers?"

A tension circled her. "No. I'm an only child."

He grinned. "That's why you're so bossy. You never learned to share."

Her lips twitched. "And you're the eldest of four which is why you insist on getting your own way."

He thought about the years between seventeen and twenty-two and how nothing had gone his way then or in the last few days. "I spent five years helping raise my sisters. It should have been three but when Lori hit eighteen, she married Carl and left home so what on earth makes you think I get things my own way?"

She rested her chin on her hands. "The way you deal with women now."

He didn't like the insightful gleam in her eyes. "You make it sound like poker. I don't 'deal' with women."

"Sure you do. You either charm them or bribe them with money."

The words hit with partial accuracy and he couldn't deny that charm and his good looks opened doors and his money helped to make life easier. But indignation burned at her other accusation. "I've never bribed anyone and I've *employed* you. I believe it was you who hustled me for a computer and a phone."

"That wasn't hustling. It was negotiating terms and conditions." She winked and took a sip of her drink before peering at his plans. "What's this?"

He leaned forward over the plans. "Living space."

She trailed her fingers across the plans. "You design apartments?"

"I design all sorts of things but heritage restoration with modern space is my specialty."

"I thought New York City was all modern glass skyscrapers?"

"Parts of it are." He clicked an icon on his laptop and opened up the presentation he'd shown his mother. "Other parts of it are like this."

She walked around to view the screen and breathed out a blissful sigh. "Oh, that's gorgeous. I love the character of those Victorian buildings and what a brilliant way of preserving the old and incorporating the new. What do they look like inside?"

He clicked again and displayed a picture of the apartment he'd bought in the complex.

Her face clouded. "Oh."

"Oh?" He'd gotten a lot of feedback on this presentation from colleagues and potential buyers but he'd never heard that particular tone. "What does 'oh' mean?"

She wriggled her snub nose and pointed to the screen. "I know this is probably just the display model for selling purposes but the design's a bit soulless, don't you think?"

Her comment surprised him. "It was decorated by one of the top New York interior designers."

"Still, it could do with a bit of 'lived-in clutter.' What's its energy rating?"

"Lived-in clutter" was exactly what he'd grown up in and up until this last week had since managed to avoid. His apartment suited him perfectly. He responded to her question on the energy rating. "Extremely green. That's always my goal and by the end of the consultation process it's part of the customer's as well."

Admiration lit across her face. "Excellent. So what's your plan for your current project?"

He scratched his head. "Good question. I've been asking myself the very same for the last month."

She stared at the plans for a bit longer before walking over to the large window, gazing out into the grove of trees silhouetted by the light of the moon. "Perhaps inspiration will strike you now you're out of the concrete jungle."

He laughed out loud. "I doubt it. Corn fields don't really do it for me." He stared at his screen knowing that he needed something to kickstart the project because the client was expecting a briefing soon after Thanksgiving and so far he had squat.

"Oh my God!" Matilda suddenly shrieked, and raced out of the room.

"Matilda?" He called after but the only reply was the squeak of the front door being opened. He strode to the entrance hall and a blast of cold hit him in the chest, rushing through the open door. Grabbing his scarf and coat he headed into the dark, still night.

She stood in the middle of Lori's lawn in her fleece socks, her head thrown back and her slender, alabaster neck illuminated by the white moonlight. With outstretched arms she twirled around and around, a look of wondrous rapture on her face.

He walked over to her as the thick flakes of snow fell in tiny spirals to the ground. She stuck out her tongue, catching a feathery frozen droplet on the pink tip and a moment later laughed delightedly. "This is so amazing. I've never tasted snow before. In fact I've never *seen* snow before."

Breathless, she stopped twirling and looked up at him, excitement skating on pink cheeks. Snowflakes tangled in her hair, clung to her lashes and balanced on the tip of her nose. She didn't look like a woman who'd had her life plan crumble at her feet. Instead her eyes radiated childlike exhilaration and sheer optimism.

"You're like a kid in a candy store," he teased but he envied her ability to experience such joy from something as simple as snow. When had he last felt like that?

She stood perfectly still. "Listen."

He did. "I can't hear a thing."

"I know, how awesome is this? Who knew snow was silent."

Luminous eyes the color of rainforest pools hit him with a look so bright and clear that he imagined he could dive right into them and surface changed somehow. He veered away from the thought.

"You'll freeze." He slung his scarf around her neck, pulling her close as he knotted the fine wool around her before brushing her icy cheeks with his thumbs.

She shuddered and the flakes dissolved on her lips, forming perfect orbs of water.

Need, hot and hard, ripped along his veins stronger than ever before. More insistent and less able to be ignored. Like everything in his life, he used logic to fight it. This lust-fest reaction made no sense. Matilda didn't even come close to fitting the mold of the women he found attractive. She was far too bossy and opinionated for that, but he couldn't ignore his tight pants much longer. This reaction had to be an aberration, an out-of-sync response by his body to his lack of recent action and now compounded by his forced stay in Hobin. The only way to deal with it was to face it straight on. If he kissed her, his body would instantly realize its mistake and be shocked back into sync. Matilda would return to being the short, plain woman she was and this attraction would disappear. End of story.

Her mouth's not plain. He ignored the voice, confident of his plan. His thumb brushed a droplet of water, smearing it against her full bottom lip which quivered with a ruby sheen.

Her eyes widened to inky discs and a pulse fluttered in her throat but she stayed perfectly still.

Wordlessly, he brought his mouth down gently onto the edge of her mouth, stage one of a planned assault to assuage his desire and reclaim much-needed order back into his life. She tasted of cold and ice—a flavorless combination that numbed his lips and cooled his blood. He instantly relaxed, cocooned in a bubble of knowledge that he'd been right all along about Matilda. She didn't do it for him.

He brushed his lips across hers well on his way to ending the perfunctory caress, while his mind toyed with a quip about snow to keep things light. Suddenly the ice cracked. Chocolate and chili collided in a rich heady rush, spilling over his lips in a sweet, tangy promise. Fire lit through him and his tongue flicked against pillow softness, desperate to taste more.

Cupping her face in his hands, he used his tongue to tickle and cajole, using every trick in his arsenal of seduction to enter the secret cave. Her lips parted on a sigh and he dove in like a pirate seeking treasure, absolutely certain it waited there just for him.

Heat met him, scorched him and swallowed him up.

His blood pounded fast, roaring like a flood through a canyon and his breath came in short rafts but still he explored, needing to taste and touch every part of that wondrous mouth.

His tongue found hers, colliding, dueling, taking, but he wanted more. Needed more. He wanted to taste the salt on her skin, bury his face in the softness of her hair, and feel the touch of her silky skin against the length of him.

He just wanted her.

Pulling her closer, needing to feel her body caressing his, he was frustrated by thick sweaters and coats diluting the touch. He dropped his hands to her hips, his fingers gripping the hem of her sweater, well on their way to their target—the soft skin underneath.

She unexpectedly broke away and gazed up at him, her mouth crushed crimson, its moistness shimmering in the moonlight. Curls bounced around her head as she lifted her chin even higher, her expression wry. "Just as well you told me I'm not your type, Blondie, or else I might be about to hurt your feelings."

His blood was a very long way from his brain and he struggled to think. "What are you talking about?"

"As a kiss it wasn't half-bad, but—" She shrugged and opened her hands palm up. "It's just, well, I'm not that into you." She leaned forward, giving his shoulder a friendly squeeze before pressing her lips against his cheek in a sisterly kiss. Then she spun around on her soggy socks and walked inside.

He stood staring, still hard, still craving the treasure he hadn't yet found, and knowing that the kiss was just an appetizer.

I'm not that into you. No woman had ever said that to him and he'd never chased a woman in his life. Usually he chose whoever caught his eye from the parade of women who passed through his life indicating their interest in him by a range of responses from flirting glances to the complete come-on of pushed-up cleavages and pouting lips.

But not Matilda. Sure, she'd never fluttered her eyelashes or hung off his every word but the kiss they'd just shared had been unlike any kiss he could remember. Given the number of kisses he'd received since Sue-Ellen Voss had jumped him under the bleachers in middle school, that was saying something. But it had been a long time since the game with women had been fun and recently he'd given up completely. But twice in two days with Matilda he'd gotten hard and that was two times more than the nothing it had been for weeks. That had to mean he was back in the game.

He thrived on challenges. He'd won awards for creating brilliance out of dereliction, for designing buildings to fit the landscape and making them living, breathable spaces no matter what the obstacles. *I'm just not that into you.*

He laughed out loud at the absurd thought. For a recently dumped bride, she'd returned his kiss without too much hesitation. He wasn't certain what was going on here but one thing he did know—he was stuck in Hobin so he might as well make it work for him. Matilda Geoffrey, Australian-with-attitude, might not know it, but she'd just issued him with a challenge and he could never resist one of those.

CHAPTER TEN

Matilda opened the curtains in Lori's room after assisting with a sponge bath and let the morning sunshine stream in. She couldn't believe how different everything looked from the day before. Gone were the bare trees and the brown-black earth. Instead, blue skies met with white ground for as far as she could see and trees stood dusted in sparkling crystals catching the beams of sunlight. On the top of a tall branch, a bright red bird perched, unlike any bird from Australia. "It's a beautiful day and that view alone should cheer you up."

Lori smiled. "The first snow of the season is always magical."

She immediately thought about Marc's kiss. Snow had fallen gently on them but there'd been nothing gentle about his kiss. It had raced through her like an Australian bushfire, lighting everything in its path until it exploded in one massive fireball, blowing apart every single intention to keep a safe distance from him. She realized that up until this point in her life she'd never been thoroughly kissed. At university she'd been kissed by youths who'd had no clue, and Jason's kisses had been tinged with an air of distraction as if he was looking over her shoulder for something or someone better to come along. Barry's kisses had been perfunctory at best, but Marc's kiss had all the hallmarks of a man who knew exactly what he was doing, and who knew how to do it very, very well.

It had only taken one well-placed flick of his tongue to turn her legs liquid and then she'd sunk into his chest with a sigh, almost begging him to never stop.

But something had made her stop. Perhaps the last few days had activated a core survival response but somehow she'd managed to mesh her quivering body and boneless legs into supporting her, and she'd managed to walk away. She was clueless about men, and her salary which was paid by him was the *only* reliable thing keeping her afloat. Nothing could jeopardize that, so kissing Marc Olsen again wasn't an option.

She shifted her thoughts to something a lot safer—her job. "What's ambrosia salad?"

"It's pineapple, mandarins, cherries and marshmallows all mixed with sour cream and coconut."

She'd expected something with lettuce and tomatoes. "Why is it called a salad then when it sounds like dessert?"

"It's not a dessert and it's always served with a meal such as Fourth of July or Christmas. Why did you want to know?"

"Because your mum has left three messages on your machine since yesterday and the last one said she's bringing ambrosia salad for Thanksgiving."

Lori's open and relaxed expression shut down tightly and she closed her eyes, remaining silent.

Matilda swallowed a sigh. It was one thing not to tell the

town about the surgery, but another to keep it from family. "You haven't told your mother, have you?"

"No." Lori's eyes remained closed.

Matilda's mother had never been very maternal and she virtually never telephoned. Granted, she usually wasn't where a phone was but even when she had been, she didn't call. Theirs wasn't a close relationship. So to have a mother who called and left caring messages on a machine seemed to Matilda not to be something to ignore. "She's going to get a hell of a fright if she turns up here on Thursday and finds an Australian in the kitchen totally clueless about cooking a turkey and thanking her for bringing dessert." She gave Lori's hand a gentle prod. "That's not really fair now, is it?"

One blue eye opened and then the other, followed by a resigned sigh. "She's not well and I thought I could wait until I'd been told the full pathology report."

She nodded in understanding. "Usually a good plan except with a public holiday in the middle associated with an en masse family gathering, it's going to be a bit hard to hide your mastectomy."

"Ask Marc to tell her and cancel Thanksgiving." Her blond bob swung around her face as she turned her head toward the pillow.

Matilda spoke to the back of Lori's head. "I suppose he could tell her but your mum will want to see you as soon as she hears the news, just to make sure you're okay."

"But I'm not okay, am I?"

She ignored the inference. "You're a lot better than you were yesterday and you could cope with a quick visit."

"I don't want anyone to see me like this." The pain in her voice couldn't be muffled by the pillow.

"This isn't anyone, Lori. It's your mum. The longer you put it off the harder it's going to be to tell her. If we plan it then you have more control. If you tell her today then we can let Thanksgiving Day slide by if that's what you want."

Lori remained silent and as much as she hated it, Matilda let the silence roll out and waited for her patient's decision.

Very slowly, Lori's head turned back toward her and she sighed. "Okay, ask Marc to bring her over this afternoon."

Matilda straightened the top sheet. "Good idea. Nana always said, 'Don't put off tomorrow what you can do today.' She also said, 'Food feeds the soul' so I'll bake us all a huge afternoon tea."

At least that would keep her occupied and out of harm's way.

The sweet scent of baking wafted into the dining room, rousing Marc from the plethora of problems he faced with his work project. The sugary aroma instantly took him back to when he was a kid on the farm, to a time before his father had died and his mother baked angel food cakes and chocolate-chip cookies. He'd tumble into the warm kitchen having walked from the bus stop, his cheeks burning with cold, and a glass of milk would be waiting along with a piece of fruit. He'd drink the milk fast and then sneak chocolate-chip cookies straight from the wire cooling rack, the chocolate melting hot, spreading deliciously over his tongue. He couldn't recall a time since then when his mother had baked. Sure she'd assembled meals but she hadn't baked.

But Matilda must be baking. The thought of sneaking something more than just a cookie had him flicking his computer over to standby and heading into the kitchen. She stood at the counter and irritation swept through him at the sight of her now-familiar T-shirt and jeans. She'd spent enough of his money on new clothes so why wasn't she wearing them?

Her hands sank deep into a bowl of gooey mixture and traces of flour could be seen in her hair and some had streaked across her cheek. He walked straight over and leaned in next to her, breathing in her scent of tropical fruit as he scooped his finger into the mixture.

"Hey!" She bumped her hip against the top of his thigh, as if to move him away. "No stealing the mixture."

He smiled down at her as he slowly put his cookie-dough-covered finger into his mouth and sucked it clean.

Her gaze darkened and fixed on his mouth, her plump bottom lip vibrating with the slightest quiver. "If you get salmonella from eating raw egg, don't blame me."

"I'll risk it." His hand darted forward for a second taste.

"Aren't you supposed to be collecting your mother?" Her small hands worked quickly rolling the pale yellow dough into balls.

"Soon." He tried for a third raid but she moved the bowl.

"You're a grumpy cook."

"No, I'm not. The deal in my kitchen is if you help you get to lick the bowl at the end."

"Were they your mother's kitchen rules?" He put the whistling kettle that Matilda had insisted he buy onto the stove, and turned on the burner.

"No, they were Nana's. Mum didn't really have a kitchen."

He thought about how much he'd loved the farmhouse kitchen and right up to the accident he'd always associated it with security and the warmth of his mother before she lost her spark. "You grew up in a house without a kitchen?"

She pressed each dough ball down with a fork, leaving an

imprint of neat lines. "I didn't really grow up in a house. My parents had a van and we lived in that and traveled around the outback. A one-burner stove isn't really a kitchen but she could cook just about anything in a camp oven over an open fire and Dad was pretty good on the barbecue."

He couldn't imagine such a life and the only thing he could think of that came close were carnival operators or circus families. "Is traveling around like that common in Australia?"

She laughed as she picked up the cookie sheet, but it came out tinged with something he couldn't quite put his finger on.

"No. Life in Australia is in the most part very urban with the bulk of the population clinging desperately to the East Coast. My parents are..." She seemed to be searching for a word.

"Unique?" he offered.

"Passionate." She slid the tray into the oven. "They met at a university rally towards the end of the Vietnam War and from that moment they've never been apart."

"Are they another example of your 'love at first sight' theory?"

The oven door slammed shut. "It works very well for a lot of people. My parents found each other and are a strong team. They've lived their life following what they believe in and right now they're living and working in a village in the jungles of Papua New Guinea."

Flicking out a cloth, she briskly wiped down the counter, clearing away the mess of bits of butter, sugar crystals and flour before pouring cream into a bowl. Every action bristled as if keeping busy was important.

He suddenly remembered her tension in the car when she'd

mentioned her parents. "So how did growing up like that work out for you as a kid?"

Her hand paused on the switch of the beater. "What do you mean?"

"Well, I got on a yellow school bus every morning for thirteen years. I doubt you did that."

"No Aussie kid does that because we don't have yellow school buses," she replied as she turned the beater on low.

He recognized the comment as a red stop sign so he lifted the boiling kettle off the stove, poured the water over the tea bag that rested in the mug and added milk before passing it to Matilda. "But you obviously got educated or you wouldn't be a nurse."

The beater went silent. "I did correspondence classes and School of the Air, where you talk to a teacher on a radio who's hundreds of kilometers away although today they use computers. A few times I went to real school but it never lasted longer than six months before Mum and Dad felt they were being 'called' somewhere else."

Before college he'd only ever lived at the farm and then in the house in Hobin but both had kept him in the same community. Her upbringing might account for her "take-no-prisoners" attitude. "That would have made it difficult to make friends."

She nodded. "After the third school I stopped trying. There was no point because I knew we'd move. At sixteen I pleaded to go to high school and I couldn't believe it when my parents agreed. I was beside myself with happiness thinking that for the first time we'd be in one place for two years, in a house with a garden and friends over to visit."

Whipped cream plopped onto one half of a pale white cake

and she jabbed at it with a spatula held by white-knuckled hands.

They packed their bags and left on numerous occasions.

Her offhand comment the other day played through his head and it didn't sound good. "So where did you all end up living?"

"Nana's. *I* lived with Nana." She balanced the second half of the cake on top of its creamed partner. "My parents enrolled me in school and then promptly left for Thailand to work with the Karen refugees up near the border of Burma."

"That's tough."

"True, but that's what they love doing and they're good at it. NGOs seek them out to run programs because they're so experienced."

He shook his head. "No, I meant that would have been tough on you."

She sifted confectionary sugar over the top of the cake. "I wasn't a little kid."

He wondered at her parents' decision, knowing his parents would never have done such a thing. "You were sixteen. You weren't exactly grown-up either."

"Perhaps." She dragged her teeth across her bottom lip as she arranged sliced strawberries around the edges of the cake before standing back and admiring her work. "Nana's sponge cake was always the centerpiece of afternoon tea."

"So, it was Nana who taught you the rule of licking the bowl if you helped." He grinned as he eyed the beaters and the remains of the cookie dough. "Does making you a cup of tea count?"

She tilted her head as if this required serious thought. "If it had been leaf tea in a teapot then that would qualify."

He had no idea what she was talking about. "Leaf tea? I thought tea came in tea bags."

She looked aghast. "That's dust. I'm talking about real tea. The actual dried camellia leaves which are put in a pre-warmed teapot and left to steep."

"Who knew tea was such serious stuff?" He grabbed a beater from the bowl.

She lunged for his arm. "I believe this country fought a war over tea or have you forgotten your roots?"

Her lack of height was no match for him and he easily held the beater out of her reach. "I don't think there were any Vikings at the Boston Tea Party."

"You were probably too busy pilfering." Her right hand continued to reach for the beater while the fingers of her other hand curved into the spaces between his ribs.

Laughter bubbled up, brought to the surface by the tickling onslaught. "Convicts pilfered. Vikings pillaged. Get your history right."

"So brawn versus brain, eh?" She swung sideways, grabbing his car keys off the hook by the pantry door and toying with them in her hand. "You've tucked your baby up in the warm garage, away from all that lovely snow but it might want to be a real car and get its pretty tires dirty just like the truck you rented."

He almost said, "You wouldn't dare" but this was Matilda and if he'd learned one thing, she did dare. He put the beater down in the sink. "Sweetheart, you have trouble finding the driver's side of a car, let alone working the shift so I'll save you the embarrassment."

She grinned and tossed him the keys. "Before you collect

your mother, Blondie, you might want to replace that preppy shirt with flannel so the truck respects you."

He caught the keys as a lightness rolled through him. She might be as aggravating as hell but she made him laugh and even before the news of Lori's illness, that was something he hadn't done much of lately.

Matilda walked into Peggy's shop at 4:30 p.m., still surprised by how early it got dark. Even in midwinter, dusk didn't come to Narranbool until well after five o'clock. She was feeling pretty proud of herself having got into town safely driving on what felt to her like the wrong side of the road, as well as driving in snow. When she'd left Narranbool she'd wanted new experiences and although she hadn't envisaged snow or being poverty-stricken, she had to admit, it was all new and different.

On the sound of the bell, Peggy came out of the storeroom and smiled. "You made it! I was beginning to worry."

"I'm sorry it's a bit later than we planned but it took ages for Marc and Kyle to shovel the driveway." Marc had actually paid a contractor to shovel it but she couldn't say she'd been taking care of Lori and this was the first opportunity she'd had to leave the house. Marc had arrived with his mother and his sister Jennifer and after a quick introduction she'd left them to it, wanting to give the family some time alone.

"Watching Marc Olsen shovel a driveway wouldn't be a hardship." Peggy winked and giggled. "Although it would be much more fun watching him work in summer with his shirt off, don't you think?"

"I hadn't really noticed." *Yeah, you keep kidding yourself.*

"Oh, I'm sorry, that was thoughtless of me given your situation, but really Matilda." Her lips pursed. "Don't waste any time thinking about that terrible Barry-man."

"Thanks." A flash of guilt stabbed her that the loss of Barry-the-Bastard didn't hurt in the way Peggy thought so she accepted the kindness thinking about the loss of her financial independence instead.

Peggy patted her arm. "You're better off without him and there's nothing wrong with consoling yourself by watching a bit of eye candy like Marc."

Consoling herself with Marc? Is that what she'd been doing when she'd let him kiss her until mind-altering lust had sucked every single thought out of her brain? *Don't think about him. Just focus on work.* "I've spoken to Vanessa on the phone and she's given me her choices and backup choices so I'll get on to the computer and order them now."

Matilda sat down behind the counter and created a folder in Favorites called "Vanessa's Wedding." Marc was organizing a laptop for her to use but she'd wanted to come into the shop today in case Peggy had decided to come by the house.

Peggy perched on a stool beside her, watching the screen. "I'm sure Lori wouldn't have minded you using her computer seeing as it snowed."

She hoped that when Lori realized telling her family about her surgery wasn't as awful as she imagined it would be, then she'd tell a couple of close friends. This way the news would hopefully slowly filter into Hobin because she hated having to lie by omission. "It's bad enough I've landed on her doorstep right on Thanksgiving without tying up her computer as well. Besides this is business and it's best to do it here."

"Would you be interested in doing another wedding?"

Her fingers paused on the keyboard. She didn't quite believe what she'd heard and tried not to sound too excited. "Sure."

Peggy beamed. "Great, because I've had two more wedding inquiries today. One bride is a friend of Vanessa's. I overheard her raving to Brittany about you last night at the Spotted Cow so I left my card and Brittany called me first thing. She's getting married in July."

"At the old log church?"

Peggy nodded. "It's a popular place for Hobin girls to marry."

"What about the other bride?"

"That's a funny story. One couple drove through very lost on their way to Mystery Lake. I don't know why they didn't question their GPS when it had them heading north instead of west, but—" Peggy's hands flew up in the air "—they're from Illinois." Apparently the mention of their home state explained their navigating incompetence.

Peggy continued. "Anyway, they ended up taking Church Road and they told me the moment they saw the old log church they fell in love with it. They rang the reverend on their cell and booked it on the spot. He, God bless him, sent them to me and I told them about you. They want to make an appointment tomorrow."

A worry line creased her brow. "Will that be okay? I know it's Thanksgiving but generally people don't serve the meal before three."

Or not at all. "I should be able to meet them here at the store at eleven." That would give her time to help Lori with her sponge bath, redress the drain tubes and get back in time for a late lunch.

Peggy chewed the end of a pencil before scribbling a note.

"That will work. I was planning to open in the morning because after today you never know, someone else might get lost."

"Or people visiting their relatives from interstate—"

Peggy interrupted. "From where? I don't think that's a place, honey, but the interstate is a highway going from Wisconsin to Illinois or Iowa."

The parallel universe struck again and Matilda smiled. "By interstate I mean they live in another state, say Iowa, and they come to Hobin to visit."

"Oh, we say 'out-of-state' here." Peggy chuckled. "You have some cute words for things."

She didn't point out that she could say the same about Peggy. "So people from out-of-state might want to get an early start on their Christmas shopping. You have some lovely stuff here."

"Do you really think so?" Peggy looked anxiously around the tiny store groaning with holiday stock. "It's so hard to know what to get in at this time of year when the choice is so huge."

"I think you have a great blend and a good range of prices. Yesterday I went into every store in town and yours and Gracie's stood out, although I was very taken with Grayson's."

Peggy's eyes widened in surprise. "All that junk."

"It's got potential." She could picture gardens in summer decorated with old implements that showcased the flowerbeds.

"You think? All I see is rusty old junk, and Stefan Grayson is my biggest naysayer on the chamber of commerce. Most other people just fall in behind him when he blocks every attempt at civic improvement. I just know if I could get around him and get the chamber of commerce off their butts, we could make Hobin really something." She gave a long exasperated sigh filled with the disappointment of battles past. "Anyway, this year I don't care and I'm opening from ten until one."

Ideas started popping into Matilda's head. "Peggy, do you think we could create a corner space in the shop? Just enough space for three chairs and a small table to hold a laptop, a plate of nibbles and drinks? Then the brides can sit and have coffee or even champagne while I run through their requirements."

Peggy stood up quickly and pointed to the window display. "I can clear the Thanksgiving table and decorate it with white bridal tulle. I'll get a sign made and—" She stopped. "What are we going to call this business?"

"We have a business?" Matilda's head spun. Did she really have the start of a business?

"Of course we do. We have three customers and by the end of the weekend, who knows, we might have four."

Matilda tapped a pencil against her yellow legal pad. "So far they all have the log church in common. Do you think that could be a selling point? I mean the out-of-staters fell in love with the church and are prepared to make their relatives schlep to Hobin to see them get married and that's going to spin off into the town."

Peggy stared at her, her face slowly creasing into a huge smile as an idea hit. "We need to talk to the reverend. If we become the exclusive agent to manage the weddings at the church then we, the church and Hobin would benefit. Oh, Matilda, you might just have hit on the one thing that will put Hobin firmly on the tourist map. What do you think of Hobin Weddings?"

"Well, if we're thinking bigger than just ordering people their favors, cake slices and champagne flutes, and we end up booking churches, reception venues and accommodation, then what about Weddings *Are* Hobin?"

"Yes!" Peggy punched the air. "And to think you're not even from here!"

Matilda experienced a rush of something close to relief. She'd just been given another reason to stay a bit longer in Hobin and more time to save money before she had to face the big world again.

CHAPTER ELEVEN

Restlessness clawed at Marc. His mother and sister were upstairs visiting Lori. Matilda had retreated to her room and he had the overwhelming urge to go for a run. But it was dark and the ice on the road made it treacherous so he'd been pounding Lori's treadmill. Now he was wet with sweat and exhaustion, but still calm eluded him.

He reassured himself that once he got back to New York City this unsettled feeling would vanish. *Why? It's been hanging around since the summer.* He increased the speed of the treadmill, turned up his MP3 player and kept running. Half an hour later, he hit the stop button on the console and stepped off the machine. Walking around the partition into the main part of the basement, he found Kyle sitting in the dark, watching TV.

Marc flicked on the light. "Hey."

"Hey."

Perhaps they could bond over the fact they were currently outnumbered by women. "You're in the right place, a woman-free zone." He caught sight of the posters. "These gorgeous girls excepted of course."

Kyle shrugged disinterestedly. "Tildy was just in the laundry room drying her jeans. Can you turn off the light when you go." It wasn't a question and just in case Marc was thinking of replying, he immediately turned up the volume on the TV effectively cutting off conversation, his gaze glued to yet another screen.

No matter what Marc had tried in his attempts to engage Kyle over the last three days, nothing seemed to be working and he was running out of ideas. He flicked his towel around his neck and headed back upstairs wondering why Matilda was washing her jeans at this time of night? Hell, why was she still wearing the faded denim when she had plenty of other clothes?

As he reached the landing, the phone in the kitchen started ringing and he answered the call.

"Oh, hi, Marc. It's Vanessa Jacobson."

"Hey, Vanessa." He traded pleasantries about being back in Hobin for the holidays and half listened to her excited chatter about wedding plans.

"Say, Marc, can you tell me if Tildy's car's been found yet? I so want to buy that wedding tiara of hers and I can't wait to try on the dress."

He immediately snapped to attention. Buy the tiara? What dress? Surely not Nana's dress? He couldn't imagine Matilda wanting to part with her grandmother's dress even though her own wedding hadn't taken place. It seemed to him that Nana represented family to Matilda more than her own parents. So why was she selling the dress?

"No news yet, Vanessa, but as soon as she hears anything, I'm sure she'll call you."

"Remember to give her the message," the bride-to-be instructed firmly.

"Oh don't you worry, Vanessa, I will." He hung up the phone, his mind working overtime. At supper time when he'd given Matilda the laptop she'd "negotiated" out of him, she'd taken it and excused herself, mentioning she had work to do on another wedding. He still thought it odd that a rejected bride would choose to organize someone else's wedding but she'd never once mentioned any plans of selling her own bridal accessories.

On his way to the bathroom, he passed her partially open door. The Gracie's bags lay in a tossed heap on the floor and laid out neatly on the bed and on the rug in coordinated order were all the clothes, complete with price tags. Kyle's camera sat discarded on the bed, its memory card cover open, and Matilda faced her computer. He caught sight of the distinctive red-blue-yellow-and-green logo of eBay on the screen and an uploaded picture of one of the outfits on the bed.

An outfit he'd bought for her.

What the hell? She'd always been cagey or flippant when he'd pressed her for information but now things seemed to be falling into place. First the job, then the bridal accessories and now eBay. It all pointed to money. Without a second thought he strode through the door. "Why the hell are you selling your clothes?"

A tremor of surprise tinged with guilt shot through Matilda. She swung around to see a very suspicious Viking dressed in running togs, and staring at her with blue eyes flashing.

Her blood rushed to her feet as her brain creaked like a rusty cog trying to come up with a quick and witty answer, but the combination of being caught red-handed and the sight of sculpted muscular legs left her with nothing. She attacked instead. "Why are you in my room without an invitation?"

A muscle ticked in his jaw. "Cut the politician's crap of answering a question with a question."

Oh, God, he had an intransigent look she hadn't seen before but she gave it another shot. "You bought the clothes for me so therefore they're mine to do with what I want."

"I bought them for you to *wear* not sell."

She flicked her hand airily. "I won't need them when my car comes back."

His eyes took on the steely blue of flint. "Your car might never come back. It's probably been torched in south Chicago along with everything in it including that tiara you're planning on selling."

Every trace of the urbane man she thought she knew had vanished, stripped away until all that was left was the essence of a street fighter. She recognized the attitude—the survivor streak she'd come to know in herself—and she gulped. "How did you know about that?"

"Vanessa just called asking about your wedding tiara and your wedding dress, and now I find you selling your clothes. That line about staying and working in Hobin and experiencing the real U.S. was complete bullshit, wasn't it?" His voice rumbled deep and ominous. "Even if your car hadn't been stolen, you don't have any money,do you?"

She grasped at splintering straws. "Look, I didn't want the clothes but you insisted and Gracie needed the sale, so it was easier to buy them, keep you off my back and make Gracie happy. I'd always planned to sell them and return your money."

He crossed his arms over the broad expanse of glistening

skin, a menacing Viking who didn't believe a word she was saying. "That doesn't explain the tiara. It's time for the truth, Matilda."

She bit on her lip, welcoming the pain. A type of pain that hurt a lot less than the truth which would expose her completely. Up until now, having Marc think she was slightly deranged had been okay because people got dumped every day. But this was so much more than that.

Sucking in a breath, she spoke quickly. "Barry didn't just vanish from a marriage. He took…" Her mouth clogged at the starkness of the word *money*. "He took advantage of me."

A wave of fury rolled off him, almost knocking her off her feet. "You told me he didn't have sex with you."

She shook her head, steeling herself against the pummeling of her own humiliation. "He didn't. He didn't want *me* in any way at all. He only wanted my money." She forced herself to keep talking so she wouldn't fall apart. "I'd invested in his business, in what I'd been led to believe was *our* business, but it turned out it was all a very smooth, six-month con. That night in the diner, when I used your phone, I discovered he'd emptied our joint bank account and taken all my money."

His lip curled in derision and she hated the look on his face—one that heralded her a grand sucker of the most foolish kind, and another kind of hurt pierced her. "I know, that sort of thing doesn't happen to a sensible, independent woman who is always careful with her money, but sometimes it just does, okay."

His eyes narrowed. "Con men pick their targets."

She dropped her gaze. "Meaning stupid women."

"No, empathetic, compassionate people with a sense of adventure."

Her head jerked back at the unexpected words and she caught a glimmer of understanding in the depths of his eyes. "Oh it's been an adventure, all right."

The understanding disappeared. "You lied to me."

"No, I just omitted some of the truth in the same way you did with Lori. Before the car was stolen I'd agreed to sell the tiara to Vanessa to raise money to survive."

"And the dress?"

She forced herself to meet his gaze. "I might be broke but I'm not a charity case."

"I never said you were." He pushed off the doorjamb, his cheekbones sharp in relief. "You needed a place to stay and I needed help with Lori and Kyle. You're earning money now so you don't need to sell the dress."

She should be relieved but still she held her breath. "So we're even?"

"The agreement we negotiated can pretty much stay the same. I'm just adding two caveats to your employment and board."

Her chest tightened and she tried to read him but his face remained as blank as an empty canvas. Not that it mattered because she was in no position to negotiate.

She chewed her lip. "What things?"

"Keep the clothes from Gracie's and start wearing them."

The girly-girl squealed and clapped. The survivor went on alert. "Why?"

"Because I'm sick to death of seeing you in those jeans and that T-shirt."

She ignored the traitorous zip of heat and folded her arms across her chest. "Perhaps I like these clothes."

He snorted. "You wash them one more time they're going

to fall apart. Mind you, that wouldn't be all bad because then I'd get more than a glimpse of those lace panties of yours."

"You so can't see my undies when I wear my jeans."

A wicked but knowing grin rolled across his wide and generous mouth sending a rip of desire through her and liquefying her knees. She made a hasty grab for her jeans, pulling them off the back of a chair.

"Take a look where the right pocket meets the denim."

His laugh teased her as her fingers found the rent in the aging and weak material. He'd been copping an eyeful for days.

"I figure you bend over one more time and they're history."

"Then I guess after that I wear my white granny panties." But she knew she'd lost the argument. She couldn't wear ripped clothing and she forced herself to look into his handsome face. "I can't afford to buy those clothes."

"No one is asking you to do that."

"I'm not comfortable accepting them."

He held up his hand, the smiling banter from a minute ago replaced with a frown. "If you can't accept a gift then payment is keeping the cookie jar filled with those Yo-Yo cookies you made the other day. The second thing you need to do is report Barry Severson to the police."

Blood pounded loud in her ears. "I can't do that. It's bad enough being the jilted bride without everyone in Hobin knowing the rest. I just want to forget and start over."

He spoke quietly, but his words cut as deep as the sharpest knife. "Do you want one other woman to have to go through this?"

Of course she didn't but going public meant reliving the degradation and having it label her permanently. Even though she knew what was right, every single part of her railed at his ethical stance. "Why do you have to be so bloody rational and logical?"

He grinned and dimples carved deep into his cheeks. "Because I'm a man."

Standing before her, bare-chested except for a workout towel, there was not a single doubt of that fact. A gorgeous, golden man, who with one glance of his sky-blue eyes reduced her to a quivering mess.

A man who was very accustomed to getting his own way.

A man who insisted she do the right thing.

Then it struck her. Despite the fact Marc Olsen appeared to use money to bulldoze any obstacle that stood between him and what he wanted, integrity and honesty coexisted, clearly radiating from him and touching everything around him.

The fact he could also see clear down to her soul, faults and all, scared her more than anything.

Thanksgiving had dawned a dismal day, socked in with gray clouds, and wind blew the snow hard against the windows. The following hours hadn't brought much change and Lori thought the weather must have absorbed her mood. If she had to give a color to the limbo she was living in then dark and gray was exactly how she'd describe it. Had the cancer spread from her breasts into her lymph nodes? As she lay in her bed were malignant cells exploding inside her, traveling to every part of her body? She wouldn't know for sure for a few more long days.

The unfamiliar words of her doctor rumbled in her head. Chemotherapy. Radiotherapy. Clear margins. Reconstruction. She pushed her fingers against her temples, wishing she could erase the last ten days of her life and that she could will everything back to normal. Or at least back to what she'd accepted as normal after Carl had left. She'd finally found a quiet rhythm to her life—her teaching job, mothering Kyle and being a basketball parent, Sunday lunches with her mom, midweek coffee with Gracie and the occasional drink or party at the Spotted Cow.

She turned to look at the scrawled note that lay on her dressing table, the one she'd been turning toward since coming home. Brian's letter.

Brian. He'd been on the edge of her life for years—same school, different classes, same town, different circle of friends, and although they'd bumped into each other one night during sophomore year and had spent an enjoyable evening laughing and talking, she'd met Carl the next day and life had changed forever. Five years her senior, Carl, with his Latino good looks and athletic prowess, had swept her off her feet and into an early marriage. Brian had left Hobin soon after.

For ten years she'd thought she was the luckiest woman alive until she'd discovered she'd been sharing Carl with a series of women. Young women. All had been students of his at the university. Every one of them had long, blond hair, blue eyes and tight, lush bodies, just as she had when she'd met Carl at seventeen.

When she'd asked him why he was having affairs he'd told her bluntly, "I don't find you attractive anymore."

She forced the bitter memories back into the vault she'd managed to keep them contained in until it had ruptured last week. Cracked wide open by being forced to make a decision that either had her keeping her breasts and dying, or allowing her body to be mutilated and hopefully saving her life.

Brian had returned to Hobin last year. He was still quiet

and reserved, but they'd spent time together professionally as part of the Police In Schools program. He also coached basketball and she'd chatted with him at the games and at a couple of social gatherings. She knew he took a special interest in Kyle and that Kyle respected him.

A month ago, if she'd been asked to describe him she would have used the words *polite, professional, a friend.* Except for the increasing times she'd caught him looking at her, his gray eyes filled with an intensity that made her feel like a totally desirable woman. She in turn had started to wonder what he was like when he took off his uniform. Three weeks ago she'd found out when she'd turned up at the Spotted Cow on the wrong night and none of her girlfriends were there. Brian was.

It had started with a drink and ended unexpectedly but momentously with her panties on his bedroom floor and her body both sated and wildly alive for the first time in years. The quiet man out of uniform had turned out to be a talented and generous lover.

But none of that mattered now because everything for her had changed.

Everything.

A shaft of sunshine broke through the cloud, slowly widening until her bedroom was filled with light and the gray clouds scudded away leaving blue sky in their wake. She hadn't needed as many painkillers this morning and as a result the dizziness had faded, and her concentration had returned in a fashion. The sound of conversation drifted through the door which Kyle had left open after he'd taken her lunch tray back to the kitchen. She could hear the deep voice of her brother, the soft tones of her mother and Matilda's crazy accent sometimes strident sometimes soft, and suddenly loneliness pierced her. She was stuck here in her bedroom and everyone else was free to come and go. She was usually the command center of her house but right now she wasn't and it sat like a lead weight in her belly.

Thanksgiving. The house was always full at Thanksgiving and normally she loved everything about the day—the noise, the food, the chaos, just being with her family. Jennifer's kids would always arrive excited and happy and play a game of tag between the trees, squealing with delight when Kyle chased them. But today they were on a plane bound for Brunei. Sheryl would normally sit in the kitchen waving whatever kitchen implement she'd picked up so she could "help," and all the while talking nonstop but today she was in California. Her mom would alternate between playing with the grandchildren and helping in the kitchen and Marc would roll his eyes at all the noise and head off for a walk in the woods with anyone who cared to join him.

But today Marc hadn't gone out for a walk and her mom had alternated between sitting with her and then leaving her to rest. But Lori had napped this morning and this afternoon. She'd done her special arm exercises and now as she listened to the voices she had a sensation of being a prisoner in a pool of afternoon sunlight. She'd told Marc and her mother she wanted to ignore Thanksgiving this year and it seemed they'd respected her wishes but she hated this empty feeling.

Matilda barreled through the door wearing clay-brown trousers and a jersey top decorated with geometric splashes of all shades of brown from chocolate through to golden-beige, each color outlined by peacock-blue. The colors suited her making her eyes greener than ever and giving her chaotic hair, which was unusually tamed into a neat braid, a burnished gloss.

With her trademark smile she sat down laughing. "Your mum is a fabulous storyteller. She's killing me with stories about you, your sisters and Marc growing up. I especially liked the time Marc fell into the manure pile when he was trying to hide his report card."

A rush of jealousy tore into her that everyone else was enjoying themselves and she wasn't. "I'm glad everyone's having fun."

Matilda crooked up a brow. "Someone's sounding stroppy."

Lori wanted to sulk but Matilda's accent always made her smile. "I'm sounding what?"

"Stroppy. Tetchy, cross."

"Oh, that's a good word, can I use it?"

"Sure, it's yours but you have to leave the stroppy mood here 'cos you're going out to—" she did a fake drum roll "—the front room!"

A surge of excitement shot through her before fear doused it. "I can't do that."

Tildy whipped back the sheets. "Sure you can. You must be going stir-crazy in here and it will do you good to get out of these four walls for an hour."

The idea of leaving her bedroom pulled strongly but she looked at her dressing gown and frowned. "I don't want to sit out there in this."

"No worries. Wear these." Tildy handed her a loose top and a pair of drawstring pants that she'd pulled from a drawer. "Getting dressed is an important first step in recovery. I know these are probably your work-out clothes but they're comfortable and we won't be grading you on your fashion statement." She grinned. "Not today anyway and besides Marc out-dresses and outshines us all so it doesn't matter what we wear, no one will notice."

Lori laughed at the accurate description of her brother. "You noticed. He's always dressed well, even when he didn't have much money. Growing up I used to raid his stuff and he'd get really— What was that word again?"

"Stroppy."

"Yeah, super stroppy."

With Tildy's help she managed to get the shirt over her head and the pants on. The top of the pressure bandage peeked above the neckline of the T-shirt but she didn't worry about that. Just being in clothes made her feel more like herself and a buzz of excitement vibrated through her. "It's silly but I feel like a kid at Christmas."

"It's not silly. It's all part of the recovery process. We don't think twice about the normal stuff in our life until we've lost it or it's been taken away from us."

The catch in her voice made Lori look up, and for the first time since she'd heard the word *cancer* she looked outside of herself realizing other people had pain too. The memory of Carl leaving was something she chose not to think about, but it surfaced in sympathy. "I'm so sorry you lost your money and your heart to Barry."

"No, my heart isn't lost." She sighed. "I only lost the dream. I realized in the long cold night I spent in the car that I hadn't fallen in love with Barry, but I had fallen in love with the idea of someone loving me." Matilda slid a pair of shoes on to Lori's feet. "But that's all over. Three men have left me and the dream is in a thousand pieces and there's not enough superglue in the world to put it back together."

Carl had taught Lori a lot about rejection and she squeezed Matilda's hand. "I'm sorry for what Barry did to you and it's no consolation, but you being here is helping me a lot."

Tildy gave a wry smile. "I'm happy to be here too. We women have to stick together, right?"

Lori rose to her feet on wobbly legs. "Absolutely."

Walking out of the bedroom was like entering a new world. Everything looked the same but different. Marc had removed her fall decorations from the dining room table and installed his laptop and plans, although there seemed to be a pile of black and gray Lego blocks pushed to one side. Her mother sat quilting on the sofa, her material bag and sewing box wedged against the cushions and Kyle lounged on the other sofa, earphones in place and eyes glued to his handheld game console, having broken the rule about no technology above stairs. The room was silent except for the ticking of the clock.

Three large white platters sat on the coffee table groaning with fingerfood. One was filled with a variety of Wisconsin cheeses, another had asparagus rolled in thin layers of bread and the other had a selection of crudités, dips and nuts. Party food.

"Look who's here," said Matilda as they entered the room.

Marc immediately stood up as did Kyle, both giving Lori a tight smile—one that questioningly asked, "This is a good thing, right?"

Her mother set down her quilting, worry clear in her gaze. "Are you sure you should be out of bed?"

Only Matilda looked at her as if she was a person able to make her own decisions. "I'm fine, Mom."

The moment she sat on the reclining chair, Matilda pulled the lever to bring up the footrest. "Elsa, it's important for Lori to spend more and more time out of bed." She then turned to Marc and nodded.

Marc pulled a bottle of champagne from an ice bucket and the loud pop of the cork echoed around the room.

Matilda grinned. "Now that's what I call a great sound." She quickly lifted champagne flutes toward the bottle and the foaming fluid cascaded into the fine glass. "Kyle, do you want your lemonade in a champers glass?"

Kyle shot her a look that only a teenager can give to a clueless adult. "It's soda or pop, remember?"

"Kyle!" Lori blushed with embarrassment. "Apologize to Matilda for being so rude."

But Matilda just winked at Kyle and handed a glass of champagne to Elsa. "Don't stress, Lori. Kyle's been translating for me and teaching me all the American words for things that have different names in Australia." She laughed. "I wish you could have seen his face earlier when I offered him what we call cordial. That was the one time he didn't correct me but his face fell a million miles when I served him up what you all call lemonade."

A sheepish expression crossed Kyle's face. "I thought it was too good to be true."

She handed him a glass. "So right now drink your Australian lemonade, aka pop, and when you're eighteen—"

"Twenty-one," his uncle interjected firmly.

"Really?" Disbelief scored Matilda's face. "Wow, that wouldn't go down well at home. Okay, well, when you're twenty-one you can have cordial."

"I think I'll move to Australia," Kyle grumbled with a grin.

Marc returned the champagne bottle to the bucket and carried a thimble-sized amount over to Lori. "Here you go, sis."

First the fingerfood and now the champagne. A feeling of betrayal set in. "I can't drink this."

"Two sips won't hurt. The French think champagne has medicinal purposes."

"Doesn't anyone listen to me? I asked you not to do Thanksgiving this year."

Marc looked toward Matilda, his expression one of "I told you so."

"Lori, as an Australian and the current cook in the house I have no idea about pies made out of pumpkin. At home, that's a vegetable you roast and what on earth is a candied yam?" Tildy shook her head in bemusement, her curls bouncing. "But I do know that today we have something to celebrate and that's you being out of bed and on the road to recovery."

The foggy unknown loomed before her and Lori stared at the bubbles in the glass as they continuously rose in a fine bead. "It's too early to know anything."

"That depends on what you're celebrating. Now your family might be treading on eggshells around you but that's not my style. There're always going to be challenges ahead but you've made it through the first one and *that's* worth celebrating." She raised her glass. "And besides, any excuse is a good excuse for drinking champagne and that tiny amount you have won't hurt. Cheers." Matilda raised her glass and then took a long sip.

Marc gave a wry smile and clinked his glass against Lori's. "I'm thankful you're home and even more thankful I didn't have to cook a turkey."

"We're all thankful for that, honey," Elsa added dryly and stood to clink Lori's glass, her eyes filled with love and concern.

"I'm starving, Mom. Can you *please* take a sip so we can eat the food?"

Right then she realized how important it was for things to return to normal as soon as possible, not just for Kyle but for herself even though she had no idea if normal was even possible. She took a tiny sip of the amber fluid and savored the fizz of bubbles on her tongue before setting down the glass. "Kyle Perez, you serve everyone else before yourself and then I'm judging charades."

Marc and Kyle groaned simultaneously.

"Awesome, I love charades." Matilda popped a cracker and cheese in her mouth.

Marc eyed the tzatziki dip Matilda had made. "I thought you said we weren't doing Thanksgiving this year which meant not only no huge meal but no games."

She found herself grinning for the first time in days. "I changed my mind."

"I'll go first." Matilda formed a fist with her left hand and rolled her right hand next to it.

"Movie." Marc sampled the asparagus rolls, keeping his gaze fixed on Matilda. "Two words, first word."

The Australian grinned, put her hands up in front of her like paws and started to jump.

"Kangaroo." Kyle mumbled his answer through a mouthful of potato chips.

Matilda gave him the thumbs-up.

"*Kangaroo Jack*." Marc shot Matilda a triumphant look. "Too easy."

Her small white hands slapped her hips. "I'm just warming up the crowd, Blondie. The competition starts now."

Lori nearly choked on her cheeseball. She'd never heard

anyone give her brother a nickname before. "Careful, Tildy, my big brother likes to win."

"Really? I'm glad you told me because I'd never have guessed." Laughter twirled along her cheeks. "Still, I reckon I can give him a run for his money. After all, he's never played against the Narranbool charades champion of 2010."

The glint of the challenge sparkled in Marc's eyes. "Lori, you keep score."

"Can do." Lori relaxed into the chair, nibbling on the lovely food and enjoying the show.

One laughter-filled hour later, Lori announced the scores. "Elsa one, Kyle three, Matilda and Marc tied at seven."

Marc grinned and rubbed his hands together. "Up you get, Kyle. It's time for a play-off. One more charade will do it and tip the score in my favor."

Matilda rolled her eyes. "Kyle, tell him he's dreaming."

"This is getting boring. I'm going sledding." Kyle got up abruptly and headed toward the door.

Matilda shot to her feet. "Sledding. I've never done that, can I come?"

The teenager shrugged. "Sure."

Marc immediately followed them to the door. "I better come and make sure neither of you break a leg."

"Lori, do you want me to help you back to bed before we go out?" Matilda asked pausing at the coat rack.

She shook her head. "I'd like to stay up just a bit longer."

Elsa glanced up from her stitching. "I can help Lori, Tildy. You go take a well-earned break. You've hardly stopped all day."

Still Matilda hesitated. "If you're sure?"

Lori waved her away. "Go have fun, and Kyle, come tell me all about it when you get back."

She watched them grab coats and disappear into the garage to collect the sleds before heading around the back of the house to the best hill. She heard the grind of the garage door closing and the voices slowly fading as they walked farther away from the house.

A wave of well-earned fatigue washed over her, distinctly different from the tiredness she'd experienced since her surgery, but she wasn't quite ready to go back to the solitude of her room. Being part of things again had been fun and she had to thank Matilda later for making her get up and acknowledge Thanksgiving. Her mind wandered over the conversations of the last hour and she thought about the charades. "Mom, have you noticed anything between Marc and Matilda?"

Her mother's needle flashed in and out of the brightly colored material. "Your brother is his own man, Lori, and up until a few days ago Tildy thought she was marrying another man. Don't meddle."

"I'm not meddling. I'm just asking."

"I'll go make us some coffee and then you need to rest." Elsa set aside the quilt and walked toward the kitchen.

Lori tried to squash the irritation that rumbled through her. She should have known better than to ask her mother a question like that. Elsa had never been one to discuss relationships or feelings. Growing up, that had been something she'd done with her sisters or, if they weren't around, with Marc. She smiled at the memory. Poor Marc, no wonder he'd been grumpy a lot of the time.

She heard the peal of the doorbell. "Mom, can you get the door?"

But Elsa didn't appear and a persistent rap on the front door followed.

"Mom?" she called again but was greeted by silence. Perhaps her mother had gone to the bathroom. Moving slowly, Lori managed to stand up and walk to the door. "Just a minute." With great difficulty and the burn of pain, she opened the door expecting to see one of the sledders back to collect something they'd forgotten. Instead Brian stood on her stoop, his police badge shining on his broad chest and his shirt tucked neatly against a washboard-flat stomach.

She froze.

His mouth curved up into a smile packed with undisguised desire. "Hello, Lori." He always spoke her name softly as if it was a velvet caress. "I've come to tell Ms. Geoffrey that—" His pupils suddenly widened into black discs of shock as if the message from his eyes had just been fully computed by his brain. He stared at her very un-Thanksgiving type clothes. "Are you ill?"

A sob stalled in her throat as her hand flew to the neckline of her shirt, uselessly trying to hide the top of the pressure bandage and the unmistakable concave tilt of her chest. She hated that he stood there, wordlessly staring at her. Hated that he'd seen her like this.

With a strangled cry she kicked the door shut in his face and with tears scalding her eyes she somehow managed to stumble back to her room.

CHAPTER TWELVE

Marc stood at the bottom of the hill, watching Matilda squeal-ing with delight as she raced Kyle down the slope for the fifth time. Kyle kept beating her but she'd just laugh and say, "Bring it on" and trudge back up the hill to try again.

The woman was tenacious, he had to give her that, and standing by watching her cute butt wiggling as she pulled the sled was no hardship. He grinned as he wrapped his coat around him, closing out the increasing chill now the sun was dropping.

He heard her call out to Kyle, "Aussie, Aussie, Aussie, Oi, Oi, Oi," and then couldn't believe his ears when Kyle's laugh echoed around the hill.

He both admired and resented the seemingly effortless way she'd befriended his family and connected with Kyle. The kid was a different person with Matilda but with him he remained an often sullen and very aloof teenager. He'd tried the Lego idea but it hadn't worked like he'd hoped. Kyle had just stuck his nose into his handheld game console, not even glancing in his direction. All that had happened was he'd been left with a mass of tiny gray blocks cluttering up his work space so he'd returned his attention to his current design with as little success as he'd had with Kyle.

As Matilda came closer he could see the determined set of her mouth as she tilted her weight and the sled sped up, overtaking Kyle. With a whoop, she lifted her arms in victory only to miscalculate the distance required to stop and she hit a snow drift with a thud, catapulting into deep, soggy snow.

He ran over, picturing a broken neck and broken limbs, but by the time he got to her she was on her knees. Snow clung to her coat, her hair and had turned her trousers the color of wet. His hands patted her shoulders, arms and legs. "Are you hurt?"

"I don't think so." She took his hand and rose to her feet, her cheeks pink with exertion and her eyes sparkling like the facets of an emerald. "That was the most sensational rush."

Kyle walked over carrying his sled. "Cool stack, Tildy."

She high-fived him. "Thanks, mate, but I need to work on my stops."

Marc's rush of adrenaline eased now she was safe but he couldn't shake the niggle of fear that she'd taken such a risk. "You need to work on being an adult before you kill yourself."

Her eyes widened with a glimmer of mischievousness. "And you need to work on being a kid again. Come on, Kyle, help me out here." She scooped up a handful of snow and hurled it at him.

Her snowball hit him full on the shoulder, the spray tipping over his collar, and ice instantly melted to cold water, which trickled down his neck. A second snowball hit from behind.

"Good shot, Kyle, keep going," Matilda encouraged the teen as she turned to pick up more snow.

"You're gonna regret that." Marc grinned. She knew squat about snowball fights. The first rule was never turn your back on the enemy. His ball hit her right at the coat-line which matched up with the hip-band of her jeans.

Her indignant shriek was music to his ears. He shot a ball back at Kyle who dodged it with the agility and light-footedness of a good basketball player. He ran toward him and tried another shot, but Kyle's return fire collided with his and the snow hit the ground with a plop.

"Hey, Blondie."

He swung around, easily dodging the sucker ball she lobbed in his direction. "You'll have to do better than—hey!" A snowball hit him on the side, followed by another two.

"Gotcha." Kyle gave a half boy, half man laugh, the thrill of the victory clear on his face.

"Go, Kyle!" Matilda clapped her hands and ducked Marc's return fire.

Marc gave a long, slow smile. "Two against one, eh? Well, you're both in for it now." He followed up the threat with snowy fire.

Snowballs flew through the air, some hitting, many missing but all accompanied by laughter. Marc ran, dodged and circled trees. His chest heaved, blood pounded and muscles strained in a totally different way from his gym workouts. This felt real.

Unlike Matilda, Kyle knew how to snowball fight. He knew the tricks and the nuances, and he ran and weaved like a professional, lobbing well-placed balls. Matilda, on the other hand, was a soft target. She hadn't grown up in the long Wisconsin winters and she didn't have a clue. He easily caught her around the waist, lifted her petite frame off the ground and shoved a snowball down her collar.

"That will teach you to tangle with the master."

She squealed in protest and squirmed against him.

His already pounding blood surged with desire and he quickly set her on her feet.

She brushed herself down. "The master? Ah yeah, very masterful. You picked on the Aussie girl who's never had a snowball fight in her life." Her ruby-red lips tried to pout but she was laughing too much.

His gaze fixed on her lips that begged to be kissed and he lowered his head, anticipation rolling through him at revisiting that wondrous mouth. He breathed in deeply savoring the scent of sunshine and tropical flowers so deliciously at odds with the snow-covered environment.

A snowball hit them square on their cheeks. Matilda jumped back like she'd been shot.

"Gotcha." Kyle stood a few feet away, triumph beaming from his face.

Marc turned with a roar and ran toward his nephew, scraping up snow as he went, firing it as quickly as he could firm it up into a ball. Matilda cheered them both on.

The boy was fit and nimble and Marc pulled on every reserve he had as snow dragged at his heels. Kyle stumbled, giving Marc a momentary advantage. He threw himself forward, catching the boy in a football tackle and bringing him down into a drift. Panting, he forced out the word. "Gotcha."

The boy's laughing face suddenly blanked. "Yeah."

Kyle rolled away, stood up and silently trudged toward the house.

Shit. "Kyle, come back."

But the boy didn't acknowledge him and just kept walking.

A surge of disappointment whipped Marc hard, chased by

something he couldn't pin down. The kid had actually been enjoying himself and suddenly it was like a switch had been thrown and he'd gone sullen. Man, he didn't get teenagers.

Matilda jogged over to Marc. "What happened?"

He brushed snow from his jeans. "I don't know."

Her brows drew together. "Well something did."

"I guess he didn't like getting drifted."

She stared at him, her gaze thoughtful. "He's fourteen and not a kid but he's not an adult either. He needs you to be more than an uncle. He needs you to be a friend and mentor."

He ran his hand through his hair. "I've been trying."

"Maybe not hard enough." She picked up the sled and started walking up the hill without a single glance back, leaving him feeling more out of sorts than ever.

Matilda's feet kept sinking into the snow and she was making slow progress back to the house, but her frustration with Marc kept her moving forward.

"Ms. Geoffrey. You're looking mighty snowy."

Matilda looked up and laughed. "G'day, Lieutenant. Kyle's introduced me to sledding but I need to work on my stops."

"It's an inexact science." Brian fingered the brim of his winter hat. "I came out to tell you I've got some news about your car."

She held her breath. "Good news?"

"Well, it's been found."

She squealed with delight and without thinking threw her arms around his neck. His embarrassment thundered through her and she instantly stepped back. "Thank you for coming to tell me on a holiday! You could have phoned."

He shrugged. "I was in the area."

Marc appeared by her side, standing so close that she could smell the peppermint scent of his shampoo and feel the touch of his arm against her own. Her body absorbed his touch like a parched plant absorbs water.

He gave the policeman a curt nod. "Brian."

"Marc." The nod was returned. "The car's been found down near Manitowoc in a snow drift. Its condition at this point is unknown because it needs digging out and that's not something the police can do for you."

"Where's Manitowoc?" Matilda couldn't remember driving through there on her way from Chicago.

"It's southeast of here, on Lake Michigan. It will be a full day trip there and back in this weather."

"A day? But I can't leave—" She stopped herself just as she was about to blurt out Lori's name.

Marc's arm curved around her wet waist, pulling her against him, his heat warming her instantly and generating a steaming rush of her own lusty heat. "Don't be silly, of course Peggy's shop can do without you for a day. We'll head down there, dig the car out and get it back to the company rep in Manitowoc and show you a bit more of Wisconsin."

She gazed up momentarily stunned at this unexpected foray into tourism as well as his "cozy couple" impersonation, before she realized he'd just stepped up and covered her blunder. She played along, ignoring the "tarty girl" and the "sensible girl" in her brain who were slugging it out, and arguing over if she should step away from his delicious warmth *right now,* or just snuggle in closer.

Brian held out a piece of paper. "This is the location of the vehicle."

"Thanks for letting us know." Marc took the document.

"I'm sorry we can't ask you in but we need to get in for a hot shower and be ready for a late turkey."

The lieutenant glanced up at the house before turning back to them. "I'm on duty, Marc, so either way I couldn't stop. Please give my best wishes to Lori." He turned abruptly and headed away from the hill and the house, back toward his car.

Her body shivered involuntarily against Marc's, a combination of cold, the close call and the rush of sensations that grew stronger every time he touched her. Tingling and shimmering vibrations unlike anything she'd experienced before. "This is *all* getting too hard."

His head gave a sharp nod but he didn't drop his arm. "I know. You need to convince Lori it's time to tell the town."

Her head jerked back from the tempting breadth of his chest and she stepped away. "I'm not sure that falls into my job description. In fact, I think it's more in keeping with what a brother would do."

His face creased into his charming smile. The smile she knew he used with effortless ease to get what he wanted. "But you did such a great job convincing her to tell my mother and sisters, so I figured you getting her to tell Gracie and her work friends is just an extension of that."

She locked eyes with him thinking about the oh-so-many ways he effectively distanced himself from his family. From the women who came on to him. From people altogether? He'd employed her to make his life easier and this request fell easily under that banner but she felt there was more to it. "You really don't want to have this conversation with Lori, do you?"

Like shutters blocking the light, his eyes darkened. "That has nothing to do with it. This has everything to do with playing to strengths. You'll do it better."

She ignored the compliment, knowing it was just one of the many tools in his kit of devices designed to get his own way, and to avoid dealing with his family and anything remotely emotional. She should push him to do it himself but she was learning that the Viking was like a hydraulic resistance exercise machine at the gym—the harder the push, the stronger the opposition. She'd tried to push him the other day to spend time with Kyle and that hadn't worked out as well as she'd hoped, although someone had been fiddling with the Lego set as it had grown slightly.

It rankled to just give in and where was the fun in that? "I tell you what, I'll talk to her about it if you go dig out and retrieve my car."

Marc knew that the sensation in his gut was relief tinged with guilt. He was still struggling with the fact his baby sister had cancer and Matilda coped with the understandably more emotional Lori better than he ever could. But as usual, Matilda never readily agreed to anything and negotiating and bargaining with her was all part of the fun. He had a plan that fit in perfectly with his seduction of Ms. Matilda-I'm-just-not-that-into-you-Geoffrey.

He grinned down at her. "I already told you. We're doing that together." He'd half planned the trip thinking that as well as seduction he wouldn't mind showing her Schwartz House at Two Rivers. Seeing the great Frank Lloyd Wright's work again might just help him find his creative spark.

"I can't go."

He tried hard not to laugh at her stunned expression. "Of course you can."

Her small hands slapped her hips. "You hired me to look after Lori and I can't be in two places at once."

Looping his arm through hers, he propelled her toward the house. "So convince Lori to tell Gracie and then Mom and Gracie can spend a day with her. After all, it was you who told me at lunch that apart from her needing some help with her bath and checking the tubes, she really didn't need a nurse but she could do with some company."

She pulled her arm free and did that disapproval pouting thing with her mouth that he found so incredibly sexy. "That was a big hint for you to go and talk to her."

"She can talk to Gracie." He pressed the garage door opener and a moment later ducked under the opening door, wishing he could take Matilda into an empty house and explore that pout rather than having to go make casual conversation with his mother and sister.

"Gracie's got a big weekend at her shop."

This time he laughed out loud. "It's Thanksgiving weekend in Hobin. No stores will be open."

Matilda shook her head, her expression almost bemused. "Sorry, Blondie, but times change and both Peggy and Gracie are opening from ten until two all weekend."

"That's a waste of time. No one in town has ever shopped on this weekend." He upended the sleds so the snow could melt and drain.

"It's probably true that Hobinites don't shop but it seems out-of-town people drive through Hobin for a variety of reasons."

"Their GPS froze?"

She laughed a warm tickling sound that gnawed at his self-imposed rule of keeping all women at arm's length. Then she zapped him with a knowing look. "One couple did have that problem. But they also bought one hundred dollars' worth of gifts from Peggy and inquired about Weddings Are Hobin. Oh, and that reminds me, Peggy wants to talk to you about a renovation so can you call her?"

Weddings Are Hobin? Renovations? The conversation was like black ice—unexpected and slippery. He felt as if he'd crashed onto his butt and was unable to get a grip on anything familiar. Hobin had been a quiet, backroads town since before he was born and year after year nothing changed, but right now nothing seemed reliable. He kicked off his boots. "I'm an urban architect. I don't normally do renovations."

She raised one perfectly shaped eyebrow as she undid her coat. "I thought that was exactly what you did."

Her quiet words slashed into him, reminding him of his stagnant ideas for the current project and of how he'd struggled for inspiration for weeks. From the moment he'd left Hobin twelve years ago he'd made sure his life was on track, heading in the direction he wanted without any hiccups. He had a job he adored and he happily lived alone in a stylish apartment. He enjoyed the company of like-minded women and kept all other women who had ideas of white picket fences and rug-rats a very long way away from him. He'd never looked back.

But now it was like every part of his life was spiraling out of his control and the marsh mud of Hobin was sucking at his feet, dragging him down to a place filled with family and responsibilities. Not to mention a bossy Australian. "I meant I don't do Ma-and-Pa house renovations."

"This is a barn."

"Excuse me?"

"A big red barn. You have to admit it's totally different from your usual work." She tilted her head, curls dancing around her eyes which twinkled with a challenging look, and her plump bottom lip filled with a smile. "It might be fun."

Fun. Hell, he deserved some fun and she'd just reminded him of what he had in mind and it had nothing to do with renovating a barn. Stepping in close he pulled her against him, his body immediately molding to hers, as if tracing a memory. He spoke softly. "I can think of better ways to have fun."

Her cheeks flushed a delicious shade of pink but she didn't back down. "I just bet you can, but this way's legal."

Laughing, he wound a ringlet around his finger. "And here I was just talking about our trip to Two Rivers but, sweetheart, I like how your mind works."

Moss-green eyes widened in a combination of surprise and undisguised lust. He took it as a sign—a gift even, and he lowered his mouth to hers. Delectable snow-chilled lips met his but in an instant they burned scorching hot, sending heat thundering through him before it spiraled down to places he'd forgotten existed. God, she tasted amazing. A thousand times better than he remembered and he lost himself in her warmth, her lushness and her fire.

Her fingers wrapped themselves into the lapels of his coat as she sagged against him with a soft sigh—the definitive sound of desire and need. It echoed in perfect pitch to his own response, and he wanted her in a way he hadn't wanted anything or anyone in a long time. Her tropical-fruit scent filled his nostrils, promising the exotic, and he wanted to touch and feel more than just her mouth. His hands slid her opened coat off her shoulders and then with one hand cupping her neck, the other traced the swell of her breast through her top. Her mouth slackened for a moment before she pressed herself against his hand, and deepened the kiss.

Her mouth consumed his—taking and giving all at the same time making his head spin and his legs shake. Somehow, he pulled them both backward until he was leaning against the garage wall. His hand trailed down her sides, feeling the soft indentation of her waist and the intoxicating curves of her hips, until his fingers found the gap between her jeans and her top and hit pay dirt. Smooth, warm skin. The tips of his fingers climbed her spine, each touch registering tiny and delicious shock waves as they traversed every bump and crevice. His fingers reached her bra strap and prepared to expertly flick the fastenings open, when the distinctive grind and clank of the garage door sounded harsh and loud in his ears.

Matilda wrenched her mouth from his and jumped backward as if she'd been shocked.

Shit. Somehow one of them had pressed the garage door opener in his pocket.

"I need to check on Lori." She headed toward the door that connected with the house.

Her trembling and husky voice stalled his blood that was halfway back to his brain. "You might want to straighten your top before you go inside."

"Oh, geez." Her hands flew to her face for a moment before dropping to her blouse and tugging it back into position with brisk strokes. "Marc."

"Yes."

"This was a mistake."

He pushed off from the wall. "Not from my point of view."

She stared at him with her luminous sea-green eyes and nibbled at her bottom lip. She was killing him.

She tilted her chin in the way only Matilda could. "I'm working for you and I'm not adding 'sleeping with the boss' to the list of crazy things I've done in the last few months. That woman has gone and *this* is my new start." Without waiting for his reply, she turned abruptly and walked up the stairs, her wet clothes clinging to her tight little body and leaving nothing to the imagination.

Every part of him burned and ached and he could still taste her on his lips. He wanted her and despite her words to the contrary, her response to him clearly said she wanted him too. He just had to find a way to convince her that her new start included him.

"Mrs. Perez, it's Doctor Wernitzski."

Lori gripped the phone so hard she thought it would shatter in her palm. For days she'd believed she wanted this call. Since the surgery she'd existed in a cocoon of the unknown, spending most of her time railing against it and wanting the facts no matter how brutal because at least the facts could be dealt with. The unknown could not.

But now that her doctor was on the end of the line it took all her strength not to put the phone down and cut off the call and its uncompromising truth.

"Hello, Doctor." She wanted to say more but her throat seemed clogged.

"I know the holiday has slowed down the pathology and that's been hard for you so rather than wait until your office visit I thought I'd call you today. Are you sitting down?"

Oh God, that had to mean bad news. Just tell me.

Don't tell me.

"Yes."

"It's good news, Lori. The lymph nodes are clear and the cancer was confined to the breasts and there are clear margins.

It's the best possible outcome and you won't require radio or chemotherapy."

Utter relief cascaded over her and her body shook so violently she almost dropped the phone. She wanted to cry, wanted to laugh but the good news had been so unexpected it completely paralyzed her.

"Lori, are you there?" Concern filled the doctor's voice.

"I…Yes…Thank you."

"You're most welcome. Please stay on the line because I'm transferring you to my nurse who'll run through Monday's arrangements. You enjoy the rest of your weekend with your family."

The line clicked and then the nurse was talking about saline injections, plastic surgery appointments, prostheses but it was all just a jumble of words which finished with "11:00 a.m. on Monday."

She placed the phone back in the cradle and looked at her now-barren chest, once filled with voluptuous DD breasts. From the age of fourteen she knew she'd held a certain power with men because of her breasts and she'd noticed how their eyes followed her when she walked by. In the early years of their marriage Carl had idolized her breasts but that had been before a baby had changed their shape. Even after his betrayals part of her had known men still found her and her breasts attractive, always feeling their gaze on her. Then there was Brian. He'd gazed at her naked breasts with wonder, fondled them in his hands, nuzzled them with his face and made her orgasm with the touch of his mouth against her nipples.

Now they were gone. A rogue tear escaped, dripping onto the pressure bandage. Cancer had stolen her breasts and stolen a huge chunk of her life as a sexual woman.

Stop the pity party. You're still here.

And she was. She was alive, and with the opportunity to see Kyle grow up. She'd already survived a few years of being alone, survived just as her mother had stoically done for many years more. So what was a lifetime?

She stood up and headed out to tell the news to Kyle, her mother, Marc and Matilda, in that order. Then she'd call Gracie and tell her everything.

Brian had his first day off in over a week but he'd much prefer to be at work. At least station life kept him busy, giving him scant time to think. But at home, time crawled past and now he stood staring out the window onto Main Street.

He'd shoveled the walk, salted the drive, bought the groceries and picked up and put down a book ten times. Not even the Wisconsin Badgers taking on the Minnesota Golden Gophers in the time-honored Thanksgiving weekend football game could keep his interest. The only vision he could see was Lori's gaunt face, traumatized eyes and the heritage-green of her front door as it shut abruptly in his face.

Three weeks ago, after sixteen years of waiting on the sidelines, of being the "nice guy" which had almost killed him, he'd finally held Lori Olsen in his arms. He'd kissed her, caressed her and made long, slow love to her, relishing her response to him and memorizing her glow of complete satisfaction. The long wait had all been worth it and Lori had finally been where she belonged. With him.

He'd walked on air for a few days until his euphoria had been pierced by Lori not returning any of his messages. He tugged at his hair. An embarrassing number of messages as well as a letter he now regretted writing.

Didn't the pop psychology books say all women waited and pounced on the phone call after the turning-point date?

Not the woman he wanted. He'd heard nothing.

Yesterday, after she'd slammed the door on him it had killed him not to storm her house and demand to be told what the hell was going on. Instead he'd had to face her hot-shot brother and front a blatant lie about a late Thanksgiving meal. He'd tried to get information by calling in to Gracie's on the pretext of buying his sister a scarf for Christmas. He'd come away convinced Gracie had no idea either.

There was no point calling the house because her family had circled it like a stockade, and were protecting the valuable contents from marauding outsiders. But by hell, he was going to find out. He just had to work out how.

He continued staring out the window and caught a flash of red as Matilda Geoffrey stepped out of Gracie's and walked toward her car. The outsider who'd been let in.

He grabbed his coat and a minute later he was out on the sidewalk. "Tildy."

She stopped and turned, her face breaking into a smile. "G'day, Lieutenant."

"I'm off duty. Please call me Brian."

"Right-e-o, Brian it is."

He smiled, trying really hard to be casual so that he could get the information he needed in a conversational way when he so badly wanted to interrogate her and say, "Tell me what the hell is going on with Lori." "I thought you'd be at Two Rivers today, collecting your car?"

A line creased her forehead. "I wanted to be but it just wasn't possible today."

"That's too bad." An idea exploded in his head like a Fourth of July firework. "I could drive you." Surely with a two-and-a-half-hour drive each way plus time dealing with the car, he'd learn what was going on.

She smiled. "That's very kind of you but you said digging it out wasn't a police problem."

"That's correct, but I'm on a day off and as a citizen I'm more than happy to offer my services."

"Are you sure?" She sounded as if she couldn't quite believe her luck.

"Very sure."

CHAPTER THIRTEEN

Matilda bit her lip as Brian took the turn off to Hobin. Seven hours ago, she'd sent a text message to Marc telling him she was on her way to Two Rivers. This left him at home with Lori, Elsa and Kyle, and possibly Gracie. She knew he wouldn't be happy. She'd received in return one voice-mail message and one very terse text telling her exactly how grumpy a Viking could be.

But it couldn't be helped. The idea of her and Marc spending hours alone together in a truck had such a huge danger sign hanging over it that she'd run. Not that she feared Marc at all but oh my, she was scared of herself.

After the way she'd kissed Marc last night, Brian's offer had seemed not only a gift but her only safe bet. Her life was a mess and she didn't need to complicate it with any more self-destructive behavior. Acting on the chemistry between her and Marc fell clearly and unmistakably into that camp. She chewed her bottom lip regretting that she'd told Marc that she wasn't that into him. It had backfired on her big-time.

Instead of it keeping him at arm's length, she'd unwittingly issued a challenge to a man who'd hardly ever had a woman say "no" to him. Given her lack of sexual experience since Jason combined with the fact no other man had said "yes" to her, it left both of them sailing in unfamiliar waters. She also knew that by going to Two Rivers with Brian, she'd upped the ante in their escalating game of outrageous flirting. Flirting that, even with her lack of experience, had started to feel very much like foreplay. Hell, that kiss last night had *been* foreplay and she'd almost come at the touch of his hand on her breast.

A wave of heat flooded her as she recalled just how deeply she'd explored his mouth with her tongue and the memory of it mortified her, and yet it also left her feeling strangely empty.

She'd always considered sex a commitment and an extension of love. She didn't love Marc, but whenever she thought about him, all she could think about was sex. Even her dreams were filled with hot and graphic images of a spun-gold god with tender arms and a mouth that roved over her, making her ache with need and come with a rush. Dreams aside, the reality was she could hardly think straight when they were in the same room and as much as she hated to admit it, she knew that without Lori, Elsa and Kyle around, she'd end up in his arms again and not want to stop there.

But unlike with Barry, at least this time she recognized the jeopardy she was in and surely that counted for something. Jumping into bed with Marc would complicate her shaky start at getting her life together. Right now there wasn't much between him, her salary and destitution. She gazed out the car window and tried to let the snow weave a hypnotic trance on her chaotic thoughts.

Brian tapped the top of the steering wheel in time with

the music as they sat in companionable silence. "Even though you've told me about Barry Severson you do realize you have to come down to the station and make an official report."

During the journey and the big dig out of the car they'd got along well and Brian's company was easy and straightforward compared with the sexual minefield she trod every day with Marc. They'd talked about all sorts of things and she'd eventually told him about the bridal business and about Barry. Even though she knew Brian had just spoken as a friend, his instructions made her squirm in her seat.

He shot her a perceptive glance. "If it's easier, I'll give you my schedule so you can report it to me and not to Eric. Saves you telling the story over again to a stranger."

Marc's words echoed in her head. *Do you want one other woman to go through this?*

Brian glanced at her. "How about you come down on Wednesday afternoon when Eric is off duty?"

He was being so lovely and understanding and she knew he was right. Knew Marc was right and she needed to report Barry. "I'll be there on Wednesday at 2:00 p.m."

"I'm holding you to that."

She gave him a grateful smile. "Thanks, Brian. You're a really good bloke."

"A good bloke?" He sighed. "Is that Australian for a 'nice guy'?"

Something in his voice made her study his expression. "I meant it as a compliment but I get the feeling I just offended you. Is there something wrong with being a nice guy?"

"Nice guys finish last." Unexpected bitterness laced his words. "Women say they want a nice guy but believe me they go for the bad boy every time. Even when they've divorced a bad boy and they know they get hurt."

"Are you talking from recent personal experience?"

"You might say."

She thought of how "nice" Barry had seemed, of the security and family she'd been convinced he was offering her along with his complete lack of coercion to get her into bed. He'd turned out to be a snake in the grass, and a conniving bastard who was lower than pond scum.

A vividly clear image of Marc rose in her mind, one of him standing in her doorway with a sport towel draped over one taut muscular shoulder and honesty and integrity radiating from every part of him. Unlike Barry, he was decadently handsome with ruthless and penetrating charm that he combined with unrelenting and unashamed efforts to get her into bed. But he did it all with such open relish that it made her so weak and wet with longing that she could hardly see straight. But despite it all, she knew who the nice guy was in the equation.

Brian was obviously upset about the nice guy tag. "From one friend to another, is being a nice guy a problem for you, Brian?"

"I'm a small-town cop." His tone said it all.

"Just because you're a cop doesn't mean you have to be a nice guy."

He took his eye off the road for a moment. "Excuse me?"

"Nice doesn't have to be bland and boring."

He scowled and she rushed on, "Not that I think you're either of those things but I think you interpret nice as that. Look, I'm no expert as you know, and I've been duped by a so-called nice guy who was more of a bastard than any bad boy I've ever met. All I can say is you can still be a good cop and a bad boy. Give her some of that bad-boy excitement and if you get the vibes back that she wants some bad-boy Brian, then sweep her off her feet and into your bed."

"I did that to Lori three weeks ago."

Her chest tightened and his words froze her brain. She hadn't expected that. Somehow she managed to count backward. Oh God, that must have happened just before Lori found out about her breast cancer. "And?"

"And nothing." He rubbed the back of his neck with his left hand. "I've tried to contact her but she never takes my calls, school told me she was away and you told me she was at a conference." His look was a combination of hurt and betrayal. "I finally saw her yesterday and she looked like death."

"You saw her yesterday?" She couldn't hide her astonishment because for four days they'd shielded Lori from calls and visitors.

"I rang the bell when I was looking for you. I waited awhile and then Lori answered it. She slammed the door in my face." His mouth took on a grim line. "You've been living in that house since Monday. What the hell is going on?"

She hated secrets and this was the perfect example of a secret that was hurting one, possibly two people.

Can you honestly tell me there is one man out there who'd find me attractive now? Lori's words sounded in her head. At the time she'd thought Lori had been speaking in general terms but now the words haunted her.

"How long have you been the nice guy waiting for Lori?"

He gripped the wheel hard, not looking at her. "Sixteen years."

She saw frustration, strain, hurt and love in Brian's eyes and her heart rolled over. This was the kind of bone-deep love that Grandpa Hank and Nana knew and that her parents shared. The type of love that eluded her, although unlike her parents the love she wanted included a family. So help her she probably shouldn't interfere but she was a sucker for a love story.

"I can't tell you Lori's private information but I will tell you this. Waiting for her is not going to work for you this time and the nice guy will get hammered. So bring on the bad boy and, Brian, be prepared for a fight."

"I'll bear that in mind." A silver glint she'd never seen before appeared in his gray eyes, giving him the look of a warrior on a mission.

Forgive me, Lori, but it's for your own good.

Ninety minutes later after transferring all her stuff from Brian's car to hers, Matilda stood under the yellow glow of a porch light and waved goodbye to Vanessa. Walking back down the path, she caught the flicker of curtains in the next house. *Close out the night, Tildy.*

Nana had said that every winter's evening and she would close all the curtains to keep the heat in and the cold air out. She smiled because although Narranbool nights could be cold they were positively balmy compared with Hobin and it technically wasn't even winter yet. Perhaps the expression had come from the two years Nana and Grandpa Hank had lived in Michigan before Grandpa Hank had brought her home so he could live in the Narranbool heat.

She jammed her fingers into her coat pockets to keep her hands warm, and they flicked against the crisp greenbacks which were payment for the tiara.

She'd told Vanessa she needed to check the condition of

Nana's dress and work out a price but really she just wanted to try it on one more time before she parted with it. She stifled a yawn as the effects of the huge day caught up with her but it had been worth it. Now she had some more cash and she planned to use it to buy a web design package, and create a site for Weddings Are Hobin.

She couldn't wait to get started on the website. Weddings Are Hobin seemed too good an idea to walk away from and it would hopefully generate the money she needed to sit her nursing registration exams. Not that she was certain she wanted to do that but as she had no clue from one day to the next it was best to keep her options open. Right now she needed as much money as she could save to give her security.

She glanced at her watch. Nine o'clock. On cue her stomach rumbled. If she got something to eat that would delay her arrival at Lori's and there'd be more chance that the Olsen-Perez clan would have gone to bed. Even if Marc was still up she was pretty confident he wouldn't make a scene about her bailing on their arrangement to dig out the car because the house with its thin walls afforded little privacy.

As she crossed the snow-covered road she tried not to let the long moon-cast shadows of the trees dancing against the snow, spook her.

A deep booming voice came out of the darkness. "I never took you for a coward."

She shrieked and her heart lurched, trying hard to escape through her ribcage as her legs tensed, ready to run. Her brain finally got a message through her fear and she recognized the familiar voice.

Marc strode around the side of a truck, dark shadows looming around him and no light to fire his usual golden aura.

Her heart slowed some and as she walked toward him her body stirred, eager to see him. Her head immediately tried to shut it down. "What are you doing here? How did you know I was here?"

He smiled. "This is Hobin. Everyone knows everything and it only takes one phone call to find out all sorts of things." He stepped in close. "I've been waiting for you."

His deep voice wrapped around her like the seductive warmth of malt whiskey on a cold night. "Waiting for me?" Her words squeaked and she cleared her throat so she could sound more in control. "You just gave me the fright of my life."

He opened the truck door for her. "Perhaps that's payback for running out on me and leaving me stuck out at Lori's with an endless parade of visitors."

She glimpsed a hint of hurt in his eyes and a twinge of guilt scored her. "Poor Blondie. Sounds like you had a tough day."

"You don't know the half of it. I made seven pots of coffee in seven hours and endured mind-numbing moments of chitchat with people I haven't seen in years and have no plans to see for twice as long again. Meanwhile you abandoned me to spend the day with Hobin's upstanding law-enforcement officer."

He closed in on her, his movements almost predatory, and she involuntarily stepped back, feeling the cold metal of the truck doorway through her coat. She should feel intimidated but instead a rush of exhilaration pounded through her, rekindling all of yesterday's desire and making her feel truly alive for the first time in…forever.

His coat-covered arm came up beside her head as he rested

it on the seat and his head dropped close to hers. "I bet he bored you rigid."

She couldn't believe it—the Viking was jealous. Excitement skated through her, making her giddy.

Sensible girl sent out a strong, sharp warning: *He's just stroppy you outplayed him. With him it's the thrill of the chase. Get out now.*

But it felt so good. *Just a little bit of flirting will be okay.* "At least Brian's well mannered and treats me like a lady."

He moved closer still, leaning in until his arms corralled her, his right leg caressed hers and his arousal pressed hard against the top of her legs. "He's dull and boring and you know it."

Her blood hammered through her, making her body ache with need. Sizzling heat shot down between her legs almost making her cry out. "Believe me, after this past week, dull and boring is exactly what I need."

"Is that so?"

"Absolutely." But the word held a tremor as his scent of coffee and earthy musk swirled around her, almost draining her brain of all coherent thought.

It's time to get out. Game over.

But her body had taken control of her ears and she was deaf to everything except the touch of his hand which had slipped into her coat and was slowly moving upward under her blouse. Every brush of his fingers made a promise and unfurled the same delicious and addictive ribbons of sensation from yesterday and then built on them. His thumb stroked her bra and she gasped as her tingling breasts instantly strained against the lace, desperate for his intimate touch. Heat flooded her, buckling her knees and wiping out every fragile defense that she'd tried to erect against him.

His lips caressed her ear. "You couldn't do dull and boring to save your life. You're an adventurer."

Tildy, darling, the Geoffrey women are born for adventure and love. The loving voice of Nana tempted her again. The last time she'd listened she'd lost everything but this time she was under no illusions, knowing without a shadow of a doubt she had *not* been born for a great love. But was this her adventure? To take a trip out of her real-life world and have sex with a man whose eyes alone made her weak with need.

His hand grasped the back of her bra and this time there was no interruption. This time he made quick work of the fastener and she felt the support fall away. Then her breast was resting in his hand, her nipple hard and quivering with sheer pleasure and demanding more.

"I want you, Matilda, and I know you want me. Ignoring it is just driving us both crazy." His usually deep and melodic voice sounded hoarse and raspy.

She tried to form the word *no* but she could no longer deny the truth of his words.

"Aren't you tired of fighting this thing between us?" His forehead touched hers. "Use me. Let me show you what that rat-bastard couldn't see. You're an incredibly sexy woman. Let me launch your new start."

No man had ever tried this hard to get her into bed. Not many men had ever wanted to and now she had a man who could have any woman he chose yet he wanted her. Her head spun but she discarded the ego trip and instead recognized what it was—lust, raw and undiluted, vibrating between them and generated by two people struggling outside of their usual environment. Love had nothing to do with it.

Recognizing that fact had to be protective, right? She'd

spent her life looking for love starting with her parents, treading water with Jason and finishing with Barry, but this time she wasn't looking and she was under no illusions.

This was just a moment in time—earthy, primal lust, a base and uncomplicated emotion. Her adventure waiting to be taken. She reached out and cupped his cheeks, pulling his mouth down onto hers.

His lips touched hers, firing her blood and dispensing with polite preliminaries. She thrust her tongue past his lips needing to taste him again, and fill herself with him.

Coffee, peppermint and hot lust rushed in and he groaned, his need shuddering through her before exploding in her mouth. His tongue flicked and caressed, touching, tasting, searing every part of her mouth and melting her body into a raging river of thundering desire.

She needed to feel him and her hands pulled at his jacket, her fingers tugging at his shirt, until her palm touched smooth hot skin stretched over taut muscle. Bliss.

His mouth trailed down her jaw—kissing, tasting, branding and all the while his hand never strayed from her breasts, now heavy and taut with desire. As his fingers circled and stroked, her need for him built to the point where she didn't care if he took her on a quiet side street with her back against a truck.

Her palms and fingers frantically explored his back, savoring every muscle and every sinew before bringing her hands around to his chest and trailing them down to the waistband of his pants.

He kissed her hard on the mouth and pulled away. "Bloody Wisconsin weather. I'm not having sex in a truck when it's twenty-five degrees out."

She laughed. "I thought we were being adventurous and there's enough outback heat between us to keep us warm."

His finger wound around one of her curls. "I don't need Eric taking us in for indecent exposure but that and the weather aside, I want to be able to see you."

Her heart turned over in a wobbly quiver and she immediately steeled it against his words. *Lust and sex, nothing more, nothing less.*

"Come on." Grabbing her hand, he pulled her away from the vehicle, slammed the truck door shut and started striding down the quiet and empty street.

She stumbled after him. "Where are we going?"

"A friend's house."

"What? I don't think I'm *that* adventurous."

He grinned. "He's out of town."

"Well now, that is convenient."

He had the grace to look sheepish. "My plan had been to get you inside the house before anything happened but I blame that accent of yours. It does it to me every time."

"My accent turns you on?" She found the idea incredulous.

"Totally." He turned and tugged her up a snowy path toward a house with its porch light on and he pulled a key from his jacket pocket.

Completely empowered in a way she'd never known, she leaned up against him and whispered a suggestion into his ear.

An expletive shattered the Hobin night air. His key missed the lock.

She unsuccessfully tried to stifle a giggle. "And here I thought that American men were so much more polite than Australians. But then again, you are a Viking."

Eyes simmering with barely controlled desire hooked her

gaze and his voice ground out the words low and terse. "If you want the best sex of your life you'd best keep that trashy mouth closed until we're both naked."

Half a dozen retorts rose to her lips but she zipped her mouth shut with a laugh. She didn't want her big adventure ending before it started. Putting her palm over the top of his hand she pushed, and together they slid the key into the lock.

They fell through into the entrance, pulling at each other's jackets and coats, struggling with cold and shaking fingers that tried to unlace boots and cast layers of clothing frantically onto the floor.

"Summer sex is so much easier," Marc quipped as he tossed her boots by the door and drew her into the master bedroom where two bedside table lamps threw a warm glow across a white jacquard quilt partially turned down as if expecting guests. A champagne bottle in an ice bucket sat on small table with two fine glass flutes on a tray and she immediately glanced at the bedside tables looking for chocolates but instead saw a distinctive square foil pack.

She appreciated his thoughtfulness. "You're all prepared, Blondie."

"You want an adventure, not a disaster, right?"

She nodded against a tiny seed of longing and stared at the golden man in front of her. Naked except for a pair of boxers that were pushed forward with a distinctive and impressive bulge, he was six feet two of sculptured and chiseled gorgeousness and tonight he was hers. She planned to explore every millimeter of him and then go back and do it again in U.S. inches.

Marc gazed at her as if his eyes were absorbing every molecule of her body. She stood before him in her lacy panties and stocking feet, determined not to feel overwhelmed, but trying to keep her arms from crossing over her chest. "My breasts are a bit pathetic really."

He shook his head and reached forward running his fingers through her hair. "I'll be the judge of that."

"And what's your criteria?"

He grinned, a wicked glint in his eyes. "More than a mouthful's a waste."

"Ah, so you're a minimalist?"

"At work and at play." With a grin he rolled her onto the bed and pressed his mouth to her breast. He suckled her already pulsating breasts, sending her arousal into overdrive. Then his tongue abraded her nipple.

Her body, coiled tight with anticipation and running wet with need, arched up toward him, seeking him as she threw back her head in a gasp of wondrous surprise.

"Hang in there, sweetheart. I still have to judge the other one."

His mouth continued its exploration making her blood a river of hungry need, and ramping up sensation on sensation until her body almost melted from overload and she realized the moaning noise was coming from her. Her breath came fast and hard, her hands pulled frenetically at his shoulders and her hips rose from the bed, demanding to feel him hard between her legs. "Now, please, Marc, now."

He lifted his head from her breasts, his expression one of lazy indulgence. "Now?"

How could he look so calm when she was ragged with need and desperate to feel him buried deep inside her? "Now!"

His hands lifted her hips and with a gentleness that made

her want to scream he slowly drew her panties down her legs, caressing her along the way.

Her hands reached for the waistband of his boxers, desperate to touch him, hold him and guide him into her so he could fill the throbbing need that screamed inside of her. But he caught her hands by the wrists and drew them above her head. Frustration surged and she wanted to howl in protest but his mouth covered hers and his fingers dawdled down her stomach in a journey that seemed to take an eternity until they finally reached the place where her flesh burned hottest.

Her muscles screamed, desperate to grip him, to feel him, and she sucked his fingers deep inside her as his thumb stroked her body's most sensitive place.

She shattered instantly—an explosive ball pouring through her, melting everything in its path, obliterating all until she no longer existed. On a sob of wonder, she felt her body reassemble until she was whole again.

She slapped him.

"Ouch." He rubbed his shoulder. "Hey, what was that for?"

"Because, you're a control freak."

A look of bewilderment hovered in his bluer-than-blue eyes. "I just gave you an orgasm but I'm a control freak? Is this some sort of sick Australian joke?"

She shook her head, half-crazy with sated lust and yet yearning with disappointment. "I wanted to come with you."

He grinned, understanding immediately demolishing his incomprehension. "I'm sorry, that was very thoughtless of me."

"Yes, Blondie, it was. Remember, this is *my* adventure."

He faked contrition. "What can I do to make it up to you?"

She pushed at his shoulders until he rolled onto his back and she shucked his boxers. Straddling him, she whispered what she planned to do to him as she ran her hands down his chest, reveling in the tremors against her palms. She reached golden hair and gently cupped his tight scrotum in her hands, feeling him moving against her palm.

"Steady." The word sounded rough and barely controlled.

She trailed her fingers down his beautiful, erect shaft and lightly kissed the tip.

He shuddered and grabbed her arms, a sheen of sweat glistening on his top lip. "Unless you want to wait fifteen minutes…"

She smiled a smile of victory and raised a brow. "Now?"

He dexterously fitted the condom and with strong hands on her hips, he lifted her up and then lowered her gently down. She felt the hard tip of him firm against her and swallowed hard. But she need not have worried. Her body, so well prepared and ready, opened layer upon layer until she blissfully impaled herself completely upon her Viking warrior. "Oh, Marc."

His desire-filled eyes held her gaze and his hands held her buttocks as he moved inside her, thrusting deeply, and creating the most incredible mini-shocks that tore through her. Her muscles tightened convulsively around him, demanding more, and she rose and fell with him, as his breath came hard and fast and he drove her higher and higher.

Throwing her head back, she called out his name as she unraveled and was flung out into the stars with him. For a moment, they orbited together as one before falling to earth separately, pulled back by the reality of gravity.

"Nine marks for an awesome adventure, Blondie."

Marc laughed as Matilda's hair tickled his face. The last

three hours had been amazing. Sex with Matilda was as unpredictable as everyday life was with her. One minute she was all sexual ingénue and the next she was the vamp, bringing him to his knees with the touch of her mouth. He'd explored almost every part of that tight little body and Matilda in turn had demanded her own investigations which usually ended with him flipping her onto her back or pulling her down onto him and losing himself in her. Something he planned to do again very soon. "Nine? I'm getting a nine? Where did I lose two points?"

"You're so full of it." Green eyes sparkled as she half-heartedly jabbed him in the chest before converting the motion into a caress of decreasing circles. "Ten is the maximum number of points allocated and you lost one for not having any tea in the house."

He leaned back on the pillows, his arm curved around her, feeling deliciously relaxed and content—a state he couldn't remember feeling in a very long time. "It's not my house so that's one point I get back. Besides, I bought you French champagne. Isn't that a fair substitute?"

"It's more than good enough, especially as I can't afford to buy it myself so I'm even more of a fool to pass it up." Her fingers trailed across his belly, dawdling at his belly button. "But I have to drive back to Lori's and I can't risk being caught drunk driving."

He pressed a kiss into her hair, breathing in the scent of sunshine. "Don't worry about that, we have loads of time and one glass won't be a problem."

She sighed, her lips pushing into a pout. "You and your champagne are just so tempting and although it's been too much fun, I have to be up for work early in the morning."

He caressed her silky back. "You can do both."

"Not if I don't get any sleep I can't." She kissed his chest and sat up. "This was all just lovely, thank you but I have to go."

"Don't go." His arms instinctively tightened around her, holding her captive with her back against his chest. His arms brushed her nipples which instantly pebbled and he immediately hardened. God she was the most responsive woman he'd ever known. "Stay. There's a spa in the bathroom we haven't tested."

She hesitated and he grinned, already thinking of the amazing things her hands could do to him and what he could do for her in return. But then she gathered the quilt to her, slid out of the bed and padded toward the door.

He lazily stretched out an arm. "The bathroom's the other direction."

She bent down picking up the tiny triangle of lace that represented her panties. "I'd love to stay but tomorrow is busy. I promised Kyle the full catastrophe brekkie with bacon, eggs and pancakes. Lori wants her hair washed, and Elsa invited me to her quilt guild meeting. Then I've got the—"

His mother's quilt meeting? "I'll make Kyle brunch at ten. See, I just saved you an hour."

"I promised him."

A deep rumble of disgruntlement jetted up. "My family won't mind waiting, you know."

A fine crease formed on the bridge of her nose and she gave him a taut smile. "Sorry, Marc, but I don't want to let them down."

What about me? The roar of frustration built, straining against years of his family coming first. "Of course you don't want to let them down. While you're at it you might want to send Jennifer and Sheryl a care package so you've made sure you've taken care of *everyone* in my family."

Her eyes widened in surprise. "Now you're just being juvenile." She pulled on her socks.

Disappointment rammed him hard. Matilda was leaving because of his family. This was just another example in a long line of episodes where his family took over his life. One more thing to add to a very long list chronicling why he stayed away from Hobin fifty-one weeks of the year.

"Damn it, Matilda, who are you working for, them or me?"

He heard the words leave his mouth and immediately realized the implications of what he'd said. He wanted to grab them back but it was too late and instead, as if in slow motion, he watched as her ears received and delivered the message.

Her arm stopped halfway into the sleeve of her blouse and her lush and tender body stiffened, rigid with tension. "As from this moment, I'm off your payroll."

He plowed his hand through his hair. "Matilda, I didn't mean that the way it sounded."

Her green eyes flashed. "I think you did. I mean why wouldn't you? After all, you've bought me every step of the way. First as your housekeeper then as your sister's nurse and now as a sex toy."

"I'm sorry. I guess that comment was out of line."

"You guess?" She leveled him with a look that said dirt was preferable to him and left the room.

He leaped off the bed and followed her into the hall. "I did *not* buy you as a sex toy."

She was struggling into her pants, her actions furious and uncoordinated. "Oh, and that's supposed to make me feel better? You pay for what you want all the time, Marc, and I'm not so sure this is any different. You might not have held out a wad of cash but you obviously feel entitled."

Her accusations rained down on him and the ground felt slippery under his feet. "I don't feel entitled. Hell, look at me. I'm the one standing here naked and begging." The realization stunned him. "Look, the last three fantastic hours have been nothing to do with your job at the house, absolutely nothing to do with money but the last five minutes have been everything to do with my family."

She shoved her feet into her boots, her face incredulous. "Your family? You're going to have to explain that one."

He sighed. "My family is complicated. Since I was seventeen they've depended on me. I gave them five years of my life and now I help out with money and advice, which I can usually do from New York. With Lori being sick I've been hauled back again to sort things out, which I've been doing. All I'm asking for right now is that we take a little bit of time out just for us. Hell, you're the one who keeps telling me I need to relax more and lighten up."

Pity scored her face as she grabbed her coat and opened the door. "I'm leaving because I'm doing *my* job caring for Lori and Kyle. The job you delegated to me because you didn't want to do it. You have a lovely family, Marc, and I think it's time you grew up and saw them through adult eyes."

Years of hurt unleashed. "I've always been the adult!"

"Then you might want to ask yourself why you're acting like a spoiled child." The door closed behind her with a loud click.

He stared at the door in disbelief. For the first time in his life a woman had just walked out on him and he didn't like it one little bit.

CHAPTER FOURTEEN

Lori was grateful for the Wisconsin cold. Bulky winter clothing was the perfect foil to her lack of breasts although her chest was no longer totally flat. She was on her way home from another doctor's visit and she'd just received more saline injections into the pockets of skin that the surgeon had created. The salty solution stretched her pectoral muscles in preparation for her future implants, but the hard balls of saline were a long way from soft breast tissue.

"Where do you want me to drop you? Gracie's?" Marc's clipped voice broke into her thoughts.

He'd been grouchy since Thanksgiving and she was running out of patience with him. "Norsk's, but if you're going to be—what does Tildy call it—stroppy, then don't bother. I can walk from wherever you need to be."

"It's a long walk from New York," he grumbled.

She threw her hands up. "See, this is what I mean."

He sighed. "Sorry, just ignore me. I got a work call and I was thinking about that."

"Problems?"

He grimaced. "Nothing your big brother can't handle."

She glanced at the tightness around his mouth in stark contrast to his words. "Do you need to go back to New York?"

He shook his head. "You asked me to stay and I sorted things so I could be here for you. You're not even driving yet."

"True, but I can ask Tildy to drive me."

He snorted. "She has lapses and drifts left."

"She does not drift left, although she has put stickers on the dashboard that say Left and Right in big print so she remembers to stay right."

She turned in her seat to face him. "It's funny how one person's disaster turns into another person's good fortune. You have to admit that Tildy being dumped in Hobin was the best thing that could have happened to all of us. She cooks like a dream. Kyle loves her and I've appreciated her straightforward, no-nonsense style. I needed that."

"I'm glad it's all worked out for you." A scowl darkened the unfamiliar shadows on his face.

Not for the first time she wondered what was going on in that stubborn head of his, but he'd never shared much of his life with her or her sisters since he'd left home all those years ago. As a brother to rely upon, he was rock-solid but he held so much of himself back that she couldn't call him a friend. She'd noticed Kyle, who generally got along with adults and had once worshipped Marc, was now responding to that same aloofness by being particularly sullen.

He slowed down outside Norsk's. "You've got appointments with your doctor in Wausau over the next few weeks and I plan to drive you to them. I'm staying in Hobin until you're back at work."

She appreciated him but he still needed a kick. "Thanks, but be happy or you can go and be grumpy at Mom's place."

His huff turned into a laugh and he gave her his reassuring big-brother smile. "It's great that you're starting to feel more yourself."

Her muscles forced a return smile. She didn't know what herself felt like anymore. The woman she'd been before the surgery didn't exist and she hadn't been in this new version of her body long enough to know what she should feel. All she knew was that she had a chest with no sensation at all which in itself was the oddest feeling.

She opened the door. "How about you go and hit a home run with your project that's gathering dust on my dining room table."

"Yes, ma'am."

Lori watched him speed off in flurry of sludgy snow and turned toward the canopied entrance of Norsk's. She was meeting Gracie for lunch as if it was any other week. Her friend had been wonderful and although Lori appreciated her insistence at resuming normal activities again, it didn't mean she wasn't anxious about being out in public.

She opened the door to a lunchtime crowd and took a deep breath. Not everyone knew yet—her friends and colleagues had done a great job keeping it quiet and if people had put two and two together they'd been polite enough not to ask.

Astrid greeted her with a busy wave which she quickly returned before walking past the soda fountain and rosy-red diner stools, and headed to a booth at the very back of the restaurant. Lori slid in behind the empty table and checked her watch. Gracie should be here any minute. Needing something to do, she picked up the menu even though she knew it back to front and sideways. The food at Norsk's was always good but the selection stayed constant.

Five minutes later she was still sitting in her coat and the warmth of the diner had her imagining she was in a sauna. She wanted to keep her coat on but she risked melting into a puddle of inelegant sweat so she reluctantly slid it off. Feeling extremely self-conscious, even though today she'd worn the prosthetics for the first time, she glanced down at her chest.

God, what if one of them had moved and she was crooked?

She wished Gracie was here to tell her. *Come on, Gracie.* She checked her watch again. The longer she sat here alone the greater the chance someone would come sit with her and want to chat. She wasn't ready for that so she buried her nose in the menu again.

"Hello, Lori."

Brian. Her heart hiccupped then stalled as she wished herself anywhere but here in a back booth that should have hidden her from view. She'd thought she'd be safe from running into him for a while longer. *Damn it, Gracie.* But her friend was nowhere to be seen and she was on her own.

Taking in a deep breath, she told herself she could do this, she could get through the first uncomfortable meeting. After all, this was Brian and if anything, he was *always* polite. Once she told him she was expecting Gracie any minute he wouldn't linger. She slowly put down the menu. "Hello, Brian. Gracie's due any minute."

He gave her a curt nod, his clear gray eyes fixed resolutely on her face. She counted through the uncomfortable silence, expecting him to turn and leave well before she got to five.

His solid bulk slid across the bench seat opposite her, his uniformed knees brushing hers through her slacks.

Shock fizzed through her making her head spin. People didn't sit down unless they were invited to and Brian was the last person in the world to break protocol. Somehow she managed to stammer, "A private lunch."

His expression didn't alter. "I just passed the store and it was brimming with women wearing red hats."

"Red hats?"

"Yep. They've come to Hobin in a bus for an excursion. Quite a few of them are in Peggy's as well so I don't think Gracie will be making it in for lunch." He picked up the menu and held it in both hands.

Broad hands with half-moon cuticles and clean, well-kept nails. The last time she'd seen those hands they'd been touching her, caressing her and drawing responses from her she'd never thought possible. Responses that would never be possible again.

"Thanks for letting me know." She picked up her coat and hugged it to her chest.

His eyes didn't leave the menu. "You're not leaving."

There was no inflection in the stern tone and it couldn't be confused with a question. Her heart kicked up as a thread of uneasiness wound through her and she started to slide along the bench. "I have to go."

His foot hit her seat effectively blocking her exit and he lowered the menu, the plastic covering hitting the tabletop with a snap. "You have a choice. You can go but I'll follow you everywhere until you tell me what's going on. If you take that option, the town gossips will have a field day so the sensible option is to stay and have lunch with me."

"This is a joke, right?" The courteous and accommodating man she thought she knew so well had vanished. She blinked to clear her vision but again all she could see was the same steely purpose in his eyes reflecting back at her, and no sign of humor on his square-jawed face.

"Oh, hi, Mrs. Perez, Lieutenant Rogerson." Cindy-Louise, one of Lori's ex-students, smiled expectantly at them both, notepad in hand. "I'm guessing you'll be having your usual, Mrs. Perez, but what can I get you, sir?"

"What's her usual?" Brian asked with a smile at the waitress.

"Norwegian meatballs." Cindy giggled. "They sure look funny but they taste really good."

Lori hated being talked about as if she wasn't actually sitting right there. "Hello, Brian, I'm here. You can ask me."

"I take it that means you're staying for lunch." His eyes flicked over her before he turned back to the waitress. "I'll have the same, as well as coffee with cream." He tucked the menu behind the condiments. "Oh and, Cindy, can you please hang Lori's coat up for her?"

"You bet." The waitress put her hand out for the coat.

Fury at his high-handed and blatant blackmail spun through Lori making her breathless. She didn't recognize this man at all. Holding on to her coat would look ridiculous so he had her well and truly backed into a corner—the booth corner she'd chosen because she thought it would be safe.

They sat in silence while Cindy hung up the coat, poured their water and brought them a basket of bread. Not remotely hungry but desperate to do something, Lori buttered a slice of bread and savagely bit into it, taking her frustration out on the crunchy crust.

"You're looking better than when I saw you at Thanksgiving." Brian's voice was the only soft thing about him.

"That's not saying much." She took a sip of the water.

"You've lost weight."

She automatically glanced at her chest, panicked and then forced herself to look directly at him. "I have."

"Are you going to tell me why?"

"No."

The soft voice developed an edge. "You owe me an explanation."

The hand in her lap fisted as she forced herself to block him out of her life, knowing she was hurting him but that had to happen before he hurt her. "I don't owe you anything. We're both consenting adults and we had—" she dropped her voice "—we had sex. Once. In retrospect, had I realized you were so small town in your thinking I would never have gotten into bed with you. Stop being a needy wimp, Brian. Once doesn't mean forever."

He didn't even flinch. It was like the words hit a brick wall and just fell at his feet not making a dent in his demeanor. Not even his eyes hinted that her words had caused him any pain.

His head moved almost imperceptively. "And this from a woman who hadn't been laid in two years."

The crude slang word, so inaccurately describing what they'd shared, pierced her and she steeled herself against the convulsive flinch that rocked through her.

He leaned forward, his voice low. "You're conveniently forgetting a few details. I was there too, Lori. I heard the begging. I heard the ecstatic moaning and it took a few days for the scratches on my back to heal. There's no way you've forgotten lying in my arms so long you almost left it too late to get home. The only reason you didn't stay all night was because of Kyle."

The truth of his words rained down on her, burning like

acid but she couldn't buckle. "Think whatever you want to think but I'm not putting up with this." She moved to rise.

His hand came down over hers in a firm human-handcuff grip. "You're running scared, Lori, and I'm not going away, so tell me now."

For a moment, a spark of heat set off a coil of need spiraling deep inside her, and then pain and despair shrouded her in a suffocating cloak. With shocking clarity she realized that nothing could get any worse than this. She'd lost him anyway and the only thing left was to deal with the inevitable look of pity from those intelligent gray eyes.

"I've got breast cancer."

Brian dropped his hand as his stomach turned over and bile scalded his throat. *Cancer.* Of all the things that had caused her to walk away from him that scenario had never even entered his head. *Cancer. His Lori. No!*

Fear exploded inside him, the terror rolling through him until it touched and stained every part of him. He wanted to haul her close, hold her tight and protect her from the malignant harm.

She didn't tell you. Pain cramped his heart. She'd deliberately shut him out of her life during a time of enormous need. But he shouldn't focus on that. He had to treat this like work and stay on task, finding out all the details so he knew exactly what he was dealing with.

"Are you having treatment? Are the doctors hopeful you'll recover?"

She nodded, her mouth tight. "The prognosis is very good."

"Thank God." He blew out a long breath, wanting to punch the air but he heard her sharp intake of breath and caught her look of utter anguish which tore him apart. He immediately clarified. "This is a good thing, right?"

She struck her chest with the side of her hand, her face lined with pain. "Brian, the reason the prognosis is good is because I no longer have any breasts."

Her raw emotion stuck him in the gut like a jagged knife and words seemed useless. "I'm sorry."

Her cheeks hollowed and her voice developed an edge. "I knew you would be."

He frowned, suddenly feeling like he was in a dark building with an unpredictable armed fugitive who could open fire at any moment. "Of course I'm sorry."

"Exactly, and to save you the embarrassment of making up some excuse I didn't return your calls."

No matter how he reconstructed her reply, it made no sense. "What the hell are you talking about? What excuse?"

Her nostrils flared as she spoke in a whispered hiss. "As you so adroitly reminded me five minutes ago I was there in bed with you. Your face and hands spent more time against my breasts than any other part of my body and let's not forget the glowing testimony you gave to them before you painted them with chocolate and licked them clean."

Shock slugged him so hard he thought he'd been hit by a bullet from his service revolver. He leaned forward, pulling on every fiber of restraint so he didn't yell. "You think I had sex with you because you were stacked?"

Her fingers gripped the table edge. "You do the math."

"Here're your Norwegian meatballs." Cindy giggled as she set down the plates in front of them—two large round meatballs together on each plate with sauce dribbled on the very top. They looked like a set of pert breasts complete with nipples.

With a muffled cry Lori slid to the end of the bench, pushed past the waitress, grabbed her coat off the rack and fled.

He didn't try to stop her. If she thought that little of him then what was the point?

Cindy turned to him, questions and curiosity in her eyes.

"She got a call and had to leave."

"Oh, will she be back?"

He shook his head and pulled money out of his wallet. "I have to leave as well."

"I can put these in a take-out box?"

"No thanks." The thought of eating curdled his stomach. "I'll take the coffee to go." He moved through the diner, nodding to people, taking his change, answering questions about the new winter-parking regulations and all the time gut-clenching anger churned through him.

Somehow he made it out of the diner and into the squad car. With the siren blaring and a squeal of tires he drove out of town heading nowhere, the control of the speeding car blessedly taking all his attention. He finally turned into the empty rest area where Tildy's car had been stolen, remembering the morning report of a fallen tree across the exit, and he cut the engine.

Not caring about the driving wind or the stinging snow, he got out of the car, slamming the door so hard that the vehicle rocked. His chest burned tight and he threw his head back letting his mouth fall open, finally releasing the roar he'd kept in for too long. A ragged sound came back to him, hollow and desolate like the barren trees around him.

He stomped around to the trunk, opened it, hauled out an

axe before heading toward the fallen tree. Raising the wooden handle high above his head, he brought the blade down with a thwack. The head buried itself deep into the wood.

The woman he loved had reduced his feelings for her down to being dependent on a pair of breasts.

He raised the axe high above his head. *Thwack.* Wood splinters flew into the air and then fell back to earth, beating the snow.

He'd loved her for so long he could hardly remember a time when he hadn't. He'd come back to Hobin the moment he'd heard her divorce was final and had subjugated all his sexual feelings with exercise and cold showers so as not to go too fast and scare her.

The low creak of cracking wood resonated as the log broke apart. Shit, he'd gone slowly. He'd been understanding and had got to know her kid which was no hardship. He loved Kyle. He'd never rushed her, and she'd eventually come to him on her terms. Now he was the one being accused of only seeing her as body parts? As a set of breasts.

He roared again but this time in the echo he heard Tildy's distinctive voice. *Waiting for her is not going to work for you this time.*

Well, duh! It hadn't worked the first time. He'd waited for years and where had that got him? He should have been a prick and jumped her like he'd wanted to the moment he'd arrived back in Hobin. Breathing hard, he heaved a section of the now-split log to the side of the road. Four back-breaking, lung-burning trips later, the exit was clear and his heart rate started to slow. He stared around at the isolated picnic area—stark and empty just like his life.

The nice guy will get hammered. He stowed the axe and

slammed the trunk shut. Hell, his bad guy had got hammered too. He thought of his tough tactics in the diner, the stunned expression on Lori's beautiful face and how her eyes had pooled with sadness when he'd blackmailed her. A jet of remorse spurted up at the memory of her look when his hand had cuffed hers.

It was immediately overlaid with a memory of the softness of her skin under his fingers and, like a movie reeling through his head, he suddenly saw it all again in slow motion—his arm reaching across the table, his hand circling her wrist and her baby-blue eyes flaring with momentary heat before flooding with misery.

Heat. He revisited the image again, convinced he hadn't imagined it. She'd wanted his touch, so why the hell was she pushing him away?

He welcomed the snow whipping his skin, the pain being so much less than the mess of uncompleted and perplexing thoughts spinning in his head and leading him nowhere. He had nothing. Rubbing his temples, he drew on hard-learned lessons from years of being a cop. Police work came down to facts and intuition.

Lori had been diagnosed with cancer. The cancer was being treated. Lori was in less danger than she'd been before and the prognosis was good. She still wanted him and, so help him, he wanted her. He needed her in his life like his body needed oxygen. So what was the problem?

The testimony to my breasts.

To save you the embarrassment of making up some excuse.

I have no breasts.

The verdict came clanging in loud and ringing like the closing of cell doors.

Brian, be prepared for a fight.

Oh, he'd fight but what tactics did he use to fight for a woman he loved who no longer saw herself as desirable and believed he didn't either?

"Why do you call it tuna fish when the only thing in the world called tuna is a fish?" Matilda laughed as she slapped mayonnaise on bread in preparation for lunch.

Elsa smiled in her quiet way as she set the table. "I guess for the same reason you call beets, beetroot. Is Marc home for lunch?"

Matilda glanced at the fridge, searching for the ubiquitous note; their communication having gone from as intimate as a couple could get, to bullet-point memos held in place by an advertising magnet. But then they'd never been a couple. They'd just had sex.

Mind-blowing, amazing sex and then, in a heartbeat, he'd gone from a generous, giving and considerate lover to a man who couldn't see past his own wants and it made no sense.

She'd been furious with him.

He had a loving mother and caring sisters, all who took great interest in him and his life. How could he not see that and value it? Instead, he could only see them in terms of unwanted reliance which confined and restrained him.

And she was still furious at herself. At the time she'd been so livid at him for the way he threw away the love of family—a thing she'd always craved—and at the same time she'd been so insecure about her own desirability that she'd let his jibe about "who was she working for" take on a sexual tone.

She'd deliberately misconstrued him which was totally unfair. He hadn't bought her. She'd gone with him willingly. Oh-so willingly that it scared her.

She'd maintained her rage for a day—the day he'd apologized by letter, paid her salary in full and tried to give her a ridiculously expensive pendant. She'd refused the lot. She didn't for a moment regret refusing the money or the jewelry but she should have accepted his apology because despite his lapse and his immature attitude to his family he was a good and decent man, which was more than could be said for the other men she'd let into her life.

He in turn had become polite and distant and she missed his laugh, his teasing and, God help her, she missed the sex. No, she craved it. It was as if he'd flicked a switch in her body, bringing it alive in a way it never had been before. She ached for it. Ached for him. But it was all too hard so she'd gone into protective mode, trying to keep sane living in close proximity to a man who'd rocked her world.

For almost a week she'd deliberately kept herself very busy and surrounded by people so there'd been no time to think. She'd spring-cleaned Lori's house even though it was winter, filled the freezer with food, and created a website for Weddings Are Hobin. She'd also taken two phone meetings with prospective clients, placated Vanessa who'd returned to Philly but still wanted to try on Nana's dress, assisted Elsa with her blood-pressure monitor and medication, as well as helped Kyle get his book report beyond the opening line of, "This book totally sucks." But still her thoughts strayed to Marc.

Her eyes finally found his firm, clear script on the yellow sticky note attached to the fridge. "The memo says, 'No for lunch.'" Just as it had for most of the week. She slid the sandwiches into the sandwich maker.

Elsa nodded. "He's always been concise and precise which probably lends itself to all those intricate calculations required for architecture." Her face took on a pensive look where happiness and sadness dueled. "When Hal died, Marc drove his sisters mad with his chore board and black and red marker pens, but he kept us afloat, kept the family wheels turning. It was enough for me just to get to work and home again."

The older woman's disclosure was unexpected and Matilda could hear both the gratitude she held for her son as well as painful memories in her voice. "It must have been a tough time for you."

"It was. Sometimes it still is. I miss Hal every day but I have the joy of knowing I was one of the lucky ones to have experienced a wonderful love. I wish all my children could find that."

Matilda immediately thought of Brian and the determined warrior look in his enigmatic gray eyes. "There's always hope."

Elsa sighed. "Lori's scars run a lot deeper than the surgeon's knife and Marc is far too independent for love, just like you are."

The knife Matilda held clattered to the bench and she covered by sliding the toasted sandwiches onto a plate. The usually reserved woman was full of surprises today. "Elsa, I was so caught up with Nana's crazy dream for me that I let a man steal all my money. How is that independent?"

The older woman patted her hand. "That was a grief-induced lapse."

And what would you call having sex with your son in so many different ways we could hardly walk, let alone see straight?

Elsa continued. "The real you is here in this kitchen, doing everything for everyone and not letting anyone do anything for you."

The touch and words of the reticent woman sent traitor-

ous feelings of belonging winding through her. She jumped
on them instantly, and savagely cut through the toasted sandwiches. "I'm no saint, Elsa. This arrangement was purely business. I needed the money and Marc paid me to care for the
family."

"I know, honey. He paid you to do a job he believes he
should be doing but doesn't want to." She folded the napkins.
"Marc doesn't let anyone do anything for him either. I know
because I've tried many times. I think he believes by not letting anyone get close it keeps him safe. The thing is, if the
heart is kept safe, it just shrivels."

Matilda turned the words over in her head as Lori walked
into the kitchen.

"What shrivels, Mom?"

Elsa didn't skip a beat. "Green tender shoots with an early
frost."

Matilda chewed her lip. Elsa had opened up to the wrong
person in the household. She should be having the "great
love" conversation with her daughter because at least Lori
still had a chance.

CHAPTER FIFTEEN

In stark contrast to his usual site meetings where the buzz of traffic, the head-jarring sound of jackhammers and the sheer life-force of New York City surrounded him, Marc stood knee-deep in snow, gazing up at the distinctive gambrel roof of an old red barn. His fingers scraped across the field stone wall as he breathed in the fading scent of cattle, hay and milk which clung determinedly to the barn, dredging up buried memories he hadn't visited in years. Like recollections of helping his father in a similar barn, milking cows and learning how to plane wood and bevel edges. Not to mention the endless hours of painting the exterior wood so it survived yet another long and tough winter.

With a huff of surprise he realized his love for buildings had probably started in a place just like this and had taken him a world away to New York City. That got him thinking about the office, and he checked his watch seeing he still had ten minutes before the daily conference call. Not that he had anything new to report on the Matheson account.

He walked back inside the barn where Peggy and Matilda waited. For half an hour he'd examined every part of the barn inside and out, including clambering into the loft up a rickety wooden ladder. Throughout it all he'd listened to Peggy's vision for the icon in a stream of nonstop chatter.

Matilda however had been remarkably silent and surprisingly lacking in opinion. Twice he'd needed to stop himself from asking her what she thought, and that really irked him. He should be happy that for once she wasn't giving out unsolicited and unwanted advice, so he couldn't believe he'd almost requested it.

He dragged his hand through his hair as he snuck a long look at her. Her down coat covered her torso giving her the distinctive androgynous lumpy look that only winter in Wisconsin could generate, but he could too easily picture what was underneath and his brain took him there in an instant— small but pert breasts nestled in lace and an ocean of creamy skin that he'd touched, tasted and explored six days ago.

Six days of unrelenting irritation, intermittent hard-ons and numerous cold showers. Initial fury at her for dishing out unqualified advice had turned into a bone-deep frustration at himself that not work, exercise or even a night at the Spotted Cow could douse. His body craved to have her wrapped around him again and his mind wanted the buzz that came from having sex with Matilda. Unlike the other women he allowed into his life for short sojourns, Matilda didn't seem to want anything from him and that put him on shaky ground. Jewelry had always worked for him in the past but she'd refused the pendant in the pale blue box, and he knew that the only reason she'd cashed his check was because she'd be destitute without it. But damn it, she made it hard to apologize and he really regretted what he'd said.

He would have moved out of Lori's except that would have caused more questions than it was worth so instead, sick of the treadmill, he bought a rowing machine and installed it in the basement. If he wasn't getting any then at least he'd be fit.

But what the hell was he doing letting her get away with this? It wasn't his life that was totally screwed, having been conned out of everything he owned. As for her jibe about him needing to grow up she had no idea about family life or the responsibilities of being the eldest, seeing she was an only child with parents who seemed disinterested in her life.

He, unlike her, was at least in charge of his life. He steered it and that was why he was a successful architect with a proven design record and a proven track record with women. All he needed to fix this was some one-on-one time alone with her. He just had to get rid of Peggy.

"So, is it possible?" Peggy Hendrix, Hobin's mayor, clapped her gloved hands against the cold, her expression expectant.

He tilted his head in thought. "Well, anything's possible, but does that mean it should be done?"

"Marc, this is Hobin's new dawn. People from Chicago, Madison and Minneapolis want a rural experience."

"Next you'll be asking me to cover the bridge."

Matilda suddenly turned around. "That's an excellent idea, Blondie. Now you're really thinking."

Her use of his nickname made him smile. Did he detect a thaw? Was the ice melting after all? So it should given the amount of heat they generated just standing next to each other.

Matilda pointed across a frozen brook lined with frost-encrusted gnarly maples. "Peggy's vision's a good one. The log church is just through that grove of trees and from late spring to autumn the bridal party and guests can walk through a wonderland of shadowy foliage, shards of sunlight and pretty wildflowers to get to here. Then we wow them with the barn where rustic ambience meets modern elegance and style."

Her eyes glowed with wonder, as if she had a vivid 3-D picture in her head, holding all the details from the vastness of a clear blue sky down to the minutia of the ladybug landing on the vivid yellow black-eyed Susans that dotted the meadows in spring. All he could see was endless snow and cold and that annoyed the hell out of him. Damn it, he was the architect. He was the one with vision but it had eluded him for weeks.

After what Barry-the-Bastard had done to her, how could she still see things through rose-colored glasses? "How do you even know about foliage and wildflowers? You've never been here in spring or summer." He could hear the irritability in his voice and that made him feel even more out of sorts.

She grinned. "I've read *Wisconsin's Rustic Roads* and studied the pictures."

"Hah. Did you tell her about the spring mud, Peggy?"

Peggy laughed. "Marc, we can work our way around a bit of mud. We have a church people want to use and this project would add value to that and bring money into Hobin."

Sunlight crept through the gaps in the barn wall, dancing on the exposed beams that bore the history of a hundred years of use. A rapid play of ideas for the barn ran through his head which he immediately closed his mind against. His concentration needed to be on the conversion of the Matheson building.

"This place has soul." Matilda leaned up against a supporting beam, her head tilted back, staring up into the forty-foot ceiling, as a dreamy look rolled across her face. "I reckon you could come up with something that retained the rustic charm and history of the place but gave it a classic elegance with modern conveniences to satisfy the punters."

Matilda's words mirrored his half-thought-out ideas that he'd dumped because he didn't do work like this. "Unfortunately, I'm too busy with a project."

She pushed off the beam, and a furrow creased her brow. "The one that's been gathering dust on the table for almost two weeks?"

He didn't like her inference that nothing much seemed to be happening with the Matheson account even though it was the truth. "That's the one. I've just had a breakthrough." *Liar.*

Peggy checked her watch. "I have to head back to the shop but what do you think?"

It's a crazy idea. "I've got a pretty big project on in New York at the moment, Peggy. Why not try one of the Wausau firms?"

She wriggled her nose. "I suppose, I could. It's just that someone local would be best."

His open palm hit a wooden upright. "I've lived in New York for a decade!"

Matilda raised one quizzical brow but Peggy didn't react at all to his overly loud voice, instead she just smiled. "Yes, but Hobin's home. No one expects you to decide right this minute, Marc. You think on it and I'll call you in a few days to get your answer then."

He resisted the urge to slam his forehead into a beam. Instead he leaned his head back against the wall, silently groaning.

Peggy walked toward the door and Matilda pushed off the beam she'd been leaning against and followed her.

Peggy stopped abruptly, her face creasing in consternation.

"Oh, I got so caught up with the barn I forgot to show you the house." She pulled a key off the bunch around her neck. "Marc, if you go through it with Tildy then can you drop her back in town?"

Thank you, Peggy. He forgave the pushy mayor on the spot and tried hard not to grin wide and long. "I can do that."

Matilda's shoulders squared in the now-familiar intransigent position. "Peggy, I've got an appointment with Rosie Girtin."

"At three o'clock, which is four hours away, so you have plenty of time." Peggy was in full flight and handed the key to Marc while instructing Matilda. "Tell him the idea, Tildy, so he can get the full picture. Even though the house would be stage two of the project it all has to flow."

"You heard Marc. He's far too busy." Matilda swung around to him, her eyes screaming, "You say yes and you're dead meat."

He met her gaze and smiled. Finally the planets in his world were aligning. "I'll return Matilda and your key this afternoon, Peggy."

But the busy mayor was already out the door, heading toward her car, her arm in the air giving them a backward wave.

He stepped in next to Matilda wanting to pull her close and kiss her hard but he kept his arms by his side. "I've missed you."

Her chin shot up but not fast enough to hide the glint of desire that fired the emerald facets in her eyes. "You see me every day."

"Along with your rent-a-crowd."

"That would be your family."

"And Peggy and Gracie. Not to mention yesterday's sudden conversation with Stefan Grayson when I came out of Norsk's."

Her head tilted stubbornly but her lips twitched guiltily. "We were having a long awaited business discussion about a line of folk art."

"You were avoiding me." He closed the slight distance between them so his side connected with hers, touching all the way from shoulder to ankle. "We had a fight. Both of us said things we regret, hell I know I did." His hand tugged at his hair. "I've tried to apologize in every way I know how and I'm asking you, please don't let one mistake get in the way of something that's good for both of us."

She didn't step away but her eyes widened. "And let me guess, that something would be hot sex."

"Well, I was going to say your *adventure* but your words work so much better." Grinning, he gently nudged her hip with his. "Besides, you know you want me."

The muscles on her face fought but the smile won. "Yeah, right. I dream of spoiled egocentric architects every night."

"I know you do." He whispered the words into her ear and felt her body shudder and then go slack against his for the briefest moment.

Yes.

She straightened up. "Come on, let's go and look at this house."

"Good idea. We'll look at the house and then we'll get naked and make up for a week of lost time."

"You are so dreaming."

"Sweetheart, this isn't about me. It's all about you. I'm your temporary lover, helping you have the adventure you deserve."

She shot him a wry smile. "You're all heart."

He hooked her gaze. "No, not all of me."

Her pupils dilated into inky discs of desire as her gaze swept him, before she turned abruptly and stalked to the door.

Laughing, he followed her out of the barn, his step light. Matilda's permafrost had thawed and the thought of the next few weeks in Hobin suddenly seemed pleasant. They turned in the opposite direction from the church, and she led him along a wire fence before striking out through a second grove of trees. The path was narrow and the snow deep, forcing him to walk behind her in single file.

As he followed her into a clearing, he got his first glimpse of a steeply pitched and shingled asymmetrical roof. Then he saw the distinctive Queen Anne tower with its conical crown, a two-storey wraparound porch and the remains of what had once been delicate turned porch posts and lacy, ornamental spindles. In sharp contrast to the clean lines of the Prairie School which he favored, he couldn't help but have a surge of affection for the old girl and her architectural excesses. "This is the old Gutherson House."

She flicked up her coat collar against the cold wind that had sprung up. "It's gorgeous, isn't it?"

"She's a grand old dame, that's for sure, and was once the most expensive house ever built in Hobin."

He caught her hand as he stepped past her and up onto the worn stone steps. Tugging her with him, he strode across the wide porch and into the entrance hall, and wondered about all the people who'd crossed the house's threshold in the last one hundred and twenty years. "Does Peggy own her?"

They walked into a large room which would have been the parlor. "Not yet. The current owners are in Chicago and are thinking of selling. Peggy's leased it and has been subletting it over the summer as a self-contained vacation home. It reminds me of Nana's place with its overstuffed couches and faded carpet runners. Can't you just imagine kids charging around on the lawn playing cricket?"

She slid her hand out of his and leaned her palms against the huge window seat, staring out onto the snow.

Her face wore the same dreamy look he'd seen in the barn and a tug of something indefinable pulled at him, making waves in his perennial restlessness. He ignored it. "Nah, they wouldn't be playing cricket. No one even knows what that is here, and anyway, it's far too dangerous."

Her head turned to the side so fast, her curls whipped her face. "How is cricket dangerous?"

"You can get badly burned drinking tea."

Her laugh tinkled around the shabby room and he realized how much he'd missed the sound. "The kids would be playing baseball in the summer and tackling each other in early fall as they worked on their football skills."

"No matter the sports, this house is designed for a family." A moment later she seemed to give herself a shake. "Come and see the rest of it."

Matilda walked him through all the downstairs rooms. "Peggy sees this as a bed-and-breakfast and honeymoon suite to go along with the barn reception center and the log church. With a lot of love, this house could shine again."

He knew all Peggy could see was dollar signs and shrewd business decisions. He looked around at the large, once-elegant rooms now tattered with age and a lack of care and suddenly a flash of images shot across his mind showing him how it could look again. "With a lot of money poured into it this house could shine again."

She ran her hand along the carved wooden staircase. "Money would help but without love in the detail it's just bricks and mortar."

He knew what she meant and for some reason he instantly thought about the Matheson project. A project where money was no object but his ideas for the design were slow in coming.

His phone rang. "Sorry, I need to take this call. It's the office."

"No worries, you take the call and I'll go make some coffee." She walked off toward the kitchen.

"Marc, how's the dairy heartland treating you?" The booming voice of Phillip Evans, the senior partner of the firm, came down the line. "Got your fill of deep-fried cheese curds?"

Marc forced a laugh. It was one thing for him to joke about his childhood state and another for people who'd never lived here. "It's as cold and snowbound as I remember."

"Look, I'll get straight to the point. Matheson is antsy about the delay on his project and you're tied up with family so we need you to hand it over to Richard so he can cut his teeth on it."

A whoosh of cold air hit his lungs, instantly cramping them. Richard was the new associate. "That won't be necessary, Phillip. I've got it under control."

A sigh sounded down the line. "Marc, you've had the project since September and nothing has moved."

"Good work takes time."

"Everyone has a dry spell—"

"I'm not having a dry spell," he hissed down the phone, his voice low.

"Suit yourself, but your sister's ill and that can take the edge off your game, which is why Richard's taking over the project. Meanwhile, focus on your family, Marc, and relax into the bucolic experience. It might just be what you need."

Before he could speak he heard a click and the long beep of a disconnected line. He'd just been screwed by the senior partner.

Fury ricocheted through him, raging against the unjust decision. He swung around, crouching down into a low squat, pulling his arms over his head, before pushing them forward and rising with a roar.

"Fuck!"

Hobin had done it again—detained him against his will, plunged him into the heartland of his family and now for the first time in his career he'd lost an account.

The bellow brought Matilda running from the kitchen.

Marc stood staring out the window, his glittering golden aura unusually dim like tarnished brass, and his sky-blue eyes now the steely color of a heavy snow-filled cloud. She'd seen him laughing. She'd seen him furious and frustrated but she'd never seen him look like this—as if something monumental had just dropped out of his well-ordered world.

Her stomach rolled for him. She was all too familiar with that feeling.

He pushed off the window sill, a look of torment clear in his eyes. "Don't even think about asking."

Her heart spasmed for him inside its protective box. Marc defined himself by his work and its rewards, and every fiber in her gut told her this was to do with work. Perhaps with the plans that he'd avoided more than worked on. "Okay."

"I *don't* want to talk about it."

Of course you don't. It involves your feelings. She bit her lip hard to keep from asking. "Fair enough."

In two strides he was by her side, pulling her into his arms and slamming his lips against hers—stealing a kiss, stealing her breath, and when he finally raised his head he'd taken a part of her with him. Then grabbing her hand, he marched her out of the room and up the stairs.

She stumbled, trying to keep up with him, and his arm shot out to steady her but he didn't slow his pace as he stormed past the minor bedrooms with their single beds and mismatched quilts until he found the master bedroom.

The room screamed retro-cozy, reminiscent of less complicated times. Faded braided rugs covered the floorboards, lace curtains hung on the windows, and a two-seater couch covered in a riot of brightly covered cushions sat in the bay window, a perfect place to snuggle up with someone and enjoy the view across the fields and down toward the lake. A large pine box was positioned at the end of an old standard double bed with a utilitarian wooden headboard. Freshly made, and covered with a wedding-ring quilt, it sat as if it was waiting for the next occupants. She bit her lip. Nana and Grandpa Hank's bed had looked just like this. A bed for love.

He unzipped his jacket and kicked off his shoes, the actions brisk and purposeful. "Take off your coat."

She reminded herself this wasn't anything to do with love. "You're such a romantic."

"Matilda." He growled her name in a low warning but there was no threat in his expression. His face held only pain. "Are you getting naked or not?"

She should have been outraged but her Viking, the man always in control and in charge, was unraveling before her.

Gone was the façade of urbanity, gone was the silver-tongued charmer—all of it had been stripped away. Instead he stood before her bereft as if he'd lost his anchor and been set adrift at sea. Her heart ached for him as his hurt tore into her.

He needed her. She slipped off her coat, pulled her sweater over her head and unbuttoned her blouse until she stood shivering in her underwear so she dived under the feather quilt.

"About damn time." He pulled off the rest of his clothes and followed her into bed. His hands immediately reached for her and he pulled her against him, holding her tightly as if he couldn't let her go. Burying his face in her hair, he took in a long, deep breath and his body slackened for the briefest of moments before the tension returned with a slam that rocked right through her. Then he rolled her over until she lay underneath him, pinned against the soft mattress.

There was nothing soft about his kisses. He had his eyes shut tight as if he was in a trance, and his chest heaved as he rained hard and urgent kisses down on her mouth. Kisses filled with the air of desperation. It was as if every touch of his lips against hers would expunge whatever was driving him. Kissing her to gain back control. Kissing her to block out pain. His pain.

Her heart bled—not for herself but for him. She wrapped her arms around him, needing to give him something to ease the turmoil in his soul. Wanting to comfort and protect him. Gently, she slid her hands along his back, slowly skimming the tips of her fingers against his hot skin in a way she knew he loved. In a way she loved, and she traversed his entire back touching every sinew, bone and muscle until she'd caressed every inch of glorious skin. She held him in her arms, keeping him close and giving him the shelter and protection she was certain he needed but from exactly what, she had no idea. All she knew was that she had to do this for him.

A sigh shuddered into her mouth and the pressure of his lips eased but she could still feel the hammering of his heart. "Marc?"

"Hmm." His tongue was tracing a gentle line along her cheek exactly the way she liked it.

She fought to focus. "Better now?"

But he didn't raise his head or reply. Instead, his hand found her breast and her nipple instantly puckered, lapping up his touch as it always did. With long shards of intoxicating sensation shooting through her like an arrow heading straight down deep to vibrate between her legs, her body took over on a pleasure mission and she lost all conscious thought. His tongue, which had unhurriedly roved across her cheek, reached her ear. With deliberate strokes of his tongue and tiny nibbles of his teeth, he outlined her ear, pausing now and then until she wanted to scream, "Just keep going." Then his mouth zeroed on the one spot that made her buck toward him. Every. Single. Time.

She pressed her hips against his, feeling his erection against her thigh, wanting to have him inside her. "Please, Marc."

But instead of moving into her, he silenced her again only this time with a kiss that gave as much as it took. When he finally broke the touch, it was like part of her had gone with him and she wanted to haul his lips back to hers to stop the bereft feeling in its tracks. She reached for his head but a second later his mouth touched the hollow in her neck and started journeying downward and her arms fell to her side, weak with need. With every flick of his tongue, every nip of his teeth and every press of his lips, excruciating pleasure built on itself until the sensations morphed into a huge ball of ecstatic promise that had her head thrashing against the pillow and her begging for release. "Marc, you're killing me."

Again, he didn't reply. Instead, he slid two fingers inside her and with a whoop of gratitude, her muscles gripped them and she instantly shattered with a scream. As the last waves of her orgasm ebbed away she pulled him close, angling her now wet and ready body to receive him. "Your turn now."

He stared down at her for a moment with lust-filled eyes. "Our turn."

He entered her and she cried out with the joy of having him fill her. Filling the aching void that had been part of her for so long. With long, rhythmic thrusts he rose over her, driving her higher and higher until she spun out and exploded again on a wave of bliss. She seemed to float over him in a myriad of parts before she reassembled around him as he continued to move in her—harder, faster and more and more frantic. It was like he was sucking her up as if his life depended on it.

She wanted to watch him. Wanted to see his face when he shattered so she cupped his cheek with her hand. He shuddered over her with an anguished cry that tore through her and she caught the moment raw pain broke through his lust and he stared blindly down at her. His hurt burned through her fingers and scorched her all the way down to her toes. A trickle of dampness rolled down her cheek and she realized she was crying. His pain had become her pain. His hurt was her hurt. It was as if something unknown had somehow linked them together, forging a bond she'd never experienced with anyone.

That's love.

He sagged against her, pulling her close and burying his face in her hair, and her breath stalled. She couldn't possibly love Marc. She couldn't possibly be that stupid. Love went together with the dream of marriage and a family. What was going on here had nothing to do with either. He was her adventure, hot sex for the taking. A gorgeous man to play with, a man who in everyday circumstances wouldn't even look at her. This was her opportunity to do something for herself amidst the detritus of her life.

What just happened wasn't just hot sex. There was raw, primal pain.

She squeezed her eyes shut against the swirl of unfamiliar emotions that battered her—pleasure, pain and an intensely heavy feeling that rolled through her, a feeling she couldn't recognize or decipher. She'd been in love before and it felt nothing like this.

You only thought you were in love.

No! She railed against the thought. Of course she'd been in love. She hadn't loved Barry but she'd loved Jason. She'd invested in the dream with him and had been left with a crumpled and crushed reality. Then Barry had put the icing on the cake. Now she'd retired the dream and love was something that happened to other people.

I don't love Marc!

A tiny part of her heart quivered, and right then she knew she might be in serious trouble.

CHAPTER SIXTEEN

"That lipstick's new and it suits the new top I brought over." Gracie sat in Lori's kitchen, sipping coffee. "Did you pick it up in Wausau?"

Since running into Brian at Norsk's, Lori had blamed not driving for avoiding town and had suggested Gracie come visit her at home. "It got delivered here yesterday with a heap of stuff for Marc. I'm figuring he threw out the advertising brochure that came with it which is a shame because I really like it. Not only does the color suit me, it tastes like raspberry chocolate."

Gracie laughed. "That's perfect for you. You've always been a sucker for chocolate." She nibbled on one of Tildy's buttery Yo-Yos. "When do you think you'll be back at work?"

"Straight after winter break, although now my concentration's coming back I promised to do some English grading next week."

"That's a good way to ease back into the job." Gracie refilled her coffee mug. "So how are you planning to ease back into the rest of your life?"

Lori tried to duck the direct look from her friend's chocolate-brown eyes. "My life is Kyle and school so there's nothing else to ease back into."

"Peggy and I missed you at the Spotted Cow last night."

She shrugged. "By the end of the day I'm exhausted."

"So we'll do lunch."

She immediately thought of the last disastrous time she'd tried to do lunch. "And if the shop gets busy?"

"Sunday lunch then, when the shop is closed. Come on, Lori, you'll get cabin fever if you don't get out."

"I'll think about it." But she had no intention of doing any such thing. Right now it was enough just to get up each morning and put one foot in front of the other.

"You do that." Gracie drained her mug, rose and set it on the counter.

Lori heard the chirruping of her cell, the tone telling her she had a message. "I better get that. It might be Kyle." She crossed the kitchen to her purse and plucked the phone from inside its depths. Reading the message, she half laughed but couldn't quite stop a sigh of regret.

"Something wrong?" Gracie peered over her shoulder.

She shook her head. "It's got to be a wrong number."

"Why? What does it say?"

"'I'll never forget the taste of your lips against mine.'"

"Whoa, let me see that?" Gracie grabbed the phone and studied the screen. "I'd be smiling all day if I had someone sending me a text like that. But who is it? It just says the number, no name."

"Like I said, not from anyone in my contacts so a wrong number."

"Pity." Gracie winked. "Especially as you taste like chocolate."

"Don't be ridiculous, Gracie." The words came out harsher than she intended.

Gracie's mouth firmed into a hard line. "You lost your breasts and I'm real sorry about that but you still have every other erogenous zone on your body, Lori Perez, so you remember that."

The shock of her friend's words made her flinch, and she didn't know quite what to say or feel. Gracie was her oldest girlfriend and had always been there for her in every high and low of her life, always supporting and understanding. Until this moment. "Just delete the message, okay."

"I'll leave that to you after you've enjoyed it some more." Gracie handed her back the phone and kissed her on the cheek. "I've gotta run. Tildy put a Gracie's icon on the wedding website and linked it to my new site. Now the bride from Chicago wants a phone meeting about honeymoon fashions."

Lori's mouth twitched. "Isn't that the naked look?"

Gracie laughed. "Sweetie, if I have anything to do with it, this bride is going to have eight different outfits to get naked from."

She waved goodbye to her friend, happy that Gracie's store seemed to finally be taking off. Wiping the table and putting the uneaten cookies back in their airtight container took about two minutes and then she looked around for something to do. But all she could see was a neat and tidy house. Tildy had the laundry under control, supper gently cooking in the slow cooker and she'd mopped the bathrooms before driving into town.

Lori passed the dining room table, the one place Tildy's cleaning never seemed to touch. Someone had added a few more pieces to the hardly started spaceship model but going on the pile of plastic bricks scattered across one end of the table it still had a very long way to go. She resisted the strong temptation to brush it all neatly into its box. Marc had always been very particular about anyone touching his things and he'd finally seemed a bit happier the last few days so she didn't want to rock the boat.

Maybe he'd finally got his current project finished. His laptop computer was shut off and all the plans had vanished so she was surprised to see sketches of a barn littering the table. Another page had measurements scribbled all over it and she found a series of photographs both long shots and close-ups of Gutherson House. He'd mentioned it in passing a few times, usually linking it with the words, "Peggy's crazy scheme" yet he seemed to be going there most days, which seemed odd when he'd been so determined a week ago not to have anything to do with the project.

The doorbell rang, interrupting her thoughts, and she walked out to answer it.

"Package for Lori Perez. Can you sign please?" A delivery man, dressed in a distinctive brown uniform, pushed a pen into her hand.

"Thanks." She accepted the parcel and as she closed the door, the words of a song from *The Sound of Music* played in her head. Usually deliveries were marked clearly with a store logo or brand but this had nothing stamped on the plain brown paper package bound up with string, other than a computer-printed address label.

She hadn't been expecting anything and a zip of excitement rushed through her. She marched to the kitchen and using scissors, snipped the string, automatically winding it around her fingers as her father had taught her. Then she ripped back the paper, revealing a small cardboard box. The heady scent of gardenia and vanilla immediately wafted into the room and she breathed in deeply, enjoying the rich intoxicating fragrance.

The box was sealed with clear packing tape so she quickly slid the point of the scissors along the gutter between the box edges. The flaps lifted back and four candles in frosted glasses lay snuggled in tissue paper along with a bottle of bubble bath.

Tildy barreled through the door clutching a sack of groceries, her face glowing pink and her eyes bright. "Wow. Where is that gorgeous fragrance coming from?"

Lori gazed at the box. "It's from these candles that just arrived."

"What a lovely gift." Tildy picked up a candle and breathed in deeply before exhaling a blissful sigh. "That's divine. Who sent them to you?"

"I'm still looking for the card." She searched the edges of the box for a note wondering who had sent such a thoughtful gift. She'd appreciated the flowers that had arrived from friends and colleagues but candles and bath gel were just that bit more personal. "Perhaps the card's at the bottom."

She unpacked the rest of the candles, flattened out the tissue paper and the packaging straw until all she had was an empty box. "Now that's odd. There's no note. Who would send something this thoughtful without a note?"

Tildy inspected the box and the paper. "I've seen candles

similar to this at Peggy's but she doesn't stock this brand so I guess that rules out someone in Hobin."

"But whoever sent them is going to think I'm rude for not saying thank you." She reexamined the candles and box looking for clues.

"Maybe the card's coming separately. Has the postie been yet? It might just be waiting in the letter box?"

She smiled at Tildy's Australian words for *mailbox* and *mailman*. "He's been and he only brought bills, but you're right. It might come tomorrow in the regular mail."

Tildy grabbed a pen and paper and started jotting herself a note. "Whoever sent them has great taste. I'm going to find out where they're made and add them to the website as ideas for honeymoon ambience."

Lori thought of the mistaken text and a twinge of regret pierced her. "These particular candles aren't going to have any romantic use."

"Oh, I don't know. If they make you feel special that's romantic. Why don't you go and light one now and have a bubble bath with that new book you've just started."

The farm-raised girl deep down inside her was scandalized. "It's four in the afternoon!"

Tildy laughed. "So? Sometimes you need to steal an afternoon. See it as being part of your convalescence now that all your tubes and stitches are out and everything is healed."

The thought appealed to her and she needed to feel normal again, whatever that was. But seeing herself naked still shocked her. What if she ran the bath deep and used the bubbles? That way she could hide the scars and just luxuriate in the fragrant air. Yet four in the afternoon seemed too decadent. "You're so busy I bet you never steal yourself an afternoon."

But Tildy was putting away groceries and had her head deep in the cupboard, and didn't reply.

Marc ran his hand through Tildy's hair as she lay snuggled up against him, her head resting on his chest. "This house is growing on me."

She laughed. "You've rented out the whole house but you're only using the bedroom."

"Not true. I used the shower with you just yesterday."

Her eyes immediately darkened to moss-green, a color he now associated with lust and unfettered desire. He immediately went hard. Again. It was amazing, given all the women he'd dated over the years, not one of them with their long legs, and catwalk good looks had ever aroused him as much as Matilda. She threw herself into sex with the same enthusiasm and passion she applied to everything else in her life and he appreciated her inventiveness and bigheartedness. Losing himself in her every afternoon as they shared uncomplicated sex in the gable bedroom of this old house was something he looked forward to each day.

Matilda wrapped her leg around his. "I can't believe Peggy just handed you over the keys without giving you the third degree on why you wanted them."

"I told her without the house I wouldn't consider the barn project."

She raised herself up on her elbow, her mouth pouting with disapproval. "You're using her."

He laughed thinking back over the haggling conversation he'd shared with the mayor. "No, she's a very savvy businesswoman and we're helping each other."

"Have you told your firm about the barn?"

He sighed. "I told you. This is nothing like the work we do and they won't be interested."

Lying in bed with her like this each afternoon, he'd discovered he enjoyed talking to her about all sorts of things, even topics he usually didn't discuss with the women he dated. But telling Matilda about the loss of the Matheson account had been unexpectedly easy. Not that it meant she didn't have an opinion about it.

She wriggled her nose. "So? Peggy's a client and this is an account just like any other. Evans, Gaynor and Associates can only benefit from being associated with Wisconsin's future top wedding venue."

A streak of envy tore through him at her belief and passion for the project. When had he last experienced that sort of all-encompassing buzz about his work? *Your life?*

"Matilda, it's a drafty old barn that will only be able to be used five months of the year."

"It's a design that your partners need to know about." She nudged him. "At the very least it's a billable account."

He laughed. "I forgot you're the budding businesswoman with your eye on the bottom line. Okay, I'll think about it."

"You do that." But her expression told him she saw too much. "You know you can pretend all you want that this project is a big drag and that you're only doing it because you're in town for Lori, but I've seen your drawings and I think you're enjoying yourself."

How had she managed to work that out? He was still surprised by the flickers of excitement that stirred and built every time he worked on the barn project and he wasn't sure he wanted to be that excited about it. It didn't come close to the work he was known for. But he didn't want to think or talk about work. For the first time since he'd left Hobin as a twenty-two-year-old with a clear vision of his future, the path ahead was filled with misty fog and visibility was down to zero. So he did the only thing that made sense. He kissed her.

Lori put down the brochures on breast reconstruction and sipped her coffee. She had to set a date for surgery and her doctor had suggested the spring. The thought of more surgery wasn't something she wanted to put her hand up for but surely silicone breasts had to feel more real than the rock-hard tennis-ball lumps of saline she had in her chest right now.

She'd had times of feeling completely normal, like the day she'd taken the bubble bath. Luxuriating in the fragrant water, surrounded by scented air and being massaged by the bubbling water of the spa, she'd been stunned to experience the faint stirrings of need. She'd burst into tears, a mixture of relief and grief. Gracie had been right about erogenous zones but that didn't change the fact that no man would find her sexy.

Her cell phone beeped with a message. A shimmer of excitement raced through her which was ridiculous, but yesterday at the same time in the afternoon another misdirected text had come through. She knew the words, "The scent of you intoxicates me," were not for her but right now she needed to pretend they were.

She opened up the text and disappointment sank through her. It was from Tildy asking if she needed anything from the grocery store. She texted back, "milk."

A text immediately sounded and she expected an okay from Tildy. She pressed the button—it wasn't from Tildy.

"The memory of your silken body wrapped around mine makes my day less gray."

A surge of heat burned between her legs despite common sense telling her not to be so damn stupid. A wave of guilt immediately followed. This guy deserved to know he was missing his target and the woman he was romancing deserved the buzz of receiving these texts. She owed the unknown woman that much.

Decision made, her fingers flew across the phone keys. "Sorry, this is not the woman you think it is. You have the wrong number." With a wave of sadness she pressed Send and immediately picked up the information sheet again, grounding herself in her own life not some unbelievable fantasy.

The front door slammed. "Mom?"

"In the kitchen, honey." She quickly put the brochures in a file and slid it under some papers. Although Kyle knew she needed more surgery he didn't want to know the ins and outs, and she didn't really blame him. "How was your day?"

Kyle dropped his bag and poured a glass of milk before slicing a large hunk of chocolate cake. "History's heinous but I got an A on my math test. Oh, and Brian's taking the team for ice-cream sundaes after basketball practice but he'll still drop me home as usual. Only later."

As usual? Her stomach dropped to her feet. "I thought Uncle Marc had been picking you up from practice."

He shook his head. "Nuh. He takes me and Sam like you did, but Brian drops us home same as always."

Just the same as it had been for the last year. A sharp pain throbbed at her temples. Ever since her surgery, she'd been going to bed early and she'd assumed Marc was doing both the drop-off and the pick-up basketball run. After everything that had happened between her and Brian, it never occurred to her that he'd still be bringing Kyle home. That he would still want to bring Kyle home.

After their last conversation he was supposed to have walked away hating her, not wanting to have anything to do with her because that was the only way it could be. She'd had to reject him before he could reject her. But he hadn't walked away from Kyle. She rubbed her temples hard with her fingers as guilt shredded her. Damn it, but he was too nice.

He wasn't nice last time you saw him. The memory of his hand clamping her wrist and the roar of longing that had poured through her at his touch, washed over her. Regret at losing something so good clawed at her gut. "Marc will pick you up from the ice-cream parlor." Her words snapped out harsh and loud.

"Aw, Mom, why? He hates driving me around. At least Brian talks about sports. Uncle Marc just plays lousy CDs."

A need to protect her loving but difficult brother surged inside her and she wished Kyle could see past Marc's aloofness. "Your uncle loves you and is happy to drive you around. If he hates anything, it's the truck. I think he misses driving his sports car, is all."

Her son shrugged as if to say, "whatever," as he rummaged through his bag before handing her a parcel wrapped in familiar brown paper and string. "Here's a package for you."

Surprise rocked her. "Who gave you this?"

"The delivery guy was about to pull into the driveway when I got off the bus so I signed for it. It feels like papers from school."

The sound of Marc honking the truck's horn blasted into the room.

"Gotta go, Mom. Coach hates it if we're late and don't forget I'm going to the ice-cream parlor." Kyle gave her a quick kiss and, shoving the cake into his mouth, he dashed out the door.

Lori reached out to touch the soft package. No card had ever arrived mentioning the candles and bath gel, and she'd gone through her address book trying to work out who might have sent them but had drawn a blank. She could account for everyone she knew really well and all had sent her flowers or a card.

The floppy package might be the papers she was to grade but she was ninety-nine percent certain the school would have put them in a padded envelope, and not wrapped them in brown paper. With trembling fingers, she unknotted the string and opened the paper. Two separate gifts came wrapped in pale blue tissue. She pulled at the multiple layers of the first until her hand touched cool, soft silk, the color of rich Swiss milk chocolate.

She gasped in wonder as she picked up a camisole top with wide pleats, which fell luxuriously from a high neck. Full-length pants sat neatly folded underneath. She raised the pajamas to her face, breathing in the light scent of vanilla, and loving the cool smoothness of the material against her cheeks. She'd never owned anything this gorgeous in her life and she could imagine how deliciously the silk would caress her body.

She opened the other package. A bolt of surprise rocked her and she was glad she was sitting down. Neatly folded in the layers of tissue was a set of gray silk men's pajamas. She picked them up and inhaled a faint scent of fresh pine.

The memory of your silken body wrapped around mine makes my day less gray.

She dropped the pajamas as if they were on fire and rustled her hands through the tissue paper looking for a note.

Nothing.

She shook out both tops and both bottoms expecting a gift tag but nothing fluttered to the floor. Not a single clue as to who had sent the pajamas. Just like the candles and bath gel.

The scent of you intoxicates me.

She flipped open her phone and somehow managed to get her fingers to cooperate and she located the first message. "The taste of your lips against mine is all I need."

Her tongue ran over her lips and she tasted raspberry chocolate. Her breath stalled in her throat as connections started synapsing. Marc hadn't thrown out any advertising brochures because this lip gloss wasn't a sample—it was a gift. Each text message was preceded by a gift.

As if completely in tune with her thoughts, her phone beeped again and her heart pounded so hard, she thought her ribs would bruise. The black text read, "Lori, your body's made for mine."

She stared at the words. Even though the phone number was completely new, the use of her name, the gifts so individual to her personal tastes and the amazing thoughtfulness left her in no doubt of the sender.

Brian. The man she'd tried so hard to drive away still wanted her.

Traitorous coils of warmth spread through her just like when his hand had cuffed hers, and just like when the bath gel and fragrant candles had surrounded her. Like an addict seeking her next hit, she immediately reread all the messages again. Jets of arousal surged through her, heating her face, making her skin tingle all over and pooling moisture between her legs.

She heard the clock chime and she realized she was sitting in her kitchen half-wild with longing which wasn't something she wanted to share with Marc, Tildy or heaven forbid, her mother, should any of them arrive. Grabbing the pajamas, she managed to rise on wobbly legs and stumble to her room.

She caught sight of herself in the mirror—eyes as wide as the Pacific, cheeks flushed pink and she knew right then that the cancer had only taken her breasts and had left the rest of her intact and that was the kicker. When she could hardly bear to look at herself, how could she let Brian look and touch her?

Her phone beeped with another text. Her heart kicked and another bolt of heat raced through her.

"Tell me what it feels like with the silk against your skin."

She started to text, "It's only 4:30 p.m." Good farm girls, responsible mothers and women recovering from mastectomies didn't lock their bedroom doors in the afternoon.

Steal an afternoon. Her fingers stopped working as excitement and guilt tangoed inside her making her dizzy. Could she really do this? She strained her ears and heard only silence. Should the others come home they'd assume she was resting and leave her be. On a surge of guilty pleasure she locked her bedroom door, stripped off all her clothes and let the decadent pajamas slide over her body.

She twirled in front of the mirror. The only exposed skin was on her arms. The halter-style top of the camisole curved around the base of her throat, totally covering her chest, and the trousers fell to her ankles. For the first time she saw more than just a woman who had lost her breasts. She lay down on her bed and messaged back, "Every part of me is stroked by silk."

A moment later Brian replied. "I want to stroke you. Where shall I start?"

A shiver of anticipation buzzed through her and she smiled a secret smile. That was easy and her fingers tapped out, "My feet."

"I remember the sounds you made when my tongue traced your arch."

The reminiscence flooded her and she lost herself in the memory of his firm fingers massaging her soles and the exquisite trails of sensation his mouth had created. Matching shimmers now vibrated along her legs and she managed to tap out, "Your kisses feel divine behind my knee."

"You're lying on your back watching me through smoky-blue eyes."

"I want you to keep touching me."

"I know. My hands are stroking your thighs with silk. Long firm sweeps, then soft tantalizing touches. Put your hands on mine."

The smoldering heat that had coiled inside her suddenly ignited. Brian's hands had coaxed her body alive when they'd made love and now his words were doing it again. Her own hands ran along the silk, trailing from her knee to her inner thigh, the touch excruciatingly divine. Her body ached and somehow through a haze of need she managed to type out, "I want to hear your voice."

The phone rang a moment later. "Brian."

"Lori." His husky voice matched hers. "Are your hands on mine?"

She managed to breathe out, "Yes."

"Do you feel safe?"

Oddly, she did. She felt cocooned in silky safety. "I do."

"Darling, you're the most gorgeous woman I've ever known. Today every part of you I touch is through silk and I'm only caressing you where you guide my hands. So where are my hands right now?"

Part of her wanted to cry but most of her pulsed with ragged need. "Your fingers are trailing up my inner thigh."

"How does it feel?"

"Wonderful."

"How far do you want my hands to go?"

"I want your hand to cup me and your thumb to caress me."

She heard the strain in his voice. "Is the silk sliding against your wetness?"

"Yes." It came out on a moan as her legs fell apart.

"God, Lori, you're beautiful."

Then she lost herself in his words and the touch of her hand which was his hand until nothing existed except the rush of sensation that took her away from every idea of herself.

CHAPTER SEVENTEEN

Matilda thought she was having a life-imitating-art moment except it suddenly occurred to her that perhaps her view was back to front. She'd always believed that American high school basketball games complete with cheerleaders strutting their stuff was totally made up for the movies. "I can't believe how much that was like *High School Musical*."

Marc and Lori laughed as they filed out of the gym after the game and Lori quipped, "Except none of the jocks broke out in song."

Marc's hand brushed the small of her back as she passed through the doorway. "Don't Aussie kids play basketball?"

"They do, but not quite like this." She pointed to a student who was struggling to see where he was going whilst wearing the moose head of Hobin High's mascot. "I never realized all those high school movies were just telling it like it is. I mean look at all these lockers. The corridors really are the social hub of school and I can just imagine jock corner actually exists."

Lori had moved ahead in the crowd, chatting to Gracie,

and Marc suddenly grabbed Matilda's hand and pulled her in the opposite direction.

"Where are we going?"

He just grinned at her and kept walking away from the crowd.

A flash of anticipation followed her initial surprise. It had been a mutually unspoken agreement that when they were in public or with his family, they kept their hands off each other, although that got harder every day and came with an increasing dose of regret. But it avoided unwanted questions and scrutiny by well-meaning but nosy Hobinites, especially when what they had wasn't forever.

Her heart quivered and she ignored it.

She jogged beside him, having learned over the last couple of weeks that when he didn't feel confined by Hobin and his family, he had a fun streak a mile wide. She hung on to that and took every ride with him because she knew they had a pre-ordained end-date—she just didn't know when it would be activated.

After a couple of turns they were in yet another corridor that looked identical to all the others she'd walked down, from the central clock hanging from the ceiling to the closed classroom doors, but Marc seemed to know where he was and strode purposefully to a bank of red-and-white lockers on an intersecting corner. Opposite them was a bulletin board full of sports notices and a large trophy cupboard filled with shining cups.

He gently backed her up against a locker in the center bank and then leaned in against her, his body molding to hers in a deliciously familiar way. With a quick glance in either direction, as if he was checking the coast was clear, he kissed her with a teasing kiss that caressed her lips and left the imprint of a promise of things to come.

Everything inside her melted, just as it always did when he touched her.

He rested his forehead on hers, his voice deep and smooth like warm chocolate sauce. "Welcome to jock corner."

She hooked her thumbs around the lapels of his coat, pulling him even closer. "Is this where the bad boys hang out?"

He shook his head. "Nah, that's down near shop."

She laughed. "This is all so weird. It's like being on a film set. Actually so much of life in Hobin is like a film set."

"Only to you. For us it's a perfectly normal Midwestern high school. I was on the basketball team and this was my locker."

She traced his jaw with her finger, thinking of all the American films she'd watched over the years, and spoke without thinking. "Kissing a girl at your locker, mate. Doesn't that mean you have to give her your pin?"

The fun in his blue eyes flickered slightly. "I never stayed with one girl long enough for that."

A jagged pain unexpectedly caught her under her ribs and she bit her lip. *Of course you didn't. Giving a pin would mean an emotional attachment. Risking a part of yourself.* "So how many girls did you kiss at this locker?"

But he didn't answer. Instead he pressed his lips against hers so neither of them could speak or think and then he slid his hand under her coat, seeking her already tingling and aching breast.

Her body pulled in two directions—half of her craving him with an intensity that terrified her and the other half sternly warning her that no matter her daydreams, Marc Olsen wasn't for keeps. He didn't want to be keeps with her or with anyone.

Reluctantly, she slid her lips away from his. "We better get back to the others before we need to move down to the lockers near shop."

Marc sighed as he stole one more kiss, trying to make up for the ninety minutes he'd had to sit next to Matilda, breathe in her scent of flowers, sunshine and simmering desire, but not be able to touch her. "You're probably right. Lori will want to get home."

As they walked back toward the gym he told her stories about his years at the school, enjoying the recollections, and a warm cozy feeling settled over him. "So, what about your high school? No cafeteria food, no homecoming, no yellow school bus?"

Her eyes danced. "Yeah, it was seriously different from here. For starters, I rode a kangaroo to school most days."

He laughed, recognizing her teasing. "And you caught an emu home, right?"

"It's Eeem-U, not E-moo."

He concentrated on flattening his vowels. "Eeem-u, mate."

She laughed. "Not bad. Did you ever have an Australian exchange student here?"

He shook his head. "No, but if you'd been here I would have asked you to prom."

She stopped walking so fast she almost over balanced. Her long, intense gaze sent a ripple of unease through him. "Marc, I had red hair and freckles and my mother made my clothes. You wouldn't have even noticed me."

He wanted to deny it but she had him. Every girlfriend of

his had been tall, blonde and voluptuous. "You're probably right but that would have been my loss."

Her eyes widened in surprise for a fraction of a second but then she cocked one knowing brow. "It's okay, Marc. You don't have to pretend to make me feel better because I'm not under any illusions here. If we'd met in New York we wouldn't be burning up the sheets every afternoon in the old Gutherson House."

"That would be because it's a one thousand mile journey." He deliberately kept it light, not wanting to go where the conversation was heading, not wanting to admit that her statement was one hundred percent accurate. That he didn't want to go there worried the hell out of him because the fact Matilda knew this was just no-strings-attached sex should be making him whoop for joy. Instead, his usually cast-iron stomach rolled as if he was on a boat in pitching seas. A sensation he'd experienced more and more over the last two weeks.

The one place his life seemed calm was when he was lying in bed with Matilda straight after sex, when they talked about anything and everything. "Talking of Gutherson House, we missed this afternoon because of the early game so how about we drop Lori home and sneak—"

"There you two are!" Lori came around the corner, with Gracie and Kyle following. "Where have you been?"

Matilda stepped toward them, her face open and smiling. "Sorry, I asked Marc for a quick tour of the school. Great game, Kyle, and your shooting was awesome." She held up her hand and slapped him a high-five.

Marc grinned at her performance which didn't even hint at the fact that less than five minutes ago they'd been making out against the lockers like two teenagers. The woman should be on the stage. Except the way everyone was responding to her belied his cynical thought. Kyle's slightly embarrassed but mostly proud smile transformed his face and Lori's appreciative mother-glance had genuine warmth and care. Even Gracie, who often disparaged other women who didn't dress to kill like she did, smiled indulgently.

There was no disputing their regard and respect for Matilda but there was more to it than that. He recognized an extended tenderness and with abrupt clarity realized it didn't encompass both of them. It stopped at her.

"Great game, buddy." Brian appeared next to Kyle, clapping his hand on the boy's shoulder.

"Thanks." Kyle grinned.

A shot of regret hit the back of Marc's throat. He was pretty certain if he'd clapped his hand on Kyle's shoulder the kid would have ducked out from under the touch.

Brian then turned to Lori, his hand brushing the small of her back as he smiled down at her in a way that excluded everyone else. "So are you ready to go to the Spotted Cow?"

What the hell? Brian Rogerson was hitting on his sister. A protective instinct hurled itself through him. "Lori, are you sure you're feeling well enough for this?"

"Yes, Marc, I am. In fact I'm looking forward to it."

He heard strength in his sister's voice that had been missing for a long time and he took a second look at her. A real look. Her eyes shone blue-on-blue, her cheeks glowed but the biggest change was in her posture. For the first time since her surgery she held herself almost tall and straight. Damn it, but he'd bet his last dollar she didn't find the upstanding lieutenant boring at all.

Lori touched his arm. "You don't mind taking Kyle home, do you?"

Shit. Taking Kyle home put an end to his idea of sneaking out with Matilda but Lori had been through hell and now she was looking so happy that there was no way he could say no. Besides, once Kyle had gone to bed, he and Matilda could brush up on their kissing and he never tired of exploring that lush mouth. "You bet. Happy to."

Gracie slung her arm through Matilda's and Marc didn't like the cagey look in his sister's best friend's eyes. "You're coming with us, Tildy."

"Awesome." Matilda gave a genuine smile of delight to the group.

A brilliant green bolt of pure jealousy tore through Marc. Hobin had just circled in around Matilda and completely shut him out. *But you left, never wanting to belong again.* And hell, he didn't want to belong now but that didn't seem enough to stop him feeling like a kid who hadn't been picked for the team. He managed to force a smile and grind out the Wisconsin farewell of, "Dress warm, drive safe" before he spun on his heel. "Come on, Kyle. It's getting late and you've got school tomorrow."

Marc flicked through the zillion channels of nothing that was cable TV, turned it off, tossed the remote onto the couch and decided he had to find something else to do. He could hear Kyle in the kitchen making himself a snack. As usual, the drive home with Kyle had been pretty silent and the kid had gone straight to the shower.

With a mute teenager in the house, Matilda and Lori out, and his mother surprisingly not visiting, he opened his computer, deciding to do the final touches on the barn plans and start work on Gutherson House. The computer took its time to boot up so while he waited he added a few more bricks to the Lego spaceship without glancing at the instructions.

Kyle ambled in holding a bowl brimming with ice cream and stood watching.

Marc continued with the Lego pieces. "Hey."

"Hey."

He'd tried the good-game compliment in the car and had got a grunt in reply. He clicked in another piece of the spaceship.

"That doesn't go there." Kyle put his bowl down on top of the barn plans and flicked forward a few pages in the build guide.

Don't spill food on my plans. Marc managed to bite back the sentence that teetered dangerously on his lips. He stared at the model and noticed the piece Kyle had added changed the line. "You might be right."

"I *am* right."

Marc heard the burgeoning man in Kyle's voice as well as the challenge.

Gotcha, I win. With regret he recalled the snowball fight— the last time Kyle had faced him down and this time he was determined not to screw things up but to get them right. Make them right, but to do that he had to find the correct path to tread with this half boy, half man.

I am right. He took in a long, deep breath, remembering the first time he'd made a similar declaration to his dad when they'd been working on a carpentry project. That moment had been a rite of passage. "What makes you so sure you're right?"

Kyle passed the booklet and pointed to the correct layout. "See."

Marc saw, but he also knew that the instruction book had been open pages behind where the model was at. "That's your proof but you knew before you saw it in print. Tell me, what made you so sure."

Kyle stared at him for a moment as if checking Marc's question was serious. "That's easy. Most of this is uneven, except for this part. See the smooth curve?" His finger traced across the model. "So this piece here sets up the wrong line."

Marc was impressed. "You've got a good eye, Kyle, just like your grandpa."

The boy's head came up, as undisguised delight shot across his face. "Yeah?"

"Yeah. It's a shame you never knew him because he could build just about anything. Anyone who was interested in wood and building would be invited to his workshop in the barn. If you passed the 'sweeping the floor' job he'd teach you all he knew."

"I would have liked that. My dad never wanted to build anything." He shot Marc a hostile look. "He just sends me stuff to build on my own."

Carl was a prick. But as he immediately sentenced his ex-brother-in-law, Marc faced the knowledge that he too was guilty of sending unaccompanied gifts. However, he'd never sent models through the mail. He'd always brought them with him. "You and I have always built Legos."

Kyle's breath came out on a huff. "Just at Thanksgiving."

The words hit like a jagged barb and suddenly Kyle's antagonism toward him this year made some sort of sense. "You think I should come more often?"

He shrugged casually as if it didn't matter. "Maybe." He immediately picked up his ice cream and spooned up a mouthful.

The memory of freshly shaved wood in his father's workshop tickled his nostrils. One of his earliest memories was sitting up on the scarred workbench next to the vise, watching his father's hands make magic with wood. The closest he'd got lately was his work with Habitat for Humanity and that had been months ago. "Would you be interested in some real building?"

"Like what?"

Ignoring Kyle's tone that shrieked, "This better be good or I'll crap all over it," he pulled off the offending bit of Lego. "I was thinking a barn."

The spark of interest returned. "You mean that job you're doing for Mayor Hendrix?"

He couldn't quite manage to hide his surprise. "That's the one, but how did you know about that?"

Kyle rolled his eyes. "Uncle Marc, you and Tildy talk about it *all* the time and—" His jaw jutted in a way that said, "I don't care if it was wrong." "I've looked at the plans you've been leaving on the table."

A dose of reality hit him hard in the solar plexus and he couldn't believe how blind he'd been. He'd spent three weeks missing every damn sign the kid might have given him. Instead, he'd only seen the hostility. But Kyle had the Olsen gene for building and behind those white earbuds, he'd been listening and really paying attention. "So, what do you think of the plans?"

"Dunno." He put his ice-cream bowl back on the table.

But Marc wasn't having any of that monosyllabic crap. He'd finally found a way to connect with Kyle and he was holding on to it with both hands. He knew that deciphering plans took time and learning, so he clicked on his computer's mouse and opened up a 3-D drawing of the barn, making it slowly rotate. "This is what it will end up looking like inside."

Kyle's eyes widened. "That's awesome. How did you do that?"

Marc grinned. "I can show you if you like?"

"Yeah? That'd be cool."

Lori sat at a booth in the Spotted Cow, but she could have been on the moon for all the attention she was paying to her surroundings. She saw Gracie's mouth moving and Tildy's curls bobbing but the only awareness she had was the touch of Brian's leg against hers, and the river of heat pouring through her that threatened to slide her under the table in a pool of unsated need.

Over the last few days gifts had continued to arrive. Body butter, her favorite perfume and silky panties with a matching camisole. Each gift came with an accompanying text message that made her bones melt and had her walking around in a constant state of desire, making it impossible to concentrate on anything. Anything except Brian.

But even though they'd shared phone calls every night, tonight was the first time they'd met in person and the first time he'd touched her since before her surgery. All evening he'd been relaxed, his touch casual and momentary, as he chatted to everyone. She on the other hand was wound so tight she thought she'd explode any minute. She wanted to be with him on his own, not sharing him with half the town.

"Come and dance, Lori." Brian's hand caught hers and she slid along the bench. As they walked toward the tiny dance floor, an old Vanessa Williams song started playing on the jukebox.

Brian smiled. "That takes me back to the first time I saw you. Mrs. Bauer's math class."

He moved opposite her, dancing without touching her. She felt like there was an elephant between them. They'd said the most intimate things to each other over the phone, and now he was behaving like she was porcelain and this was their first date.

"We spent a lot of high school passing in corridors."

"We've spent years passing each other, Lori."

"Not so much this last year." She moved in closer to him thinking about the year past where they'd spent a lot of time together as friends.

He smiled at her, his eyes crinkling at the edges. "This year's been special."

This no-touch dancing was driving her insane. "Can we go now?"

He frowned and stopped dancing. "You're tired? Sure, I'll take you home."

She gripped his upper arm and shook her head. "No, I don't want to go home. I want to go to *your* home."

His body stiffened under her touch and for the first time all evening she detected a crack in his relaxed demeanor.

Intense gray eyes studied her. "Are you sure?"

She swallowed. "Yes and no."

His smile, one of complete understanding mixed with un-disguised desire, rained down on her. "We'll tell the others I'm taking you home."

Ten minutes later she'd had long enough to think about what she'd done and panic fizzed and popped inside her. She shivered as Brian slid her coat off her shoulders and hung it on his coat rack.

A moment later he came up behind her and rested his hands on her shoulders. He spoke softly. "You can change your mind, Lori. I can make coffee and we can just talk because we're not doing this until you're ready."

She wrung her hands, loving that he was so caring, and hating that her own fear could destroy what she wanted so much. She turned to face him. "No, I think I'm ready."

He cupped her cheek with his palm and his face filled with tenderness. "Lori, I love you. I've loved you for years. I'd love you if you had one leg or three arms and I'm not going to walk away from you because of some scars on your chest."

Her naked fear jetted up. "But you haven't seen them. They're awful."

His voice quietly chided. "Surely over this last week you've learned you don't need breasts to be incredibly sexual."

Her cheeks blazed with heat at the memory of the things they'd said to each other, the things they'd done in the privacy of their own rooms. "Yes but—"

He tilted her chin, his determined gaze meeting hers. "No matter what, I'm never going to leave you and if you want to have sex wearing a sexy silk camisole for the rest of our lives, that's fine by me."

"The…the rest of our lives?" She couldn't believe she'd heard right.

He nodded. "Marry me."

But a tiny kernel of fear still lingered. "Let's have sex first."

He folded his arms across his chest. "I'm a well-respected police officer and if people find out what you and I've been up to over the last week my reputation will be shot. And then there's Kyle to think about. He doesn't need a scandal like that about his mother."

She heard a half strangled, half hysterical laugh and realized it had come from her. "You're saying you won't have sex with me until I agree to marry you?"

"That's right."

"That's insane. Besides it's the girl who always pulls that blackmail stunt not the guy."

His hand suddenly caught his shirt and he pulled it over his head fast and then let it drop to the floor. Sculpted muscles carved down from his wide shoulders to a narrow waist.

Her breath caught in her throat.

"You calling me a girl?" His long fingers languidly undid his belt buckle and tantalizingly slowly, he brought the leather strap out of the loops. His trousers fell to his ankles and he kicked them aside so he stood magnificent in a pair of silk boxers. "Still calling me a girl?"

A rush of pure love, filled with absolute trust, raced through her like a river gushing after rain. This wonderful, caring man, her very dear friend and friend to her son, loved her in a way she'd never been loved before. She'd be a fool to walk away from this. With trembling fingers she unbuttoned her blouse and stepped out of her trousers until she stood in the silk panties and camisole top he'd sent her yesterday.

A tremor ran across his toned body and his eyes immediately darkened to the color of polished iron ore.

A fresh green shoot of belief opened inside her. "I'm calling you mine."

With one step he was beside her and then she was in his

arms, cocooned in silk and in love. He carried her to the bedroom and slowly and tenderly made love to her, forging his pledge to her and making them one.

CHAPTER EIGHTEEN

Matilda carried a thermos of hot chocolate, a basket of hot homemade sausage rolls and a tea-cake still warm and buttery from the Gutherson House oven, up toward the barn, loving the sensation of sunshine on her back and the crisp sound of snow crunching beneath her boots. A run of milder weather meant blue skies, the lightest of breezes and days in the high twenties. She chuckled at how she'd been thinking the weather was almost a heat wave. It never got close to this cold at home and the average Australian would be in total shock if it did.

She stepped inside the barn and breathed in the sweet aroma of freshly cut wood. Marc had rented some huge blow heaters, purchased lumber and started work on the interior of the barn, surprising everyone in Hobin except herself. She'd watched his initial reluctance at taking on the barn project turn into benign interest, before ramping up into full-on enjoyment and excitement. He lived and breathed this job and was always discussing his ideas with her. That had been a surprise and even more so was that he'd given consideration to all of her thoughts. She'd been both stunned and thrilled that he'd taken on board some of her opinions and incorporated them into the plans, but most of all she loved that he was happy. All the strain and tension that had surrounded him for weeks had faded and he'd finally relaxed into Hobin. Not that he'd admit it.

He'd needed the barn project as much as Peggy had needed his vision and expertise. She only wished she had the money to be in partnership with Peggy because every time she stepped into this wondrous building she could picture a magical place for couples to pledge their love to each other as well as a glorious setting to celebrate with their loved ones. This place would be the jewel in Weddings Are Hobin's crown.

But in all of this there'd been *one* thing that had astonished her, but it was in the best possible way. Kyle was working with Marc on the barn after school and on weekends. Marc had finally found a way to relax and be himself around his nephew and Kyle had responded to it with the enthusiasm of youth.

As she slid the huge barn door open, she called out, "G'day. I've brought you guys lunch."

"Just guy," Marc called down from the scaffolding.

She openly gazed at him as he climbed down the ladder. Gone were the designer trousers, shirts and handmade Italian leather shoes. In their place were snug blue jeans, a thick sweater and metal-capped work boots, and to complete the picture a tool belt slung low from his hips. He jumped the last step, landing firmly on his feet, a lock of blond hair falling over his forehead and a wide smile carving dimples into his cheeks.

She put down her basket. "Why is it that even in work wear you look prettier than me?"

"It's a gift." Grinning, he whipped off his work gloves and

pulled her into his arms, his lips stroking hers with a kiss. "As are you. You smell of pastry and spices and good enough to eat."

She laughed and leaned her head against his shoulder, breathing deeply. He smelled of hard work and pine. "Where's your quasi apprentice?"

"Didn't Lori tell you when you were baking?"

"I haven't been back to Lori's since breakfast. Peggy and I did some stock ordering and then my phone conference with a supplier in St. Paul was all messed up. I keep forgetting you guys put the month first and the day second. So rather than drive back I baked at Gutherson House." She didn't mention how much she adored the house or that she'd pretended that the kitchen was truly hers. Instead, she winked at him. "I thought another room of the house should be used to justify your rent."

He stroked a crazy curl from her eyes and his own eyes simmered with undisguised lust. "We're using the house. Remember the other day we lit the fire in the front room and then lay down in front of it just to prove the chimney doesn't smoke. I'm a responsible tenant and I'm sure we should check all the other fireplaces too."

A shimmer of need stirred.

An imaginative glint flickered in his eyes. "We could start now."

"Hot food first." She slipped out of his arms, flipped out a cloth and set out the food. "So where's Kyle?"

Marc dunked a sausage roll in ketchup as if he was a true Aussie. "He and I found a great tree so we cut it down and lashed it to the car for Lori. When he's finished unloading and setting it up for her, he'll be back."

"Oh." Delight that Lori was now "doing Christmas" collided with irrational disappointment that she'd missed out on being part of the tree decorating which was ridiculous because no matter how much she might want it, this wasn't her family.

"Oh?" Marc raised a brow.

"Oh, nothing." She tried to cover her slip and ignore the silly, childish feeling inside her. Her parents had always ignored Christmas, claiming it to be commercial and fake. December had always been spent in far-flung places full of heat and dust. She wryly acknowledged that in its own way it was a tradition for her family, but it wasn't the one she'd wanted. Only Nana had understood how much she'd craved a normal childhood with family traditions and bless her, she'd done her best but often by the time her gifts had arrived at the post office, they'd moved on.

"Matilda, I know you and that 'oh' meant something, so out with it."

She shook her head. "It's silly."

Blue eyes lasered her with teasing in their depths. "And it's not like you've ever done anything silly before. Come on, tell me."

She interlaced her fingers and shrugged. "Traveling around as a kid, I didn't get to do a lot of the Christmas stuff but more than that, December is in the middle of summer in Australia. None of the traditions of plum pudding, mince pies and a huge roast dinner make any sense in one hundred degree heat. But here, with the snow, it's magical. I guess I was hoping to have the experience of cutting down a tree in the snow, dragging it home, decorating it and drinking eggnog."

"What's a plum pudding?"

She'd expected him to laugh but instead interest played

across his cheeks. "It's alcohol-infused fruit similar to Nana's cake but cooked in muslin, hung for a while and then served with the most divine brandy-cream sauce, which is similar to eggnog."

He looked skeptical. "And a mince pie?"

She laughed. "More alcohol-infused fruit but instead of in a cake, it's in pastry."

He shook his head, laughter lines carving deep around his mouth. "You Aussies sure have a thing for liquored fruit."

"Hey, don't knock it until you try it."

He snuck another sausage roll. "I might just have to do that after we've cut you down a tree."

A zing of incredulity shot through her for a moment before common sense prevailed. "But Lori doesn't need two trees."

He shrugged. "So we'll set up our own tree in the dining room of Gutherson House, and toast it with eggnog. Sounds like you've got a lot of catching up to do, Christmas-wise."

Our own tree. He'd mentioned the other day he never bothered with a tree in his apartment in New York and she knew he never spent Christmas in Hobin with his family. She couldn't believe he was offering to do this for her.

The part of her heart that had quivered the day he'd lost the Matheson account, quivered again in that odd and funny way, a combination of weight and incredible lightness. Only this time the rest of her heart followed with a resounding shudder.

Despair hit her and she bit her lip unable to hide from the truth any longer. *I love him.* She loved Marc. Despite everything she knew about herself, despite everything that had gone before, despite her total commitment that this was only adventure and sex, she'd fallen deeply and hopelessly in love.

She'd been a complete fool. How could she have ever

thought she'd been in love before and that would protect her? Compared with this feeling of pleasure, pain, heartache and unadulterated joy, what she'd felt before had only been superficial dross.

Oh, Nana, what have I done? I locked up the dream and threw away the key and I've still managed to stuff up and fail.

You're always looking for complications, Tildy. Just live each day as it comes.

I don't think it works like that, Nana!

But her grandmother had gone off the air and now all she could hear was white noise. She managed to stammer out, "You want us to put a tree up in the house?"

"Sure, it'll be fun. Plus it will satisfy your current obsession about me getting 'value for money' for that house, which by the way, I really am."

With twinkling eyes, he leaned forward and kissed her lightly but with affection, like a couple who'd been together for years.

Her bewilderment intensified but before she could even try and sort out her thoughts, he'd grabbed a hunk of cake in one hand and with her hand in the other he pulled her to her feet. "Come on. Let's see what you're like on the other end of a cross-saw."

"You're eating more than you're threading," Marc laughingly accused Matilda as they sat on the floor making popcorn garlands, in front of a crackling open fire.

She raised a brow. "Did I comment on how many mince pies you ate?"

"They were surprisingly good."

"Nana's recipes always are."

He lay back by the fire, startlingly content, his belly filled with good food and the mellowing effects of the eggnog's brandy warming him from the inside out. He hadn't cut down a tree in twelve years and today he'd cut two. He didn't know who had been more surprised, Matilda or himself when he'd offered to get her a tree but he did know that his muscles felt well used and satisfied in a way the gym never quite managed. She'd been a quick study on the cross-saw, and had laughed so delightedly when they'd towed the tree home in the sled that he'd found himself drawn into the spirit of the season by her enthusiasm.

She was making his time in Hobin more than bearable. *And what after that?* The random thought blindsided him and he instantly set it aside because it wasn't a question he wanted to think about. Lori needed him until she went back to school in the New Year. The start of the year seemed a fitting time for him to resume his normal lifestyle. He'd return to New York, to his uncluttered and spacious apartment, and his complication-free life. But right now that was still a week or so away. "So we've cut you down your tree. What's next on your childhood Christmas fantasy list?"

"What did you do as a kid?"

He searched his memories. "Dad had an old sleigh that he'd harness up if the weather was fine and on Christmas Eve we'd take the sugar cookies and gingerbread men Mom had made us bake and decorate, and give them to the neighbors."

Her eyes lit up. "That sounds wonderful."

"It was usually freezing cold."

She poked him in the ribs. "Yeah but you loved it anyway."

He captured her fingers with his hand and didn't argue. He'd always enjoyed putting the snowbell harness on the horses and riding next to his father.

She pulled away and draped her popcorn garland over the tree before lying down beside him, her belly resting on the floor and her eyes gazing at the orange-red-and-blue flames.

"I like to imagine this old house was filled with family traditions like baking and Friday-night quiz night."

He caught the dreamy look in her eyes, the one that always made his gut clench.

"Life isn't all happy families, Matilda. My father died. God, I miss him." He heard himself speak the words and realized he'd never said them to anyone before. More words poured out. "It was his love of wood and his skill with it that made me want to become an architect. When he died, I didn't just lose him. I lost his knowledge. I went from being a carefree kid who was being taught how to be a man and still had a bunch of lessons to learn, to instantly being the man of the family. My role of older brother suddenly became quasi parent to three younger sisters and I had no clue what I was doing."

Matilda's heart ached for him and for all that he'd lost when his father had died. She reached out, squeezing his hand. "That would have been beyond tough, Marc."

"Yeah." He linked his fingers through hers and stared down at their entwined hands as if he was back in the past. "I didn't want to be my sisters' keeper and they hated that I wasn't Dad."

She doubted they'd ever hated him. "You must have done okay because if Jennifer and Sheryl are anything like Lori, then they're both strong women."

"Yeah, they are." He smiled at her with deep and seductive dimples in his cheeks. "But growing up they hogged the bathroom, refused to do their share of the chores and borrowed my stuff and never returned it. Be thankful you were an only child, Matilda. Families aren't a fairy tale, which is why I've never carried on the tradition."

His expression was teasing but his belief was stark and uncompromising in his words, and they sliced through her heart, tearing it in two. Somehow, she managed a smile and said, "Blondie, you're not telling me anything I don't already know." But it was the biggest lie she'd ever told. All she'd ever wanted was a family of her own and now she'd fallen in love with a man who held himself apart from everyone and didn't want to love anyone. She'd thought that the last few weeks might have given him a different view of his own family but obviously she'd been very wrong.

Most of her wanted to hit him over the head, tell him how blind he was but the last time she'd confronted him about his family, the fallout had been ugly. She wasn't usually shy about voicing her opinions but today had been such a wondrous day—a day she'd hug to herself and revisit in the years ahead, long after he'd returned to New York. So help her but she didn't want to spoil it by arguing. Going against everything she believed, she let him do what he did every time their con-versation strayed toward anything remotely emotional. She let him pull her into his arms, roll her onto the rug and kiss her until every thought slid away on a rush of glorious sensation, and nothing existed except bliss.

"Your phone's ringing, Uncle Marc."

"Can you grab it, Kyle?" Marc shot the final few nails into the framework for the bathrooms, the whoosh, hiss and thump of the nail-gun ringing in his ears. As the echo faded he heard Kyle talking into the phone about the barn.

Marc mouthed, "Is it Peggy?" He'd been waiting to hear

back from her about the contractors, none of whom probably wanted to work on the job until March.

"He's here now, Mr. Evans."

Marc wiped his forehead against his sleeve and accepted the phone. "Phillip, you got the plans?"

"I did." The senior partner sounded happy. "It's one hell of a good idea. The more strings we have to our bow in these economic times the better and this would diversify us out of Manhattan. There're a hell of a lot of aging Queen Anne houses in Connecticut and upstate New York. We've already got one prospective client who wants to meet with you as soon as possible. When can you get back to the city?"

A buzz of excitement stirred in his belly. The sort of excitement he used to have for work. "My sister needs me until after New Year's."

"Any way you can get away sooner? This client's really anxious to get started and requested a meeting straight after Christmas."

Marc rubbed his forehead expecting to feel really torn but he knew where he had to be for another nine days. Lori needed him. *And Matilda?*

Matilda doesn't need anyone. She was the strongest woman he knew.

"All I can promise is that if anything changes on this end, I'll be on a plane but, Phillip, the chances of that are pretty much zilch."

Matilda stood at Lori's kitchen window, staring out into the night. Lori had asked her if she would mind cooking on Christmas Eve for a small party of family and close friends. As she'd fallen in love not only with Marc but his entire family, of course she'd said yes. The evening had been easy and relaxed and she'd been thrilled when she'd opened the door to find that Brian had been invited. He'd hugged her so hard she thought he'd break her arms.

Marc had appeared by her side and welcomed the policeman with an unusual amount of warmth and at one point in the evening she'd overheard him asking if there was any news on tracking down Barry-the-Bastard. She'd kept walking not wanting to be reminded of her folly but was secretly touched that he'd thought to ask. When he did things like that it made it even harder to accept what she knew, and that was that they had no future together.

She'd left the noisy dinner table a few minutes ago to serve the dessert. Kyle had requested Pavlova, the Australian concoction of crunchy meringue on the outside and light-as-air fluffy meringue on the inside, and all of it coated in whipped cream and fresh fruit.

"You snow-gazing again?"

Matilda felt Marc's arms slide around her waist and she leaned back against him, loving the fact that he wanted to touch her despite the fact the house was full of people. "It's hypnotizing."

"Just like you."

She turned in his arms, trying to steel her already-lost heart a tiny bit against his words. Words which fell so effortlessly from a man born with a charm spoon in his mouth but meant little because the moment New Year's was over he'd be leaving Hobin. Leaving her. Just like everyone she ever loved eventually left her.

He produced a tiny green branch from behind his back and held it over her head. "It's mistletoe so you *have* to kiss me."

She would have kissed him with or without the mistletoe but sometimes egotistical architects needed a bit of leveling. "Lost your touch, have you, Blondie. It's too sad that you're depending on vegetation to score."

"Sweetheart, I'm only thinking of you and saving you the public embarrassment of having to stand in line, or as you say, 'stand in a queue,' later tonight with all the other women in the room."

Her hand trailed up to his jaw. "And to think some people call you conceited."

His face deadpanned but his eyes teased with wicked intent. "So are you putting out or not?"

She laughed, loving him too much, and pressed her lips softly against his before plunging her tongue inside his mouth with a quick and erotic flick. "We need to get back to the party."

He swallowed hard. "I'm not sure I can walk. Let's make polite conversation for a minute on topics such as our tree is heaps better than Lori's."

But she didn't want to talk about the tree at the house or even think about it. Nor did she want to think about the wreath that now graced the front door and she definitely wasn't thinking about the stocking that had appeared tacked to the mantelpiece. It was as if Marc had a list of every Christmas tradition she'd ever missed out on and was working his way through it so she could have the full North American Christmas experience. But as much as she loved it all, every tradition tore at her heart and reminded her that he wouldn't be doing it with her this time next year. Or ever again.

"Can you carry some plates?"

"Sure. You know, it's really good of you to do this for Lori."

He started eating a slice of Pavlova. "Thank you. She's a different woman these couple of weeks."

"I love to cook and it's the least I can do seeing as I'm living here rent free."

His jaw stiffened. "If you weren't so stubborn you could be being paid for *all* you do around here. None of us could have got through this time without you and we're all guilty of asking too much of you."

Her heart bled a bit. He thought he was being her champion but he had no idea that it was him who was taking advantage of her the most. He'd used her as a shield against his family getting too close and as a buffer to deal with being back in Hobin.

"I'm not being taken advantage of and if it bothers you so much then donate to a Christmas charity in my name." They'd had this conversation over and over but no way was she taking money from Marc or any of the Olsen family. Love didn't work that way.

Kyle walked into the kitchen with an indignant look on his face. "Hey, Uncle Marc! You punked me. There's no present in the basement. You just wanted to get at the Pavlova first."

Marc had the decency to look sheepish. "My bad, but it's so good." He slung his arm around his nephew. "But I put in a good word for you and Tildy's saved you thirds."

Matilda laughed. "He's still scamming you, Kyle, but I have plenty." She listened to the two of them giving each other a hard time underpinned by mutual love and respect as they carried the dessert to the dining room. They'd come a long way since the first time they'd all sat down to supper together.

The moment the plates were laid down in front of everyone, Brian stood up, placing his napkin carefully on the table.

Everyone at the table fell silent, including Gracie who'd been working very hard trying to convince Marc to go cross-country skiing with her.

Before he spoke, Brian glanced down at Lori, and Matilda had to blink hard and fast as she wondered what it must feel like to be worshipped like that by a man.

Brian cleared his throat. "I'd like to thank Tildy for an amazing meal so far, and Kyle tells me I haven't lived until I've tasted this dessert."

A chuckle of laughter amidst scattered "thank yous" echoed around the room and Marc raised his glass to her and smiled. A smile of shared times, of tangled sheets and friendship. Her heart spasmed. She wanted so much more than friendship but that was never going to happen.

Brian continued, his hand resting on Lori's shoulder. "I'd also like to say that after a man-to-man talk, Kyle has given his blessing and Lori and I are getting married in the spring."

Joy bounced through Matilda at her friends' happiness, reinforcing her belief that love did really exist even if it never found her the way she wanted it to. Lori and Brian were so right together. Her gaze immediately shot to Marc. Surprise clung to his face but it was soon pushed away by a warm smile. He caught her looking at him and mouthed, "Did you know?"

As she shook her head, the room erupted into hoots and hoorays and clapping. Brian grinned, then kissed Lori and hugged Kyle before accepting congratulations from a damp-eyed Elsa and a beaming Marc.

Matilda hugged Lori and teased, "So you found yourself a leg man, after all?"

Her friend blushed. "It's not just my legs he adores. It's all of me, scars included."

"Just as it should be. I'm so happy for you."

"Thanks for everything, Tildy. I mean it. I thought a part of my life was over but it's just starting. Come spring I'll have a new husband and a new set of size B breasts."

"You're downsizing?"

"I had a love-hate relationship with my old boobs and Brian says he doesn't care what I get as long as I'm happy. So it's a new start with perfect B's." Lori laughed and then her eyes, so similar to her brother's, gave her a keen look. "Now we just need to find you someone."

Why did brides always want to make sure everyone else was coupled up? She tried to joke. "No point, Lori, you know everyone leaves me."

"Barry didn't count, Tildy." Her friend looked and sounded like the school teacher she was, reprimanding a difficult student. "Perhaps people leave you because you never ask them to stay."

The memory of begging her parents to stay loomed large and she pushed it back down. She'd begged and they'd still left her. She'd asked Jason and he'd still gone. Since then she'd never asked anyone to stay because there was no point; it made no difference to their decision. "Life's not that black-and-white, Lori."

"Brian said you told him to fight for me and thank goodness you did." The engaged woman tilted her head toward Marc who stood on the edge of the party, his cell phone unexpectedly in his hand. The aura of reserve he'd had when she first met him, which had faded to almost nothing over the last few weeks, had suddenly shot back firmly in place. "Isn't it time you took your own advice?"

"Lori! Tell all!"

Gracie's squeal of delight and her demand of "girlfriend exclusive rights" to all of the information about the engagement gave Matilda a chance to step away from Lori's far too intuitive gaze. Her own gaze returned to Marc but he no longer stood near his mother and Brian.

He'd been the perfect host all evening, taking coats, refilling people's glasses and making sure Lori was free to mingle with her guests. He'd even taken all the jibes about how New Yorkers had lost touch with the real America, with a smile and good humor. Now with Lori's great news, he must be opening more champagne.

She went room to room looking for him. Kyle sat alone at the table eating Pavlova with another two plates lined up next to him, completely oblivious to all the kisses, hand-pumping and back slapping that went with such a big announcement. Lori's teaching colleagues had put on a CD and started dancing, and Peggy had cornered Brian's boss, Eric, in the kitchen, probably haranguing him about the winter-parking restrictions outside her shop. She passed the bathroom, which was empty, then she checked the garage where the drinks were being chilled by the subzero air before she ran down the stairs to the basement.

Unaccountable goose bumps shot swiftly down her spine, quickly radiating to her entire body. Marc was nowhere to be seen.

CHAPTER NINETEEN

Matilda found Marc in his room, a suitcase on the bed, a handful of socks in one hand and in the other his phone was pressed firmly to his ear. She stood in the doorway, watching him end the call and drop the socks into the case and all the while tried to stop the trembling that followed the goose bumps. It looked like he was leaving.

She stepped uninvited into the room determined not to lose control, not to beg him to stay with her. Her heartache burned hot enough without adding humiliation to the mix. No, she was going out the same way she came in, using sass to hide her feelings. "Going somewhere?"

He nodded, his handsome face devoid of any discernable emotion. "Home."

Gutherson House immediately sprang to mind, instantly overrun by reality.

"I've just managed to book an afternoon flight back to New York and I'll arrange for the car to be trucked back next week because there's no way I'm driving it on salty roads. I figure if I pack now then you and I can spend tonight at Gutherson House and Christmas morning together." His voice matched the matter-of-fact way he scooped silk boxers out of a drawer and dumped them next to the socks.

"You're flying out on Christmas Day?" She plonked down on the bed, unable to hide the incredulity from her voice as her heart hammered so fast her head swam. But she fought the feeling. "If I'd known you didn't want to eat my plum pudding this much I'd have made another Christmas dessert."

He caressed her cheek with the soft pad of his thumb. "Don't worry. We'll still have time for a special breakfast and a Christmas skate on the lake."

A surreal feeling circled her, not dissimilar to when she'd first stepped off the plane into a foreign country. "A Christmas skate?"

He smiled. "Sure. You didn't think I'd leave before we'd finished your Christmas list."

I'd leave. No hint, no ambiguity about that at all, and no invitation for her to go with him to New York. She steeled herself against the tremors of shock that had started in her legs. She stared at him, her heart shattering at the final three items on his Christmas list for her. Breakfast, skating and leaving her. "Actually, I wasn't expecting you to leave tomorrow."

Discomposure scaled his cheeks for a moment. "Work wants me back on the twenty-sixth."

"Who works on Boxing Day?"

He looked nonplussed. "Boxing Day? No idea what that is but the twenty-sixth is a work day here and I've got a client meeting."

A client? He hadn't mentioned a project or a client to her in any of their conversations. The realization that he'd kept that a secret pricked her sharply. "I'm sure if you'd explained to your client that you're interstate and spending Christmas with your family, he or she would have been happy to delay the meeting by twenty-four hours."

"I never celebrate Christmas in Hobin."

Her befuddled mind started making connections. "But I thought you'd told Lori you'd be here until after New Year's."

He smiled. "I did and I was happy to but her engagement's a game changer. Now I can take the client meeting at the time they requested and Lori has Brian to be her 'go-to' guy. I'm not needed here anymore."

I need you.

But he didn't need her anymore. He was leaving like she'd always known he would. So this was it. Her adventure was ending, ironically on the eve of a day that represented love and family. But given Marc's feelings about family it wasn't ironic at all. It was painfully real and totally accurate.

And it was wrong. He was so totally wrong about his family and she'd stayed silent long enough and now she had nothing to lose because he was going no matter what she said or didn't say.

In five weeks she'd watched Marc relax, slowly carve out a friendship with his nephew, and enjoy his family despite his protestations about their dependence on him. Not that she'd seen a lot of evidence of overreliance apart from Lori's recent and understandable need although she'd heard the stories of a grieving family twelve years ago.

She stood up, and folded her arms across her chest for support. "So you're not needed anymore and you're running away?"

His jaw tightened. "I'm going home."

"I think you're going back to the place you live."

He shrugged. "Home, my apartment, it's the same thing."

She vigorously shook her head. "No, it isn't home. The place you live in is a soulless box."

"How would you know?"

"I've seen pictures and there's not a thing out of place."

He shoved shoes into sealable bags. "So sue me for having an uncluttered home with a multimillion-dollar view."

She thought of Gutherson House and Lori's place. "A home is noisy, a bit tattered from use and filled with people, love and a thousand messy emotions in between. You design living spaces, not homes. That's why your apartment's so sterile, isn't it?"

"I win awards for those living spaces!" His eyes flashed the blue-gray of thunder clouds. "And remind me, when did it become an offense to live in a neat and ordered house?"

She threw her arms out wide. "It's not an offense but it isn't just the house that's ordered, it's your whole life. You keep everyone at a safe distance, not allowing anyone to get close because it makes you too vulnerable. Although for some reason you broke that rule the day you stole my car keys."

"That's a ridiculous statement." He stormed to the door and closed it against the hum of the party.

She shook her head slowly. "No, it's what you do. I agree, at seventeen it totally sucked for you to have to set aside college and be the father-figure and part financial contributor to your family. Of course you wanted to escape that unwanted responsibility when you hadn't even started your adult life."

"Tell me something I don't know."

"Okay, you're emotionally stuck at twenty. You resent your family and keep them at a distance. But here's the kicker,

Marc. Yes, Lori needed you these last few weeks but ask yourself this. How many times in the last twelve years have any of your family ever really asked you for anything other than an opinion? And has your mother ever asked you for *one* single thing in twelve years? She doesn't even ask you to be here at Christmas."

His mouth which she knew so intimately—lips that could curve upward into a smile that changed her world—flattened into a hard line. "Have you finished?"

"Not quite." She resisted the overwhelming urge to bite her bottom lip but she had to keep going. She loved him and she wanted him to be happy. "Think about what's happened between you and Kyle when you gave a bit of yourself. Look at your life with new eyes, Marc. Take a risk. Let people in because when you do they give back more than they take."

He started pulling shirts off hangers with sharp tugs. "Oh, this is sweet coming from someone who let a con man into her life and lost everything. Before you go trying to fix up my life take a long look at your own."

His words stung but she faced up to them. "I have. Yes, I made a huge mistake and I screwed up big-time, but at least I had a go at life and took a risk."

"And where did it get you, Matilda? Believing in your grandmother's mumbo jumbo about great love and trying to live through other people's experiences? You lost everything and that wasn't even love. Real love is worse. I'm happy Lori's happy but God knows why she'd risk marriage again when she's already had her heart kicked out by a prick of an ex-husband. I watched my mother shrivel to a shadow of her vibrant self when Dad died. She stopped baking, stopped gardening, stopped singing. She just existed and she's never recovered."

"That's not true, she—"

His hand shot up hard and firm. "I listened to you deconstruct my life, so now it's your turn. Let's turn the spotlight onto your family, shall we? Your parents' love for each other was so great that it left no room for you."

Her mouth opened, intending to hotly deny it but the truth swirled within her as well as staring starkly back at her from steel-blue eyes.

"And here's the kicker, Matilda." He paused for a moment letting the words she'd used against him zing her. "Your parents abandoned you and yet you still have stars in your eyes that love and family is everything. As for this business you're creating, how can you perpetrate this illusion of great love?"

She spoke quietly, mustering all her dignity against his words that pummeled her like storm waves on a beach. "Because, just like you I have to live and pay my way." But as she spoke the words she realized although it had started off as survival, now it had changed. It had taken her from homeless to having a connection with Hobin, and given her a sense of belonging. It also connected her to Marc through the barn project.

"You should be nursing. I've offered to pay your exam fees but you're too stubborn to accept." He slammed the case shut and then unexpectedly his shoulders slumped and his voice wavered. "Hell, Matilda, why are we doing this?"

He turned around, reaching for her, and she reluctantly stepped into his arms, resting her head against his shoulder, telling herself she was only doing this because it was her one last chance to breathe in his clean, woodsy scent and feel his warmth against her.

His fingers trailed absently through her curls. "I'm going to miss you."

Her head tilted back slowly at the unexpected words and with a jolt she saw true regret in his eyes.

I'm going to miss you. Why are we doing this?

Lori's voice played through her bruised and battered mind. *Perhaps people leave you because you never ask them to stay.*

The fear of rejection surged through her so strongly she tasted the sharp burn of acid in the back of her throat. Her pummeled heart hurt enough without her mouth issuing an invitation to force him to say the words she knew he would say. *"I don't love you and I won't stay."*

But she thought about Lori, Elsa, Kyle and Brian. How they'd hugged her so hard like she was part of their family. Of the conversations over the last few weeks, of the words they'd spoken, and she realized they valued her in their lives as much as she loved and valued them. Wasn't it time she valued herself?

She could take the safe way, say nothing and let Marc leave believing both of them thought their time together had all been about sex and fun. Five weeks ago that's exactly what she would have done. But now she knew that wasn't good enough and she had to do the one thing a woman who truly loves a man does.

Her hand rose up to his cheek, his stubble deliciously rough against her palm. "I'm going to miss you too because you're a good man, because you make me laugh and because I love you. I'd like you to stay."

She hated how shock stole the smile from his face, sucked in his cheeks and vibrated through his body, making him rigid and still under her touch.

He gently set her aside from him and plowed his hands

through his hair. "You don't love me, Matilda. You just think you do."

She shook her head. "No, actually the one thing I've learned from all of this is that what I feel for you is the real deal. But unlike my parents' love for each other, I want to expand my love for you to encompass children."

His face paled. "I can't—"

"I know." A sigh rattled out of her. "It's okay, Marc. You don't have to panic. You don't have to say or do anything. I know you don't love me. I know you don't want a family."

"I'm sorry—"

"Don't be. I've never expected you to love me back but a long time ago I stopped telling people how I felt about them because I didn't want to be rejected. But that didn't change a thing so I'm not doing it anymore. Now I'm telling it like it is even though I know it won't change how you feel, because more importantly, it changes how I feel about myself."

She wrapped her hand around the door handle and summoned up a small smile from deep down inside her, because with all her heart she really did believe what she was about to say. "Merry Christmas, Marc. I wish you a long and happy life."

"Matilda, I—"

But she closed the door against the sound of his voice. She managed to walk across the hall to her room, pick up her phone and text Peggy two rooms away. Then she telephoned Vanessa.

Somehow Matilda got through Christmas day. Lori unexpectedly arrived at Peggy's that afternoon, squeezed her hand and simply said, "My brother's a fool." Then, although the plan had always been for the Christmas meal to be held at Lori's, she drove Matilda to Elsa's house. Matilda had walked in to find Elsa, Brian and Kyle, a table set for lunch and gifts with her name on them under the tree. That was the only time she'd cried.

On New Year's Eve she'd written a long letter to her parents. She told them everything that had happened since she'd left Australia, and then she told them she loved them. She also said she'd be writing a long letter each month and asked them to consider writing monthly as well so they could keep in closer contact.

Midway through January, Brian had told her that a woman from Florida had filed a report about a man named Brent who'd used a similar modus operandi as Barry, only this time he'd left a trail leading to Arkansas.

"I'm confident we'll get him, Tildy, just like the German police got that guy who blackmailed one too many heiresses."

She'd hugged him and thanked him but most of her didn't care about retribution except to save more women from bankruptcy. She'd lost far worse than money since that fateful Sunday when she'd arrived in Hobin.

The rest of the time she'd thrown herself into work, devising a business plan that would incorporate many of Hobin's existing businesses into Weddings Are Hobin, so the ultimate in complete wedding packages could be offered to customers.

Through January and into early February she lived on the computer, the phone, and conducted face-to-face meetings with all the Hobin businessmen and women during the day, and at night she lay in a bed above Peggy's shop counting the hours until dawn. The temperature plummeted to a viciously cold minus forty, the point where Fahrenheit and Celsius are equal. She no longer had to mentally convert but did it matter? She'd never known cold like it. Ironically it was over forty degrees Celsius in Narranbool, one hundred and four degrees Fahrenheit, and even though she didn't quite have the money for a fare yet, the idea of returning didn't play a huge part in her thoughts. She had more of a connection to Hobin now and she believed she had a viable business. Even in the early days it was earning enough to pay board and feed her.

Her phone rang. "Matilda Geoffrey."

"Tildy, the courier's arrived and I can't believe it." Vanessa Jacobson squealed down the phone. "It's a perfect fit! And where did you find that cleaner? The sixty-year-old fabric's come alive! I'm so excited."

She waited for the rush of sadness to swamp her as it had when she'd slid the dress into the courier's transit bag but it didn't come. "That's great, Vanessa. I'm pleased you adore it so much because it deserves to be worn with love and hope."

"It will be, Tildy. I couldn't believe how it almost spoke to me when I put it on." Vanessa rushed on in her usual bulldozer style. "Oh, and I've deposited the money in your account and I've been thinking about the barn. Can you promise me that it will be operating in June?"

Matilda hadn't been out to the barn but Peggy talked about it constantly so she knew the contractors had moved in and taken over from the solid start Marc and Kyle had made. "It has to be ready because we've taken a booking for late May, and Lori and Brian are the first weekend of June. If you want to switch venues you're going to have to decide by the end of this week."

"Okay. I'll call you on Friday. Now about the mini-heart place card frames…"

Matilda jotted down Vanessa's instructions but her mind was focused on the fact that the sale of Nana's dress would now allow her to write a check and pay for her phone and computer, completely separating her from Marc.

Marc gazed out the window, watching the blur of white-and-red lights against the inky night as the traffic snarled far below him. Mellow jazz crooned from the speakers, filling the apartment along with a slight citrus fragrance that lingered from the zealous efforts of his housekeeper.

Since returning from Hobin he hadn't spent much time here. Work had gone crazy with his new interest in Queen Annes and that meant traveling a lot farther to site meetings now he had clients in upstate New York. So he planned to enjoy his *home* tonight. Bending down, he randomly selected a bottle of wine from the rack, reading the yellow label as he stood up. Petaluma Coonawarra Cabernet Merlot. Australian wine.

He put it straight back and tugged out a bottle from the Napa Valley. For a month he'd used work to keep Matilda out of his thoughts but nothing kept her out of his dreams. Her scent, her touch and her lush body screened every night in the theater of his mind, in complete digitalized, cinematic widescreen clarity.

But work hadn't totally done the job either. Every Queen Anne he stepped into reminded him of their time in Gutherson House. Of course he remembered the amazing sex but that wasn't what he thought of most. Matilda was the most giving person he'd ever met. She had an amazing capacity to care and a heart the size of Australia. Even when her own life wasn't going the way she planned she put other people first.

When she smiled at him with her head tilted, curls brushing her cheek and her emerald eyes fixed on his face filled with genuine interest and—

Love.

He pulled back sharply on the corkscrew, bringing the cork out of the bottle with a loud plop. He poured a glass and, ignoring his internal wine critic, he took a long slug without pausing first to inhale the bouquet of the wine. All that time in Hobin and he hadn't realized that special way she looked at him had been love.

He hated that he'd hurt her but falling in love had never been open for discussion. He didn't want the things out of life that she wanted, and despite what she'd accused him of he was happy with his life. All that restlessness he'd had last year had obviously been due to being burned out at work and ironically his time in Hobin had given him a new direction and new zeal.

Yeah you tell yourself that.

Picking up the bottle of wine and his glass, he wandered into his home office and started attacking the pile of mail with his system. There was *nothing* wrong with being neat! Flyers got tossed into the recycling pile, circulars and magazines moved into the reading box and that left a small pile of letters. As he slid the letter opener into the first envelope he recognized Matilda's large looping writing. He immediately pictured her smile and heard her laughter. But missing her laugh and her smile wasn't love. He separated the sides of the envelope and pulled out a check with a Weddings Are Hobin sticky note stuck to it.

Please find attached check to fully payout the loan against cell and computer. Thank you for your assistance. M.

Fury blew through him, scorching his guilt. Buying her the computer and phone hadn't been a freaking loan but part of an employment contract. One she'd broken when she'd refused to accept a weekly paycheck and yet had kept on working anyway. The woman was impossible. The only things she'd accepted from him were the clothes and even then only because he'd intervened to prevent her from selling her grandmother's dress.

Where had she got this money from? He couldn't imagine she would have borrowed money from Peggy and it was far too early days to be earning more than a basic living allowance from her business unless—

The thought stopped him cold. No matter how fanciful he thought her nana's ideas about love were, that dress was the only thing Matilda had left of her grandmother.

He refilled his glass and downed half of it in one gulp. Surely she wouldn't have sold the dress, but he couldn't shed himself of that nagging feeling. No matter how she'd got the money, there was no way he was accepting it. He ripped the check up into tiny pieces and dumped them into the trash can.

The rest of the mail was mostly bills but there were two invitations—one to an opening at the Met and the other to the AIA's New York Annual Design Awards. He didn't feel like finding a date and going to either. He had a hankering instead to see Kyle play basketball, or play air hockey with him, or better yet, chat with him as he supervised him on the jigsaw. He'd been a quick study.

His cell beeped and Peggy's name lit up on the liquid display. They communicated every few days about the barn project and, as he scanned the text, his fingers plowed through his hair. The contractors required a site visit before they could proceed to the next phase. That meant a return trip to Hobin. Even flying, he'd have to stay *one* night. Peggy never mentioned Matilda in their phone calls and he didn't ask but she was obviously still very much part of this wedding business and living in Hobin.

Send an associate. He squelched the thought immediately knowing he had to attend. The barn project was his and his business was with Peggy, not Matilda. Well, at least he'd get to see Kyle.

His finger pressed against the phone's touch screen, confirming the suggested date with Peggy. Then he scrolled down his contact list and clicked on his mother's number. Although Lori hadn't said anything to him, he'd sensed from her complete lack of emails that she knew about him and Matilda, and she disagreed with his decision. Not needing a lecture, he decided instead to call his mother to let her know the date he'd be in Hobin.

As he waited for her to pick up, Matilda's words jumped uninvited into his head. *Has your mother ever asked you for one single thing in twelve years?*

"Hello."

"Hi, Mom. It's me."

"Marc, how lovely to hear from you." His mother's voice sounded warm and strong. "How's everything?"

Their conversations always started exactly the same way every time he called. *You call. You always call her.* The thought struck him so hard his breath caught in his throat, snatching back his standard reply of "fine." His mother never phoned him. He always called her.

"Honey, are you still there?" Concern wove through her voice.

"Yes, Mom. I'm here." He glanced at his watch. "Is it an okay time to talk?"

"Sure, although I might have to pull some chocolate-chip cookies out of the oven in a few minutes."

He thought he'd misheard. "Cookies?" He'd loved her chocolate-chip cookies. "I thought you didn't bake anymore, Mom."

She laughed, her bemusement tinkling down the phone. "Of course I bake, honey. I guess when you're in Hobin it's Thanksgiving and with all the family together we're at Jennifer's or Lori's and the girls take over in the kitchen." She paused for a moment. "I guess this year with me feeling so dizzy, what with the new medication, I wasn't my usual self but I'm feeling great again now."

He shook his head trying to clear his thoughts. This year his mother had seemed to be exactly the same as every other year—quiet. But now she was telling him she was baking and feeling great. He tried to reconcile what she was saying with his very strong memories. "But when Dad died and we left the farm, you didn't bake."

A heavy silence hung for a moment before she spoke. "You're right, Marc. For quite a while I stopped baking. I missed the farm. I missed your dad and I was too exhausted just going to work and putting one foot in front of the other. But I recovered, Marc. It took me a while but I've carved out a new life with good friends and the family."

She paused for a few seconds. "I know that I relied on you far too much, and you took the brunt of that time. If I could make it up to you I would. I'm so sorry you had to grow up too fast."

I recovered, Marc. His chest hurt and he rubbed it with his free hand. All these years his mother had been busy living her life but he'd never noticed because he'd been stuck fast at a resentful seventeen, reliving unwanted responsibilities and never visiting long enough to really see.

"Mom, I'm not sure I've grown up at all."

"Perhaps now's your chance."

Her quiet words packed a punch and somehow he managed to tell her he'd see her on Friday and then he rang off, completely poleaxed as everything he'd believed and held on to for twelve years fell away. Matilda had been right all along. In twelve years his mother had never asked him for anything, never expected anything of him, never once tried to draw him back into the family. Hell, she'd never even told him she'd been unwell in October. She'd tried to make up those five years by leaving him free to have the life he wanted. And he'd taken that freedom with both hands and what had it got him? He'd held back from his family, jeopardized his relationship with his nephew and rebuffed the people of Hobin to the point where they no longer even tried to include him. Life had gone on and he was the one missing out. He was the one disconnected, unsettled and alone.

I love you.

His gut clenched. Matilda had offered him love even though she knew he hadn't a clue how to love her. He'd tossed her precious gift back at her.

I want to expand my love for you to encompass children.

He dropped his head in his hands. He'd been such a fool. She'd offered him a chance for his own family but he hadn't understood what a precious bequest that was and he'd rejected it out of hand. Now he understood. Now he wanted that very same thing.

I love you.

Realization rushed in. He loved Matilda. The months of restlessness stilled.

He loved her and she loved him. It was that simple.

The urge to get straight onto a plane and tell Matilda he loved her burned through him but before he could do that he needed to call Peggy. He took a deep breath because for that conversation he'd need every bit of his New York hustle.

CHAPTER TWENTY

"I need a favor."

"Hmm?" Matilda glanced up at Peggy, her mind spinning on the idea of how she could introduce the Australian tradition of satin-and-lace-covered horseshoes to the website and have her American clients think they were the new must-have bridal accessory. "Which one? We're currently offering forty-five selections."

Peggy laughed. "Not a wedding favor, and not even really a business favor. I need you to go to Gutherson House and show a prospective vacationer through it. He wants to use it in the summer."

Matilda's heart lurched. Peggy had no idea what Gutherson House meant to her, or how it represented everything she'd lost. Lori, Brian and Elsa were the only people who had any real idea and she'd only given them a bare sketch outline. Like the barn, Matilda hadn't been back to the house. The rental agreement had been between Marc and Peggy and she knew as part of the contract a cleaner had gone in and taken out the tree, stripped the linen and cleaned up, erasing any evidence of her time there with Marc.

She had no plans to go back. "How about I mind the shop while you show the holidaymaker through?"

Peggy absently straightened a Valentine's Day ornament. "That's the reason this is a favor. I've got a meeting with the rep from the supplier whose shipment of mugs arrived more broken than intact, and I intend to nail him to the wall. He's still claiming 'no responsibility.'"

A sliver of guilt zapped her but she wasn't prepared to risk her fragile hold on the control that she'd fought so hard for this last month. "What about shifting the show-through time?"

"Illinoisans." Peggy threw up her hands. "You know those brash Chicago types. They're almost as bad as New Yorkers. I know it's an imposition and not part of our business but just this once, as a friend?"

Just like that, Peggy had her. Swallowing a sigh, she pushed back from the desk. "Okay, Peggy, but you realize it involves me driving your car."

Peggy just smiled and handed her the keys.

The road was thick with snow and she drove carefully, missing the safety of the truck she'd driven when Marc had been in town. The Queen Anne's turret came into view and she bit her lip. She loved this house but it hurt too much to think about it, just like it hurt too much to think about Marc. She missed him so much it ached.

She gripped the wheel, refusing to let her mind wander to the automatic follow-up thought of did he miss her? He hadn't wanted her love, hadn't been prepared to open his heart and take a risk with his safe and controlled life and sadly, that was his loss.

She pulled in beside a rental car with Wisconsin plates. The cabin was empty and footsteps led through the snow up to the front porch. That was odd. She had the key to the house and waiting inside the car had to be warmer than huddling on the verandah.

Taking in a deep breath, she got out of the car. She could do this. Snow crunched under her boots as she marched determinedly toward the steps. She called out, "Hello?"

No reply. As she negotiated the icy entrance, she called out again before walking around the verandah and doubling back to the front door. She brought her hands up around her mouth and bellowed the Aussie outback shout of "Coo-eee," in an attempt to find the missing vacationer who'd obviously gone exploring.

Except there were no footprints in the snow leading away from the house.

She heard the squeak of the front door opening behind her and she swung around with a start.

She forgot to breathe.

Marc stood in front of her, his hair gleaming golden in the narrow band of sunlight that had sneaked past the clouds. He was a gorgeous mismatch of designer chic and country Wisconsin—fine wool pants, an ocean-blue cable sweater and the obligatory Wisconsin bulky down jacket, the one she knew he hated.

"Cooee, Matilda." Marc used every ounce of his willpower to stay standing where he was. He stared at her, soaking her up, from the recalcitrant curls escaping from under her black felt hat to her heavy, snow-covered boots. She was beautiful. She was the missing piece in the jigsaw of his life, the key to his heart and his bridge to fulfillment. He wanted to gather her close, press his face into her hair and then kiss her until the sun went down.

But her perfect pout had flattened into a disapproving line. "You're not from Chicago."

It sounded like a crime. "Ah, no, should I be?"

She pushed past him into the entrance hall. "Peggy asked me to meet a prospective vacationer here from Chicago."

"Ah." He'd told Peggy to get Matilda here any way she could. "I've made tea."

Green sparks shot from her eyes as her intelligent mind worked out what was going on. "So no one is coming to look at the house."

He tried a smile. "Just you."

Her hands slapped her hips. "I don't need to look at the house, Marc. If you need an inspection then you certainly don't need me here to show you around."

He'd thought because she loved him she'd at least be prepared to sit down for a few minutes so he could tell her what a fool he'd been. But nothing about her stance showed any sign of conciliation. This wasn't going quite the way he'd planned. They'd always teased each other so he tried that. "I've never known you to refuse a cup of Earl Grey tea."

She closed her eyes for a moment and sighed. When she opened them it was resignation that slugged him. "What are you doing here, Marc?"

He opened his hands. "I wanted to see you."

"So get a photo." The quip didn't come with her usual teasing smile—instead her face wore a stony and uncompromising expression. "The thing is, I don't want to see you. I sure as hell don't want to listen to you. I don't want to hear about your latest job and how it excites you. I don't want to know that you've bought a new model to build with Kyle. I do *not* want to hear you say you're sad we parted like we did, and you're sorry that things can't be different but you'd like for us to be friends." She gulped in a breath and her voice hardened. "You broke my heart, Marc. No way am I staying here to let you appease your guilt over a cup of tea."

She spun toward the door and reached for the handle.

You broke my heart. Panic thundered through him. He was losing her and every plan he had for how this meeting would unfold vanished. All he knew was that he couldn't let her leave. "Marry me."

Her hand stalled and she turned around slowly, her eyes shockingly empty. "I beg your pardon?"

"Marry me." He grabbed the huge white box he brought with him off a chair and shoved it into her hands.

"What's this?"

"Just open it." He tried to settle his agitation by telling himself this would prove to her how serious he was.

Watching her slowly lower the box onto the floor, undo the white chiffon ribbon, lift the lid off the box and leaf-by-leaf fold back the blue tissue paper was killing him, and it took every grain of self-control not to lean forward and rip the paper apart to show her what it was.

Finally she saw the contents. "Nana's dress." Her voice sounded hollow and she stared at him, her eyes wide with disbelief. "But I sold this to Vanessa Jacobsen."

"I know." He smiled at her, loving her with every part of him. "I bought it back, for you."

"No."

No? Accusing eyes fried him.

She stood up fast, shoving the box into his stomach. "How could you? How could you bulldoze her into selling you *her* wedding dress?"

Bewilderment swirled through him, tilting his world so sharply he felt like he was clinging to a precipice by his fingernails. He'd probably just paid half the cost of Vanessa's entire wedding to get that dress back, as the definitive gesture to prove to Matilda he really did love her. He put the box back onto the chair. "I don't understand. You always said you wanted to wear your grandmother's wedding dress. I'm sorry it took so long for me to work out that I love you, but I do love you, Matilda, and this dress is a token of my love for you."

She folded her arms. "No, it isn't."

Her words stung like an open slap. "Yes, it is." He didn't understand why she couldn't see the symbolism. "Peggy and Vanessa thought it was a romantic gesture."

The moment the words left his mouth he wanted to grab them back.

Matilda seared him with a look of pity that squeezed his heart so hard his vision blurred.

"They don't know that you buy things instead of feeling things."

But he was feeling things now. Pain and despair swirled through him leaving a trail of destruction. She gazed at him with such resolve it scared him and the floor seemed to tilt underneath him, changing everything he'd ever believed in and held dear. He'd spent his adult life keeping people at a distance and now he'd pushed away the one person he wanted. The one person he needed as much as life itself. The one person he might not be able to get back. He had no clue what to do or say but he had to try something. "If you want, I'll return it to Vanessa."

She sighed. "Do that, Marc. It isn't my dress anymore. For so long I'd imagined myself gliding down the aisle in Nana's dress to meet my own great love. But this dress has never fitted me and that's because it was Nana's dress, and Nana's life. Not mine. A month ago you told me that I can't live my life through other people's dreams for me and, sadly, you were right." Her fist pressed against her heart. "I have my own life to live and my own experiences to have."

His legs turned to rubber and he gripped the banister for support as a crushing sense of loss poured through him. Her reply sounded very much like a life that didn't include him at all. He'd screwed up everything with Matilda and hurt her so badly and now, no apology, no gesture however big or small, would be enough to come back from it. His loss almost choked him.

"I know I was a fool. I know I don't deserve you but I'll do whatever it takes to win you back, Matilda. Just tell me what to say or do."

"That's not how it works, Marc." With shaking hands Matilda pulled off her hat as heat and chills racked her body and her heart careened in her chest like a drunk trying to find his way. He said he loved her. Was that true? She wasn't sure he'd really learned anything given he was asking her what to say and do, but his anguished expression when she hadn't squealed with delight over the dress had the same pain-tinged feel to it as the love she held so closely for him. But it was all way too confusing, this about-face from not loving her to loving her. From not wanting marriage to proposing, from not wanting family to—

The thought flung her heart against her ribs. She wanted children and he avoided family. As much as she loved him, she knew she couldn't compromise on that. Not now when she'd finally realized she had a right to what she wanted in life.

He ran his hands through his hair, his face ragged. "I get it. Grand gestures are not what you want. I'll tell Peggy I'm putting the house back on the market."

Her fingers gripped the brim of her hat. "What house?"

"This house."

Her jaw dropped. She couldn't believe she'd heard right. Why would he have bought it when he hated Hobin? "You bought this house?"

"Yes, three days ago. The same day I bought the dress."

Thoughts hammered her and she tried to make sense of what he was saying. "But you hate Hobin. You don't enjoy being here and—"

He tugged at the crewneck of his sweater as if it was too tight against his throat.

"I had this crazy dream of spending summers here."

She stared at him. "You? Vacationing in Hobin?"

"Yes, in Hobin with you, and teaching our children how to play baseball and cricket."

Our children. White noise roared in her head. Her breath caught fast in her chest and her heart just quivered like jelly. "But you don't want a family. You don't want that sort of commitment."

His heartfelt sigh vibrated with regret. "You once accused me of being juvenile when it came to my family and you were right. I was stuck in time and it took you to show me exactly what I've been missing and I've missed out on so much. But you've taught me well and I think I'm finally on the way to being a grown-up."

He's learned. Somehow she managed to stammer out, "And you want to marry me and have children?"

His tortured expression intensified. "What do you think 'I love you' and 'marry me' means? Or is this one of those Australian differences things like *supper?*" His blue eyes studied her hard, seeking confirmation. "Am I supposed to hop like a kangaroo or grunt like a koala to get you to believe that I really do love you? To get you to believe that you're my best friend, my conscience and my lover, and I want to be with you for the rest of our lives?"

The emotions in his eyes and his tightly controlled voice told her everything she wanted to know and her heart sang. Marc truly loved her. He'd just said exactly what he needed to say and what she needed to hear.

Happiness unlike anything she'd ever known flowed through her. "Off you go then, start hopping."

His eyes narrowed. "You're not serious?"

"Oh I'm very serious, Blondie. You know how important traditions are to me so we need to start off right." But try as she might she couldn't keep the smile off her face or the laughter out of her voice. "I'll marry you, Marc Olsen."

He pulled her into his arms, relief and love clear on his handsome face. "You're a shocking tease, Matilda Geoffrey."

"And you're the most maddening man I've ever known." She laid her head on his chest for a moment and breathed him in, knowing she was exactly where she belonged and then a thought struck her and she stiffened. "I thought Peggy had first option to buy this house. She wanted it so badly to be a Honeymoon Inn and part of Weddings Are Hobin."

A worried look crossed his face. "She did and I promise you, Matilda, I didn't throw money at the house and outbid her. We've come to a business arrangement. You and I get Gutherson House and we're financing a new-to-look-old Queen Anne which will be custom built to meet the requirements of Weddings Are Hobin. This way you're an equal partner in the whole business, rather than just owning the website."

She gazed up at him, stunned at what he'd done. "I can't believe you did that. I can't believe you bought this house for us."

He trailed his fingers through her hair, winding a curl around his finger. "Buying the house was a no brainer. This is where I fell in love with you and where I intend to keep loving you."

"Really?" She trusted him absolutely but given everything he'd put her through she thought she was entitled to a bit of fun. "I think you might have to show me."

He grinned down at her and lowered his lips to hers, kissing her as softly as if she was treasured porcelain. As his lips played across hers in a sweet dance of adoration, he swung her into his arms and climbed the stairs to the bedroom. The scent of rose and sandalwood wafted over her from lit pillar candles.

"Candles?"

"I can blow them out."

"So you thought you'd get lucky."

"I hoped with all my heart you'd forgive me."

He looked so contrite and slightly green with anxiety that she immediately stopped her teasing. "It's a lovely gesture."

"Not grand." He lowered her onto the bed. "I promise you I won't do grand again."

She cupped his cheek. "Marc, I love you. I know you love me. You don't have to tiptoe around me. We're both going to make mistakes and do the wrong things but we'll work through them together."

"Always."

She pulled his head down to hers and kissed him. Hard. Soft. Lovingly. He groaned as her tongue found his and their taste and touch merged, and a heady rush of joy consumed her—she could make this gorgeous man, her man, weak with need for her. His hands started to pull at her coat and hers found the zipper on his vest.

As they struggled with clothing, he pulled his mouth from hers. "I can't wait for summer when you're wearing the skimpiest bikini I can buy."

She laughed and tugged off her clothes and dropped them in a heap next to his.

Diving under the wedding-ring quilt she pulled it up over their heads and rolled into his arms. "There's something to be said for being cuddled up in our very own cocoon."

His bluer-than-blue eyes burned with love for her. "I've got more than cuddling on my mind."

"I was depending on it—oh!"

His mouth found her breast and conversation lapsed as he suckled her—his tongue abrading her nipple in a way that made her breasts heavy and full, and sent glorious shimmers through her that set every part of her alight with need. Using his hands and his mouth, he worshipped her slowly, intently and with so much love she cried out from overwhelming happiness.

She was loved and adored. Wholly and completely.

And she loved him. She showed him in all the ways she knew he hungered for until he moaned with the guttural sound of need that matched her own. He entered her and she knew she was home. They each soared to new heights, spiraling out on a pledge of love and commitment, and returning together as one.

EPILOGUE

Summer in Hobin meant blue skies, emerald-green grass, corn as far as the eye could see and weddings. From late May to early September, brides and grooms and their families came to Hobin to marry in rustic elegance and to soak up the small town's welcome.

The Olsens came too, to work and play.

"Bowled!" Clancy Olsen, aged eight, ran around the garden, punching the air.

"No way." His twin brother Lukas's hands shot straight to his hips. "The bails are still on the wicket."

"I'm sick of standing here," their younger sister, Emily, called out from third base as Dingo the kelpie charged around trying to round up the kids as if they were sheep. "It's my turn next."

Her brothers ignored her.

"You're still out, Lukas, 'cos the bases are loaded and you didn't run." Clancy turned to his father for confirmation. "That's right, isn't it, Dad?"

Marc laughed as he cuddled his youngest child, baby Krista, on his shoulder. "You guys are the ones who invented Base-Crick and the rules seem to change all the time." Since the most recent family holiday in Australia, and backed up by screenings on the cable sports channel, the twins were now avid cricket fans and had invented a combination game of baseball and cricket.

The unexpected roar of a motorbike silenced the boys' argument, and they turned and stared. The low-slung machine came to a crunching halt on the driveway and the black-leathered rider pulled off his helmet, grinned and gave a wave.

"Kyle!" Emily ditched the base, running across the lawn as fast as her sturdy five-year-old legs could carry her. Her brothers immediately forgot their dispute and raced after her, keen to check out the new motorcycle and hoping that Kyle would give them a ride.

Matilda appeared by Marc's side having just walked back from trouble-shooting a small wedding glitch at the barn. She slid her arm through her husband's as she stroked her sleeping baby's head with her free hand. "Brian and Lori are going to have a fit."

He smiled down at his wife whose auburn curls still disobeyed orders and rioted around her face. Motherhood had etched small lines around her eyes and deepened the laughter brackets around her mouth but in his eyes that only made her more beautiful.

He moved his free arm and curled it around her shoulder, pulling her gently against him, loving the way her body curved so naturally into his. "That's probably why he's come straight here. He thinks they won't say anything to him with the entire clan coming for a barbecue."

Matilda laughed. "Tell him he's dreaming, even if he is twenty-three and just graduated from M.I.T."

But before he could answer, a line of cars snaked down the drive. Elsa alighted from the first one, her gentle smile full of happiness. "Happy anniversary, my darlings. Sheryl sends her love from sunny California and hopes her card arrived." She kissed them both. "How's my gorgeous Krista?"

Marc smiled and passed the baby to his mother. "Needing a cuddle from her nana."

Elsa cooed to the pink-cheeked cherub and walked toward the house calling over her shoulder, "Can you please get the ambrosia salad out of the trunk?"

"Dude!" Mason, Lori and Brian's younger son, streaked from the second car, his eyes wide as saucers as he ran straight toward his older brother, cousins and the gleaming bike.

Brian opened the door for his wife and squeezed her hand as she hopped out. "Kyle's a man now and you have to give it to him that he's wearing a helmet for you."

Lori didn't look totally convinced but she stroked his face and gave a wry smile. "As police chief, are you sure you can't arrest him for stressing out his poor mom?"

Jennifer, Ty and their children arrived next, calling out their greetings in unusual accents—a blend of Midwest and the world, honed by years at international schools all over Asia. Then Peggy Hendrix, Hobin's most successful resident businesswoman, arrived. She mouthed to Marc, "We have to talk" and he smiled knowing that meant another project to fill the coffers of Evans, Gaynor, Olsen and Associates, but that could happen tomorrow or the next day because today was a party.

Everyone gathered on the lawn and tea was served with Elsa's chewy chocolate-chip cookies and Marc managed to eat as many as the kids. Then the children whipped the adults at T-ball until Kyle hit the ball high into the cornfield next door and they found a new game of running through the corn like it was a maze. The lazy afternoon rolled into evening and drinks were served, the men choosing the Northwoods' beer and many of the women did too, although it made Marc chuckle that Matilda, who came from a country with the record for the most beer consumed per capita, always drank champagne.

She rose on her tiptoes and kissed his cheek. "Why wouldn't I drink champagne when I have so much in my life to celebrate?"

And he couldn't disagree with that. Even his in-laws had sent them an email from Vietnam earlier that day, wishing them well.

Lori sat under a shady market umbrella with Emily cuddled in her lap. "Now you know what today is, don't you?"

Emily clapped her hands. "The day my mommy married my daddy in the log church, and Mommy wore a dress that made her look like a princess."

Matilda caught Marc's eye while setting down a huge bowl of green salad onto a trestle table and answering Clancy's third question about when the food was going to be ready. The look in her almond-shaped eyes was of shared memories of a glorious day, one that was carved into both of their hearts. But it also carried a clear message.

Marc immediately leaned forward to his daughter. "And what does every bride have to have?"

Emily frowned in concentration, her face serious. "Her own dreams and her very own dress."

He smiled and patted her knee. "That's right, sweetheart. You remember that because it's very important."

"And Gracie would agree with you on that." Lori smiled as her friend appeared.

"Agree on what?" Gracie sank into the Adirondack chair and gratefully accepted a glass of champagne.

"On every bride having her very own dress."

"You bet." She raised her glass. "To Weddings Are Hobin."

Weddings Are Hobin had flourished and Gracie's dress shop had expanded, incorporating a well-patronized bridal range that suited the Old World charm of a Hobin wedding. The red barn reception center and the Honeymoon Inn were booked solid each spring through fall but who would have guessed that part of the business would turn out to be a minor one. It was Matilda's worldwide business success with the website, which she ran from New York nine months of the year, that made Marc's chest swell with pride.

"Daddy, I'm starving!" Clancy pulled at his father's arms.

Marc grinned and put on his best Australian accent. "Right oh, mate. Let's fire up the barbie!"

In the Aussie tradition of "bring a plate," there was a wide range of salads from the sweet ambrosia, the traditional potato to the Aussie favorite of mangoes, macadamia nuts and avocado. Marc and Brian grilled the Wisconsin brats, burgers and Australian lamb chops to perfection. Everyone agreed there was nothing like Pavlova for dessert except Marc who preferred the rich and heavy fruitcake which tasted like solid vintage port. He gave his annual silent toast of thanks to Matilda's Nana for making the original cake that had sent her halfway around the world and into his arms.

Scarlet rolled across the sky and the kids chased fireflies while the bonfire crackled and young and old made s'mores, an American tradition Matilda had taken to with gusto. Finally under the white light of a three-quarter moon, the younger kids fell asleep in their parents' laps and slowly people headed home or to one of the many comfy spare beds that Gutherson House was known for, leaving Matilda and Marc cuddled up on the verandah swing.

Matilda sighed in contentment, her head resting on his chest. "That was fun. Most couples don't have a crowd like this at their wedding anniversary every year."

He wound a curl of her hair around his finger. "Most people don't get married on the Fourth of July."

"True, but who knew that would be the only free Saturday in our first year of business when we could actually get a booking for the barn. Now it's one of our most popular dates."

He pressed a kiss into her hair. "I always think our anniversary's February tenth, the day I made the best decision of my life."

She raised her head, emerald-green eyes filled with love. "And I love the way you always write me a letter on that day and take me out to a swanky New York City restaurant."

He smiled wryly, knowing his wife so very well. "I'm thinking diamonds next year to go along with the card and the dinner, so you have six months to get used to the idea."

"Am I that difficult to give gifts to?"

"Yes, but I understand where you're coming from." Life had been good to them, from his architectural successes to her thriving business, as well as a loving, extended family. But most of all life had given them the four blessings asleep upstairs. "We have everything we need whether we're here or in New York."

She wriggled against him, a teasing glint in her eyes. "Actually I *have* been thinking about something you could give me."

"Really?" He gave her a lazy smile as his hand found its way under her blouse to caress the hollow at the base of her spine, loving her involuntary shudder of delight. "Now I wonder what that could be?"

She leaned her very kissable mouth against his ear and, in her distinctive Australian accent that he still found incredibly sexy, she whispered a wickedly erotic invitation that a Viking couldn't possibly refuse.

★ ★ ★ ★ ★

ABOUT THE AUTHOR

Books have always been a big part of Fiona's life and her first teenage rebellion was refusing to go on a hike with her parents because she was halfway through *Gone With the Wind*. As an adult, Fiona read her way around the world, always trying to read a book that related to where she was at the time… The Brontës in Yorkshire, Jane Austen in Bath, *The Godfather* in Italy, Michener in Hawaii…you get the picture. It was when she was living in Madison, Wisconsin, and at home with a baby, that she started writing romance fiction.

Now multi-published with Harlequin Mills & Boon and Carina Press, she's been the recipient of the CataRomance Reviewers' Award and has been nominated for Australian Romantic Book of the Year. She loves creating characters you could meet on the street and enjoys putting them in unique situations where they eventually fall in love. Fiona currently lives in Australia, which is a lot warmer than Wisconsin, and she attempts to juggle her writing career with her own real-life hero, a rambling garden with 80 rose bushes and two heroes in the making.

Fiona loves to hear from her readers and you can contact her at fiona@fionalowe.com. She also hangs out at www.fionalowe.com, www.facebook.com/FionaLowe RomanceAuthor and twitter.com/#!/FionaLowe.

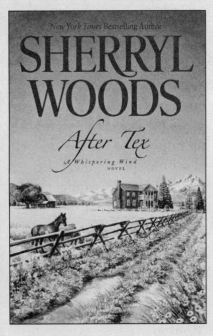

#1 *New York Times* Bestselling Author

DEBBIE MACOMBER

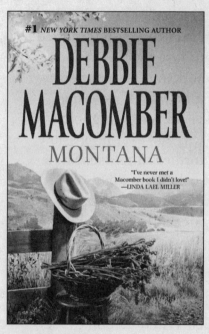

Her grandfather wants her to come home, and Molly thinks she just might. His ranch will be a good place for her sons to grow up, a place to escape big-city influences. Then she learns—from a stranger named Sam—that her grandfather is ill. Possibly dying. Molly packs up the kids without a second thought and makes the long drive to Sweetgrass, Montana.

She immediately has questions about Sam Dakota. Why is he working on her grandfather's ranch? Why doesn't the sheriff trust him? Just who is he? But despite everything, Molly can't deny her attraction to Sam—until her ailing grandfather tries to push them into marriage.

Some borders aren't so easy to cross....

Available wherever books are sold.

HARLEQUIN® MIRA®
www.Harlequin.com

Plan on falling in love again with this charming story
from author Christi Barth!

Wedding planner Ivy Rhodes is the best in the business, and she's not
about to let a personal problem stop her from getting ahead. So when
she's asked to star in the reality TV show *Planning for Love,* it doesn't
matter that the show's videographer Bennett Westcott happens to be
a recent—and heartbreaking—one-night stand. The more time they
spend together, the more Ben realizes Ivy isn't the wedding-crazed
bridezilla he'd imagined....

Planning for Love

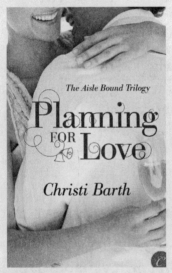

The Aisle Bound Trilogy

Planning
FOR Love

Christi Barth

Available now in ebook!

Then don't miss the next installments in The Aisle Bound trilogy:
A Fine Romance, available in ebook March 2013
Friends to Lovers, available in ebook July 2013

Connect with us for info on our new releases,
access to exclusive offers and much more!

Visit **CarinaPress.com**

We like you—why not like us on Facebook:
Facebook.com/CarinaPress

Follow us on Twitter: **Twitter.com/CarinaPress**

If you enjoyed *Boomerang Bride* by RITA® Award-winning author Fiona Lowe, then don't miss her new *Wedding Fever* series available in ebook, starting in April 2013!

Saved by the Bride

Annika Jacobson, the acting mayor of Whitetail, Wisconsin, is determined to do everything she can to save her beloved hometown from financial ruin, even if that means crashing an exclusive engagement party to get an audience with the one man in town who can help Whitetail create more jobs.

Finn Callahan is determined to avoid being the cliché third-generation who loses the business, and no one is going to derail him from that goal. Not a parent who's decided to act like a father twenty years too late, or a completely uncoordinated-yet-sexy mayor who will do anything to save her town....

Then don't miss the next installments:

Picture Perfect Wedding, available August 2013
Runaway Groom, available December 2013

Connect with us for info on our new releases,
access to exclusive offers and much more!

Visit **CarinaPress.com**

We like you—why not like us on Facebook:
Facebook.com/CarinaPress

Follow us on Twitter: **Twitter.com/CarinaPress**